THE LOST CHRONICLES
VOLUME ONE

DRAGONS OF THE DWARVEN DEPTHS

Margaret Weis and Tracy Hickman

The Lost Chronicles, Volume One
DRAGONS OF THE DWARVEN DEPTHS

©2006 Wizards of the Coast, Inc.

Published by Wizards of the Coast, Inc. DRAGONLANCE, WIZARDS OF THE COAST, and their respective logos are trademarks of Wizards of the Coast, Inc., in the U.S.A. and other countries.

Printed in the U.S.A.

Cover art by Matt Stawicki
Map by Sean MacDonald
First Printing: July 2006
Library of Congress Catalog Card Number: 2005935527

9 8 7 6 5 4 3 2 1

ISBN-10: 0-7869-4099-9
ISBN-13: 978-0-7869-4099-8
620-95646720-001-EN

U.S., CANADA,   EUROPEAN HEADQUARTERS
ASIA, PACIFIC, & LATIN AMERICA   Hasbro UK Ltd
Wizards of the Coast, Inc.   Caswell Way
P.O. Box 707   Newport, Gwent NP9 0YH
Renton, WA 98057-0707   GREAT BRITAIN
+1-800-324-6496   Save this address for your records.

Visit our web site at www.wizards.com

By Margaret Weis and Tracy Hickman

CHRONICLES

Dragons of Autumn Twilight

Dragons of Winter Night

Dragons of Spring Dawning

LEGENDS

Time of the Twins

War of the Twins

Test of the Twins

The Second Generation

Dragons of Summer Flame

THE WAR OF SOULS

Dragons of a Fallen Sun

Dragons of a Lost Star

Dragons of a Vanished Moon

THE LOST CHRONICLES

Dragons of the Dwarven Depths

Dragons of the Highlord Skies
July 2007

Dragons of the Hourglass Mage
July 2008

To the memory of my father, George Edward Weis, this book is lovingly dedicated.

—Margaret Weis

To all those whose sacrifices are praised only in the heavens.

—Tracy Hickman

FOREWORD

Joseph Campbell charts the course of the epic myth as a circle.

It begins at the comforts of the hero's home—the top of the circle, if you will—and the Call of the Adventure. From those safe and familiar surroundings, he sets off, perhaps urged along by a Helper character, and encounters the Threshold of Adventure. There, passing the obstacles of the Guardians that protect the way, he then crosses into the Realms of Power. In that wondrous new land he encounters both more helpers to support him on his journey, and tests and adversaries that seek to deter him from the path. He obtains the great prize—Sacred Marriage, Father Atonement, Apotheosis, or Elixir Theft. Yet having attained his goal, the hero is only halfway through his true journey. Then comes the flight from the realms of power, the crossing back over the threshold into the mundane world, and, like Odysseus of old, the return to home, where he started—only to find that either home has changed in his absence—or that his absence has changed him.

The journeys of Tanis, Laurana, Flint, Tasslehoff, Raistlin, Caramon, Sturm, and Tika—our Heroes of the Lance—began in similar fashion over twenty years ago. They, too, were motivated to leave their home, forge a path into mysterious, powerful, and unknown realms, so that they, too, might gain a great prize—though not without tremendous cost. And they might have come home to a place changed irreparably, as they, too, were changed.

So it was with Margaret and I as we set out on our own epic path over two decades ago. We forged into unknown realms far from the security of our familiar lives. There were many helpers along the way; we remember and honor you all. So, too, were there many trials that stood to dissuade us from our course. These came in many shapes and forms. Each cost us—sometimes dearly—and still we pressed on.

Now, we find ourselves returning again to that home from which we started on our adventure, all those many years ago.

We fear to find it changed: we remember it as it was when it was wild and unexplored—before so many thousands of words described so much of this world.

We fear to find ourselves changed: we vaguely recall how young we were, how we could not conceive of failure in those days, and how raw our craft, then, seemed to us.

Yet, as we stand here on the hillside, the sunrise illuminates the Vallenwood Trees one more time. The brass fixtures gleam again on the Inn of the Last Home, restored magically to its previous glory. The clock and calendar have rewound here in Krynn. We have returned to find the world truly as it was in the beginning—our heroes are as yet unproven, innocent yet filled with strength and hope. Here, through the eye of our memory, the world is reborn.

And we, for a time, are young again.

—Tracy Hickman, January, 2006

The Song of Kharas

by Michael Williams

Three were the thoughts of
  those in Thorbardin
In the dark after Dergoth when
  the ogres danced.
One was the lost light, the
  limping darkness
In the caves of the kingdom
  where light crumbles.
One the despair of the
  Dwarfthane Derkin
Gone to the gloom of the tower
  of Glory.
One the world, weary and
  wounded
Down to the deep of the
  Darkling's waters.
    Under the heart of the
     highland,
      Under the ceiling of
       stone,
       Under the wane of the
        world's glory.
         Home under home.

Then was Kharas among us, the
  Keeper of Kings.
The Hand on the Hammer, Arm of
  the Hylar.
At the gleaming gravesite of
  gold and garnet
Three sons of the thane he
  buried thereunder.
While Derkin saw dark upon dark
  in the tunnels,
In the halls of the nation saw
  nooses and knives,

killers and kingmakers came to
  Kharas
With agate and amethyst, asking
  allegiance.
    Under the heart of the
     highland,
      Under the ceiling of
       stone,
        Under the wane of the
        world's glory.
          Home under home.

But the stalwart in heart is
  strong as a stone.
And bold and unbending his mind
  to the better:
The Hammer of Hylar was firm in
  the halls,
Denying all discord, all doubt
  and division,
He turned from intrigue, from
  the wild tunnels,
Out to the open, one oath
  swearing
That time not treachery shall
  ever tarnish
The Hammer's return in a time of
  great troubles.
    Under the heart of the
     highland,
      Under the ceiling of
       stone,
        Under the wane of the
        world's glory.
          Home under home.

King Duncan's Floating Tomb

1. Hall of Enemies
2. Duncan's Tomb
3. Antechamber
4. Grand Promenade
5. Ruby Tower
   of Singing Light
6. Courtyard
7. Vestibule
8. Ruby Chamber
   of the Hammer

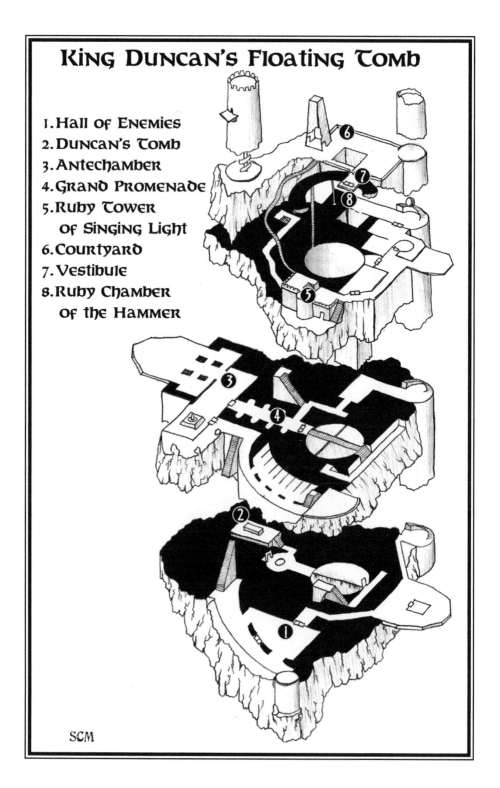

SCM

BOOK I

PROLOGUE

Standing over the bloody body of the fallen Dragon Highlord Verminaard, the aurak draconian, Dray-yan, saw his destiny flare before him.

The brilliant flash hit him with the force of a comet falling from the sky, burning his blood and sending a tingling sensation throughout his scaly body down to his clawed fingers. After the initial burst, a cascade of more ideas followed, showering down on him. His entire plan formed in seconds.

Dray-yan whipped off his ornate cloak and dropped it over the body of the Dragon Highlord, hiding the corpse and the large pool of blood beneath it from view. The aurak draconian was panicked, or so it must appear to those watching. Shouting furiously for help, he grabbed several baaz (draconians of lowly stature, notable for their obtuse gullibility) and ordered them to fetch a litter.

"Make haste! Lord Verminaard is grievously wounded! We must carry Lord Verminaard to his chambers! Swiftly! Swiftly, before his lordship succumbs to his wounds."

Fortunately for Dray-yan, the situation inside the fortress of Pax

Tharkas was chaotic: escaping slaves, two red dragons battling each other, the sudden thunderous fall of tons of rocks blocking the pass and crushing a vast number of soldiers. No one was paying any attention to the fallen Highlord being carried inside the fortress or to the aurak who was accompanying him.

When Verminaard's corpse was safely inside his chambers, Dray-yan shut the doors, posted the baaz draconians who had carried the litter outside as guards, and gave orders that no one was to enter.

Dray-yan then helped himself to a bottle of Verminaard's finest wine and sat down at Verminaard's desk and began to go through Verminaard's secret papers. What Dray-yan read intrigued and impressed him. He sipped the wine, studied the situation, and went over his plans in his mind. Occasionally someone would come to the door demanding orders. Dray-yan would shout that his lordship was not to be disturbed. Hours passed and then, when night had fallen, Dray-yan opened the door a crack.

"Tell Commander Grag that he is wanted in Lord Verminaard's chambers."

It took some time before the large bozak commander arrived. During the interval, Dray-yan pondered whether or not to take Grag into his confidence. His instinct was to trust no one, particularly a draconian Dray-yan considered inferior to himself. Dray-yan was forced to concede, however, that he could not do this alone. He was going to need help, and though he held Grag in disdain, he had to admit that Grag was not as stupid or incompetent as most other bozaks Dray-yan had encountered. Grag was, in fact, quite intelligent, an excellent military commander. If Grag had been in charge of Pax Tharkas instead of that muscle-bound, muscle-headed human Verminaard, there would have been no slave uprising. This disaster would have never happened.

Unfortunately, no one would have even considered putting Grag in command of humans, who believed that the "lizard-men," with their shining scales, wings, and tails, were bred for killing and nothing else. Draconians were incapable of rational thought, unfit for any type of leadership role in the Dark Queen's army. Dray-yan knew Takhisis herself believed this, and he secretly despised his goddess for it.

He would show her. Draconians would prove themselves to her. If he succeeded, he might well be the next Dragon Highlord.

One clawed step at a time, however.

"Commander Grag," announced one of the baaz.

The door opened, and Grag walked inside. The bozak stood well over six feet in height, and his large wings made him appear far taller. He had bronze scales covered by minimal armor, for he relied on his scales and tough hide to protect him. His scales at the moment were smeared with dirt and dust and streaked with blood. He was obviously exhausted. His long tail swept slowly from side to side. His lips were tightly pressed over his fangs. His yellow eyes narrowed as they stared hard at Dray-yan.

"What do *you* want?" Grag demanded churlishly. He waved a claw. "It had better be important. I'm needed out there." Then he caught sight of the figure on the bed. "I heard his lordship was wounded. Are you treating him?"

Grag neither liked nor trusted the aurak, as Dray-yan well knew. Bozak draconians were bred to be warriors. Like auraks, bozaks were granted magical spells by their Queen, but bozak magic was martial in nature and not nearly as powerful as that of the auraks. In personality, the large and burly bozaks tended to be open, forthright, blunt, and to the point.

Auraks, by contrast, were not intended to fight battles. Tall and slender, they were secretive by nature, sly and subtle, their magic extremely powerful.

Aurak and bozak draconians had been raised to hate and mistrust each other by humans who feared they would otherwise become too powerful—or at least that's what Dray-yan had come to believe.

"His lordship is grievously wounded," said Dray-yan, loudly for the benefit of the baaz, who were probably eavesdropping, "but I am praying to Her Dark Majesty and there is every hope he will recover. Please come in, Commander, and shut the door behind you."

Grag hesitated then did as he was told.

"Make certain that door is shut and bolted," Dray-yan added. "Now, come here."

Dray-yan motioned Grag to Verminaard's bedside.

Grag looked down then looked back up.

"He's not wounded," said Grag. "He's dead."

"Yes, he is," said Dray-yan dispassionately.

"Then why tell me he's alive?"

"I wasn't telling you so much as I was telling the baaz guards."

"What slime you auraks are," Grag sneered. "You have to twist everything—"

"The point is," said Dray-yan, "we're the only two who know he's dead.

Grag stared, puzzled.

"Let me make this clear, Commander," Dray-yan said. "We—you and I—are the only two beings in this world who know that Lord Verminaard is no more. Even those baaz who carried his lordship inside this room think he still lives."

"I still don't see your point—"

"Verminaard is dead. There is no Highlord, no one in command of the Red Dragonarmy," said Dray-yan.

Grag shrugged then said bitterly, "Once Emperor Ariakas finds out Verminaard is dead, another human will be sent to take over. It's only a matter of time."

"You and I both know that would be a mistake," said Dray-yan. "You and I both know there are others who are better qualified."

Grag looked at Dray-yan and the bozak's yellow eyes flickered. "Who did you have in mind?"

"The two of us," said Dray-yan.

"Us?" Grag repeated with a curl of his lip

"Yes, us," said Dray-yan coolly. "I know very little of military tactics and strategies. I would leave all that up to your wise expertise."

Grag's eyes flickered again, this time with amusement at the aurak's attempt at flattery. He glanced back at the corpse. "So I am to command the Red Dragonarmy, while you are doing . . . what?"

"I will be Lord Verminaard," said the aurak.

Grag turned to ask Dray-yan what in the Abyss he meant by that last remark, only to find Lord Verminaard standing beside him. His lordship, in all his hulking glory, stood glaring at Grag.

"Well, what do you think, Commander?" Dray-yan asked in a perfect imitation of Verminaard's deep, rasping voice.

The illusion cast by the aurak was so perfect, so compelling, that Grag glanced involuntarily back at the corpse to reassure himself the human was, indeed, truly dead. When he looked back, Dray-yan was himself once more—golden scales, small wings, stubby tail, pretentious arrogance and all.

"How would this work?" Grag asked, still not trusting the aurak.

"You and I will determine our course of action. We make plans for the disposition of the armies, prosecute the battles, etc. I would, of course, defer to you in such matters," Dray-yan added smoothly.

Grag grunted.

"I issue the commands and take his lordship's place whenever he needs to be seen in public."

Grag thought this over. "We put out the word that Verminaard was wounded but that, with the Dark Queen's blessing, he's recovering. Meanwhile you act in his place, relaying his commands from his 'sick bed'."

"Within a short time," Dray-yan said, "with the Dark Queen's blessing his lordship will be fit enough to resume his normal duties."

Grag was intrigued. "It just might work." He regarded Dray-yan with grudging admiration

Dray-yan didn't notice. "Our biggest problem will be disposing of the body." He cast a scathing glance at the corpse. "There was such a lot of him."

Lord Verminaard had been an enormous human—standing nearly seven feet tall, big-boned, fleshy, and heavily muscled.

"The mines," suggested Grag. "Dump the body in a mine shaft and then bring down the shaft on top of it."

"The mines are outside the fortress walls. How do we smuggle out the body?"

"You auraks can walk through air, or so I've heard," Grag replied. "You should have no trouble carrying the body out of here unseen."

"We walk the halls of magic, of time and space," said Dray-yan reprovingly. "I could carry the bastard, I suppose, though he weighs a ton. Still, one must make sacrifices for the cause. I'll dispose of him tonight. Now, tell me what's going on in the fortress. Have the escaped slaves been recaptured?"

"No," said Grag, adding bluntly, "and they won't be. Both Pyros and Flamestrike are dead. The fool dragons killed each other. The triggering of the defense mechanism caused the boulders to clog the pass, effectively blocking our troops who are now trapped on other side."

"You could send the forces we have here after the slaves," suggested Dray-yan.

"Most of my men lie buried under the rock fall," said Grag grimly. "That's where I was when you summoned me—trying to dig them out. It would take days, maybe weeks of work even if we had the manpower, which we don't."

Grag shook his head. "We need dragons to help us; that would make a difference. There are eight red dragons assigned to this army, but I have no idea where they are—Qualinesti, maybe, or Abanasinia."

"I can find out." Dray-yan jerked a claw at the piles of papers that lay scattered about on the desk. "I'll summon them in the name of Lord Verminaard."

"The dragons won't take orders from the likes of us," Grag pointed out. "Dragons despise us, even those who are on our side, fighting for the same cause. The reds would just as soon fry us as not. Your Verminaard illusion had better be able to fool them. Either that or . . ."

He paused, thoughtful.

"Or?" Dray-yan asked worriedly. The aurak was confident his illusion would fool humans and other draconians. He was not all that certain about dragons.

"We could ask Her Dark Majesty for help. The dragons would obey her, if not us."

"True," Dray-yan conceded. "Unfortunately, our queen's opinion of us is almost as low as that of her dragons."

"I have some ideas." Grag was starting to grow enthusiastic. "Ideas about how dragons and draconians can work together in ways that humans cannot. I could speak to Her Majesty, if you like. I think that once I explain—"

"You do that!" said Dray-yan hastily, glad to be relieved of this burden.

Bozak were known for their devotion to the goddess. If Takhisis would listen to anyone, it would be Grag.

Dray-yan went back to the original topic under discussion. "So the humans escaped. How did that happen?"

"My men tried to stop them," Grag said defensively. He felt he was being blamed. "There were too few of us. This fortress is undermanned. I repeatedly requested more troops, but his lordship said they were needed elsewhere. Some human warriors, led by an accursed Solamnic knight and an elven female, held off my forces, while other humans ransacked the supply room and hauled off whatever they could lay their hands on in stolen wagons. I had to let them go. I didn't have enough men to send after them."

"The humans have to travel south, a route that will take them into the Kharolis mountains. With winter coming on, they will need to find shelter and food. How many got away?"

"About eight hundred. Those who worked in the mines. Men, women, children."

"Ah, they have children with them." Dray-yan was pleased. "That will slow them down. We can take our time, Commander, pursue them at our leisure."

"What about the mines? The army needs steel. The emperor will be upset if the mines close."

"I have some thoughts on that. As to the humans—"

"Unfortunately, they have leaders now," Grag complained. "Intelligent leaders, not like those doddering old idiots, the Seekers. The same leaders who planned the slave revolt and fought and killed his lordship."

"That was luck, not skill," Dray-yan said dismissively. "I saw those so-called leaders of yours—a half-breed elf, a sickly mage, and a barbarian savage. The others are even less worthy of note. I don't think we need worry overmuch about them."

"We have to pursue the humans," Grag insisted. "We have to find them and bring them back here, not only to work in the mines. There is something about them that is vitally important to Her Dark Majesty. She has ordered me to go after them."

"I know what that is," said Dray-yan triumphantly. "Verminaard has it in his notes. She fears they might dig up some moldy old artifact, a hammer or something. I forget what it is called."

Grag shook his head. He had no interest in artifacts.

"We will go after them, Grag, I promise you," Dray-yan said. "We will bring back the men to work in the mines. We won't bother with the women and children. They only cause trouble. We'll simply dispose of them—"

"Don't dispose of all the women," Grag said with a leer. "My men need some amusement—"

Dray-yan grimaced. He found the unnatural lust some draconians had for human females disgusting.

"In the meantime, there are other more important events happening in the world, events that could have a significant impact on the war and on us."

Dray-yan poured Grag a glass of wine, sat him down at the table, and shoved forward a stack of papers.

"Look through these. Take special note of a place labeled, 'Thorbardin'. . ."

I

The coughing spell. Hot tea.
Chickens aren't eagles.

Wearily, Raistlin Majere wrapped himself in a blanket and lay down on the dirt floor of the pitch dark cave and tried to go to sleep. Almost immediately, he began coughing. He hoped this would be a brief spasm, as some were, and would soon end, but the tight, constricted feeling in his chest did not abate. Rather, the cough grew worse. He sat upright, struggling to breathe, a taste of iron in his mouth. Fumbling for a handkerchief, he pressed it to his lips. He could not see in the utter darkness of the smallish cave, but he had no need to see. He knew quite well when he removed the cloth it would be stained with red.

Raistlin was a young man in his early twenties, yet he felt sometimes as if he had lived a hundred years and that each of those years had taken its toll on him. The shattering of his health had happened in a matter of moments during the dread Test in the Tower of High Sorcery. He'd gone into that test a young man, physically weak, perhaps, but relatively healthy. He'd emerged an old one—his health irretrievably impaired—not even the gods could heal him; his brownish red hair gone white, his skin turned glistening gold; his vision cursed.

The mundane were horrified. A test that left a young man crippled was not a test at all, they said. It was sadistic torture. The wise wizards knew better. Magic is a powerful force, a gift of the gods of magic, and with such a force comes a powerful responsibility. In the past, this power had been misused. Wizards had once come perilously close to destroying the world. The gods of magic had intervened, establishing rules and laws for the use of magic, and now only those mortals capable of handling such responsibility were permitted to wield it.

All mages who wanted to advance in their profession were required to take a test given to them by the wizards high in the Order. To ensure that every wizard who went into this test was serious about the art, the Orders of High Sorcery decreed that each wizard must be willing to bet his or her life on the outcome. Failure meant death. Even success did not come without sacrifice. The test was designed to teach the mage something about himself.

Raistlin had learned a great deal about himself, more than he wanted to know. He had committed a terrible act in that Tower, an act from which part of him recoiled in horror, yet there was another part of him that knew quite well he would do the same again. The act had not been real, though it had seemed quite real to him at the time. The test consisted of dropping the mage into a world of illusion. The choices he made in this world would affect him the rest of his life—might even end up costing him his life.

The terrible deed Raistlin had committed involved his twin brother, Caramon, who had been a horrified witness to it. The two never spoke of what had happened, but the knowledge was always there, casting its shadow over them.

The Test in the Tower is designed to help the mage learn more about his strengths and his weaknesses in order for him to improve himself. Thus, the punishment. Thus, the rewards. The punishment had been severe in Raistlin's case—his health wrecked, his vision cursed. He had emerged from the Test with pupils the shape of hourglasses. To teach him humility and compassion, he saw the passage of time speeded up. Whatever he looked upon, be it fair maiden or a newly picked apple, withered with age as he gazed at it.

Yet the rewards were worth it. Raistlin had power now, power that astonished, awed, and frightened those who knew the young mage best. Par-Salian, head of the Conclave, had given Raistlin the Staff of Magius, a rare and valuable artifact. Even as he bent double coughing,

Raistlin put out his hand to touch the staff. Its presence was comforting, reassuring. His suffering was worth it. The magical staff had been crafted by Magius, one of the most gifted mages who had ever lived. Raistlin had owned the staff for several years now, and he still did not know the full extent of the staff's powers.

He coughed again, the cough tearing at him, rending flesh and bone. The only remedy for one of these spasms was a special herbal tea. The tea should be drunk hot for best effect. The cave that was his current home had no fire pit, no means to warm the water. Raistlin would have to leave the warmth of his blanket and go out into the night in search of hot water.

Ordinarily, Caramon would have been on hand to fetch the water and brew the tea. Caramon was not here, however. Hale and healthy, big of heart and body, generous of spirit, Raistlin's twin was somewhere out there in the night, capering light-heartedly with the other guests at the wedding of Riverwind and Goldmoon.

The hour was late—well after midnight. Raistlin could still hear the laughter and music from the celebration. He was angry with Caramon for abandoning him, going off to make merry with some girl—Tika Waylan most likely—leaving his ill twin to fend for himself.

Half suffocated, Raistlin tried to stand and almost collapsed. He grabbed hold of a chair, eased himself into it and crumpled over, laying his head on the rickety table Caramon had cobbled together from a packing crate.

"Raistlin?" cried a cheerful voice from outside. "Are you asleep? I have a question I need to ask you!"

"Tas!" Raistlin tried to call out the kender's name, but another spasm of coughing interrupted him.

"Oh, good," the cheery voice went on, hearing the coughing, "you're still awake."

Tas—short for Tasslehoff—Burrfoot bounded into the cave.

The kender had been told repeatedly that, in polite society, one always knocked on the door (or, in this instance, the lattice-work screen of branches that covered the cave entrance) and waited to be invited inside before one entered. Tas had difficulty adapting to this custom, which was not the norm in kender society, where doors are shut against inclement weather and marauding bugbears (and sometimes not even the bugbears, if they are interesting bugbears). When

Tas remembered to knock at all, he generally did so simultaneous with entering if the occupant was lucky. Otherwise, he entered first and then remembered to knock, which is what he did on this occasion.

Tas lifted the screen and slipped nimbly inside, bringing with him light flaring from a lantern.

"Hullo, Raistlin," said Tas. He came to stand beside the young mage and thrust both a grubby hand and the lantern into Raistlin's face. "What kind of a feather is this?"

Kender are a diminutive race said to be distantly related to dwarves (by everyone except the dwarves). Kender are fearless, intensely curious, fond of bright-colored clothing, leather pouches, and collecting interesting objects to put in those pouches. Kender are a race of optimists and sadly a race that tends to be a bit light-fingered. To call a kender a thief is misnomer. Kender never mean to steal. They borrow, always with the best intentions of returning what they've picked up. It is hard to persuade a closed-minded person to understand this, however, particularly when he finds the kender's hand in his purse.

Tasslehoff was representative of his race. He stood somewhere near four feet in height, depending on how high his topknot of hair was on any particular day. Tas was quite proud of his topknot and often decorated it as he'd done tonight, having adorned it with several red maple leaves. He faced Raistlin with a grin on his face, his slightly slanted eyes shining and his pointed ears quivering with excitement.

Raistlin glared at Tasslehoff with as much fury as he could muster, given that he was blinded by the sudden light and choking to death. He reached out his own hand and seized hold of the kender's wrist and squeezed.

"Hot water!" Raistlin gasped. "Tea!"

"Tea?" said Tas, just catching the last word. "No, thanks, I just ate."

Raistlin coughed into the handkerchief. It came away from his lips stained red with blood. He glared at Tas again and this time the kender caught on.

"Oh, *you* want the tea! The tea Caramon always makes for your cough. Caramon's not here to make it, and you can't make it, because you're coughing. Which means . . ." Tas hesitated. He didn't want to get this wrong.

Raistlin pointed a trembling hand at the empty mug on the table.

"You want me to fetch the water!" Tas jumped to his feet. "I won't be gone a minute!"

The kender dashed outside, leaving the screen of branches open so that cold air blew in, causing Raistlin to shiver. He clutched the blanket around his shoulders and went into a another fit of coughing.

Tas was back in an instant.

"Forgot the mug."

He grabbed the mug and ran off again.

"Shut the—" Raistlin tried, but he couldn't manage to say it quickly enough. The kender was gone, the screen standing open.

Raistlin gazed out into the night. The sound of merriment was louder now. He could see firelight and the silhouettes of people dancing. The bride and groom, Riverwind and Goldmoon, would have gone to their wedding bed by now. They would be wrapped in each other's arms; their love for each other, their trials, their sorrows and griefs, their long and dark journey together culminating in this moment of joy.

That's all it will be, Raistlin thought—a moment—a spark that will flare for an instant then be stamped out by the doom that was fast approaching. He was the only one with the brains to see it. Even Tanis Half-Elven, who had more sense than most of this lot, had been lulled into a false sense of peace and security.

"The Queen of Darkness is not defeated," Raistlin had told Tanis not so many hours ago.

"We may not have won the war," Tanis had said in reply, "but we have won a major battle—"

Raistlin had shaken his head at such stupidity.

"Do you see no hope?" Tanis had asked.

"Hope is the denial of reality," Raistlin had said in return. "Hope is the carrot dangled before the draft horse to keep him plodding along in a vain attempt to reach it."

He was rather proud of that imagery, and he smiled as he thought back on it. Another fit of coughing ended his smile and interrupted his thoughts. When he had recovered, he stared again out the door, trying to see the kender in the moonlight. Raistlin was leaning on a weak reed and he knew it. There was every possibility that the rattle-brained kender would get distracted by something and forget about him completely.

"In which case I'll be dead by morning," Raistlin muttered. His irritation at Caramon grew.

His thoughts went back to his conversation with Tanis.

"Are you saying we should just give up?" Tanis had asked him.

"I'm saying we should remove the carrot and walk forward with our eyes open," Raistlin had answered. "How will you fight the dragons, Tanis? For there will be more! More than you can imagine! Where now is Huma? Where now are the fabled dragonlances?"

The half-elf had no answer. Tanis had been impressed with Raistlin's remarks, though. He'd gone off to think about them, and now that this wedding was over, perhaps the people could be made to take a good hard look at the grim reality of their situation. Autumn was ending. The chill wind blowing into the door, coming from the mountains, presaged the winter months that lay ahead.

Raistlin went into another fit of coughing. When he lifted his head, there was the kender.

"I'm back," said Tasslehoff brightly and unnecessarily. "Sorry to be so slow, but I didn't want to spill any."

He gingerly set the steaming mug on the table and then looked about for the sack of herbs. Finding it lying nearby, he grabbed hold of it and yanked it open.

"Do I just dump this whole bag in here—"

Raistlin snatched the precious herbs away from the kender. Carefully, he shook out some of the leaves into the hot water and watched intently as they swirled about and then drifted to the bottom of the cup. When the color of the water had darkened and the pungent smell filled the air, Raistlin took the mug in his shaking hands and brought it to his lips.

The brew had been a gift from the archmage, Par-Salian—a gift to ease his guilty conscience, so Raistlin had always thought bitterly. The soothing concoction slid down Raistlin's throat and almost immediately the spasms ceased. The smothering feeling, like cobwebs in his lungs, eased. He drew in a deep breath.

Tas wrinkled his nose. "That stuff smells like a gully dwarf picnic. Are you sure it makes you better?"

Raistlin sipped the tea, reveling in its warmth.

"Now that you can talk," Tas continued, "I have a question about this feather. Where did I put it—"

Tas began to search through the pockets of his jacket.

Raistlin eyed the kender coldly. "I am exhausted, and I would like to return to my bed, but I don't suppose I will be able to get rid of you, will I?"

"I *did* fetch the hot water for you," Tas reminded him. He suddenly looked worried. "My feather's not here."

Raistlin sighed deeply as he watched the kender continue to rummage through his pockets decorated with gold braiding "borrowed" from a ceremonial cloak the kender had come across somewhere. Not finding what he sought, Tas rummaged through the pockets of his loose-fitting trousers and then started in on his boots. Raistlin lacked the strength, or he would have thrown the kender out bodily.

"It's this new jacket," Tas complained. "I never know where to find things."

He had discarded the clothes he had been wearing for an entirely new set, collected over the past few weeks from the leavings and cast-offs of the refugees from Pax Tharkas in whose company they were now traveling.

The refugees had been slaves, forced to work in the iron mines for the Dragon Highlord Verminaard. The Highlord had been killed in an uprising led by Raistlin and his friends. They had freed the slaves and fled with them into the mountainous region south of the city of Pax Tharkas. Though it was hard to believe, this annoying kender, Tasslehoff Burrfoot, had been one of the heroes of that uprising. He and the elderly and befuddled wizard, who called himself by the grandiose name of Fizban the Fabulous, had inadvertently triggered a mechanism that sent hundreds of tons of boulders dropping down into a mountain pass, blocking the draconian army on the other side of the pass from entering Pax Tharkas to put down the uprising.

Verminaard had died at the hands of Tanis and Sturm Brightblade. The magical sword of the legendary elven king, Kith-Kanan, and the hereditary sword of the Solamnic knight, Sturm Brightblade, pierced the Highlord's armor and stabbed deep into the man's body. Up above them, two red dragons fought and two red dragons died, their blood falling like horrible rain upon the terrified observers.

Tanis and the others had acted quickly to take charge of the chaotic situation. Some of the slaves had wanted to take out their revenge against the monstrous draconians who had been their masters. Knowing their only hope for survival lay in flight, Tanis, Sturm, and

Elistan had persuaded the men and women that they had a god-given opportunity to escape, taking their families to safety.

Tanis had organized work parties. The women and children had gathered what supplies they could find. They loaded up wagons used to carry ore from the mines with food, blankets, tools—whatever they thought would be needed on their trek to freedom.

The dwarf, Flint Fireforge, had been born and raised in these mountains, and he led Plainsmen scouts, who had been among the slaves, on a expedition south to find a safe haven for the refugees. They had discovered a valley nestled between the Kharolis peaks. The tops of the mountains were already white with snow, but the valley far below was still lush and green, the leaves barely touched by the reds and golds of autumn. There was game in abundance. The valley was crisscrossed with clear streams, and the foothills were honey-combed with caves that could be used for dwellings, food storage, and refuge in case of attack.

In those early days, the refugees expected at any moment to be set upon by dragons, pursued by the foul dragon-men known as draconians, and they might well have been pursued, for the draconian army was quite capable of scaling the pass leading into the valley. It had been (astonishingly) Raistlin's twin, Caramon, who had come up with the idea of blocking the pass by causing an avalanche.

It had been Raistlin's magic—a devastating lightning spell he had learned from a night-blue spellbook he had acquired in the sunken city of Xak Tsaroth—that had produced the thunder clap that had shaken loose mounds of snow and sent heavy boulders cascading into the pass. More snow had fallen on top of that, fallen for days and nights, so that the pass was soon choked with it. No creature—not even the winged and claw-footed lizard-men—could now enter the valley.

Days for the refugees had passed in peaceful tranquility, and the people relaxed. The red and gold leaves fell to the ground and turned brown. The memory of the dragons and the terror of their captivity receded. Safe, snug, and secure, the refugees talked about spending the winter here, planning to continue their journey south in the spring. They spoke of building permanent shelters. They talked of dismantling the wagons and using the wood for crude huts, or building dwellings out of rock and sod to keep them warm when the chill rain and snows of winter would eventually come to the valley.

Raistlin's lip curled in a sneer of contempt.

"I'm going to bed," he said.

"Found it!" cried Tasslehoff, remembering at the last moment that he'd stuck the feather in a safe place—his brown topknot of hair.

Tasslehoff plucked the feather from his topknot and held it out in the palm of his hand. He held it carefully, as if it were a precious jewel, and regarded it with awe.

Raistlin regarded the feather with disdain. "It's a chicken feather," he stated.

He rose to his feet, gathered his long red robes around his wasted body, and returned to his straw pallet spread out on the dirt floor.

"Ah, I thought so," said Tasslehoff, softly.

"Close the door on your way out," Raistlin ordered. Lying down on the pallet, he wrapped himself in his blanket and closed his eyes. He was sinking into slumber when a hand, shaking his shoulder, brought him back awake.

"What?" Raistlin snapped.

"This is very important," Tas said solemnly, bending over Raistlin and breathing garlic from dinner into the mage's face. "Can chickens fly?"

Raistlin shut his eyes. Maybe this was a bad dream.

"I know they have wings," Tas continued, "and I know roosters can flap to the top of the chicken coop so they can crow when the sun comes up, but what I'm wondering is if can chickens fly way up high, like eagles? Because, you see, this feather floated down from the sky and I looked up, but I didn't see any passing chickens, and then I realized that I'd never seen chickens fly—"

"Get out!" Raistlin snarled, and he reached for the Staff of Magius that lay near his bed. "Or so help me I will—"

"—turn me into a hop toad and feed me to a snake. Yes, I know." Tas sighed and stood up. "About the chickens—"

Raistlin knew the kender would never leave him alone, not even with the threat of being turned into a toad, which Raistlin lacked the strength to do anyway.

"Chickens are not eagles. They cannot fly," said Raistlin.

"Thank you!" said Tasslehoff joyously. "I knew it! Chickens aren't eagles!"

He flung aside the screen, leaving it wide open, and forgetting his lantern, which shone right in Raistlin's eyes. Raistlin was just starting to drift off, when Tas's shrill voice jolted him again to wakefulness.

"Caramon! There you are!" Tas shouted. "Guess what? Chickens aren't eagles. They *can't* fly! Raistlin said so. There's hope, Caramon! Your brother is wrong. Not about the chickens, but about the hope. This feather is a sign! Fizban cast a magic spell he called *featherfall* to save us when we were falling off the chain and we were supposed to fall like feathers, but instead the only thing that fell were feathers—chicken feathers. The feathers saved me, though not Fizban."

Tas's voice trailed off into a snuffle as he thought of his sadly deceased friend.

"Have you been pestering Raist?" Caramon demanded.

"No, I've been helping him!" Tas said proudly. "Raistlin was choking to death, like he does, you know. He was coughing up blood! I saved him. I ran to get the water that he uses to make that horrible smelling stuff he drinks. He's better now, so you don't have to fret. Hey, Caramon, don't you want to hear about the chickens—"

Caramon didn't. Raistlin heard his twin's large boots clomp hastily over the ground, running toward the hut.

"Raist!" Caramon cried anxiously. "Are you all right?"

"No thanks to you," Raistlin muttered. He hunched deeper into his blanket, kept his eyes closed. He could see Caramon well enough without looking at him.

Big, muscular, broad-shouldered, broad-smiling, genial, good-looking, his brother was everybody's friend, all the girls' darling.

"I was left to the tender mercies of a kender," Raistlin told him, "while you were out playing slap and tickle with the buxom Tika."

"Don't talk about her like that, Raist," said Caramon, and there was a harsh edge to his generally cheerful voice. "Tika's a nice girl. We were dancing. That's all."

Raistlin grunted.

Caramon stood there shuffling his big feet, then said remorsefully, "I'm sorry I wasn't here to fix your tea. I didn't realize it was so late. Can I— Can I get you anything? Do something for you?"

"You can stop talking, shut what passes for a door, and douse that blasted light!"

"Yeah, Raist. Sure." Caramon picked up the lattice-work branch screen and set it back into place. He blew out the candle inside the lantern and undressed in the darkness.

Caramon tried to be quiet, but the big man—a muscular and healthy contrast to his weaker twin—stumbled into the table, knocked over a chair, and once, to judge by the sound of swearing, bumped his head on the cavern wall while groping about in the dark, trying to find his mattress.

Raistlin grit his teeth and waited in seething silence until Caramon finally settled down. His brother was soon snoring, and Raistlin, who had been so weary, lay wide awake, unable to sleep.

He stared into the darkness, not blinded by it as his twin and all the rest of them. His eyes were open to what lived inside.

"Chicken feathers!" he muttered scathingly and began to cough again.

2

Dawn of a new day.
The longing for home.

anis Half-Elven woke with a hangover, and he hadn't even been drinking. His hangover came not from spending the night in jollity, dancing, and drinking too much ale. It came from lying awake half the night worrying.

Tanis had left the wedding early last night. The celebratory spirit grated on his soul. The loud music made him wince and glance uneasily over his shoulder, fearful that they were revealing themselves to their enemies. He longed to tell the musicians, banging and tooting on their crude instruments, not to play so loudly. There were eyes watching from the darkness, ears listening. Eventually he had sought out Raistlin, finding the company of the dark-souled, cynical mage more in keeping with his own dark and pessimistic feelings.

Tanis had paid for it, too. When he had finally fallen asleep, he dreamed of horses and carrots, dreamed he was that draft horse, plodding round and round in a never-ending circle, seeking vainly for the carrot he could never quite reach.

"First, the carrot is a blue crystal staff," he said resentfully, rubbing his aching forehead. "We have to save the staff from falling into

---

23

the wrong hands. We do and then we're told this is not good enough. We have to travel to Xak Tsaroth to find the god's greatest gift—the sacred Disks of Mishakal, only to discover that we can't read them. We have to seek out the person who can, and all the while, we are being dragged deeper and deeper into this war—a war none of knew was even going on!"

"Yes, you did," growled a largish lump, barely visible in the half-light of dawn that was slipping through the blankets covering the opening of the cave. "You had traveled enough, seen enough, heard enough to know war was brewing. You just wouldn't admit it."

"I'm sorry, Flint," said Tanis. "I didn't mean to wake you. I didn't realize I was talking out loud."

"That's a sign of madness, you know," the dwarf grumbled. "Talking to yourself. You shouldn't make a habit of it. Now go back to sleep before you wake the kender."

Tanis glanced over at another lump on the opposite side of the cave that was not so much a cave as a hole scooped out of the mountain. Tas had been relegated to a far corner by Flint, who'd been grumpily opposed to sharing his cave with the kender anyway. Tanis needed to keep an eye on Tas, however, and had finally persuaded the dwarf to allow the kender to share their dwelling.

"I think I could shout and not wake him," said Tanis, smiling.

The kender slept the peaceful and innocent sleep of dogs and children. Much like a dog, Tas twitched and whiffled in his sleep, his small fingers wiggling as if even in his dreams he was examining all sorts of curious and wondrous things. Tas's precious pouches, containing his treasure trove of "borrowed" items, lay scattered around him. He was using one as a pillow.

Tanis made a mental note to go through those pouches sometime today when Tas was off on one of his excursions. Tanis regularly searched the kender's possessions, looking for objects people had "misplaced" or "dropped." Tanis would return said objects to their owners, who would receive them in a huff and tell him he really should do something about the kender's pilfering.

Since kender had been pilfering since the day the Graygem's passing had created them (if you believed the old legends), there wasn't much Tanis could do to stop it, short of taking the kender to the top of the mountain and shoving him off, which was Flint's preferred solution to the problem.

Tanis crawled out from beneath his blanket, and moving as quietly as he could, he left the hut. He had an important decision to make today, and if he remained in his bed, trying to go back to sleep, he would only toss and turn restlessly thinking about it, risking another outraged protest from Flint. Despite the chill of the morning—and winter was definitely in the air—Tanis decided to go wash the thought of carrots out of his mind with a plunge in the stream.

His cavern was just one of many that pocked the mountainside. The refugees of Pax Tharkas were not the first people to dwell in these caves. Pictures painted on the walls of some gave indications that ancient folk had lived here before. The pictures depicted hunters with bows and arrows and animals that resembled deer yet had long pointed horns, not antlers. And in some there were creatures with wings. Enormous creatures breathing fire from their mouths. Dragons.

He stood for a moment on the ledge in front of his cave, gazing down at floor of the valley spread out before him. He could not see the stream; the valley was shrouded with a low-lying mist rising off the water. The sun lit the sky, but it had not yet risen over the mountains. The valley remained nestled in its foggy blanket, as though as loathe to wake up as the old dwarf.

A beautiful place, Tanis thought to himself, climbing down from the rocks onto the wet grass in the misty half-light, heading toward the tree-lined stream.

The red leaves of the maple and the gold of the walnut and oak trees were a brilliant contrast to the dark green of the pines, as the gray rock of the mountains was a contrast to the stark white, new-fallen snows. He could see tracks of game animals on the muddy trail leading to the stream. Nuts lay on the ground, and fruit hung glistening from the vines.

"We could shelter in this valley though the winter months," Tanis said, doing his thinking aloud. He slipped and slid down the bank until he came to the edge of the deep, swift-flowing water. "What harm would there be in that?" he asked his reflection.

The face that looked up at him grinned in answer. He had elven blood in him, but one would never know by looking. Laurana accused him of hiding it. Well, maybe he did. It made life easier. Tanis scratched at the beard that no elf could grow. Long hair covered his slightly pointed ears. His body did not have the slender delicacy of the elven form but the bulk of humans.

Stripping off his leather tunic, breeches, and boots, Tanis waded into the stream, dispersing his reflection in ripples, gasping at the shock of the cold water. He splashed water onto his chest and neck. Then, holding his breath, he braved himself for a plunge. He came up huffing and blowing water from his nose and mouth, grinning widely at the tingling sensation that spread throughout his body. Already he felt better.

After all, why shouldn't they stay here?

"The mountains protect us from the chill winds. We have food enough to see us through the winter, if we are careful." Tanis splashed water into the air, like a kid at play. "We are safe from our enemies—"

"For how long?"

Tanis had thought himself alone, and he nearly leaped out of the water in shock at hearing another voice.

"Riverwind!" Tanis exclaimed, turning around and spotting the tall man standing on the bank. "You scared me out of six years of my life!"

"Since you are half elven with a life-span of several hundred years, six of those years is not much to worry about," Riverwind remarked.

Tanis looked searchingly at the Plainsman. Riverwind had never met or even seen anyone of elven blood until he had encountered Tanis, and though Tanis was half elf and half human, Riverwind found him wholly alien. There had been occasions between the two when such a remark about Tanis's race would have been meant as an insult.

Tanis saw a smile warm in the Plainsman's brown eyes, however, and he smiled in return. He and Riverwind had gone through too much together for the old prejudices to remain. The fire of dragons had burned up mistrust and hatred. Tears of joy and of sorrow had washed away the ashes.

Tanis climbed out of the water. He used his leather tunic to dry himself then sat down beside Riverwind, shivering in the cold air. The sun, beaming through a gap in the mountains, burned away the mist and soon warmed him.

Tanis eyed Riverwind in concern that was half-mocking and half-serious. "What is the bridegroom doing up so early on his wedding morn? I did not expect to see you or Goldmoon for several days."

Riverwind gazed out over the water. The sun shone full on his face. The Plainsman was a man who kept himself to himself. His innermost feelings and thoughts were his alone, personal and private, not to be shared with anyone. His dark visage was normally set in an expressionless mask, and so it was today, but Tanis could see radiance shining from beneath.

"My joy was too great to be contained within rock walls," said Riverwind softly. "I had to come outside to share it with the earth and the wind, the water and the sun. Even now, the wide, vast world feels too small to hold it."

Tanis had to look away. He was glad for Riverwind, also envious, and he didn't want the envy to show. Tanis found himself longing for such love and joy himself. The irony was that he could have it. All he had to do was banish the memory of curly dark hair, flashing dark eyes, and a charming, crooked smile.

As if reading his thoughts, Riverwind said, "I wish the same for you, my friend. Perhaps you and Laurana . . ."

His voice trailed off.

Tanis shook his head and changed the subject.

"We have that meeting today with Elistan and the Seekers. I want you and your people to attend. We have to decide what to do, whether we stay here or leave."

Riverwind nodded but said nothing.

"I know this is bad timing," Tanis added ruefully. "If ever there was a joy-killer, it's Hederick the High Theocrat, but we have to make a decision quickly, before the snows come."

"From what you were saying, you have already decided we should stay," said Riverwind. "Is that wise? We are still very close to Pax Tharkas and the dragonarmies."

"True," said Tanis, "but the pass between here and Pax Tharkas is blocked by rocks and snow. The dragonarmy has better things to do than chase after us. They're conquering nations. We're a ragtag bunch of former slaves—"

"—who escaped them, giving them a black eye." Riverwind turned his penetrating gaze full on Tanis. "The enemy must come after us. If the people they conquer hear that others threw off their manacles and walked free, they will begin to believe they can also overthrow their masters. The armies of the Dark Queen will come after us. Maybe not soon, but they will come."

Tanis knew he was right. He knew Raistlin and his analogy

about the carrot was right. Staying here was dangerous. Every day that passed could be bringing their enemies closer. He didn't want to admit it. Tanis Half-Elven had traveled the world for five years, searching for himself. He thought he'd found himself, only to discover on his return that he wasn't who he'd thought he was.

He would have liked to have spent some time—even just a little while—in a quiet place he could call home, a place where he could think, figure out some things. A cave shared with an irascible old dwarf and a pilfering and sometimes highly annoying kender wasn't Tanis's ideal home, but—compared to the road—it seemed very attractive.

"That is good reasoning, my friend, but Hederick will say that it is not the true reason you want to leave," Tanis pointed out. "You and your people want to go back to your homeland. You want to return to the Plains of Dust."

"We want to reclaim what is ours," said Riverwind, "what was taken from us."

"There is nothing left," said Tanis gently, thinking of the burned-out village of Que-shu.

"*We* are left," said Riverwind.

Tanis shivered. The sun had ducked behind a cloud, and he was chilled. He had long feared that this was Riverwind's intent.

"So you and your people plan to strike out on your own."

"We have not yet decided," said Riverwind, "but that is the direction our thinking is tending."

"Look, Riverwind," said Tanis. "I know it's a lot to ask, but your Plainsmen have been an immense help to us. These people are not accustomed to living like this. Before they were slaves, they were shopkeepers and merchants, farmers and cobblers. They came from cities like Haven and Solace and a host of other towns and villages around Abanasinia. They've never had to live off the land. They don't know how."

"And for centuries, these city-dwellers have looked down on us," said Riverwind. "They call us barbarians, savages."

And you call me a half-elf, Tanis thought, but did not say aloud. Instead he said, "When we were all of us prisoners, you put all the old hatreds and misunderstandings aside. We worked together to help each other escape. Why dredge that up now?"

"Because others brought it up first," Riverwind said harshly.

"Hederick," said Tanis, sighing. "The man's an ass, plain and simple. You know that; although, it's because he's an ass that we met you and Goldmoon."

Riverwind smiled at the memory. "True," he said, his voice softening. "I have not forgotten."

"Hederick falls into the fire. Goldmoon's blue crystal staff heals him, and all he can do is yell that she is a witch, and he sticks his hand back into the fire, then he runs off and calls the guards. That's the sort of lunk-head he is. You can't pay any attention to what he says."

"Others do pay attention, my friend."

"I know," Tanis said gloomily. He picked up a handful of small rocks, began tossing them one-by-one into the water.

"We have done our part," Riverwind continued. "We helped scout out the land to find this valley. We showed your shopkeepers how to transform caves into dwellings. We taught them to track and bring down game, to set out snares and traps. We showed them which berries to eat and which were poisonous. Goldmoon, my wife,"—this was the first time he'd used that word and he spoke it with gentle pride—"heals their sick."

"They are grateful, though they don't say it. You and your people might be able to make it safely through the mountains and back to your homeland before the worst of the winter sets in, but you know as well as I do that it's risky. I wish you would stay with us. I have this feeling in my gut that we should all keep together.

"I know we can't stay here," Tanis added with a sigh. "I know it's dangerous." He hesitated before he went on, knowing how his proposal would be received. Then, like diving into cold water, he plunged ahead.

"I'm sure if we could find the dwarven kingdom of Thorbardin—"

"Thorbardin! The mountain fastness of the dwarves?" Riverwind scowled. "I won't consider it."

"Think about it. Hidden deep below ground, the dwarven kingdom would be a perfect refuge for our people. We could remain there during the winter, safe beneath the mountain. Not even dragon eyes could find us—"

"We would also be safe buried in a tomb!" Riverwind stated caustically. "My people will not go to Thorbardin. We will go nowhere near dwarves. We will scout out our own path. After all, we have no children with us to slow us up."

His face was shadowed. The children of the Plainsmen had all perished in the dragonarmy's attack on their villages.

"You have Elistan with you now," Riverwind went on. "He is a cleric of Paladine. He can heal the sick in Goldmoon's absence and teach your people of the return of the gods. My people and I want to go home. Can't you understand that?"

Tanis thought of his home in Solace. He wondered if his house was still standing, if it had survived the dragonarmy's assault. He liked to think it was. Though he had not been in his house for five years, knowing it was there, waiting to receive him, was a comfort.

"Yes," he answered. "I can understand."

"We have not yet made a final decision," said Riverwind, seeing his friend downcast. "Some of our people believe like you that there is safety in numbers, that we should remain together."

"Your wife among them," said Goldmoon, walking up behind them.

Riverwind rose to his feet, turning to meet his new bride as she came to him in the dawn.

Goldmoon had always been beautiful. Her long silver-gold hair— the color that was so rare among her people—had always glistened in the morning half-light. She had always worn the soft and supple leather skins of her people with a grace and elegance that would have been envied by the fine ladies of Palanthas. This morning, she made beauty seem a paltry and inadequate word to describe her. The mists seemed to part for her, the shadows lift.

"You were not worried about me, were you?" Riverwind asked, with a trace of unease.

"No, my husband," said Goldmoon, and she lingered lovingly over the word. "I knew where to find you." She glanced upward into the blue heavens. "I knew you would be out beneath the skies. Out here, where you can breathe."

He took her hands and they greeted each other by touching cheeks. The Plainsmen believed their love for each other should be expressed only in private.

"I claim the privilege of kissing the bride," said Tanis.

"You claimed that privilege last night," Riverwind protested, smiling.

"I will likely go on claiming it for the rest of my life," said Tanis. He kissed Goldmoon on the cheek.

The sun flared out from behind the mountain peak, as though to expressly admire Goldmoon, causing her silver hair to flame in its light.

"With such beauty in the world, how can there be evil?" Tanis asked.

Goldmoon laughed. "Perhaps to make me look better by contrast," she said, teasing. "You were speaking of serious subjects before I interrupted you," she added more somberly.

"Riverwind thinks you and your people should head off on your own, travel eastward toward the plains. He says you want to remain with us."

"That is true," said Goldmoon complacently. "I would like to remain with you and the others. I believe that I am needed, but my vote is just one among our people. If my husband and the others decide we should leave, then we will leave."

Tanis glanced from one to the other. He didn't quite know how to say this, so he decided just to come out with it.

"Excuse me for asking," he said awkwardly, "but what happened to Chieftain's Daughter?"

Goldmoon laughed again, laughed long and merrily, and even Riverwind smiled.

Tanis did not see the joke. When he'd first met the two, Goldmoon was Chieftain's Daughter and Riverwind, a humble shepherd, was her subject. True, they loved each other dearly, and it had often seemed to Tanis that Goldmoon would have been willing to put aside the responsibility of leadership, but Riverwind stubbornly refused to let her. He had insisted on being subservient, forcing her to make decisions. Placed in that position, she had done so.

"I don't get it," Tanis said.

"Chieftain's Daughter gave her final command last night," Goldmoon explained.

During the marriage ceremony, Riverwind had knelt before her, since she was his ruler, but Goldmoon had bidden her husband rise, indicating the two were wed as equals.

"I am Goldmoon of the Plains," she said. "Cleric of Mishakal. Priestess of the Que-shu."

"Who will be Chieftain of the Que-shu?" Tanis asked. "There are survivors from your tribe among the other Plainsmen. Will they accept Riverwind as their chieftain? He has proven himself to be a strong leader."

Goldmoon looked at Riverwind. He did not meet her gaze. He deliberately kept his eyes fixed on the bubbling stream. His lips tightened.

"The Que-shu have long memories," Goldmoon said at last, seeing her husband would not speak. "They know that my father did not accept Riverwind as my husband and ordered him stoned to death. They know that, but for the miracle of the blue crystal staff, Riverwind and I would have both perished."

"So they won't accept him as Chieftain, even though they look to him for guidance."

"The Que-shu do," said Goldmoon, "but they are not the only people here. There are some from the Que-Kiri, and they were once our bitter enemies. Our tribes met on the field of battle many times."

Tanis muttered a few words in elven.

"I won't ask you to translate that, my friend," said Goldmoon with a sad smile. "I know, and my people know, the truth of the tale about the two wolves that turned on each other and the lion who ate them both. It is not easy for people to overcome hatred that was born in them."

"You and Riverwind have done so," said Tanis.

"We still have trouble," Goldmoon admitted, "but we know where to go when we need help."

She touched the medallion she wore around her neck, the medallion that was the goddess's gift and an emblem of her faith.

"Maybe I'm being selfish," Tanis said quietly. "Maybe I don't want to say good-bye."

"We will not speak of goodbye," said Goldmoon firmly, "not on this day of joy—our first day as a married couple."

She reached for her husband's hand. Their fingers entwined, she and Riverwind walked back toward their dwelling, leaving Tanis alone by the stream.

It might be a day of joy for them, but he had the feeling it was going to be a day of aggravation and contention for him.

As if to prove him right, Tasslehoff Burrfoot burst out of the woods, running as fast as his short legs would carry him, an irate miller in hot pursuit.

"You don't understand!" Tas was yelling over his shoulder, "I was trying to put it *back*!"

3

Dissension. Letting go. From bad to worse.

The meeting of the refugees started every bit as badly as Tanis had expected.

They held the meeting in a grove of trees near the stream, for there was no cave large enough to hold eight hundred men, women, and children. The refugees had chosen representatives to speak for them, but they didn't intend to let those people speak unobserved. Thus almost everyone in the small community attended the meeting, standing on the outskirts where they could see, hear and speak up if they felt like it. Not an ideal situation, Tanis thought, for any delegates who might have been persuaded to change their thinking by reasoned argument would be forced to stand their ground because they were under the watchful eyes of those who had selected them.

The Plainsmen arrived in a body, for they had not been able to agree on a delegate—a bad sign. Riverwind was grimmer and more morose than usual. Goldmoon stood at his side, her face flushed with anger. Members of the Que-shu tribe stood apart from those of the Que-Kiri. None of the Plainsmen mingled with the other former slaves but regarded the main body of refugees with a suspicion that was whole-heartedly returned.

The refugees were also divided. Elistan came with his group of followers. Hederick arrived with his. Tanis and his friends formed yet another group.

Tanis looked around the assembly, where people were eying each other askance. Only last night, they were all dancing and singing together. So much for Goldmoon's day of joy.

Tanis looked to Elistan to start the proceedings. A former member of the Theocracy of Seekers himself, Elistan had been one of the few members of that group to actually use his power to help people. He had been the only one of them to stand up against Dragon Highlord Verminaard, warning the others that they were wrong to believe the Highlord's promises—promises that turned out to be lies and eventually landed them in the iron mines of Pax Tharkas. Though a prisoner himself, Elistan had continued to defy Verminaard and had nearly paid for his rebellion with his life. Already suffering from a wasting disease, he had been tortured by Verminaard in an effort to force him to worship the Dark Queen.

Elistan had been dying when he had met Goldmoon. She had secretly entered Pax Tharkas in company with Tanis and the other companions in a bold endeavor to free the slaves. Seeing Elistan, weak as he was, continue to work tirelessly to help the people, Goldmoon was drawn to him. She was able to heal him through the power of Mishakal, and Elistan knew that at last his life-long search had ended. He had found the true gods.

Elistan was able to read and translate the cryptic Disks of Mishakal. Elistan used the disks to teach them of the ancient gods of Krynn who, if they were remembered at all, were remembered only in legend. He told the people of Paladine, God of Light, and leader of the other gods of Light. He told them of Takhisis, Queen of Darkness, and of those gods who dwelt in the shadows. He spoke of Gilean of the Book, the God of the Scales of Balance, who, with the other Gods of Neutrality, kept the scales from tipping one way or the other, as had happened during the Age of Might, bringing about the catastrophe known as the Cataclysm that had forever changed the face of the world.

Although only in his forties, Elistan appeared older. The white robes of a Revered Son of Paladine hung on this thin frame. His recent illness, though cured, had left its mark on him. So, too, had his new-found faith. He was no longer troubled by doubts, no longer searching. His eyes were bright with intelligence and laughter. Children ran straight to his arms. People admired him and loved him, and more than a few had already accepted his teachings and were now followers of the gods.

Hederick the High Theocrat was not among them. In the absence of true gods, Hederick had devised some gods of his own. These Seeker gods had done well by Hederick, providing him with a good living, if they had done little for anyone else. Hederick had abandoned his gods when Verminaard came along, succumbing to the Highlord's blandishments and lies, ending up in the dungeons of Pax Tharkas.

Hederick had prudently taken no part in the uprising, for he thought it had little chance of success. When, to his amazement, the slaves were victorious, he was quick enough to switch sides and take advantage of the freedom others had won for him. He had always been jealous and mistrustful of Elistan and he was secretly incensed that the man was now able to perform "miracles." Hederick did not believe in these miracles. He did not believe in these new gods. He was biding his time, waiting for Elistan to be exposed as a charlatan. Meanwhile, because Hederick was loud and ingratiating and said what everyone wanted to hear, he'd manage to win over large numbers to his way of thinking.

Tanis hoped Elistan's wise counsel would prevail this day, convincing the refugees that they were not safe here. Unfortunately, before Elistan had a chance to speak, Hederick raised his arms.

"My dear friends," began the High Theocrat in well-oiled tones, "we have come together today to discuss issues important to us all."

Tanis sighed and looked at Elistan, who stood behind the High Theocrat with the rest of the Seekers. Elistan caught Tanis's glance. He shrugged and smiled ruefully. Hederick was still the leader of the people. He had a right to address them first.

"There are those among us who have been talking of leaving this valley," Hederick was saying. "This valley—that is safe, teeming with game, sheltered from the winter winds, hidden from our enemies—"

"We are *not* hidden," Tanis muttered, recalling Riverwind's words to himself only that morning. Tanis stood with his friends, apart from the main body, leaning his back against a fir tree. "Why doesn't Elistan speak up, remind him of that? Elistan should say something, do something—instead of just standing there."

"On the contrary," said Laurana, who was beside him. "Elistan is doing exactly right. He will allow Hederick to have his say, then Elistan will be able to answer all that Hederick is saying."

Tanis glanced at her. Laurana was not even listening to Hederick. Her gaze was fixed on Elistan. Her eyes, almond-shaped and bluer than the clear, cobalt sky, glowed with admiration; her voice warmed when she spoke of him. Tanis felt a twinge of jealousy. Some might say that Elistan was old enough to be Laurana's father, but in truth the beautiful elven maiden was far older than the human male. Laurana appeared to be a maid in her early twenties, as young as her friend, Tika Waylan, when, in fact, Laurana could have been Tika's great-grandmother.

I have no right to be jealous, Tanis reminded himself. I'm the one who ended our relationship. I'm in love with another woman myself, or at least, I think I might be in love with her. I should be glad Laurana has found someone else.

All very logical arguments, and yet Tanis found himself saying, "You and Elistan have certainly been spending a lot of time together."

Laurana turned to him. Her blue eyes were chill as the water in the stream. "What do you mean by that remark?" she asked sharply.

"Nothing," Tanis returned, astonished at her sudden anger. "I didn't mean anything—"

"Indeed we have been spending time together," Laurana continued. "I was a diplomat for many years in my father's court, where, as you well know, every sentence must be carefully considered lest it cause someone offense. A single word given the wrong intonation could bring about a feud that might last for centuries. I offered Elistan advice on one or two small matters, and he was grateful. Now he seeks out my counsel. *He* does not consider me a child!"

"Laurana, I didn't mean —"

She walked off, her shoulders stiff. Even angry and offended, she moved with a flowing grace that put the slender branches of willows to shame and caused Tanis's heart to stand still in awe when he looked at her.

Many watched Laurana as she walked past. Daughter of the Speaker of the Suns, ruler of the Qualinesti elves, she was the first elf maiden some of these humans had ever seen, and they never tired of gazing at her. Her beauty was exotic, alien, seemed almost ethereal. Her eyes were luminous blue, her hair a golden shower. Her voice was musical and low, her touch gentle.

This radiant, stunning woman could have been his. Tanis could have been as happy as Riverwind and Goldmoon.

"You must like the taste of shoe leather," Flint remarked, his voice low. "Your foot is in your mouth often enough these days."

"She took it the wrong way," Tanis said, annoyed.

"You *said* it the wrong way," Flint retorted. "Laurana's not the little girl who fell in love with a playmate, Tanis. She's grown up. She's a woman with a woman's heart to give, or hadn't you noticed?"

"I noticed," said Tanis, "and I still maintain that breaking our engagement was the right thing to do—for her sake, not mine."

"If you believe that, then let her go."

"I'm not holding onto her," Tanis returned heatedly.

He'd spoken too loudly. Eyes turned his way, including the almond-shaped eyes of Laurana's brother, Gilthanas. Hederick heard him too and paused, offended.

"Do you have something to say, Half-Elven?" Hederick asked reproachfully.

"Oh, Tanis, now you're in trouble!" Caramon sniggered.

Feeling like an errant school boy who has been called to the front of the class, Tanis mumbled something in apology and retreated back into the shadows. Everyone smiled knowingly, then turned back to listen to Hederick's speech, except Gilthanas, who regarded Tanis with stern disapproval.

Once, many years ago, Gilthanas had been Tanis's friend. Then Tanis had made the mistake of falling in love with Laurana, and that had ended his friendship with her brother. To make matters worse, Tanis had recently suspected and even accused Gilthanas of being a spy. Tanis had been proven wrong, and he'd made an apology, but Gilthanas found it hard to forgive the fact that Tanis had suspected him capable of such a crime. Tanis wondered irritably if there were any additional means by which he could make his life more complicated.

Then Sturm Brightblade walked to him, and Tanis smiled and relaxed. Thank goodness for Sturm. The Solamnic knight, intent on the politics of the situation, was oblivious to all else.

"Are you listening to this great idiot?" Sturm demanded. "The man talks about building houses in this valley. Even a town hall! Apparently he has forgotten that only weeks before we were fleeing for our lives."

"I'm listening," said Tanis, "and so are they, more's the pity."

Many in the crowd were smiling and murmuring assent. Hederick's word-picture of a cozy winter spent in this peaceful place was an attractive one. Tanis felt a twinge of remorse. He'd been thinking much the same himself. Perhaps it was his talk with Raistlin last night or his talk with Riverwind this morning, but Tanis was growing increasingly uneasy. The valley seemed no longer a place of peace and beauty. He felt trapped here. Thinking of Raistlin, he looked over at the mage to see his reaction.

Raistlin sat upon a blanket spread for him on the ground by his brother. He cradled his magical staff in his arms. His gaze was abstracted, turned inward. He did not appear to be listening.

Hederick closed by saying that when spring came, the refugees would continue their journey to Tarsis, the city by the sea, where they would find a ship to take them far from this war-torn land.

"Some place where *humans* can reside in peace," Hederick concluded, laying emphasis on that word. "Some place far from those sorts of people known to cause trouble and strife in the world."

"What sorts of people is he talking about?" Tas asked, interested.

"Elves," said Tanis, scratching his beard.

"Dwarves," growled Flint.

"And kender," said Caramon, giving Tas's topknot a playful tweak that made the kender yelp.

Hederick glanced in their direction and pursed his lips in disapproval, then looked out upon the audience as much as to say, "See what I mean?"

With that, he retired to great applause.

"What a short memory he has," Sturm remarked. He smoothed the long mustaches that were the hallmark of a Solamnic knight and Sturm's pride, along with his father's sword and armor, the only legacy his father had left him. "Elves and a dwarf helped save his miserable life!"

"*And* a kender!" Tas added indignantly.

"Maybe Elistan will remind him of that," Tanis said, as the Revered Son of Paladine stepped forward.

"The gods of good hold back the darkness," Elistan stated, "as they hold back the snows that must soon blanket this valley, but winter will come and so too will the forces of evil."

Hederick interrupted him.

"If, as you say, Revered Son, your god, Paladine, and the other gods of Light have protected us in the past, can't we be assured that they will continue to protect us in the future?" the High Theocrat asked.

"The gods have helped us, that is true," said Elistan, "and they will continue to help us, but we must do our part. We are not babes in arms, whose every need has to be met by the parents. We are grown men and women. We have free will, a gift given to us by the gods. We have the ability to make choices—"

"And we *choose* to remain here in this valley," said Hederick.

This drew a laugh and applause.

Flint nudged Tanis with his elbow. "Look there," he said urgently, pointing.

The Plainsmen were leaving. They had turned their backs on the speakers and on their fellow refugees and were walking out of the grove. Riverwind and Goldmoon remained, seemingly reluctant to leave, but then, with a shake of his head, Riverwind walked off. He said something to Goldmoon, but she did not immediately follow him. She sent her searching gaze through the crowd until she found Tanis.

Goldmoon looked at him long, and he saw in her sad smile an apology. Then, she, too, turned her back and went to be with her husband. Both left to join their people.

By now, everyone in the crowd was watching the Plainsmen depart. Some cried, "Good riddance," but others stated that it was a shame to let them leave in anger. Elistan tried to say something, but the clamor in the crowd drowned him out. Hederick stood in the background, smiling contentedly.

Raistlin was at Tanis's elbow, plucking at his sleeve. Tanis could smell the fragrance of dried rose petals emanating from the young mage's pouch of spell components that he wore on a belt around his waist. Tanis could also smell the scent of decay that lingered about Raistlin, a scent the sweet perfume of roses could never quite mask. Rose petals were not the only spell components the mage carried. Some were far less pleasant.

"Something is wrong," Raistlin said urgently. "Don't you feel it?"

He gave a sudden hiss. His hand seized hold of Tanis's arm, the long, slender fingers digging painfully into Tanis's flesh.

"Raistlin," said Tanis irritably, "this is no time for—"

"Hush!" Raistlin raised his head, as though listening. "Where is the kender? Quickly! I need him!"

"You do?" Tasslehoff cried, amazed. "Excuse me," he added importantly, stepping on Flint's toes. "I have to get by. Raistlin needs me—"

"You have the sharpest eyes among us," said Raistlin, grasping hold of the kender. "Look into the sky! Swiftly. What do you see?"

Tas did as he was told, craning his neck and peering up into the sky, nearly tumbling over backward in the process.

"I see a white cloud that looks like a rabbit. There, do you see it, Caramon? It has long ears and a puffy tail and—"

"Don't be ridiculous!" Raistlin snarled, giving Tas a shake that snapped his head back. "Keep looking!"

"It might help if I knew what I was looking for," Tas pointed out meekly.

"That mage shivers my skin," said Flint, scowling and rubbing his arms.

"It's not him," said Tanis. "I feel it, too. Sturm!" he called, looking about for the knight.

Sturm had been standing in the shadows of an oak, keeping himself apart from the others, especially Raistlin. The serious-minded knight, who lived by the code, *Est Sularas est Mithos*, "My honor is my life," had grown up with Raistlin and his brother, and though Sturm liked Caramon, the knight had never liked nor trusted his twin.

"I sense it as well," Sturm said.

An uneasy silence had fallen over the crowd. People turned this way and that, searching for the cause of the pricklings of fear that tingled in their arms and raised goose bumps on their flesh. The Plainspeople had halted and were gazing skyward. Riverwind had his hand on the hilt of his sword.

"This reminds me of something!" Tanis said suddenly.

"Xak Tsaroth," Sturm murmured.

"There!" Tasslehoff cried, pointing. "A dragon!"

It flew far above them, so high that the huge monster was reduced in size to a child's toy—a deadly toy. As the people watched in terror, the dragon dipped its wings and began to descend, winding downward in slow, lazy circles. The morning sun flashed off red scales and shone through the thin membrane of red wings. The fear that is part of a dragon's arsenal swept over the crowd. Primal fear from a memory of time's beginning. Deep-rooted fear that wrung the heart and made the soul shudder.

"Run!" Hederick shrieked. "Run for your lives!"

Tanis understood the terror. He felt the desire to flee, to run anywhere and nowhere in a desperate, panicked need to escape the horror, but he could see that running was the last thing they should do. Most of the people were standing beneath the trees, concealed from the dragon's sight by the overspreading branches.

"Don't move!" he managed to shout, though he had to struggle to breathe through the suffocating fear. "If no one moves, the dragon might not see us—"

"Too late," said Sturm. He gazed upward at the beast. "The dragon has seen all there is to see, and so has the rider."

The dragon had flown closer to them. They could all see the rider accoutered in heavy armor and a helm decorated with horns. The rider sat at his ease in a specially designed saddle on the dragon's back, between the wings.

Pandemonium broke out. Some people went racing for the caves. Others collapsed weeping and shivering, onto the grass.

Tanis couldn't move. He could not take his eyes from the rider. The man was huge with muscular arms that were bare, despite the cold. His helm covered his face, yet Tanis had no trouble recognizing him.

"Verminaard!" Tanis gasped, forcing out the name through clenched teeth.

"That's impossible!" Sturm said. "He's dead!"

"Look for yourself!" Tanis returned.

"He was dead, I tell you," Sturm insisted, yet he sounded shaken. "No man could survive such wounds!"

"Well, this one did, apparently," Flint said grimly.

"Remember that he himself was a powerful cleric, serving an all powerful goddess," said Raistlin. "Takhisis might well have restored him to life."

Someone barreled straight into Tanis, nearly knocking him down. The person shoved Tanis aside and kept on running.

Panic had seized hold of nearly everyone. People went haring off in every direction. Women screamed, men shouted, and children wailed. The dragon flew lower and lower.

"They've all gone mad!" Caramon shouted, trying to make himself heard above the chaos. "Someone has to do something!"

"Someone is," said Tanis.

Elistan stood firm, his hand on the medallion of faith he wore around his neck. Surrounding him were twenty of his followers and they were pale but composed, listening carefully to Elistan's instructions. Laurana was among these. She seemed to sense Tanis's gaze, for she turned her head and flashed him a quick, cool glance. Then she and the other followers of Paladine went among the crowd, taking firm hold of those who were in hysterics and ministering to those who had fallen or been knocked down or trampled.

The Plainsmen were also taking action against the dragon. They stood with bows and arrows ready. The dragon was still too far away for a good shot, but the archers were prepared in case the beast should try to harm those on the ground. Riverwind was giving orders. Standing beside him, shoulder-to-shoulder, was Gilthanas. The elf had his bow and arrow aimed and ready.

Tanis had not thought to bring his bow, but he wore his sword, the magical sword of the elven king, Kith-Kanan. He drew his weapon, thinking, as he did so that it would do little good against the enormous red dragon. Caramon had his sword drawn. Raistlin's eyes were closed. He was chanting softly to himself, readying a magical spell. Flint had his battle-axe in his hand. Tasslehoff drew his own small sword that he had named Rabbitslayer, following Caramon's remark that the small blade would be useful only if Tas were attacked by a ferocious rabbit. Tas claimed the dagger was magic, but thus far the only magic Tanis had seen was the fact that the scatter-brained kender had not yet managed to lose it.

Armed and ready for a battle they could not hope to win, the companions stood waiting in the shadow of the trees for the dragon to start the slaughter.

The Dragon Highlord, mounted on the red's back, raised his arm in a mocking salute. Even from this distance, they could hear his deep voice rumbling orders to the dragon. The red gave an easy flap of its massive wings and sailed upward. It soared over the heads of the archers, who loosed off a volley of arrows. Almost all found their mark, but none did any damage. Striking the dragon's scales, the arrows clattered off, falling to the ground. The Dragon Highlord extended his hand and pointed straight at the grove.

The dragon let out its breath in a gust of fire. The trees exploded into flames. A wave of scorching heat swept over Tanis and the rest. Thick black smoke choked the air.

Sturm caught hold of Tasslehoff, who was staring at the dragon in open-mouthed excitement, and hoisted the kender off his feet and flung him over his shoulder. Caramon and Raistlin were already running for safety, as was Flint. Tanis peered into the smoke to see if anyone was trapped inside the burning grove.

The trees burned fiercely. Blazing branches fell down all around him. The thick smoke stung his eyes, choking him. The heat from the raging fire was causing his skin to blister. If people were still in there, they were doomed.

Tanis wondered grimly if Verminaard planned to set fire to the entire valley, but apparently the Dragon Highlord was content with simply terrifying them. The dragon lifted its head and flapped its wings and soared into the sky, flying with ponderous grace up and over the mountains. Dragon and rider were soon lost to sight.

The grove of oak, maple, and fir burned white hot, belching smoke that rolled into the sky and hung on the still air above what had once been a peaceful valley, a safe haven.

4

Flint tells a tale. Sturm recalls a legend.

For several hours following the dragon's attack, all was chaos. Families had lost track of each other during the mad stampede; children separated from their parents, husbands from their wives. Tanis and his friends worked to calm everyone, shepherding them back up into the caves where they would be safe if the dragon should come again. Goldmoon and the other clerics of Mishakal treated the frightened and the wounded. Elistan helped to restore calm and order, and by afternoon, all of the lost had been found; families were back together again. No one had died, which Tanis held to be a miracle.

He called a meeting for that night to discuss the dire emergency and this time he set the rules. No more public gatherings outdoors. The meeting was held in the largest cavern that could be found which was, of course, the cave that had been chosen by Hederick for his residence. The cave had a high ceiling with a natural chimney for ventilation that permitted the Theocrat to have a fire. This time, the meeting was limited to the delegates. Tanis had been adamant on that point, and even Hederick had grudgingly acceded to the wisdom of the half-elf's arguments. From now on, no one was to venture outside the caves unless they had good reason.

The delegates crowded into the cave, occupying every available space. Tanis brought Sturm and Flint, telling the rest to remain in their dwellings. He had invited Raistlin, too, but the mage had not yet come. Caramon was under orders to keep Tasslehoff away, to chain the disruptive kender to a wall if he had to. Riverwind and Goldmoon represented the Plainsmen. The terrible revelation that Verminaard was still alive, and the fact that he had discovered their location, had caused the Plainspeople to rethink plans of setting out on their own. Elistan was here, with Laurana by his side.

Hederick, as usual, spoke first.

Tanis thought that Hederick would be the first one to advocate fleeing the valley. The half-elf was astonished to find that Hederick still insisted on remaining.

"If anything, this attack reinforces my argument that we should stay here in the valley where we are safe," Hederick said. "Can you imagine the terrible tragedy that would have occurred if that dragon had caught us traipsing along some mountain trail with no cover, nowhere to run? The beast would have slaughtered us all! As it was, the Highlord realized that he was no match for us and flew off."

"The Dragon Highlord did not come to attack us, High Theocrat," said Sturm. "Lord Verminaard came to find us, and he succeeded. He now knows where we are."

"What will he do about it?" Hederick asked, spreading his hands. His supporters, gathered around him, all sagely nodded their heads. "Nothing, that's what. Because there's nothing he can do! He cannot bring troops through the pass. If he returns with the dragon, we will simply remain in the caves. Not even Lord Verminaard can burn down this mountain!"

"Don't be too sure of that," Tanis muttered.

He exchanged glances with Riverwind. Both of them remembered vividly the destruction of Riverwind's village in Que-shu, the solid rock walls that had melted away like fresh churned butter.

Tanis glanced at Elistan, wondering when the Revered Son was going to speak. Tanis was starting to have serious doubts about Elistan and his gods of Light. Elistan had proclaimed that the Dragon Highlord had been killed with help from the gods, yet the evil Highlord was not dead. Tanis wanted very much to ask Elistan why the gods of light had not been able to prevent Verminaard from coming back from the dead. Now was not the time to question the Revered Son's faith, however. The High Theocrat was looking for an opportunity to denounce these new gods and return to the Seeker gods he and his followers had been promoting to their own private advantage. Tanis guessed that Hederick and his bunch were already at work to undermine Elistan's teachings. They didn't need his help.

I'll speak to Elistan in private, Tanis thought. Meanwhile, the Revered Son could at least give me his support, not just sit there in silence. If he's as wise as Laurana claims, he'll see that we can't stay here.

"Our danger grows by the minute, good gentlefolk," Sturm was saying, speaking to the assembly. "Verminaard knows where we are. He did not seek us out for the sake of his health! He has a plan in mind, you may be sure of that. To do nothing is to doom us all to certain death."

One of the delegates, a woman named Maritta, rose to her feet. She was middle-aged, stout, and plain looking, but she was also a woman of courage and of sense who had played a valuable role in helping the refugees escape Pax Tharkas. She admired Elistan and had little use for Hederick. Clasping her hands over her midriff, she faced the High Theocrat.

"You, sir, claim that we will be safe from the dragon if we stay here, but the dragon is not our only enemy. Winter is another foe, just as deadly. What happens when our food supplies run low and the game has vanished? When the bitter cold and lack of proper food brings sickness and death to the elderly and the young?"

She rounded on Tanis. "And you, Half-Elven. You want us to leave. Very well, then. Where do we go? Answer me that! Would you have us set out with no destination in mind, to wind up lost in the wilderness or starving to death on some frozen mountainside?"

Before Tanis could answer, there was a blast of chill air. The elaborate screen of branches and animal hides that covered Hederick's cavern rustled and was shoved aside. Torchlight flickered in the wind, the flames of the fire wavered. Everyone looked round to see who had arrived.

Raistlin entered the meeting area. The mage wore his cowl pulled low over his head.

"It has started to snow," he reported.

"Does he enjoy bringing bad news?" Sturm muttered.

"What's he doing here?" Flint demanded.

"I asked him to come. I told him what time to be here," Tanis said, irritated. "I wonder why he's late!"

"So he could make a dramatic entrance," said Sturm.

Raistlin walked over to stand near the fire. The mage moved slowly, taking his time, well aware that all eyes were on him, though few with any friendly feeling. He cared nothing about being universally disliked, however. Tanis thought that perhaps Raistlin even reveled in it.

"Don't let me interrupt, Half-Elven," Raistlin said, coughing softly. He held his hands over the blaze to warm himself. The firelight reflected eerily on his glistening golden skin. "You were about to say something regarding the dwarven kingdom."

Tanis hadn't said a word about this yet. He hadn't been going to spring it on people in this abrupt fashion.

"I *have* been thinking we could find safe haven in the kingdom of Thorbardin—" he began reluctantly.

His proposal caused an outburst.

"Dwarves!" cried Hederick, frowning. "We'll have nothing to do with dwarves!"

His sentiment was loudly echoed by his supporters. Riverwind looked grim and shook his head. "My people will not travel to Thorbardin."

"Now see here, the lot of you," said Maritta. "You guzzle dwarf spirits and you're quick to take their money when dwarves come to your shops—"

"That doesn't mean we have to live with them." Hederick made a stiff and condescending bow to Flint. "Present company excepted, of course."

Flint had nothing to say in return—a bad sign. Ordinarily he would have given the Theocrat the sharp edge of his tongue. As it was, the dwarf sat in silence, whittling on a piece of wood. Tanis gave an inward sigh. He had known all along that his biggest obstacle to his plan of traveling to the dwarven kingdom was going to be this stubborn old dwarf.

The argument raged. Tanis glanced at Raistlin, who stood by the fire, warming his hands, a slight smile on his thin lips. He tossed this fireball into our midst for a reason, Tanis thought. Raistlin has something in mind. What, I wonder?

"No one is even certain if there are still dwarves beneath the mountain," stated Hederick.

Flint stirred at that, but still said nothing.

"I have no objection to traveling to Thorbardin," said Maritta, "but it is well known that the dwarves shut the gates to their kingdom three hundred years ago."

"That is the truth," said Flint, "and I say let their gates stay shut!"

Startled silence fell. People stared at the dwarf in wonder.

"You're not helping," Tanis said in a low aside.

"You know my feelings," Flint returned dourly. "I'll not set one foot beneath the mountain! Even if we could find the gates, which we can't. They've been lost for three hundred years."

"So it is not safe to stay here, and we have no place to go. Where does that leave us?" Maritta asked.

"Here," said Hederick.

Everyone began talking at once. The cave was rapidly heating up, what with the fire and so many warm bodies. Tanis was starting to sweat. He did not like confined spaces, did not like breathing the same air that had been breathed over and over by others. He was tempted to leave, and let everyone take care of themselves. The noise level grew, the din of the arguing reverberating off the rock walls. Then Raistlin gave a gentle cough.

"If I may speak," he began in his soft, damaged voice, and a hush fell. "I know how to find the key to Thorbardin. The secret lies beneath Skullcap."

Everyone stared at him in silence, not understanding what he meant, all except Flint.

The dwarf's face was grim, his jaw clenched. His breath came in grunts, and he whittled at the wood so hard the chips flew. He kept his eyes on his work.

"You have our attention, Raistlin," said Tanis. "What is Skullcap? Where is it and what do you mean that the secret to Thorbardin lies beneath it."

"I really know very little about the place," Raistlin said. "Odd bits I've picked up in my studies over the years. Flint can tell us more—"

"Yes, but he won't," said Flint.

Raistlin opened his mouth to speak again, but he was interrupted. The screen door was once again swept aside, this time with ominous-sounding cracking noises, as though large hands were fumbling at it.

Caramon came blundering inside. "Tanis," he said worriedly, "have you seen Raist? I can't find— Oh! There you are."

He glanced around at the assembly and flushed. "Beg pardon. I didn't know—"

"What are you doing here, Brother?" Raistlin demanded.

Caramon looked sheepish. "It's just— You were with me one minute and gone the next. I didn't know where you went. I thought—"

"No, you didn't," Raistlin snapped. "You never think. You have no idea what the word means. I am not a child who dares not venture outdoors without holding my nursemaid's hand! Who is minding the kender?"

"I . . . uh . . . tied him to a table leg . . ."

This produced a laugh. Raistlin cast a furious glance at his twin, and Caramon retreated to a shadowy corner.

"I'll just . . . wait over here."

"Flint," said Tanis. "What is Skullcap? Do you know what he's talking about?"

Flint maintained his stubborn, angry silence.

Raistlin was also no longer inclined to speak. Twitching aside the skirts of his red robes, the mage sat down upon an overturned crate and drew his cowl up over his head.

"Raistlin, tell us what you meant—" Tanis said.

Raistlin shook his head. "It seems you are all more interested in laughing at my fool brother."

"Let him sulk," Sturm said, disgusted.

Flint flung down his knife and the piece of wood that was now little more than a splinter. The knife clattered on the stone floor of the cavern at his feet. Flint's eyes, in their maze of wrinkles, blazed. His long beard quivered. The dwarf was short, of stocky build, with big-boned arms and wrists and the strong, capable hands of the master craftsman. He and Tanis had been friends for countless years, their friendship dating back to the half-elf's unhappy youth. Flint's voice was gruff and deep, seeming to rise up from the bones of the earth.

"I will tell you the story of Skullcap," said Flint in fierce tones. "I'll make it short and sweet. I am a hill dwarf, a Niedar, as my people are known, and proud to be one! Centuries ago, my people left the mountain home of Thorbardin. We chose to live in the world, not under it. We opened up trade with humans and elves. Goods flowed from out of the mountain through us to others. Because of us, our cousins, the mountain dwarves, prospered. Then came the Cataclysm.

"The fall of the fiery mountain on Krynn is generations removed from most of you humans but not from me. My own grandfather lived through it. He saw the rain of fire that fell from the heavens. He felt the earth heave and shake beneath his feet, saw the land split and crack. Our homes were destroyed. Our livelihood was ruined, for no crops would grow. The human cities lay in rubble, and the elves withdrew from the world in anger.

"Our children cried with hunger and shivered with the cold. Ogres, goblins, human thugs and robbers were on the march. They raided our lands, killing many of our people. We went to our cousins who lived beneath the mountain. We begged them to take us in, save us from starvation and the other evils that now stalked the land."

Flint's voice grew grim. "The High King, Duncan, slammed the door in our beards! He would not let us inside the mountain and he sent out an army to keep us at bay.

"Then there came among us an evil greater than any we had yet known. Sadly, we mistook that evil for our salvation. His name was Fistandantilus—"

Caramon made a sound, something like a gasp. Raistlin shot his twin a warning glance from beneath his cowl, and Caramon fell silent.

"Fistandantilus was a human wizard. He wore the black robes, and that should have been a warning to us, but our own hearts were black with hatred, and we didn't question his motives. This Fistandantilus told us that we should be lying snug and safe beneath the mountain, with plenty to eat, and no fear of harm. Using powerful magic, he raised a mighty fortress near Thorbardin and then raised a mighty army of dwarves and humans and sent them to attack Thorbardin.

"The dwarves of Thorbardin left their mountain home and came to meet us in the valley. Long the battle raged, and many dwarves died on both sides. We were no match for our cousins, however. When it became clear that defeat was inevitable, Fistandantilus flew into a great rage. He swore that no dwarf would have his wondrous fortress. He used his magic to set off a blast that blew up the fortress and brought it down on top of him. The blast killed thousands of dwarves on both sides. The fortress collapsed, the ruins forming the shape of a skull, and that is how it came by its name—Skullcap."

"Seeing this, the Neidar who survived took it as a sign. My people withdrew from the valley, carrying their dead with them. The mountain dwarves shut the gates of Thorbardin and sealed them, not that any of us would have set foot inside them anyway after that," Flint added bitterly. "Not if they had begged us! And we still won't!"

He plunked down on the outcropping of rock he was using as a chair, picked up his knife, and thrust it into his belt.

"Could the key to Thorbardin lie in Skullcap?" Tanis asked.

Flint shrugged. "I don't know. It's not likely anyone will ever know. The place is cursed."

"Cursed! Bah!" Raistlin scoffed. "Skullcap is a ruined fortress, a pile of rubble, nothing more. Any ghosts that walk there do so only in the feeble minds of the ignorant."

"Feeble minds, is it!" Flint returned. "I suppose we were all feeble-minded in Darken Wood."

"That was different," Raistlin said coolly. "The only reason you think Skullcap is cursed is because it was built by an archmage, and all wizards are evil, according to you."

"Now, Raistlin, calm down," Tanis said. "None of us thinks that."

"Some of us do," Sturm muttered.

Elistan rose to his feet. "I believe I have a solution."

Hederick opened his mouth, but Elistan forestalled him. "You have had your turn, High Theocrat. I ask that you be patient for a moment to listen to me."

Hederick gave a sour smile. "Of course, Elistan. We all are eager to hear what you have to say."

"Mistress Maritta has stated our dilemma quite clearly and concisely. We face danger if we stay and do nothing but even more danger if we rush off in haste without taking proper care or knowing where we are going. Here is what I propose.

"We send representatives south to seek out the dwarven kingdom to see if we can find the gate, and if we do, ask the dwarves for their aid."

Flint snorted and opened his mouth. Tanis trod on his boot, and the dwarf kept quiet.

"If the dwarves are willing to shelter us," Elistan continued, "we can make the journey to Thorbardin before the harshest months of winter set in. Such a journey should be undertaken immediately," Elistan added gravely. "I agree with Tanis and the others that the danger we face here grows greater with every day that passes. That being said, despite the mage's suggestion—" Elistan bowed to Raistlin— "I do not think there would be time to make a side trip to Skullcap."

"You will think differently when you stand knocking on the side of a mountain that will not open," Raistlin said, his eyes narrow slits.

Before Elistan could reply, Hederick spoke up.

"That is an excellent idea, Revered Son. I propose that we send Tanis Half-Elven on this expedition, along with his friend, the dwarf. Set a dwarf to catch a dwarf, I always say."

Hederick laughed at his little joke.

Tanis was amazed at this sudden acquiescence and immediately suspicious. He'd expected Hederick to take a firm stand against any suggestion of leaving and here he was forwarding the plan. Tanis glanced around the assembly to see what the others thought. Elistan shrugged, as though to say he didn't understand either, but they should take advantage of the High Theocrat's sudden shift in position to gain their objective. Riverwind was silent and impassive. He didn't like the idea of going to Thorbardin. He and his people might still decide to set off on their own. That gave Tanis an idea.

"I agree to go," said Tanis, "and Flint will go with me—"

"He will?" Flint reared up his head in astonishment.

"He will," Tanis said, trodding again on the dwarf's boot and saying quietly, "I'll explain later."

He raised his voice. "In my absence, the High Theocrat and Elistan can handle the spiritual needs of the people. I propose that Riverwind of the Que-shu, take command of their safety."

Now it was Riverwind who looked astonished.

"An excellent idea," said Elistan. "All of us witnessed Riverwind's bravery in the battle at Pax Tharkas. Only today, we saw that he and his people overcame their terror of the dragon to attack the beast."

Hederick was thinking so hard that Tanis could see the man's thought process written on his face. First his brows came together and lips tightened. The High Theocrat wasn't sure he liked the idea now, even though he himself had proposed that Tanis and Flint go to Thorbardin. The Theocrat was certain the half-elf must have some nefarious scheme to put Riverwind in charge. Hederick's narrow-eyed gaze went to the Plainsman, went to the buckskin tunic and breeches, and then his face cleared. Riverwind was a savage, a barbarian. Untaught, unschooled, he would be easy to manipulate—or so Hederick figured. Things could be worse. Tanis might have picked that insufferable Solamnic knight, Sturm Brightblade, to be the leader in his absence. Such were Hederick's thoughts.

Tanis had almost chosen Sturm. The words had been on his lips, when he'd reconsidered. Not only did Tanis hope by this to persuade Riverwind and his people to stay, Tanis was convinced that Riverwind would be a better leader. Sturm saw everything as either black or white, nothing in shades of gray. He was too strict, unbending, unyielding. Riverwind was the better choice.

The High Theocrat smiled expansively. "If the Plainsman will accept the task, I have no objection."

Riverwind was about to reject it. Goldmoon put her hands over his arm and looked up at him. She said nothing in words, but he understood.

"I will think about it," Riverwind said, after a pause.

Goldmoon smiled at him. He clasped her hands with his own. Hederick's supporters gathered around him to discuss matters. Maritta joined Laurana and both began talking to Elistan. The meeting was breaking up.

"What is this about me going to Thorbardin?" Flint demanded. "I'll not set foot beneath the mountain!"

"Later," said Tanis.

Right now, he had to talk to Sturm, explain why he'd chosen Riverwind over the knight, when Sturm must feel that he was better qualified by education and lineage. Sturm was touchy about such things, easily offended.

Tanis made his way through the crowd. Flint was still going on about Thorbardin, dogging Tanis so closely that the dwarf kept tripping on Tanis's heels. As he tried to avoid falling in the fire pit, Tanis drew near Hederick. The Theocrat had his back turned, talking to one of his cronies.

"There is no way out of this valley except over the mountains," Hederick was explaining in a low voice. "It will take the half-elf and the dwarf weeks to make the crossing, and weeks more will pass while they search for this nonexistent dwarf kingdom. Thus we are rid of the meddlesome half-breed—"

Tanis walked on, his lips pressed tight. So that is Hederick's reason for supporting the plan to go to Thorbardin. He gets rid of me.

Once I'm gone, he thinks he can walk over Elistan and Riverwind. I wouldn't be so sure of that.

All the same, Tanis wondered uneasily if Hederick was right. He and Flint might well spend weeks trying to cross the mountains.

"Don't worry about what that windbag says, lad," Flint said, his gruff voice sounding at Tanis's elbow. "There's a way."

Tanis glanced down at his friend. "Does that mean you've had a change of heart?"

"No," the dwarf retorted grimly. "It means I can tell *you* how to find the path."

Tanis shook his head. He'd talk the dwarf around. Right now, he was worried that he'd offended Sturm.

The knight stood near the fire, staring into the flames. He did not look offended. Indeed, he did not look as if he was aware of what was going on around him. Tanis spoke his name several times before Sturm heard him.

Sturm turned to him. The knight's blue eyes glowed in the light. His face, generally set in stern and unbending lines, was animated and expressive.

"Your plan is brilliant, Tanis!" Sturm exclaimed. He grabbed Tanis's hand and gripped it tight.

Tanis regarded his friend in astonishment. "What plan?"

"Traveling to Thorbardin, of course. You can find it and bring it back."

"Find what?" Tanis was growing more confused.

"The Hammer of Kharas! That is the real reason you're going, isn't it?"

"I'm going to Thorbardin to try to find safe haven for the refugees. I don't know anything about a hammer—"

"Have you forgotten the legends?" Sturm asked, shocked. "We were speaking of it only the other night. The sacred and magical Hammer of Kharas—used to forge dragonlances!"

"Oh, yes, right. Dragonlances."

Sturm, hearing his skeptical tone, regarded him in disappointment. "The dragonlance is the only weapon capable of felling a dragon, Tanis. We need them to fight the Dark Queen and her minions. You saw what happened when arrows struck that red beast. They bounced off! A dragonlance, on the other hand, is a weapon blessed by the gods. The great Huma used a dragonlance to defeat Takhisis—"

"I remember," said Tanis hastily. "Hammer of Kharas. I'll keep it in mind."

"You should remember. This is important, Tanis," Sturm insisted, and he was grimly serious. "Perhaps it's the most important task you'll undertake in your lifetime."

"The lives of eight hundred people—"

Sturm brushed those aside with a wave of his hand. "The Hammer is the only chance we have to win this war, and it is in Thorbardin." His grip on Tanis's arm tightened. Tanis could feel him shaking with the intensity of his emotions. "You *must* ask the dwarves to lend it to us. You must!"

"I will, Sturm, I promise," said Tanis, taken aback by his friend's intensity. "Now, about Riverwind—"

But Sturm's gaze had shifted. He was looking at Raistlin and Caramon.

Caramon was talking to his twin in low tones. The big man's expression was troubled. Raistlin made an impatient gesture and then, leaning close, he said something to his twin.

"Raistlin is plotting something," Sturm said, frowning. "I wonder what? Why did he bring up Skullcap?"

Tanis tried again. "In my absence, I named Riverwind as leader—"

"A good choice, Tanis," said Sturm absently.

The twins ended their conversation. Raist was striding out of the cave, walking swiftly, with more energy than usual, leaving Caramon to stare unhappily after his brother. He shook his head and then he, too, left.

"Excuse me, Tanis," said Sturm, and he hurried off.

"What was all that about?" Flint asked.

"Beats me. Do you know anything about this hammer?"

"Hammer, schmammer," said Flint, glowering. "I'll not set foot beneath the mountain."

Tanis sighed and was about to try to make good his own escape from the stifling cavern when he saw Riverwind and Goldmoon standing near the entrance. He felt that he owed them both an explanation.

"A fine snare you laid for me, Half-Elven," Riverwind remarked. "I am caught in your trap and not even my wife will set me free."

"You made a wise choice," Goldmoon said.

Riverwind shook his head.

"I need you, my friend," said Tanis earnestly. "If I am to undertake this journey, I need to know that I have someone here I can trust.
Hederick is a dunce who will plunge us into disaster if given half
a chance. Elistan is a good man, but he knows nothing of battle. If
Verminaard and his forces attack, the people can't rely on prayers and
platinum disks to save them."

Goldmoon looked grave. "Tanis, you should not speak lightly of
such things."

"I'm sorry, Goldmoon," Tanis said as gently as he could, "but I
don't have time for sermons now. This is the hard truth, as I see it.
If you and your tribesmen go off on your own, you abandon these
people to their doom."

Riverwind still looked doubtful, but Tanis could see the man was
weakening. "I must discuss this with my people," he said at last.

"Do that," Tanis said. "I need your answer soon. Flint and I leave
in the morning."

"*You* leave in the morning!" Flint muttered.

"You will have my answer before you sleep," Riverwind promised,
and he and his wife departed, Goldmoon casting Tanis a troubled
glance as she left.

He pushed open the lattice-work screen of branches, walked outside, and drew in a deep breath of fresh air. Snowflakes tingled cold
on his skin. He stood a moment, breathing in the cold, pure air, then
walked off along the path that led down the mountainside.

"Where are you going?" Flint demanded.

"To set Tasslehoff free. Unless he's gnawed the leg off the table by
now . . ."

"Leave him tied up," Flint advised. "Less trouble for us all."

Snowflakes continued to drift down, but here and there Tanis
could see stars through the clouds. The snow fall would not be heavy
this night, just enough to whiten the ground, make tracking the deer
easier for the hunters. Deer were getting scarcer and scarcer in the
valley, more difficult to find.

"After we placate Tas," Tanis continued, hearing the dwarf's heavy
boots thump behind him, "you and I have to pack. I want to leave as
soon as it's daylight."

The thumping came to a halt. The dwarf crossed his arms over his
chest. He looked as if he intended to stand on that rock until he put
down roots.

"I'm not going. I've told you, Tanis, I'll not set foot—"

"—beneath the mountain. Yes, I heard you the first twenty times." Tanis halted, turned to face the dwarf. "You know I can't do this on my own, Flint. You know I need your help. I speak the dwarven tongue, and I suppose I understand dwarves about as much as any elf or human can, but I don't understand them as well as one of their own."

"I'm not one of their own!" Flint snarled. "I'm a hill dwarf—"

"Which means you'll be the first hill dwarf to set foot beneath the mountain in three hundred years. You'll make history, Flint. Have you thought of that? You might even be responsible for the unification of the dwarven nations! Then there's this hammer. If you were to find this Hammer of Kharas and bring it back—"

"Hammer of Kharas! Some wild tale Sturm's granny told him," Flint scoffed.

Tanis shrugged.

"It's up to you, of course," he said. "If you decide to stay, you'll be the one who has to take charge of Tasslehoff."

Flint sucked in a horrified breath. "You wouldn't!"

"Who else can I trust? Caramon?"

Tanis resumed his walking. He heard behind him a muttering, a shuffling and the occasional huffing breath.

Then came the clump of heavy boots.

"I guess I'll go," Flint called out with ill grace. "You'll never find the gate without me."

"I wouldn't stand a chance," said Tanis.

He smiled to himself in the darkness as the snow fell in lazy circles around him.

5

Raistlin's decree. Tika's ultimatum.
Caramon chooses.

istandantilus. Caramon knew that name. He had tensed when he heard his brother speak it and he remained tense during the remainder of the meeting, completely losing track of the discussion that followed. He was recalling another discussion with his twin in the ruined city of Xak Tsaroth.

Raistlin had told him that among the treasure in the dragon's hoard in that accursed city was a magical spellbook of immense value. If they managed to defeat the dragon, Raistlin had ordered Caramon to search for this book and retrieve it for him.

"What does the book look like?" Caramon had asked.

"The pages are bone-white parchment bound in night-blue leather with runes of silver stamped on the front," Raistlin had told him. "The book will feel deathly cold to the touch."

"What do the runes say?" Caramon had been suspicious. He hadn't liked the way Raistlin had described the book.

"You do not want to know . . . " Raistlin had smiled to himself, a secret smile.

"Whose book was it?"

Though Caramon was not a mage himself, he knew a great deal about the ways of mages from having been around his twin. A mage's most valued possession was his book of magical spells compiled over a lifetime of work. Written in the language of magic, each spell was recorded in detail using the precise wording, with notations as to the proper pronunciation of each word, the precise inflections and intonations, what gestures should be used, and what components might be required.

"You have never heard of this wizard, my brother," Raistlin had told Caramon after one of those strange lapses when he seemed to move inside himself, seemed to be searching for something lost, "yet he was one of the greatest who ever lived. His name was Fistandantilus."

Caramon had been reluctant to ask the next question, afraid of what he might hear in answer. Looking back, he realized now he'd known exactly what he was going to hear. He wished he'd kept silent.

"This Fistandantilus—did he wear the Black Robes?"

"Ask me no more!" Raistlin had been angry. "You are as bad as the others! How can any of you understand me?"

But Caramon had understood. He'd understood then. He understood now—or thought he did.

Caramon waited until the assembly started to break up, then he approached his twin. "Fistandantilus," he said in a low voice, looking around to make certain they were not overheard. "That's the name of the evil wizard—the one whose spellbook you found—"

"Just because a mage wears the Black Robes does not make him evil," Raistlin returned with an impatient gesture. "Why can you never get that through your thick skull?"

"Anyway," said Caramon, not wanting to have this discussion again, for it left him feeling muddled and confused, "I'm glad Tanis and Flint decided not to go to that place, that Skullcap."

"They are imbeciles, the lot of them!" Raistlin fumed. "Tanis might as well use the dwarf's head to knock on the side of the mountain for all the good it will do any of them. They will never find the way inside Thorbardin. The secret lies in Skullcap!"

A fit of coughing over came Raistlin, and he had to stop talking.

"You're getting all worked up," Caramon said. "It's not good for you."

Raistlin brought out his handkerchief, pressed it to his lips. He drew in a ragged breath, drew in another. The spasm eased. He laid his hand on his brother's arm.

"Come with me, Caramon. We have much to do and little time in which to do it."

"Raist—" Caramon could sometimes read his brother's mind. He did so now, knew exactly what Raistlin intended. Caramon tried to protest, but his brother's eyes narrowed alarmingly, and Caramon gulped back his words.

"I'm going back to our dwelling," Raistlin said coldly. "Come or not, as you choose."

Raistlin left in haste. Caramon followed more slowly.

The mage was in such a hurry and his twin in such misery that neither of them noted Sturm, walking behind.

While the meeting was taking place, Tika Waylan was in the dwelling she shared with Laurana, trying to comb her tangled mass of red curls. Tika sat on a little stool Caramon had made for her. She worked by the light of a lantern, dragging the wooden comb through a strand of hair until it hit a knot. She would try to patiently tease the knotted mass of red apart, as Laurana had taught her, but Tika had very little patience. Eventually she would give the comb a yank, pulling out the knot and a fistful of her hair along with it.

The blanket that the young women had rigged to cover the entrance opened, letting in a blast of air and a flurry of snow. Laurana entered, carrying a lantern.

Tika looked up. "How was the meeting?"

Tika had been in awe of Laurana when she'd first met her in Qualinesti. The two could not have been more different. Laurana was the daughter of a king. Tika was the daughter of a part-time illusionist and full-time thief. Laurana was an elf, a princess.

Tika had run wild for much of her life. Taking to thieving herself, she'd afoul of the law. Otik Sandeth, owner of the Inn of the Last Home in Solace, had offered to adopt the orphan, giving her gainful employment as a bar maid.

The two differed in looks. Laurana was slender and willowy. Tika was buxom and robust. Laurana's hair was golden, her skin white and rose. Tika's hair was flame red, her face covered in freckles.

Tika knew quite well that she had her own kind of beauty, and she felt good about herself most times—when she wasn't around Laurana. Laurana's blonde hair made Tika's seem that much redder by contrast, just as Laurana's graceful figure made Tika feel that she was all hips and bosom.

"How did it go?" Tika asked, glad to lay down the comb. Her arm and shoulder ached and her scalp stung.

"As you might expect," said Laurana, sighing. "There was lots of arguing. Hederick is a prize dolt—"

"You're telling me!" Tika said crisply. "I was in the inn when he stuck his hand in the fire."

"Just when it seemed that no one could agree, Elistan came up with a solution," said Laurana, and her voice softened in admiration. "His plan is brilliant. They've all agreed to it, even Hederick. Elistan suggested that we send a delegation to the dwarven kingdom of Thorbardin to see if we can find refuge there. Tanis volunteered to go, along with Flint."

"Not Caramon?" asked Tika anxiously.

"No, just Flint and Tanis. Raistlin wanted them to go first to a place called Skullcap to find the secret way into the dwarven kingdom or something like that, but Flint said Skullcap was haunted, and Elistan said they didn't have time to make the journey before winter set in. Raistlin seemed angry."

"I'll bet he did," said Tika, shivering. "A haunted place named Skullcap would suit him just fine, and he'd drag Caramon along with him. Thank the gods they're not going!"

"Even Hederick agreed that Elistan's plan was a good one," said Laurana.

"I guess wisdom comes with gray hair," Tika remarked, picking up her comb again. "Though, of course, that didn't work in Hederick's case."

"Elistan's hair is not gray," Laurana protested. "It's silver. I think silver hair makes a man look distinguished."

"Are you in love with Elistan?" Tika asked. She dug the comb into the mass of curls and began to tug.

Laurana winced at the sight. "Here, let me do that!"

Tika thankfully handed over the comb.

"You are too impatient," said Laurana reprovingly. "You're ruining your hair, and you have such beautiful hair. I envy you."

"You do?" Tika was astonished. "I can't think why! Your hair is so shimmery and golden!"

"And straight as a stick," said Laurana ruefully. The comb, in her hands, gently teased each knot until it came loose. "As for Elistan, no, I'm not in love with him, but I do admire him and respect him. He's been through so much pain and suffering. Such experiences would have made any other man bitter and cynical. They made Elistan more compassionate and understanding."

"I know someone who thinks you're in love with Elistan," said Tika with an impish smile.

"Who do you mean?" Laurana asked, blushing.

"Tanis, of course," said Tika archly. "He's jealous."

"That's impossible!" Laurana gave the comb a sharper tug than usual. "Tanis doesn't love me. He's made that extremely clear. He's in love with that human woman."

"That bitch Kitiara!" Tika sniffed. "Pardon my language. As for Tanis, he doesn't know his heart from his . . . well, I won't say *what*, but you understand. It's the same with all men."

Laurana was silent, and Tika twisted her head to glance up at her, to see if she was angry.

Laurana's face was mantled with a delicate flush, her eyes lowered. She kept combing, but she wasn't paying attention to what she was doing.

Maybe she *doesn't* understand, Tika realized suddenly. It seemed very odd to her that a woman who was a hundred years old knew less about the world and the ways of men than one who was only nineteen. Still, Laurana had lived all those years pampered and protected in her father's palace in the middle of a forest. Small wonder she was naïve.

"Do you really think Tanis is jealous?" Laurana asked, her blush deepening.

"Watch him sometime. He's goes green as a goblin whenever he sees you and Elistan together."

"He has no reason to think there is anything between us," said Laurana. "I'll speak to him."

"You will do no such thing!" Tika turned so fast the comb caught in her hair and jerked out of Laurana's hands. "Let him stew for awhile. Maybe it'll put that wildcat Kit out of his mind."

"But that would be lying, in a way," Laurana protested, retrieving the comb.

"No, it isn't," Tika said. "Besides, what if it is? All's fair in love and war, and the gods know that for us women, love *is* war. I wish there was someone around to make Caramon jealous."

"Caramon loves you dearly, Tika," said Laurana, smiling. "Anyone can see it by the way he looks at you."

"I don't want him to just stand there making great cow eyes at me! I want him to do something about it!"

"There's Raistlin—" Laurana began.

"Don't mention Raistlin to me!" Tika snapped. "Caramon's more a slave than a brother, and one day he'll wake up and find that out. Only by that time, it may be too late." She held her head high. "Some of us may have moved on with our lives."

There was no more conversation. Laurana was thinking over this new and unexpected revelation that Tanis might be jealous of her relationship with Elistan. That would certainly explain that remark he'd made to her today.

Tika sat on the stool Caramon had made for her and blinked back her tears—tears caused by the comb yanking on her hair . . .

Caramon lagged behind his brother as they made their way to their small cave. Caramon knew the signs, knew that Raistlin was plotting. His brother generally moved slowly, taking cautious steps, leaning on his staff or on his brother's arm. Raistlin walked rapidly now, the crystal held by the gold dragon claw atop his staff casting a magical light to guide his way. His red robes swished around his ankles. He did not look around to see if Caramon was following. Raistlin knew he would be.

Arriving at the cave, Raistlin shoved aside the wooden screen and ducked inside. Caramon entered more slowly, pausing to adjust the screen in place for the night. Raistlin stopped him.

"No need," he said. "You're going out again."

"Do you want me to fetch hot water for your tea?" Caramon asked.

"Am I coughing myself to death?" Raistlin demanded.

"No," Caramon said.

"Then I do not need my tea." Raistlin began to search among their belongings. He picked up a water skin and held it out to his brother.

"Go to the stream and fill this."

"There's water in the bucket—" Caramon began.

"If you want to carry water in a bucket with us on our journey, brother, then do so, by all means," Raistlin said coldly. "Most people find a water skin to be more convenient."

"What journey?" Caramon asked.

"The one we are undertaking in the morning," Raistlin returned. He thrust the water skin at Caramon. "Here, take this!"

"Where are we going?" Caramon kept his hands at his sides.

"Oh, come, now, Caramon! Even you can't be that stupid!" Raistlin flung the water skin at his brother's feet. "Do as I say. We will make an early start, and I want to study my spells before I sleep. We'll need food, too."

Raistlin sat down in the only chair in the cave. He picked up his spellbook and opened it. After a moment, however, he shut that book and, reaching deep into his pouch, drew out another—the spellbook with the night-blue binding. He did not open it but held it in his hand.

"We're going to Skullcap, aren't we?" said Caramon.

Raistlin didn't answer. He kept his hand on the closed book.

"You don't even know where it is!" Caramon said.

Raistlin looked up at his brother. His golden eyes gleamed strangely in the staff's magical light.

"That's just it, Caramon," he said softly. "I do know where it is. I know the location and I know how to reach it. I don't know why . . ." His voice trailed off.

"Why what?" Caramon demanded, bewildered.

"Why I know . . . or how I know. It's strange, as if I've been there before."

Caramon was unhappy. "Put that book away, Raist, and forget about this. The trip will be too hard for you. We can't climb the mountain—"

"We don't have to," said Raistlin.

"Even if the snow ends," Caramon continued, "the trip will be cold, wet, and dangerous. What if that Verminaard comes again and catches us out in open?"

"He won't, because we won't be in the open." Raistlin glared at his twin. "Quit arguing and go fill the water skin!"

Caramon shook his head. "No," he said. "I won't."

Raistlin drew in a seething breath, then, suddenly, he let it out.

"My brother," said Raistlin gently, "if we do not make this journey, Tanis and Flint will not find the gate, much less make their way inside the mountain."

Caramon looked into his twin's face. "Are you sure about that?"

"As sure as the death that awaits them, that awaits us all if they fail," said Raistlin, his gaze unwavering.

Caramon heaved a deep sigh. Reaching down, he picked up the water skin and went back out into the snow-filled night.

Raistlin relaxed in his chair. He put aside the night-blue spellbook and opened up his own.

"What a simple soul you are, my brother," he remarked in scathing tones.

As he left the cave, Caramon caught a glimpse of Sturm standing nearby. Caramon knew perfectly well why Sturm was here. He had seen the knight watching them. Sturm would never stoop to spying on his friends or his enemies, for that matter. Such a dishonorable act went against the Code and the Measure, the rigid guidelines by which a Solamnic knight lived his life. The Oath and the Measure said nothing about friendly persuasion, however. Sturm was here to waylay Caramon and "persuade" the truth out of him.

Caramon was hopeless at keeping secrets and worse still at lying. If he told Sturm that Raistlin was planning to go to Skullcap, Sturm would tell Tanis, and the gods alone knew what would come of it—a bitter argument at the least, a fatal breach between long-time friends at the worst. Caramon wished Sturm would just let the matter go.

A furious flurry of snow allowed him to conceal his movements, and he went the long way down the slope to the stream. The flurry ceased. The clouds parted, and the stars came out. Glancing back, he could see Sturm silhouetted in Solinari's silver light, still roaming about outside the twins' cave.

He'll give up after awhile, Caramon reasoned, and go to bed.

Caramon didn't like Raistlin's plan to go to this haunted Skullcap place, but he trusted his twin and believed Raistlin's argument that the journey was necessary to save lives. Caramon knew he was alone in his trust for his twin. Well, not quite. Tanis often turned to Raistlin for advice, and it was this knowledge more than his twin's reasoning that had induced Caramon to finally go along with his twin's scheme.

"Tanis would sanction our going, if he had time to think about it," Caramon reasoned to himself. "Everything's happened so fast, that's all, and Tanis has too much to worry about as it is."

As for how Raistlin knew where to find Skullcap and how he planned to get there, Caramon knew better than to ask, figuring he wouldn't understand anyway. He had never understood his twin, not when they were little children and certainly not now. The terrible Test in the Tower of High Sorcery had forever changed his brother in ways that Caramon could not fathom.

The Test had forever changed their relationship as well. The one secret Caramon kept was the secret he'd learned about his twin in the Tower. That secret was dark and appalling, and Caramon kept it mainly because he never let himself think about it.

Having safely avoided Sturm, Caramon lifted his head and breathed in the cool, crisp air. He felt better out in the open, away from all the voices. Here he could think. Caramon was not stupid, as some believed. Caramon liked to consider a problem from all angles, ruminate, mull it over, and this often gave him the appearance of being slow. He rarely shared his thoughts with others, fearing their mockery. No one had been more surprised than Caramon when his friends had lauded his idea of having Raistlin use his magic to create an avalanche to block the pass.

Caramon felt so much better out here by himself that, when another flurry struck, he stuck out his tongue to catch the snowflakes, as he'd done when a child. Snow always made him feel like a kid again. If the snow fall had been deeper, he would have been tempted to lie down on his back, flap his arms and legs, and make a snow-bird. The snow wasn't deep enough yet, though, and didn't look as if it would be. Stars glittered beneath the clouds.

Negotiating his way around an outcropping of rock, trying to keep his footing, Caramon nearly ran headlong into Tika.

"Caramon!" she said, pleased.

"Tika!" exclaimed Caramon, alarmed.

He felt like the warrior in the adage who had avoided the kobolds only to fall victim to goblins. He'd managed to evade Sturm's questioning, but if there was one person in this world who could wrap him around her red curls and wheedle whatever she wanted out of him, it was Tika Waylan.

"What are you doing out in the night?" she asked.

Caramon held up the water skin. "Fetching water."

He shuffled his big feet a moment then said abruptly, "I've got to go now!" and started to walk off.

"I'm going to the stream myself," said Tika, catching up with him. "I'm afraid of getting lost in the snow." She slid her hand through his arm. "I'm not afraid when I'm with you, though."

Caramon quivered from head to toe. He had once thought Tika Waylan the ugliest little girl he'd ever seen and the greatest nuisance ever born. He'd gone away for five years, doing mercenary work with his twin, and come back to find Tika the most attractive, wonderful woman he'd ever known, and he'd known quite a few.

Big, handsome, and brawny, with a cheerful smile and good-hearted nature, Caramon had never lacked female companionship. Girls liked him and he liked them. He'd indulged in numerous dalliances with countless women, spent more time snuggling in barn lofts and behind hay mounds than he could count. No woman had ever touched his heart, however. Not until Tika. And she hadn't really touched his heart—his heart had jumped out of his chest to land plop at her feet.

He wanted to be a better person for her. He wanted to be smarter, braver, yet every time he was with her, he went all addled and befuddled, especially when she pressed her body up close against his, like she was now. Caramon recalled a talk he'd had with Goldmoon. The older woman had warned him that although Tika talked and acted like a worldly woman, she was, in truth, young and innocent. Caramon must not take advantage of her or he would hurt her deeply. Caramon was determined to keep himself under strict control, but this was very hard when Tika looked at him as she was looking at him now, with snow sparkling on her red curls and her cheeks rosy with the cold and her green eyes shining.

Caramon suddenly began to suspect that she not had been out here to go the stream. She had no bucket and she certainly wasn't going to bathe. She was going to the stream because she wanted to be with him, and while this warmed him like spiced wine, the knowledge only added to his confusion.

They walked together in silence. Tika kept glancing at him, waiting for him to speak. He couldn't think of anything to say, and then, of course, she said the worst thing possible.

"I hear your brother wanted to go off to some terrible fortress called Skullcap, but Tanis wouldn't let him." Tika shivered and pressed even closer to him. "I'm glad you're not going."

Caramon mumbled something unintelligible and kept walking. His face burned. He probably had guilt written on his forehead in letters so large a gully dwarf could read them. He saw her glance at the water skin and saw her green eyes narrow. Caramon groaned inwardly.

Tika dropped his arm. She stepped back away from him to smite him with the full force of her red-haired fury.

"You're going, aren't you?!" she cried. "You're going to that dreadful place that everyone knows is haunted!"

Caramon made a feeble protest. "It's not haunted."

He realized a split second later that he should have denied going at all, but he couldn't think around her.

"Ah ha! You admit it! Flint says Skullcap's haunted!" Tika returned. "He should know. He was born and raised around these parts. Does Tanis know you're leaving?" She answered her own question. "Of course not. So you were going to go off and get yourself killed and never even say goodbye to me!"

Caramon had no idea where to begin to refute all these charges Finally, he said lamely, "I'm not going to get myself killed. Raist says—"

"Raist says!" Tika mimicked him. "Why is Raistlin going? Because it has something to do with that wizard, Fistanpoopus or whatever his name is. The one you told me about. The evil wizard who wore the Black Robes and whose wicked book Raistlin is carrying around with him. Laurana told me what Flint said about Skullcap. Only she didn't know what I know and what you know—that Raistlin has some sort of strange connection to this dead wizard."

"You didn't tell her, did you?" Caramon asked fearfully. "You didn't tell anyone?"

"No, I didn't, but maybe I should."

Tika faced him, head flung back, green eyes flaring. "If you love me, Caramon, you won't go. You'll tell that brother of yours that he can find someone else to risk his life for him and do his fetching and carrying and make his stupid tea!"

"I do love you, Tika," said Caramon desperately, "but Raist is my brother. We're all each of us has, and he says this is important. That the lives of all these people depend on it."

"And you believe him!" Tika scoffed.

"Yes," said Caramon with simple dignity. "I do."

Tika's eyes overflowed with tears, which spilled down her freckled cheeks. "I hope a ghost sucks your blood dry!" she sobbed angrily, and ran off.

"Tika!" Caramon called, heart-sick.

She did not look back but kept running, slipping and stumbling over the snow-slick rocks.

Caramon wanted desperately to go after her, but he didn't. For what could he say? He could not give her what she wanted. He could not give up his brother for her, no matter how much he adored her. Raistlin must always come first. Tika was strong. Raistlin was weak, fragile, feeble.

"He needs me," Caramon said to himself. "He relies on me and depends on me. If I wasn't there for him, he might die, just like when he was little. She doesn't understand."

He continued heading for the stream in order to fill the water skin, even though now they wouldn't be going. Tika would go straight to Tanis, then Tanis would go to Raistlin and forbid him to leave, and Raistlin would know Caramon had spilled the beans. If Caramon dawdled, perhaps his brother's fury would have cooled by the time he got back.

Caramon doubted it, but there was always that chance.

6

Sneaking off. Eyes in the sky. Laundry day.

aramon paused outside the cave to steel himself, then shoved aside the screen and went in.

"Raist, I'm sorry . . ."

He halted. His twin was sound asleep, wrapped in his blanket, his hand resting on the staff that never left his side. The pack containing his spellbooks was by the entrance. Caramon's pack was there, as well. All in readiness for an early departure.

A wave of relief flooded through Caramon.

Tika hadn't told Tanis! Perhaps she did understand, after all!

Moving as quietly as he could, Caramon deposited the full water skin on the floor, then stripped off his shirt, lay down, and his conscience clear, was almost immediately asleep.

His brother's hand shaking him by the shoulder woke him.

"Keep quiet!" Raistlin whispered. "Make haste! I want to be away before anyone is stirring!"

"What about breakfast?" Caramon asked.

Raistlin flashed him a disgusted glance.

"Well, I'm hungry," Caramon said.

"We will eat on the road," Raistlin returned.

Caramon sighed. Hefting the two packs and the water skin, he followed his brother out of the cave. The sky was black and glittering with stars. The air was cold and sharp, prickling the inside of the lungs. The snow had stopped during the night after dusting the ground. Clouds were massing over the mountains, however. There would be more snow before the day was out.

Solinari, the silver moon, was a curved blade in the sky. Lunitari, the red moon, and Raistlin's patron goddess of magic, was three-quarters full. Her red light cast eerie shadows on the snow. Raistlin looked up at the red moon and smiled.

"The goddess lights our way to dawn," he said. "A good omen."

Caramon hoped his twin was right. Now that they were committed to this, Caramon wanted to get as far away from the others as fast as possible. Raistlin, fortunately, was having one of his good days. He hardly coughed at all. He moved nimbly and rapidly along the trail.

They made good time, descending the mountainside to the valley floor and heading off to the southwest. Reaching a forested area, they walked among the trees and were soon out of sight of the encampment and any early risers.

Caramon was breathing easier when a rattle of armor and a clash of metal on metal caused him to drop the packs and reach for his sword. Raistlin's hand went to his pouch of spell components.

Sturm Brightblade stepped out from the red-tinged shadows of the tree branches. He stood in the path, blocking their way.

Raistlin shot Caramon a furious look.

"I didn't tell him, Raist! Honest!" Caramon gabbled.

"Your brother said nothing to me, Raistlin," Sturm confirmed, "so spare him your anger. As to how I found out, that was easy. I have known you for a good many years, long enough to realize that you will follow your own selfish pursuits without thought or care for others. I knew when you left the meeting last night that you intended to sneak off to Skullcap."

"Then," said Raistlin, glowering, "you should also know that you cannot stop me, so stand aside and permit me and my brother to pass." He paused, then added, "For the sake of our friendship, I would not want to do you harm."

Sturm's hand went to his sword's hilt, but he did not draw his weapon. His gaze flicked to Caramon, then back to his twin. "I have no quarrel with you risking your own life, Raistlin. Indeed, it is no secret that I think the world would be a better place if you were not in it, but there is no need for you to get your brother killed."

"Caramon goes of his own choosing," Raistlin returned, smiling a twisted smile at the knight's candor. "Don't you, my brother?"

"Raistlin says we have to go, Sturm," Caramon told the knight. "He says Flint and Tanis won't be able to find the gate to Thorbardin without the secret key that lies in Skullcap."

"There are many important reasons why they should win their way into Thorbardin, aren't there, Sturm Brightblade?" Raistlin said with a slight cough.

Sturm regarded Raistlin intently.

"I will let you go on one condition," said Sturm. Releasing his grip on his sword, he stood to one side. "I'm coming with you."

Caramon cringed, fearing Raistlin would fly into a rage.

Instead, Raistlin gave Sturm a strange, narrow-eyed look, then said quietly, "I have no objection to the knight's accompanying us. Do you, my brother?"

"No," said Caramon, astonished.

"In fact, he might actually be of some use to me." Raistlin pushed past the knight and continued along the trail that led through the woods.

Sturm retrieved a sack that, by the clanging sounds emanating from it, held the bulk of his armor. The knight wore the breastplate with the rose and kingfisher, symbol of the Solamnic knighthood, and his helm. He carried the rest.

"Does Tanis know?" Caramon asked in a low voice, as Sturm joined him on the trail.

"He does. I shared with him my suspicion that Raistlin would go off on his own," Sturm replied, positioning the sack more comfortably on his shoulder.

"Did . . . uh . . . Tika say anything to him?"

Sturm smiled. "So you told her, but did not tell Tanis?"

Caramon flushed deeply. "I wasn't going to tell anyone. Tika kind of cornered me. Is she *very* angry?" he asked wistfully.

Sturm didn't answer. He smoothed his long mustaches, the knight's way of avoiding an unpleasant discussion.

Caramon sighed and shook his head. "I'm surprised Tanis didn't try to stop Raist."

"He thinks there is something in what Raistlin claims, though he didn't want to say so in front of Hederick. If we can find the key to the gates of Thorbardin and if we can find the gates in time, we are to bring word to him immediately."

"How will we know where to find him?" Caramon asked. "He's going trekking off over the mountains with Flint."

Sturm shot Caramon a penetrating glance. "It's interesting that Raistlin didn't think to ask Tanis that, isn't it? My guess is that he plans to seek out Thorbardin himself if he finds the key. What do you think he might be after in Skullcap?"

"I . . . I don't know," Caramon said, staring down at his boots tromping over the snow-rimed grass. "I never thought about that."

Sturm gave him a sharp look. "No," he said quietly, "I don't suppose you would."

"Raist says we are going to help the people!" Caramon said defensively.

Sturm grunted. Then he said in a low voice, "How does he know where he's going? How does he know the way? Or are we wandering out here aimlessly?"

Caramon watched his twin walking confidently along the trail between the trees. The mage walked more slowly now, feeling his way along, sometimes tapping the ground with the butt of his staff like a blind man, yet, he didn't appear lost. He walked with purpose and determination, and when he did stop to look around he would stop only briefly then continue on.

"He said he knows a way, a secret way." Caramon saw Sturm's look and added. "Raist knows lots of things. He reads books."

Caramon was immediately sorry he'd spoken, for that brought up the unwelcome thought of the night-blue spellbook. He quickly banished the reminder. If Raistlin *had* found guidance in a book belonging to an evil wizard, Caramon didn't want to know about it.

"Maybe Flint told him," Caramon said, and the possibility cheered him. "Yeah, that's it. Flint must have told him."

Sturm knew it was hopeless to point out the obvious— Flint wouldn't tell Raistlin the time of day. Caramon had lied to himself about his twin for so many years that he wouldn't know the truth now if it gave him a swift kick in the backside.

Ranging ahead of the others, Raistlin knew perfectly well that his brother and the knight were talking about him. He even knew what they were saying. He could have quoted them both word for word. He didn't care. Let the knight malign him. Caramon would defend him. Caramon always defended him. It was nauseating the way Caramon always defended him. Sometimes Raistlin found himself wishing Caramon would grow a backbone, stand up to him, defy him. Then he reflected that if this happened, Caramon would be of no more use to him, and he still needed Caramon. The day would come when he would be able to live independent of his twin but not now. Not yet.

Raistlin cast an oblique glance at the two men over his shoulder—his brother trotting along like a pack animal; Sturm Brightblade, impoverished knight, carrying his nobility around in a sack.

Why is he coming along? Raistlin wondered. He found the notion intriguing. Certainly the noble knight is not worried about my well being! He professes to care for Caramon, yet Sturm knows perfectly well that Caramon is a seasoned warrior. My brother can take care of himself. Sturm has some reason of his own for tagging along with us. I wonder what that can be . . . Why is he so interested in Skullcap?

For that matter, Raistlin asked himself, why am I?

He did not know the answer.

Raistlin scanned the rock wall of the mountain that stood dead ahead of them blocking the way. He was searching for the image that was still shadowy in his mind, yet grew clearer and more distinct with every step he took. He knew what he was looking for—or rather, he would know it when he saw it. He knew a secret way that led to Skullcap, yet he didn't know it. He had walked this path before, and he'd never before set foot on it. He'd been here, and he hadn't. He'd done this without doing it.

The day of the dragon's attack on the grove, Raistlin had been writing a new spell into his spellbook when suddenly the quill pen had, seemingly of its own volition, scrawled the word *Skullcap* across the page.

Raistlin had stared at the word. He had stared at the quill and at his hand that had wielded it. He had torn out the ruined page and tried again to write down his spell. Again the pen had written *Skullcap*. Raistlin had thrown down the pen and searched his mind and at last recalled where he'd heard that name, in what connection.

Fistandantilus. Skullcap was the wizard's tomb.

An unpleasant thrill had tingled through Raistlin's body, a tingle in the blood as of a rising fever. He'd never thought about it, but Skullcap must be close to where they were camped. What wonders might he find there! Ancient magical artifacts, the wizard's spellbooks like the one he had already acquired.

That was the reward, yet Raistlin had the uneasy impression that he was being guided to Skullcap for darker and more sinister reasons. If so, he would deal with those when the time came, which was why he'd decided to take Sturm along.

Sturm Brightblade was an arrogant, insufferable prig who never took a piss but that he didn't have to pray over it. Nevertheless, he was a deft hand with a sword. Skullcap might indeed be nothing more than a crumbling old ruin, just as Raistlin had claimed to the assembly last night.

Even he didn't believe it.

———————•————————

"So Raistlin's gone off to Skullcap," said Flint, adding dourly, "Good riddance, I'd say, but he's taking two good men, Caramon and Sturm, to their deaths along with him."

"Let's hope it doesn't come to that," said Tanis. "Are you ready?"

"As I'll ever be," Flint grumbled. "I want to go on record as saying this is all a waste of time. If we do find the gate, which I doubt, the dwarves will never open it for us. If they do open it, they won't let us in. The hearts of the Thorbardin clans are hard and cold as the mountain itself. The only reason I'm going, Half-Elven, is to have the chance to say 'I told you so'."

"So much is changing in the world, perhaps the hearts of the dwarves have changed as well," Tanis suggested.

Flint gave an explosive snort and went off to finish his packing, leaving Tanis to try to placate an extremely disappointed kender.

"Please, please, please let me go, Tanis!" Tasslehoff begged. He sat on a chair—the same chair to which he had recently been tied—and kicked his feet against the legs. "It's only fair, you know. After all, you're using one of my very best maps."

"You along!" Flint rumbled from the other side of the cave. "We'd be shut out for the next three hundred years. The dwarves would never let a kender beneath the mountain."

"I think they would," Tas said eagerly. "Dwarves and kender are related, after all."

"We are not!" Flint roared.

"We are so," Tas argued. "First there were gnomes, then there was the Graygem and the gnomes tried to catch it, and something happened—I forget what—and Reorx changed some of the gnomes into dwarves and some into kender, so you see, we're first cousins, Flint."

The dwarf began to sputter.

"Why don't you wait for me outside?" Tanis said to the dwarf.

Flint glared at Tas then picked up his pack and stomped out.

"Please, Tanis," Tas begged, looking up at him with pleading eyes. "You know you need me to keep you out of trouble."

"I need you here much more, Tas," said Tanis.

Tasslehoff shook his head glumly. "You're just saying that."

"With Sturm, Caramon, and Raistlin gone, and Flint and I gone, who's going to look after Tika? And Laurana? And Riverwind and Goldmoon?"

Tas thought this over. "Riverwind has Goldmoon. Laurana's got Elistan . . . What's the matter, Tanis? Does your stomach hurt?"

"No, my stomach doesn't hurt," Tanis said irritably. He didn't know why any mention of Laurana and Elistan should suddenly put him in a bad humor. What they did was none of his concern.

"It's just you made the kind of face people make when their stomach hurts—"

"My stomach doesn't hurt!" Tanis said.

"That's good," Tas remarked. "Nothing's worse than a stomach ache when you're starting on a long journey. You're right. Tika doesn't have anyone since Caramon's gone. I'll stay to take care of her."

"Thank you, Tas," said Tanis. "That's a burden off my mind."

"I'd better go be with her right now," Tas added, charmed with his new responsibility. "She might be in danger."

Actually, the kender was the one who was in danger. Tika never woke before noon if she could help it, and dawn was only just now breaking. Tanis didn't like to think what would happen to poor Tas when he barged in on her at this time of day.

Tanis found Riverwind and Goldmoon waiting for him. She greeted him with a gentle kiss.

"I will ask the gods to walk with you, Tanis," she said to him, adding with a mischievous smile, "whether you want them to or not."

Tanis gave a somewhat sheepish grin and scratched his beard. He didn't know what to say, and to change the subject, he turned to Riverwind.

"Thank you for accepting this charge, my friend," Tanis told him. "I know the decision was not an easy one, nor will your task be easy, I'm afraid. You know what you must do, where you must go if the valley is attacked?"

"I know." Riverwind's expression was dark, though he said quietly, "The gods are with us. Hopefully such an attack will not happen."

The gods are with Verminaard more than us, Tanis thought wryly. They brought him back to life.

He merely nodded, however, and shaking Riverwind's hand, Tanis reminded him once more of the location of the meeting place they agreed upon—a village of gully dwarves at the very foot of the mountain where Flint said the legendary gate to Thorbardin could be found.

Flint had reluctantly, and only after much persuasion, revealed the presence of the village. He refused to say how he knew about it, but Tanis suspected that this was where the old dwarf had been captured by gully dwarves a few years before and imprisoned, the details of which harrowing ordeal Flint never discussed.

Riverwind indicated a rolled-up map tucked in his belt. He had drawn the map last night in consultation with Flint and one of Tasslehoff's maps.

"I know where the village is located," said Riverwind. "It is on the other side of the mountains, and as of now, we have no way of crossing those mountains."

"There's a pass," Flint said stolidly.

"You keep saying that, but my people have scouted the area and they can't find any sign of one."

"Are your people dwarves? When they are, come talk to me," Flint grunted. He carried both a battle-axe and a pick-axe in a harness on his back. He adjusted these more comfortably then glowered at Tanis. "If we're going, we should be going, not standing around here palavering."

"We'll be off, then. We'll blaze a trail for you to follow if you have to. I hope you—"

He halted in mid sentence, a shiver of fear clenching his gut. His flesh crawled, and the hair on the back of his neck prickled. The old wives would have said someone was walking across his grave. Goldmoon had gone pale and Riverwind's breath came fast, his hands clenched. Flint whipped out his axe, searching for the foe, but the feeling passed, and no enemy appeared.

"Dragons," said Flint grimly.

"They are up there," Goldmoon said, shivering and hugging her cloak close around her, "watching us."

Riverwind stood with his head tilted back, searching the skies. Tanis joined him, but neither could see anything in the pale blue dawn. Both looked at each other and acknowledged the truth.

"Whether we see them or not, they're up there. Make the people ready, Riverwind. If trouble does come, you won't have much time to escape."

Tanis stood a moment more, searching for some word of hope or comfort. He couldn't find any to give. Hefting his pack, he and the dwarf started off down the path.

Flint paused to shout back over his shoulder. "Bring pick-axes!"

"Pick-axes!" Riverwind repeated, frowning. "Does he mean for us to hack our way through the mountains? I don't like this. I begin to think I made the wrong decision. Our people should have gone off on their own."

"Your reasons for making this decision were sound, my husband. Not even the Que-Kiri warriors challenged you when you told them your decision. They are sensible enough to realize that there is safety in numbers. Do not start second guessing yourself. The chieftain who looks behind while he walks forward will stumble and fall. That is what my father always said."

"Damn your father!" Riverwind said angrily. "His decisions were not always right! He was the one who ordered the people to stone me, or have you forgotten that, Chieftain's Daughter?"

He stalked off, leaving Goldmoon to stare after him in astonishment.

"He didn't mean it," said Laurana, coming up the hillside to stand beside her. "Sorry, I couldn't help overhearing. He is worried, that is all. He bears a great responsibility."

"I know." Goldmoon sighed bleakly. "I am no help, I fear. He is right. I should not keep comparing him to my father. I meant to offer advice; that is all. My father was a wise man and a good chief. He made a mistake, but it was because he did not understand."

She looked after her husband and sighed again. "I love him so much, yet it seems I hurt him more than I would hurt my worst enemy."

"Love gives us a power to hurt that hate cannot match," Laurana said softly.

She looked after Flint and Tanis, who were shapeless forms in the gray dawn, descending into the valley.

"Did you come to say good-bye to Tanis?" Goldmoon asked, seeing the young woman watching them.

"I thought he might want to say good-bye to me," Laurana replied. "I waited, but he didn't come." She shrugged. "Apparently he doesn't care."

"He does, Laurana," said Goldmoon. "I've seen the way he looks at you. It's just . . ." She hesitated.

"I can't compete with a memory of a rival," Laurana bitterly. "Kitiara will always be perfect to him. Her kisses will always taste sweeter. She is not here to say or do the wrong thing. I cannot win."

Goldmoon was struck by what Laurana had said. Competing with a memory. That was what she was forcing Riverwind to do. Small wonder he resented it. She went to find him to make her apology, which, since they were newlyweds, she knew her tender "I am sorry" would be well received.

Laurana stood looking after Tanis.

———————————————

"Hullo, Tika!" Tas shoved open the screen to the cave and bounded inside, remembering at the last moment to knock. "Did you go shivery all over just a few moments ago? I did. It was a dragon! I thought I'd better hurry over to protect you! Ouch!" he said loudly, tumbling over a lump in the darkness.

"Tika?" Tas reached out his hand. "Is that lump you?"

"Yes, it's me." She didn't sound pleased about it.

"What are you doing sitting in the dark?"

"Thinking."

"Thinking about what?"

"That Caramon Majere is the biggest numbskull in the whole wide world." There was a pause, then she said, "He went to Skullcap with his brother, didn't he?"

"I guess so. Tanis said he did."

Tika glared at him. "I sent Sturm to Tanis to stop him from going! Why didn't he?"

"Tanis thinks there might be something important in Skullcap. I don't know about Sturm," Tas said, settling himself in the darkness beside Tika. He sighed longingly. "Skullcap. Doesn't that sound like a perfectly wonderful place to you?"

"It sounds horrid. It's a trap," said Tika.

"A trap? Now I wish I'd gone! I love traps!" Tas was disconsolate.

"Not those kind of traps," Tika said scornfully. "I mean Raistlin's leading Caramon into a trap. I've been up all night thinking through it. Raistlin's going because of that awful old dead wizard, that Fistandoodle or whatever his name is. Caramon told me all about him and about that wicked book of his—the book Raistlin sneaked out of Xak Tsaroth. That wizard was an evil man, and that place is an evil place. Raistlin knows that and he doesn't care. He's going to get Caramon killed."

"An evil place that belonged to an evil wizard, and it's filled with traps!" Tas sighed longingly. "If I hadn't given Tanis my solemn promise that I'd stay here to protect you, Tika, I'd go there in a minute."

"Protect me!" Tika was indignant. "You don't need to protect me. No one does. Caramon's the one who needs protecting. He's got about as much sense as a goatsucker bird. He has to be warned about that brother of his. Tanis won't do it, so I guess it's up to me."

Tika threw off the blanket she'd had draped over her shoulders. The cave was growing lighter by the minute, and Tas could now see that she was dressed for travel in men's trousers and a man's shirt and a leather vest that Tas thought looked rather like one that Flint had once owned. Tas remembered the dwarf complaining about it being missing. He'd actually accused the kender of walking off with it!

Tika's sword that she didn't know how to use very well lay on the table, next to her shield, which she *did* know how to use, though not in quite the way the shield's maker had intended. The shield had a dent in it from where she'd bashed a draconian over the head.

Tas leapt up in excitement. "Tanis made me promise solemnly that I'd protect you, so if you go to Skullcap, then I have to go with you!"

"I'm not going to Skullcap. I'm going to find Caramon and keep him from going. I plan to talk some sense into him."

Tas offered his opinion. "I think it might be easier to fight an evil wizard in Skullcap than talk sense into Caramon."

"You're probably right. But I have to try." Tika picked up the sword, intending to buckle it around her waist. "Have they been gone long?"

"Since before dawn, but Raistlin walks pretty slowly. We can catch up—"

"Shush!" Tika cautioned.

Someone was outside the screen. Sunlight glinted on blonde hair.

"Laurana!" Tika groaned softly and hurriedly laid the sword back on the table. "Not a word, Tas! She'll try to stop us!"

"You're awake!" Laurana said, entering the cave. She stopped to stare in amazement at Tika's garb. "Why are you dressed like that?"

"I . . . uh . . . am going to wash my clothes," said Tika. "All my clothes."

"Were you going to wash your sword, too?" asked Laurana, teasing.

Tika was spared the need to tell another lie, for Laurana kept on talking. "You're in luck. You'll have company. Maritta has deemed this laundry day. All the women are going to take their clothes and bedding down to the stream. Tas, you can help. Grab those blankets . . ."

Tas flashed Tika an agonized glance.

Tika shrugged, helpless. She couldn't think of any way out of this.

Tas, staggering beneath a mound of blankets, was leaving the cave when Tika grabbed hold of him. "We'll sneak away when the women go to lunch," she whispered. "Watch me! When I signal, you come running!"

"Don't worry about getting a late start," Tas whispered. "Caramon's big feet will be easy to track, and Raistlin walks really, really slow."

Tika trudged after Tas and Laurana down to the stream. She could only hope the kender was right.

7

Dray-yan's plan. Grag's opinion of it.

ray-yan sat at the large obsidian table in the late Lord Verminaard's chambers and drank the last of his lordship's elven wine. The aurak made a mental note to order the commander charged with battling the elves to send him another barrel. As he sipped the wine, Dray-yan reviewed the events of the past several days, judging how they would affect his future plans. The aurak draconian was pleased with how some things had turned out, not so pleased with others.

The red dragons dispatched to Pax Tharkas by Her Dark Majesty had, as expected, seen through Dray-yan's illusion of Verminaard. Insulted at the idea of being ordered about by draconians, whom the dragons called disparagingly "rotten egg yolk," the dragons had been on the verge of leaving.

Commander Grag took his prayers and plans to Queen Takhisis. She had graciously listened to him, and pleased with his ideas, she commanded the reds to remain in Pax Tharkas and to go along with Dray-yan's schemes, at least for the time being. Grag informed Dray-yan that the queen was backing him only because she had no other commander she could spare to run the Red Dragonarmy. Dray-yan's command was temporary. With success, it might become permanent.

Using the reluctant and grumbling help of the red dragons, Grag was able at last to reopen the pass blocked by the rock fall. Draconian troops marched into Pax Tharkas, though not in great numbers. The Red Dragonarmy was stretched thin. There were enough draconians to man the fortress, but not enough to use to work in the iron mines. Commanders in the field were desperate for weapons and armor. Steel was a more valuable commodity than gold. Dray-yan had to either regain his labor force or find new venues. He decided to do both.

Grag dispatched troops after the refugees. They picked up the trail immediately and followed it to a pass blocked by an avalanche and further blocked by new snow fall.

The reds declared that clearing this pass would be extremely difficult. Further, they made it clear to Dray-yan that clearing passes was tedious, boring, and unprofitable. In other parts of Ansalon, dragons were burning cities and raiding villages, not picking up rocks. The reds would not clear the pass, and if he did not come up with some sort of interesting and agreeable work for them, they were going to go elsewhere.

Dray-yan considered asking Takhisis to again intercede with the dragons, but he could not stomach the thought of once more crawling to his queen begging for help. Takhisis did not like whiners, and her supply of favors was limited. She liked commanders who took the initiative and went ahead with their own plans and ideas, leaving her free to move on with her own schemes.

Dray-yan dropped the idea of marching his army through the pass. He conceived another idea, one that he hoped would win him recognition and praise from the Dark Queen.

Dray-yan did his own reconnaissance in the guise of Lord Verminaard and discovered where the refugees were hiding. He had the pleasure of seeing them run panic-stricken before him like sheep. He could only imagine their dismay as they witnessed the return of the man they'd thought they'd killed.

Having flown over the area, Dray-yan was satisfied that his plan would work. His idea would require him to do a good deal of persuading, but he hoped the dragons might find it diverting and would agree to go along with it. He was less certain how Commander Grag would feel about it.

No time like the present to find out.

Dray-yan sent a messenger ordering Grag to attend him. Rather, Lord Verminaard sent the messenger. Dray-yan found it exhausting keeping up the charade, which required that he use his illusion magic every time he wanted to stick his head out the door and shout for a minion. He looked forward to the day when he could bury Verminaard once and for all. Hopefully, if this plan worked, that day would not be long in coming.

Grag arrived and was invited to partake of the wine. The commander refused, stating he was on duty.

"What do the blue dragon scouts report?" Dray-yan asked.

"One flew over the valley this morning at about dawn. The humans remain in the caves," Grag replied. "They appear to be planning to stay there for the winter, for the dragon saw no signs of any preparations being made to leave."

"Why should they leave?" Dray-yan asked with a shrug. "They do not think we can come through the pass."

"They're right. We can't," said Grag grimly.

"True, but there is more than one way to skin a human. I have a plan."

Dray-yan explained his idea.

Grag listened. First he was incredulous and stared at Dray-yan as though he'd gone mad. As Dray-yan elaborated, however, patiently explaining how this could be done, Grag began to realize that the aurak might be right. This *could* be done! The plan was daring, bold and dangerous but not impossible.

"What do you think?" Dray-yan asked finally.

"The reds must be convinced."

"I will undertake to speak with them myself. I believe they will agree."

Grag thought so too. "My troops will need to time to train."

Dray-yan eyed him, frowning. He hadn't counted on this.

"Is that necessary?"

"Consider what you are asking them to do, yes!" Grag returned heatedly.

Dray-yan considered, before waving a clawed hand in resignation. "Very well. How long?"

"A month."

Dray-yan snorted. "Out of the question."

"The humans are not going anywhere."

"We don't know that. You have one week."

"Two," Grag temporized, "or I will not agree."

Dray-yan eyed him. "I could find another commander who would."

"That is true," said Grag coolly, "but that would mean one more who knows your little secret, Lord Verminaard."

"You have two weeks," Dray-yan said. "Make the most of the time."

"I plan to." Grag rose to his feet. "How do negotiations come with the dwarves of Thorbardin?"

"Quite well," Dray-yan replied. "If this works out, we will have no need for the humans and you may simply kill them."

"We're going to a lot of trouble if we don't really need them," Grag pointed out.

"We cannot be seen to be weak. If nothing else, the deaths of these slaves will serve to instill fear in others who might be thinking of rebelling."

Grag nodded. He hesitated a moment, then said, "You know I do not like you, Dray-yan."

Dray-yan's lip curled. "We were not put into this world to be liked, Commander."

"And that I would never stoop to flattery," Grag continued.

"Where is all this leading, Commander? I have work to do."

"I want to say that I consider this plan of yours one of genius. We will make history. Emperor Ariakas and the other Highlords will look on our race with new respect and admiration."

"That is my hope," said Dray-yan. Though he did not say it, he was pleased by Grag's praise. He could already see himself in a Highlord's armor. "Do your job well, Commander. You have two weeks."

Grag saluted and left to start making arrangements.

"Oh, Commander," Dray-yan called after him, "if you think of it, you might mention this brilliant plan of mine to Her Dark Majesty. Just mention it in passing . . ."

8

A dwarf's knowledge. A wizard's mystery.

he valley in which the refugees sheltered formed a bowl perhaps ten miles long and ten miles wide. Flint and Tanis walked due south, keeping in the foothills at the base of the mountains, not descending into the valley. Flint set a meandering course. Tanis might have thought the dwarf was lost and wandering, but he'd traveled with Flint for many years and knew better.

A dwarf might lose his way in the desert. A dwarf would most certainly lose himself at sea, should he ever have the misfortune to wind up there, but the dwarf had not been born who could get lost among the mountains and hills of Kharolis, long trod by the boots of his ancestors. Flint kept his gaze fixed on the stone walls that thrust up from the valley floor, and every so often, he would adjust their course, shift direction.

They had been traveling for several hours when the dwarf suddenly veered to the right. Leaving the foothills, he began to climb a steep grade.

Tanis followed. He had been searching for some sign that Raistlin, Caramon, and Sturm had come this way, but he'd found none.

"Flint," said Tanis, as they started to ascend, "which way is Skullcap from here?"

Flint paused to get his bearings then pointed to the east. "That way. On the other side of that mountain. If they've gone in that direction, they won't get far. I guess we were worried for nothing."

"There's no pass in that direction?"

"Use your eyes, lad! Do you see a pass?"

Tanis shook his head, then smiled. "I don't see a pass in this direction either."

"Ah, that's because you're not a dwarf!" said Flint and continued the ascent.

⸻

Caramon, Sturm, and Raistlin were down in the valley, following a trail that was faint, overgrown, and occasionally impassable, forcing them to make detours into the forest. No matter how far they ventured from the trail, Raistlin always led them unerringly back.

The stream that ran near their campsite wound through the valley like a gleaming snake, cutting across the trail at several points. Up until now, whenever they'd been forced to cross the stream, it was shallow enough that they could wade through it. They had come to a place where the stream flowed deep and swift, and they could not cross it. Raistlin struck off to the north, following the bank, and eventually found a place where the water was only ankle deep.

Once they were on the other side, Raistlin led the way along the bank until they once more picked up the trail.

"How did he know where to find the ford?" Sturm asked in a low voice.

"Lucky guess," Caramon returned.

Sturm regarded Raistlin grimly. "He seems to make a lot of those."

"A good thing, too," Caramon muttered, "otherwise we'd be wandering around here lost."

Caramon increased his pace to catch up with his far-ranging twin.

"Don't you think you should rest, Raist?" Caramon asked solicitously as he caught up. Caramon was worried at the pace his frail twin was setting. They'd walked for hours without a break. "You've really pushed yourself this morning."

"No time," Raistlin said, walking faster. He glanced at the sky. "We must be there by sunset."

"We must be where by sunset?" Caramon asked, puzzled.

Raistlin appeared momentarily confused then brushed the question aside. "You will—"

His words were interrupted by a coughing spasm. He choked, gasping for breath.

Caramon hovered nearby, watching helplessly as Raistlin wiped his mouth then quickly crumpled the handkerchief, thrusting it back into a pocket, though not before Caramon had seen spots on the white cloth that were as red as the mage's robes.

"We're stopping," said Caramon.

Raistlin tried to protest, but he lacked the breath to argue. Glancing up at the sun, which had yet to reach its zenith, he gave in and slumped down on a fallen log. His breath came in wheezes. Caramon removed the stopper from the water skin, and as he held it out for his brother to drink, saw that Raistlin's golden-tinged skin had a feverish flush. Knowing better than to say anything about this, fearing to draw his brother's ire, Caramon took the opportunity as he handed over the water to brush his hand against his brother's. Raistlin's skin always seemed unnaturally warm to the touch, but Caramon fancied that it was hotter than normal.

"Sturm, could you gather some wood? I want to start a fire," Caramon said. "I'll brew your tea, Raist. You can take a nap."

Raistlin flashed his twin a look that caused the words to dry up in Caramon's mouth.

"A nap!" Raistlin said scathingly. "Do you think we are on a kender outing, brother?"

"No," said Caramon, unhappy. "It's just that you—"

Raistlin rose to his feet. His eyes glinted from the shadow of his cowl. "Go ahead, Caramon. Start a fire. You and the knight have your picnic. Perhaps you can go fishing, catch a trout. When the two of you are finished, you might consider catching up with me!" He pointed with his staff to his tracks in the snow. "You will have no difficulty following my trail."

He started to cough, but he managed to stifle it in the sleeve of his robes. Leaning on his staff, he strode off.

"By the gods, for a bent copper I *would* go fishing," Sturm said vehemently. "Let him end up in a wolf's belly!"

Caramon did not answer but silently gathered up his gear and that of his brother and started off in pursuit of his twin.

"For a bent copper," Sturm muttered.

Since there was no one around to offer him such an incentive, the knight hefted his own equipment and stalked grimly after them.

───────────────

Tanis was not the least bit surprised when Flint found the old dwarven trail, hidden from sight, carved out of the side of the mountain. Flint had been walking with one eye fixed on the ground and the other searching the mountain walls, looking for signs only he could see, secret marks left by his people who had lived in and around the Kharolis mountains since the time of the forging of the world by the dwarven god, Reorx.

Tanis pretended to be surprised, however, swearing he'd been certain they were lost past recovery. Flint flushed with pride, though he pretended he'd done nothing special. Tanis eyed the route of path that stretched ahead of them, meandering across the face of the mountain.

"It's narrow," he said, thinking of the refugees that might have to use it, "and steep."

"It is that," Flint agreed. "It was meant to be trod by dwarven feet, not human." He pointed ahead. "See that cleft in the walls up ahead? That's where this path leads. That's how we cross the mountains."

The cut was so narrow that it formed almost a perfect V shape. Tanis could not tell how wide it was, for they were yet some distance away, but from this vantage point, it looked as if two humans walking side-by-side would be a tight squeeze. The path on which he stood could accommodate two humans at some points, but he could see plainly that in other places people would need to walk single-file.

He and Flint had been climbing steadily since they left the foothills. The path had the solid backing of the mountain on one side, with nothing on the other except a long drop. Traversing such terrain did not bother dwarves in the least. Flint claimed that so long as they had rock beneath their feet, dwarven boots did not slip. Tanis thought of Goldmoon, who was terrified of heights, walking this path, and he wished for a moment that he believed in these new-found gods, so that he could pray to them to spare her and the people the necessity of making this terrible journey. As it was, he could only hope, and his hope was bleak.

He and Flint continued, their pace slowing, for though the dwarf marched with confidence along the trail, Tanis had to take more care.

Fortunately, the mountain had sheltered the path from the snow, so that the trail wasn't icy. Even so, Tanis had to watch his step, and though heights didn't bother him, every time he looked over the edge to the boulders below, certain parts of him shriveled.

By late afternoon, he and Flint had reached the cut that was every bit as narrow and difficult to cross as it had looked from a distance.

"We'll camp here for the night where the walls protect us from the wind," said Flint. "We cross in the morning."

As Tanis scouted out the best of a bad place in which to spend a cold night in a rock-strewn ravine, Flint stood with his hands on his hips, his lips pursed, staring up at the peak that towered above them. At length, after a good long perusal, he grunted in satisfaction.

"I thought as much," he said. "We need to leave Riverwind a sign."

"I have been leaving signs," Tanis pointed out. "You've seen me. He'll have no trouble finding the path."

"It's not the path I'm wanting to show him. Come take a look." Flint pointed at large boulder. "What do you make of that, lad?"

"It's a rock," said Tanis. "Like every other rock around here."

"Aye, but it's not!" Flint said triumphantly. "That rock is striped— red and orange. The rocks around it are gray."

"Then it must have tumbled down the side of the mountain. There's lots of loose rocks and boulders up there."

"That boulder didn't fall. Someone put it there. Now why do you suppose someone would do that?" Flint grinned. He was enjoying himself.

Tanis shook his head.

"It's a keystone," Flint stated. "Knock it out and it takes out that boulder, and that boulder takes out that one, and before you know it the whole shebang comes cascading down on your head."

"So you want me to warn Riverwind that no one should disturb this boulder," said Tanis.

Flint snorted. "The cold has frozen your brain, Half-Elf. I want you to tell him that if he's being pursued, once all the people have safely crossed, he should knock it out. It will block the pass behind him."

"Bring pick-axes, you advised." Tanis recalled their conversation that morning. He gazed thoughtfully at the rock and shook his head. "Explaining something this complicated is going to be difficult, short of leaving him a written note. You should have said something to him this morning."

"I wasn't certain I would find it. For all I knew, if my people *had* left a keystone, and sometimes they do and sometimes they don't, it might have already been triggered or tumbled down on its own."

"Which would have meant that this cut was impassable," said Tanis. "We would have come all this way for nothing, unless there is another way out."

Flint shrugged. "From the signs my people left, this is the only pass there is. There was no way of knowing if it was open without coming to see for ourselves."

"Still, you should have told Riverwind about the keystone."

Flint glowered at him. "I'm breaking faith with my people by showing it to you, Half-Elven, much less going around blabbing secrets to a pack of humans."

Irate, he stomped off, leaving Tanis to solve the problem. At length, the half-elf picked up Flint's pick-axe and laid it down beside the keystone with its point facing the boulder. Anyone happening upon it would think they had either dropped it or abandoned it. Riverwind, he hoped, would remember that Flint had specifically mentioned pick-axes and would realize that this was a clue. Whether he realized it was a clue to blocking the trail behind them if they were being pursued was another matter.

He found Flint comfortably ensconced among the rocks, chewing on strips of dried venison.

"I was thinking about what you said, about dwarves sharing their secrets with humans. It seems to me that if we could all see ourselves as one 'people', this would be a better world,"

"What are you grousing about, Half-Elven?" Flint demanded.

"I was saying it's a damn shame we can't trust each other."

"Ah, if we all trusted each other, we'd all be kender," Flint said. "Then where would we be? I'm going to sleep. You take first watch."

Flint finished his meal, then wrapped himself in his blanket, and lay down on his back among the rocks.

Tanis propped himself up against a sloping wall, and, unable to get comfortable, he gazed into the starlit night.

"If there is no other way out of the valley, how will Raistlin reach Skullcap?" he asked.

"Fly there on his broomstick, most likely," Flint muttered, and giving a great yawn, he shoved a stone out from beneath his shoulders, closed his eyes, and sighed in deep contentment.

"This feels like home," he said, lacing his fingers over his chest. He was soon snoring.

———————————◆◆◆◆———

Raistlin, Caramon, and Sturm continued their trek across the valley, walking all through the afternoon. Raistlin seemed infused with an unnatural energy that would not permit him to rest but kept driving him on. Caramon often insisted that they stop, but he wasted his time, for Raistlin would sit down for only a few moments, then he would be back on his feet, pacing restlessly, his gaze going to the sun now starting its descent into afternoon.

"Sunset," was all he would say and kept walking.

The forested part of the valley ended. Open grassland spread before them. The trail they had been following through the trees disappeared, yet Raistlin kept going, moving out onto the snow-covered grass. He walked with his head down, leaning heavily on his staff. He looked neither to the right nor the left but kept his gaze fixed on his feet, as though all his will was bent on placing one foot in front of the other. His hand pressed against his chest. His breath rattled in his lungs.

Sturm expected the mage to collapse at any moment. He knew better than to say anything, however, knowing that any attempt to try to make Raistlin rest would result in a venomous look and a sarcastic gibe.

"This will be the death of your brother," Sturm warned Caramon in a low voice.

"I know," said Caramon, worried, "but he won't stop. I've tried to talk to him. He just gets mad."

"Where is he going in such a hurry? There's nothing ahead of us but a solid stone wall!"

The grass lands, smooth and trackless, stretched on for about two miles, coming to an abrupt end at a sheer wall of rock jutting up from the valley floor. The rock wall formed a span, like a natural bridge, between two mountains.

"Once we step out from under the cover of the trees and onto the empty grasslands, a blind gully dwarf could spot us."

Caramon acknowledged the truth of this with a slow nod and kept walking.

"I don't like this, Caramon," Sturm continued. "There's something strange at work here." He had been going to say "evil," but he changed it at the last moment, fearing to upset Caramon, who nodded again and kept walking.

Sturm halted to draw breath. Gazing after the twins, he shook his head.

"I think Raistlin could order Caramon to follow him into the Abyss and he'd never hesitate," he said to himself. Loyalty to a brother was admirable, but loyalty should see with clear eyes, not stumble along blind.

Caramon peered around over his shoulder. "Sturm? You coming?"

Sturm hefted his pack and walked on. Loyalty to friends went unquestioned.

9

Pheragas who?
Wake me if you see a ghost.

s the sun waned and Flint and Tanis bedded down for the night on the mountain, Sturm, Caramon and Raistlin reached the end of their day's journey—a blank wall.

Both Caramon and Sturm could see quite clearly their sojourn across a snow-covered meadow was headed straight for a dead end. The rays of the setting sun struck the immense stone wall full on. Caramon thought they might climb it, but the bright sunlight revealed that the wall was smooth-sided with nary a hand or foot-hold in sight. The wall was slightly curved, like the side of a bowl, and so high that the tallest siege engines ever constructed would have reached only to its midpoint. There were no caves, no cracks, no way through it or over it, yet Raistlin made for the wall with dogged determination.

Caramon said nothing about the fact that they were on a journey to nowhere, for he was loathe to cross his brother. Sturm said nothing to Raistlin aloud, though he said plenty beneath his breath. Caramon could hear the knight muttering to himself as he slogged along behind him. Caramon knew Sturm was angry with him as well as his brother. Sturm believed Caramon should call a halt to this and force Raistlin to turn back. Sturm assumed that Caramon didn't because he feared his twin.

Sturm was only half-right. Caramon did fear his brother's anger, but he would have willingly risked his twin's snide comments and disparaging remarks if he thought that Raistlin was doing something wrong or putting himself in danger. Caramon was not so sure that was the case. Raistlin was acting very strangely, but he was also acting with purpose and resolve. Caramon felt compelled to respect his brother's decisions.

If it turns out he's wrong and we've come all this way for nothing, Caramon reflected wryly, Sturm will at least have the satisfaction of saying, "I told you so."

They continued to march across the grassland. Raistlin increased his pace as the shadows of coming night spread across the valley. They came at last to the base of the great gray wall.

The land was silent with that eerie, heavy silence that comes with a blanket of snow. The sky was empty, as was the land around them. They might have been the only living beings in the world.

Raistlin shoved back the cowl so that it fell around his shoulders and stared at the wall before him. He blinked and looked vaguely astonished, very much like he was seeing it for the first time, with no clear idea how he came to be here.

His confusion was not lost on Sturm.

The knight dropped his pack containing his armor with a clang and a clatter that echoed off the mountainside and jarred every tooth in Caramon's head.

"Your brother has no idea where he is, does he?" Sturm said flatly. "Or what he's doing here?" He glanced over shoulder. "It will be dark soon. We can make camp back in the woods. If we start now—"

He stopped talking because no one was listening to him. Raistlin had begun to walk along the base of the wall, his gaze intently scanning the gray rock that glimmered orange in the light of a flaring sunset. He walked several paces in one direction, then, not finding what he was seeking, he turned around and walked back. His gaze never left the wall. At length he paused. He brushed off snow that had stuck to the wall and smiled.

"This is it," he said.

Caramon walked over to look. His brother had uncovered a mark chiseled into stone at about waist-height. Caramon recognized the mark as a rune, one of the letters of the language of magic. His gut twisted, and his flesh crawled. He longed to ask his brother how he had known to trek miles across an unfamiliar, desolate valley and walk up to this vast wall of stone at precisely this location. He did not ask, however, perhaps because he feared Raistlin might tell him.

"What . . . what does it mean?" Caramon asked instead.

Sturm shoved forward. He saw the mark and said grimly, "Evil, that's what it means."

"It's not evil; it's magic," Caramon said, though he knew he was wasting his breath. In the mind of the Solamnic knight, they amounted to the same thing.

Raistlin paid no attention to either of them. The mage's long, delicate fingers rested lightly, caressingly, on the rune.

"Don't you know where you are, Pheragas?" Raistlin said suddenly. "This was to be our supply route in case we were besieged, and this was to have been our means of escape if the battle went awry. I know that you are dull-witted sometimes, Pheragas, but even you could not have forgotten something this important."

Caramon glanced around in perplexity, then stared at his brother. "Who are you talking to, Raist? Who's Pheragas?"

"You are, of course," returned Raistlin irritably. "Pheragas . . ."

He looked at Caramon and blinked. Raistlin put his hand to his forehead. His eyes lost their focus. "Why did I say that?" Seeing the rune beneath his fingers, he suddenly snatched his hand away. He looked up the wall and down, looked side to side. Turning to Caramon, Raistlin asked in a low voice. "Where are we, my brother?"

"Paladine save us," said Sturm. "He's gone mad."

Caramon licked dry lips, then said hesitantly, "Don't you know? You brought us here, Raist."

Raistlin made an impatient gesture. "Just tell me where we are!"

"The eastern end of the valley." Caramon peered at their surroundings. "By my reckoning, Skullcap must be somewhere on the other side of this wall. You said something about an 'escape route'. 'In case the battle went awry.' What . . . uh . . . did you mean by that?"

"I have no idea," Raistlin replied. He gazed at the wall and at the rune, his brow furrowed. "Yet I do seem to remember . . ."

Caramon laid a solicitous hand on his brother's arm. "Never mind, Raist. You're exhausted. You should rest."

Raistlin wasn't listening. He stared at the wall, and his expression cleared. "Yes, that's right." He spoke softly. "If I touch this rune . . ."

"Raist, don't!" Caramon grabbed hold of his brother's arm.

Raistlin whipped his staff around, giving Caramon a crack on the wrist. Caramon yelped and drew back his hand. Raistlin touched the rune and pressed on it hard.

The portion of the wall on which the rune was etched depressed, sliding into the wall about three inches. A grinding sound emanated from inside the stone wall, followed by loud snapping and groaning. The outline of a doorway, about five feet in height and rectangular, appeared etched into the wall. The door shivered, displacing the snow sticking to the side of the wall, then the noise stopped. Nothing else happened.

Raistlin stood, frowning at it.

"Something must be wrong with the mechanism. Pheragas, put your shoulder to the door and push on it. You, too, Denubis. It will take both of you to force it."

Neither man moved.

Raistlin glanced irritably at them both. "What are you waiting for? Your brains to come back? Trust me. It will not happen. Pheragas, quit standing there gaping like a gutted fish and do as I command you."

Caramon simply stared at his twin, his mouth wide open. Sturm frowned deeply and took a step backward.

"I'll have nothing to do with evil magic," he said.

Raistlin gave a mirthless laugh.

"Magic? Are you daft? This is not magic. If this door was magic, it would be reliable! This mark is not a magical rune. It is the dwarven rune for the word 'Door'. The mechanism is three hundred years old and it is stuck, that's all."

He eyed his brother. "Pheragas—"

"I'm not Pheragas, Raist," said Caramon quietly.

Raistlin stared at him. His eyes flickered, and he said quietly, "No, no, you're not. I don't know why I keep calling you that. Caramon, please, you have nothing to fear. Just put your shoulder to the door—"

"Wait a minute, Caramon." Sturm halted the big man as he was about to obey. "*This* door might not be magic, as you say—" though he gave the doorway a dark glance— "but I for one want to know how your brother knew it was here."

Raistlin glared at the knight and Caramon cringed, expecting him to lash out at Sturm. Caramon was always getting caught in the middle between his brother and his friends, and he hated it. Their fighting made his stomach twist. He cast Sturm a pleading glance, begging him to let the subject drop. After all, it was just a door . . .

His brother did not lash out. The explosion of rage Caramon feared did not happen. Raistlin's lips compressed. He looked at the door, looked at the trail they had left through the snow, the trail that stretched back to the woods and across the valley. His gaze went to Sturm, and there came a ghost of a smile to the thin lips.

"You have never trusted me, Sturm Brightblade," Raistlin said quietly, "and I do not know why. To my knowledge, I have never betrayed you. I have never lied to you. If I have kept certain information to myself from time to time, I suppose that is my right. To be honest," Raistlin added with a shrug, "I do not know how I found this door. I do not know how I knew it was here. I do not know how I knew to open it. I did, and that is all I can say."

He raised his hand, as Sturm would have spoken. "I also know this. Inside the door we will find a tunnel that will lead us directly into the fortress of Zhaman, what is now known as Skullcap."

Raistlin glanced at the door and sighed. "At least, it used to. The tunnel might have been destroyed in the blast."

"Now that you're being so open and honest," said Sturm grimly, "I suppose you assume we'll walk right in."

"Either that or spend the next several days searching for a way over these mountains, and more days after that in crossing them," Raistlin replied. "It is up to you, Sir Knight. Which would you rather do? In the interests of saving time, Caramon and I will take this route. Won't we, my brother?"

"Sure, Raist," said Caramon.

Sturm was still frowning at the door.

"C'mon, Sturm," said Caramon in low tones. "You don't want to go traipsing over these mountains. You might never find a way. Like Raist says, the door's not magic. Dwarves built it. We saw doors that worked like this in Pax Tharkas. As for how Raist knew it was here, it doesn't matter. Maybe he read about it in a book and just forgot."

Sturm regarded his friend thoughtfully. Then he smiled and laid his hand on his friend's shoulder. "If all mankind were as loyal and trusting as you are, Caramon, the world would be a better place.

Unhappily—" his gaze shifted to Raistlin— "such is not the case. Still, as you say, this saves us time and effort."

Sturm walked over to the door and put his shoulder against the stone. Caramon joined him, and both shoved on the rock. At first, they made no progress. They might have been pushing on the side of the mountain. They gave it another shove, digging their heels into the ground, and suddenly the block of stone slid backward, moving so fast on steel tracks that Caramon lost his footing and fell flat. Sturm stumbled too, barely catching himself.

The sun had vanished. The afterglow was all the light in the sky, and that would be gone soon.

"*Shirak*," said Raistlin, raising his staff. The crystal on top, held fast in the golden claw, burst into light. He walked past his brother, and Sturm, who stood hesitantly near the opening in the stone wall, and entered the tunnel.

Light gleamed on a steel rail about six feet in length, running straight into the passage until, at this juncture, the rail line split, part of it curving around to the left to come up against a wall, The rest continued on down the tunnel, disappearing in the darkness. Raistlin examined the mechanism with interest.

"Look at this," he said, pointing. "The door is mounted on wheels that run along the rail. The door can then be pushed against this wall, so that it is out of the way."

Four carts mounted on rails stood in a row. The carts were still in good condition, for the passage beneath the mountain had been sealed up tight. The floor and walls were dry. Raistlin glanced inside the carts. They were empty. By the looks of them, they had never been used.

"Supply wagons could be driven up to the tunnel, their contents unloaded onto these carts. The carts were either pushed or pulled along the rails, down the tunnel, and into Zhaman. Thus, even besieged, the fortress could still be resupplied, and in case defeat was imminent, those inside the fortress could use this route to escape."

"That doesn't make any sense," stated Caramon, entering and peering around.

"What doesn't?" asked his brother impatiently.

"According to Flint, when the wizard saw that he was about to be defeated, he decided to destroy himself and kill thousands of his own troops." Caramon gestured to the tunnel. "Why would he do that when he could have fled to safety?"

"You have a point, my brother," Raistlin said thoughtfully. "It is strange. I wonder . . ."

"Wonder what?" asked Caramon.

"Nothing." Raistlin shook his head, yet he remained thoughtful.

"Bah! The wizard was mad," said Sturm flatly, "consumed by his own evil."

"Fistandantilus was many things," said Raistlin softly, "but he was not mad." He shrugged himself out of his reverie. "We waste our time in idle speculation. It is unlikely that anyone will ever know the truth of what happened in Zhaman at the end."

Further exploration of the tunnel revealed a cache of weapons and armor of dwarven make, torches and lanterns, pick axes, and other tools, stores of food and casks of ale. The food had all been devoured by rodents. The casks were also empty, much to Caramon's disappointment, though his brother pointed out that any ale left sitting around for three centuries would hardly be drinkable.

Sturm lit one of the torches and set to out examine the area, searching for tracks or other signs that this tunnel might be inhabited. He explored the passage for about a mile and returned to report that he could find no indication that other living beings had walked the tunnel. He laid grim emphasis on the word "living," reminding them all that Skullcap was supposed to be haunted.

Raistlin smiled and said nothing.

Caramon proposed they spend the night at the entrance and proceed down the tunnel the next day. Raistlin would have pushed on, even though he knew he could not go far before he collapsed. Though weary to the point of dropping, he was restless, incapable of settling down.

He ate little and drank his tea. Caramon and Sturm sat at their ease, discussing what they knew of the Dwarfgate Wars, which knowledge came mostly from Flint's stories of the conflict. Raistlin roamed about the tunnel, staring intently into the darkness, wishing he was capable of piercing it and drawing forth its secrets. When he finally was so exhausted he could not take another step, he lay down on his bedroll and fell immediately into a deep slumber.

Caramon and Sturm debated whether or not to close and seal the tunnel by shoving the stone door back into place. They decided to leave it open, in case they needed to make a quick escape.

As Sturm said, rolling himself up in his blanket, "We know what's out there. We don't know what's in here."

"And we know we're not being followed," said Caramon with a yawn.

As it turned out, they were both wrong. Tas and Tika were out there, and they were following them.

Midway through the day, Tasslehoff and Tika had finally managed to sneak away from laundry detail. When it came time to spread the sopping wet clothes and bedding over bushes to dry, Tika had eagerly volunteered for the task. A quick poke in the ribs had caused Tas to volunteer as well. Tas had managed to retrieve their packs and hide them beneath a rotted log. Snagging these, the two of them had dumped the laundry they were supposed to be hanging and slipped away from camp.

They'd picked up the trail of the three men with ease. They could see in the snow the print of Raistlin's narrow feet, the brush-marks left by the hem of his robes, and indentations made by his staff. Caramon's large footprints were always near the smaller prints of his brother, and Sturm's heavy prints came behind, guarding the rear.

Well aware that they'd lost valuable time and that they had only half the day left before darkness overtook them, Tika tried her best to hurry along. This proved difficult, for Tasslehoff was constantly being distracted by something he saw and continually starting to venture off to investigate. Tika had to either argue him out of it, forcibly restrain him, or if she happened to be looking the other way, go chase him down.

When night fell, the two were still inside the forest.

"We have to stop," Tika said, dispirited. "If we go on, we might miss their tracks in the dark. Does this clearing look like a good place to camp?"

"As good as any," said Tas. "There are probably wolves out there ready to tear us apart, but if we build a fire we can keep them away."

"Wolves?" Tika glanced nervously around the dark forest.

She had traveled far from Solace and the Inn of the Last Home, where she had worked as a barmaid, going on a journey she had never expected to take. Neither had she expected to fall in love on this journey and certainly not with Caramon Majere, who had teased her unmercifully when she was a little girl, calling her "Carrot-top," "Freckle-face" and "Skinny Butt."

He didn't call her those names now, of course. No one did. Tika had filled out nicely; too nicely, she thought, when she compared herself to the graceful, sylph-like Laurana. Buxom and broad-shouldered, with strong, muscular arms, gleaned from years of carrying heavy trays of food and hefting mugs of ale, Tika was always amused when someone termed her "pretty". Her red curls, green eyes and flashing smile had captured more than one heart back in Solace, and now Caramon's was among them, his the most treasured.

Here she was, far from home, far from anything resembling a home, if you came down to it, spending the night in a dark—extremely dark—forest, her only companion a kender. While Tasslehoff was her best friend and she was very glad he was with her, she couldn't help wishing he wouldn't talk quite so much or so loudly and especially that he wouldn't keep jumping up at every strange noise and crying out eagerly, "Did you hear that, Tika? It sounded like a bear!"

Tika had spent many nights in the wilderness on this trip but always in company with skilled warriors who knew how to defend themselves. Tika had been in a few fights, but thus far the only weapon she had ever wielded with élan was a heavy iron skillet. She had found a sword, but she knew quite well, for she'd been told often enough, that when she wielded it, she was dangerous only to herself.

Tika had not meant to be spending this night alone. She'd meant to be spending the night with Caramon. She knew that once she'd caught up with them, neither Sturm nor Caramon would send her back alone and unprotected, no matter what Raistlin might say. They would have to take her and Tas along with them, and she would be able to keep Caramon out of whatever trouble his brother was likely to get him into.

A snapping sound nearby caused her heart to stop.

"What was that?" she gasped.

Tas had grown sleepy by this time and gone to bed.

"Probably a goblin," he said drowsily. "You're taking first watch."

Tika gave a muffled shriek and grabbed her sword.

"Don't worry," said Tas, yawning and pulling his blanket up over his head. "Goblins almost never attack by night. Ghosts and ghouls attack by night."

Tika, who had been reassured, wasn't anymore.

"You don't think there are ghosts here?" she asked, dismayed.

"There aren't any burial grounds around, at least that we've found, so I expect not," said Tas, after giving the matter some thought. He added, with another jaw-cracking yawn, "If a ghost does show up, Tika, be sure to wake me. I wouldn't want to miss it."

Tika told herself that the snapping noise she had heard was a deer, not a bear or a wolf, but she quickly threw more wood on the fire until she realized that the fire would reveal them to their enemies. Then she wondered in a panic if she should put it out.

Before she could decide, the fire began to die and there was no more fuel. Tika was afraid to go out to gather wood, and when the last flickering light from the last ember disappeared, she sat in the darkness, clutching her sword and hating Tasslehoff with all her might for sleeping so soundly and peacefully when there were ghosts, goblins, wolves, and other horrible things all around them.

Terror is exhausting, however, not to mention she'd spent half the day hauling water and wringing out wet clothes and the other half traipsing through the woods. Tika's head sank onto her chest. The hand holding the sword relaxed its grip.

Her last thought as she drifted off to sleep was that one was never ever supposed to fall asleep on watch.

10

A memory of the past.
Hope for the future. Mumblety-peg.

turm took first watch for their group that night. Caramon took second. They did not ask Raistlin to stand watch. Sturm would not have trusted him, and Caramon proclaimed his brother too weak; Raist needed his sleep.

The night passed in such profound peace and quiet that Sturm found it difficult to stay awake. He was at length forced to march up and down along the tunnel to fight off the longing to close his eyes. As he marched, his mind went, as it generally did when he was alone, to the time he'd spent in Solamnia, a bittersweet time, with more bitter than sweet.

The knighthood that had once been so revered in Solamnia had long since fallen into disrepute. The reasons for this were numerous. The Cataclysm brought death and destruction to all parts Krynn, not excluding the nation of Solamnia. Shortly after the disaster struck, rumors began to spread throughout Solamnia that the knights had been given the power by the gods to prevent the Cataclysm and had failed to stop it.

People who had lost everything—homes, livelihood, friends and family—were glad to have someone to blame, and the knights were easy targets. Add to this volatile situation those who had always been jealous of the power wielded by the knights, and those who believed, rightly or wrongly, that the knights had grown wealthy at the expense of the poor, and it was small wonder the mixture exploded.

Mobs attacked the knights' halls and castles. The knights could not win under such circumstances. If they defended themselves against the mobs and killed people, they were called murderers. If they did not stand up to the mobs, they risked losing everything, including their lives.The turmoil in Solamnia would abate for a time, then again rear its monstrous head. The knights continued to try desperately to bring stability and peace to the land, and in some places they would succeed, but because their Order was fractured, individual knights could never hold onto power for long.

Sturm's family had worked hard to maintain peace in their ancestral holding, and they had succeeded longer than most, for the Brightblades were revered and honored by those they governed. Outsiders came to the villages and towns under their control, however, and began stirring up trouble, as they were now doing over much of Solamnia. This was, in truth, a concerted effort by the forces of the Dark Queen to undermine the power of her most implacable enemies. None knew this at the time, however. Angriff Brightblade, foreseeing trouble, sent his wife and son south to the tree-top town of Solace, long known as a safe haven for those in desperate straits.

Sturm grew up in Solace, raised on his mother's tales of the past glories of the knighthood. He read and studied the Measure—the code of laws devised by the knights—and he lived by the Oath *Est sularus et mithas,* "My honor is my life." He and his mother heard little news from the north, and what they did hear was bad. Then the time came that they heard no news at all. When Sturm's mother died, he determined to seek out his father and he traveled north to Solamnia.

Sturm discovered his family's hall in ruins, for it had not only been ransacked, it had also been burned and razed. He could not find his father, nor could he discover what had happened to Angriff Brightblade. Some said this; some said that. No one knew for certain. Sturm believed his father must be dead; otherwise nothing would have kept him from returning to claim the castle of his ancestors.

While his father might be dead, his father's debts were very much alive. Angriff had borrowed heavily on his lands in order to keep them up and provide aid to the poor and destitute under his protection. The bitter irony of the fact that those who had attacked the hall were those who were alive to do so because of his father's help was not lost upon Sturm. He was forced to sell off the lands of his forefathers in order to settle the debts. All that was left when he was finished was his father's sword and armor. And his honor.

Sturm thought back to all this as he walked his watch in the darkness of the tunnel, his pacing lit by the feeble light of a lantern. The night before he left to return to Solace, the only home he had ever known, he had entered the Brightblade vault where the dead lay in repose. Located in the ruins of the family chapel, the burial chamber was accessible only by a sealed bronze door, the key to which was hidden in the chapel. There was evidence that the mob had attempted to batter down the door, probably hoping to find wealth inside. The door held firm, as had the Brightblades, down through the centuries.

Sturm found the hidden key and opened the door and went, hushed and reverent, into the vault, his eyes half-blinded by his tears. The tombs holding his forebearers stood in the gloom. Stone knights lay atop upon the sarcophagi, their graven hands holding graven swords. Sturm's father had no tomb, for none knew where his body lay buried. Sturm placed on the floor a living rose in memory of his father, and he went down on his knees and asked his ancestors for forgiveness for having failed them.

Sturm kept vigil all that night. When the light of dawn crept into the chamber, he rose stiffly to his feet and made a solemn vow on the sword, which was all he had left, that he would restore the honor and glory of the Brightblade family. He left the vault, shutting and sealing the bronze door. He kept the key with him until he was on board ship back to Abanasinia. Standing on the deck in the silver light of Solinari, Sturm consigned the key to the ocean's depths.

As yet, he'd done nothing to fulfill that oath.

He walked the tunnel with measured tread, thinking his melancholy thoughts, when he was interrupted.

"Will you stop that pacing!" Raistlin demanded peevishly. "I cannot sleep with you stomping about."

Sturm halted, turned to confront the mage.

"What is it you hope to find in this accursed place, Raistlin? What is so important that you risk all our lives to find it?"

All Sturm could see of Raistlin were his strange hourglass eyes gleaming in the lantern light. Sturm had not really expected an answer, and he was startled when Raistlin said, his voice cool and clear in the darkness, "What is it you are hoping to find in Skullcap?"

When Sturm made no reply, Raistlin continued, "You did not choose to go with us for love of me certainly. You know that both Caramon and I are capable of taking care of ourselves, so why did you come?"

"I see no need to bandy words with you, Raistlin," Sturm returned. "My reasons are my own."

"The Hammer of Kharas," said Raistlin. He drew out the last syllable into a sibilant hiss.

Sturm was startled. He had spoken of the Hammer only to Tanis. His first impulse was to turn away, but he could not resist the challenge.

"What do you know of the Hammer?" he asked in a low voice.

Raistlin made a hoarse, rasping sound that might have been a bitter chuckle, or else he was clearing his throat. "While you and my brother were smashing each other over the head with wooden swords, I pursued my studies, something for which you mocked me. Now you come running to me for answers."

"I never mocked you, Raistlin," Sturm said quietly. "Whatever else you may think of me, you must at least give me credit for that. I often protected you, as in the time the mob was about to turn you into a burnt offering to that snake god. If you must know, my dislike of you stems from the miserable way you treat your brother."

"What is between my brother and me is between my brother and me, Sturm Brightblade," Raistlin returned. "You cannot possibly understand."

"You are right. I do not understand," Sturm replied coolly. "Caramon loves you. He would lay down his life for you, and you treat him like garbage. Now I must get some sleep, so I will bid you good-night—"

"That which is now known as the Hammer of Kharas was originally known as the Hammer of Honor," said Raistlin. "The hammer was made to honor the Hammer of Reorx, used by the god to forge the world. The Hammer of Honor was a symbol of peace between the humans of Ergoth, the elves of Qualinesti, and the dwarves of Thorbardin. During the Third Dragon War, the Hammer was given to the great knight, Huma Dragonbane, to be used along with the magical Silver Arm to forge the first dragonlances. They drove the Dark Queen back into the Abyss, where she has been ever since, or rather, up until now.

"In the time of the High King Duncan and the Dwarfgate Wars, the Hammer of Honor was given into the hands of the hero, Kharas, a dwarf so revered that the Hammer's name was changed in his honor. The Hammer was last seen during the war being wielded by Kharas, but he departed the field of battle early, grieved at being forced to fight his own kind. He carried the Hammer with him back into Thorbardin, and there it has been lost to all knowledge, for the gates of the mountain kingdom were sealed shut and hidden from the world."

Raistlin paused to draw breath then added, "The one who recovers the Hammer and uses it to forge dragonlances will be lauded a hero. He will find fame and fortune, honor, and glory."

Sturm cast Raistlin an uneasy glance. Was the mage speaking in generalities, or he had been prying into the knight's innermost thoughts?

"I must get some sleep," Sturm said, and he walked over to wake up the loudly snoring Caramon.

"The Hammer is not in Skullcap," Raistlin told him. "If it still exists, it is in Thorbardin. If you are seeking the Hammer, you should have gone with Tanis and Flint."

"You said the key to Thorbardin lies in Skullcap," said Sturm.

"I did," Raistlin replied, "but since when does anyone ever listen to me?"

"Tanis listens," said Sturm, "and that is why he sent me with you and your brother, to make sure that if you do find the key, you deliver it."

The mage had nothing to say to that, for which Sturm was grateful. Conversations with Raistlin always upset him, left him with feeling that all his sterling notions of the world were in reality blackened and tarnished.

Sturm woke Caramon. The big man, yawning and stretching, took up the watch. Sturm was weary, and he sank almost immediately into a deep sleep. In his dreams, he used the Hammer of Kharas to batter down the bronze door of his family's vault.

———————————————

The night passed without event for all those who wandered. Those who kept watch saw nothing and heard nothing. Those who did not keep watch—Tika and Tasslehoff—slept undisturbed. All-seeing eyes kept watch over them.

Day dawned slowly and reluctantly. The sun struggled to pierce thick, gray clouds and ended up failing miserably and eventually went, sulking, into hiding. The sky threatened rain or snow, though it did neither.

When a gray and feeble sun lit the tunnel entrance, Sturm, Caramon, and Raistlin resumed their journey. They discussed shutting the entrance behind them, shoving the stone door back in place.

Upon examination, none of them, not even Raistlin, could determine how to operate the mechanism and open the door once it was shut. Even if they did finally figure it out, the mechanism had broken down once. It might do so again. Then they would be trapped, and they had no idea what they would find farther on. The tunnel might be blocked, in which case they would have to admit defeat and retrace their steps. They agreed to leave the door open.

The three proceeded down the tunnel, the light of the crystal atop Raistlin's staff illuminating their way. Sturm carried a lantern, for he disliked intensely the idea that Raistlin could suddenly, with a single word, plunge them into darkness.

The tunnel, constructed by dwarven engineers, cut straight through the mountain. The walls were rough hewn, the floor relatively smooth. There were no signs that anyone had ever been inside it.

"If the dwarves had been fleeing their besieged fortress, we'd find discarded armor, broken weapons, bodies," said Caramon. "This was never used."

"Which proves the theory that Fistandantilus did not bring down Zhaman deliberately," Raistlin stated. "The blast was accidental."

"Then what caused it?" Caramon asked, interested.

"Foul magic," Sturm stated.

Raistlin shook his head. "I know of no magic, foul or otherwise, that has the power to level such a mighty fortress. According to Flint, the blast laid waste to the land for miles around Zhaman. The wise have long wondered what really happened in that fortress. Perhaps we will be the ones to discover the truth."

"You will write a treatise on the subject, no doubt," said Sturm, "and read it aloud at the next Wizard's Conclave."

"I might at that," Raistlin said with a smile.

The three walked on.

Tasslehoff woke Tika by scolding her for having fallen asleep. She had undoubtedly missed any number of ghosts that could have visited them in the night.

Tika scolded herself, flushing to think how Caramon would have berated her for sleeping on watch. Tika told Tas irritably to shut up and get a move on. They picked up the trail of the three ahead of them and set out in dogged pursuit.

She and Tas also got an early start to their day, making up for lost time. Lack of sleep and the knowledge that she was far from home and help put Tika in a bad mood. She was grumpy with Tas and did not want to chat, even about such interesting tidbits of gossip as the fact that Tasslehoff had discovered Hederick the High Seeker had his own secret stash of food hidden away.

Tika stalked along the trail, keeping her gaze on the ground, following the tracks in the snow and fighting the strong urge to turn around and run back to the settlement. If she'd been able to think of a way to sneak back without anyone knowing she'd been gone, she would have.

Tika could have come up with a plausible tale, but she knew that Tasslehoff would never be able to keep from blurting out the truth, and she dreaded the idea that people would laugh at her and say she'd gone running after Caramon like some infatuated school girl.

To give her credit, it wasn't all fear of being ridiculed that kept her going. Tika's heart was warm, her love for Caramon deep, and her fear for him very real. The idea that she might be able to save Caramon from Raistlin's machinations kept her slogging along the trail.

As for Tas, he was happy to be on the road to adventure once more.

The two reached the edge of the forest about midmorning and saw the trail snake across the barren, snow-covered field.

"Look, Tika!" Tas pointed excitedly, as they drew near the mountain. "There's a cave. Their trail leads into a cave!"

Tas grabbed Tika's hand and tugged at her, trying to hurry her along.

"I'm very fond of caves. You never know what you're going to find inside. Did I ever tell you about the time I went into this cave and there were two ogres and they were playing at mumblety-peg, and at first they were going to tear me limb from limb and eat me, starting with my toes. I didn't know this, but kender toes are considered a delicacy among ogres. Anyway, I told the ogres I was really good at mumblety-peg, better than either of them, and I wagered them that if I won, they wouldn't eat me. Of course they had to play, because I had made a wager. The ogres handed me a knife, which I was supposed to throw, but instead I used the knife to stab the ogres in the knees. That way they couldn't chase after me, and I escaped being eaten. Can you play mumblety-peg, Tika, in case ogres inside the cave want to eat us?"

"No," said Tika. She did *not* like caves at all, and her heart was beating fast at the thought of going into one.

Tas was about to launch into more details about the ogres, but Tika ordered him to hush up and when he didn't, she gave his topknot a yank and threatened to pull it out by the roots if he didn't for mercy's sake keep quiet and let her think.

Tas wasn't sure what it was she had to think about, but he was fond of his topknot, and while he didn't really believe Tika would pull it out, he didn't want to take any chances. She'd gone very pale and tight-lipped, and whenever she thought he wasn't looking, she wiped away a tear.

The footprints they were following led straight to the cave, which turned out to be a tunnel. There were muddy boot prints inside, large muddy boot prints. Tika knew Caramon and the others had come this way.

"Light the lantern!" Tas said. "Let's see what's down here."

"I didn't bring a lantern," Tika said in dismay.

"Never mind!" cried Tas, rooting around in the darkness. "I found a whole stack of torches."

"Oh, good," said Tika. She stared into the darkness that stretched on and on ahead of them, and she felt her knees go weak and her stomach turn to jelly.

Tas had managed to light one of the torches, and he was walking all around the cave, peering into the carts and stopping to scan the walls. "Hey, look, Tika! Come here! Look at this!"

Tika didn't want to look. She wanted to turn and run, run all the way back to camp. Then Tas would tell everyone that Tika had run away like a big scared baby. Gritting her teeth, Tika went to see what he'd found, hoping it wasn't too horrible.

Tas was pointing at the wall. There, scrawled in charcoal, was a heart. In the middle of the heart was the word "Tika".

"I'll bet Caramon drew that," said Tas, grinning.

"I'll bet he did, too," said Tika softly. She reached out and took the flaring torch from the kender.

"Follow me," she said, and feeling her own heart soar to the heavens with happiness, she led the way along the tunnel, deeper into the darkness.

II

A Question of Faith. End of the Tunnel. The Man-eating Stalig Mite.

lint and Tanis edged their way through the pass that wasn't so much as a pass as a large gap. Tanis envisioned the refugees trying to cross this rocky, narrow defile, their children in tow, and he hoped fervently it wouldn't come to that. They spent most of the morning navigating among the boulders and scrambling over rock slides, finally emerging after hours of toil on the other side.

Using his battle-axe, Flint pointed. "Well, there you are, Half-Elven," he said. "Thorbardin."

Tanis looked down at the landscape spread beneath him. Ash-gray plains led into dark green foothills, thick with pine trees, from which soared the gray blank face of the tallest mountain peak in the Kharolis chain.

Tanis regarded the mountain in bleak dismay. "There's nothing there."

"Aye," said Flint in gloomy satisfaction. "Just like I told you."

The dwarf had indeed told him, but Flint had a tendency to exaggerate and embellish his tales a mite now and then, particularly those tales having to do with the wrongs, perceived or otherwise, suffered by his people. Search as Tanis might, he could see no sign of anything resembling a gate on the mountain side or even a place where one might put a gate.

"Are you sure Thorbardin is there?" Tanis asked.

Flint rested his weight on the battle-axe and gazed steadily at the mountain.

"I was born and raised hereabouts. The bones of my ancestors lie on the plains below us. They died because our cousins closed the gates of that mountain on them. Cloudseeker casts a shadow over us all. Each and every one of us hill dwarves sees it loom large in his dreams. I'm not likely to forget this place."

Flint spit on the ground. "That's Thorbardin."

Tanis sighed deeply, scratched his beard and asked himself, "What in the Abyss do I do now?"

He had no hope at all that he would be successful in his mission. Neither he nor Flint had any idea where to even start looking for the lost gate to the dwarven kingdom. They could spend years traipsing across the face of Cloudseeker. The greedy and the desperate had been searching for this gate for three hundred years and never found it. There was no reason to think he and Flint would be the ones to succeed where so many had failed.

Tanis considered giving up. He went so far as to half-turn, look back the way they'd come, and even take a step in that direction, but he found he couldn't do it. He could not admit defeat, not yet.

Flint stood leaning on the battle-axe, watching his friend turn first one way and then the other. When Tanis turned around again, Flint nodded.

"We're to keep going then," he said.

"You know as well as I do that it's only a matter of time before Verminaard attacks," Tanis said, adding in frustration, "There *must* be a way inside Thorbardin! Just because no one else has discovered it . . ."

"After all, the gods are with us," Flint observed.

Tanis eyed his friend to see if the dwarf had spoken sarcastically or if he was serious. Tanis couldn't tell. The dwarf's expression was unreadable, much of it hidden behind his full beard and shaggy eyebrows.

"Do you believe the gods are with us?" Tanis asked. "Do you believe what Elistan and Goldmoon have been teaching?"

"Hard to say," said Flint, and he appeared uncomfortable talking about it. He cast Tanis a sidelong glance. "I take you don't?"

"I want to." Tanis shook his head. "But I can't."

"We've seen miracles," Flint pointed out. "Riverwind was burnt to a crisp by a black dragon. Elistan was brought back from the brink of death."

"And Verminaard brought back from the dead, as well," said Tanis dryly. "I've seen Raistlin scatter a few rose petals and cause goblins to fall sound asleep at his feet."

"That's different," Flint growled.

"Why? Because it's magic? Magic or no, one could call such things 'miraculous'."

"I call them accursed," Flint muttered.

"All I know for certain," Tanis said, smiling, "is that the only being who walks with me is you, my friend." He clapped Flint on the shoulder. "I could not ask for a better companion. Gods included."

Flint flushed in pleasure, but he only said gruffly that Tanis was a silly ass and he shouldn't talk in such a flippant manner about things beyond his understanding.

"I think we should keep going," Tanis said. "Raistlin may find the key to the gate in Skullcap."

"Do you think he's planning to bring it to us if he does?" Flint snorted in derision. "And you claim you don't believe in miracles."

The two started what Tanis feared would be a slow and laborious journey down the side of the mountain when Flint came to a sudden halt.

"Would you look at this," he said.

Tanis looked and marveled. It wasn't a miracle. It was a road. Built by dwarves, centuries old, the road had been carved out of the side of the mountain. Winding back and forth across the face of the mountain, the road led down and into the foothills then climbed back up the other side. All the refugees had to do was make it this far, and the way after that would be smooth.

"Provided this road leads to the gate," said Flint, reading Tanis's thoughts.

"It must," said Tanis. "Where else would it go?"

"Just what people have been asking themselves these last three hundred years," Flint remarked dryly.

⸻

Sturm, Caramon, and Raistlin, traveling beneath the mountain, found their journey long, tedious and uneventful. The area was prone to earthquakes, but the dwarf-built tunnel had survived hundreds of these shocks almost unscathed. Occasionally they noticed places where the walls had cracks, and here and there a small rock slide impeded their path, but that was all.

The tunnel ran straight, no twists or turns. It was neither haunted nor otherwise inhabited. They walked for several hours and made good time. Raistlin was again strangely energized. He set a swift pace, ranging ahead of his brother and Sturm, his staff thumping the tunnel floor, his red robes swirling about his ankles. When the other two called a halt to take a breather, Raistlin would caustically remind them that lives depended on their progress.

Down here in the darkness, with no way to tell time, none of them had any idea how long they walked or how many miles they traveled. Every so often, they came upon marks on the wall that appeared to be some type of indicator of distance. The marks were in dwarven, however, and none of them knew what they meant.

They traveled so long that Caramon began to secretly wonder if they might not have missed Skullcap altogether. Perhaps they had walked across the continent and would emerge to find themselves in some distant realm—the far southern reaches of Ice Wall, maybe. He was deep in his imaginings, dreaming of vast expanses of white wastes, when Sturm called their attention to the increased amount of debris and rubble in the passage.

"We must be nearing the end," said Raistlin. "The destruction we see is a result of the blast that leveled the fortress."

"What do we do if the blast destroyed the tunnel?" Sturm asked.

"We must hope that it was protected," Raistlin said. "As you can see, the beams shoring up the ceiling have not been damaged. That is a good sign."

They trudged wearily on. The light of Sturm's torch and Raistlin's staff did not extend far, and Raistlin almost walked headlong into a stone wall before he realized it was there. He came to an abrupt halt, shining the light this way and that.

"I hope this is a hidden door like that other one," said Caramon. "Otherwise we've come all this way for nothing."

"You have no faith in me, do you, Pheragas?" Raistlin murmured. Holding his staff to light his task, he began to search the wall for marks.

"Who is this Pheragas?" Caramon muttered.

"Probably better you don't know," Sturm said grimly.

"Found it!" Raistlin announced. He pointed, and there was the same mark that they had seen on the door at the other end—the dwarven rune for 'door.'

He pressed on the rune. As before, the mark depressed, sliding into the wall. There came a grinding sound, then a cracking sound as the stone separated, forming the outline of a doorway. This time the mechanism worked. The heavy door rumbled back so fast that it almost ran Raistlin down, and he was forced to scramble out of its way in a flurry of red robes, causing Sturm to pull at his mustaches to hide his smile.

The heavy door rumbled and screeched on the rusted tracks and flattened itself against the wall with a resounding boom that echoed back down the passageway.

"Nothing like announcing our arrival," Sturm remarked.

"Hush!" Raistlin held up his hand.

"It's a little late for that," Caramon said, with a wink at Sturm.

Raistlin glared at him. "Take off your helm and you might find your brain inside! The sounds I hear are coming from out there." He pointed through the opening of the tunnel and, now that the echoes had faded, they could hear harsh shouts and the clash of arms.

Caramon and Sturm both drew their swords. Raistlin reached into his pouch.

"*Dulak*," he murmured, and the glow from his staff blinked out, leaving only Sturm's torch to light the way.

"What did you do that for?" Sturm demanded, adding grudgingly, "Much as I hate to admit it, we could use that light of yours."

"It is never wise to proclaim to your enemies that you are a wizard," Raistlin said quietly.

"Magic works best by stealth and darkness, is that it?" Sturm said.

"C'mon, you two, cut it out," Caramon said.

They stood unmoving, listening to the sounds of battle that were distant, far away.

"Someone else is interested in the secrets of Skullcap," Sturm said at last.

Raistlin stirred at this. "I'm going to go find out what is happening. You two can stay here."

"No," said Sturm. "We all go together."

Moving cautiously, holding his torch in one hand and his sword in the other, Sturm walked through the door. Raistlin came after him and Caramon brought up the rear, keeping a look-out over his shoulder.

———————————————

Traveling down the dark tunnel, Tasslehoff Burrfoot reached the conclusion that if he never saw another rock in his life, it would be too soon. At first, tramping along a secret tunnel underneath a mountain was exciting. A skeletal warrior might be lurking just around the corner, ready to leap out and throttle them. A wight might decide to try to suck out their souls, or whatever it was that wights did to people.

Tika, on the other hand, didn't appear to find the tunnel in the least exciting. She was nervous and unhappy.

Tas considered it his duty to try keep up her spirits and so he livened the journey by telling her all the gruesome, creepy, scary stories he'd ever heard about the things that lived in secret tunnels underneath mountains. Far from having the desired effect, the stories seemed to simply plunge Tika deeper in gloom. Once she actually turned around and tried to smack the kender. Accustomed to this sort of behavior in his companions, Tas ducked in time. He decided to change the subject.

"How long do you suppose we've been walking, Tika?"

"Weeks, I should imagine," she said glumly.

"I think it's only been a few hours," Tas said.

"Oh, what do you know?" she snapped.

"I know it certainly is boring," said the kender. He kicked at a rock, sent it bounding over the stone floor. "Do we have any more food left?"

"You just ate!"

"That seems like days ago!" Tas waved his arms. "You said yourself we've been walking for weeks . . ."

"Oh, shut up—" Tika began then froze in place.

A hideous sound thundered down the passageway—a loud rumbling, accompanied by shrill screeching. The ground shook, and dust fell from the walls. The rumbling and screeching lasted for several heart-thudding moments, then ended abruptly.

"What . . . what was that?" Tika quavered.

Tas reflected. "I think it was a Stalig Mite," he said in hushed tones.

"A what kind of mite?" Tika whispered, her hands shaking so that the flame of the torch bounced all over the cavern.

"A Stalig Mite," Tas said solemnly. "I've heard stories about them. They live in caves, and they're huge and quite ferocious. I'm sorry to tell you this, Tika, but you should prepare yourself for the worst. That sound we heard was probably the Stalig Mite devouring Caramon."

"No!" Tika cried wildly. "I don't believe—" She paused, eying the kender. "Wait a minute. *I've* never heard of a Stalig Mite."

"You should really get out more, Tika."

"You mean stalagmite!" Tika was so mad she very nearly threw the torch at him.

"That's what I said." Tas was hurt. "Stalig Mite. Found only in caves."

"A stalagmite is a rock formation found in caves, you doorknob! What do you mean scaring me like that?" Tika wiped sweat from her forehead.

"Are you sure?" Tas was loathe to give up the idea of a ferocious man-eating Stalig Mite.

"Yes, I'm sure." Tika sounded very cross.

"Well, if that noise wasn't made by a Stalig Mite devouring Caramon, then what was it?" Tas asked practically.

Tika had no answer for that, and she wished he hadn't brought it up. She turned around. "Maybe we should go back . . ."

"We've been back, Tika," Tas pointed out. "We know what's back there—a lot of very dark darkness—and we *don't* know what's up ahead. Maybe Caramon hasn't been eaten by a rock formation, but he and his brother could still be in trouble and need our help. Wouldn't it be wonderful if we—you and I—rescued Caramon and Raistlin? They'd respect us then. No more pulling my topknot or slapping my hand when all I wanted to do was to touch his stupid old staff."

Tika envisioned Raistlin humbled and meek, thanking her profusely for saving his life, and Caramon hugging her tightly, telling her over and over how proud he was of her.

Tas was right. Behind them was nothing but darkness.

Fearful but resolute, Tika continued on her way through the tunnel, accompanied by Tasslehoff, who was hoping Tika turned out to be wrong about the Stalig Mites.

12

Death in the Darkness. A Ghostly Messenger.

turm had taken only a few steps into the room beyond before he found his way blocked by a heavy beam that had fallen down from the ceiling. Standing in the small pool of light cast by his torch, he saw that he'd encountered destruction so complete he could make out few details of what it was he was even looking at. Fire had swept the room. The floor was ankle-deep in debris, most of it blackened and burnt. Charred lumps might have once been furniture.

Sturm circled around the heavy beam, kicking aside debris, and found another doorway.

"The sounds are coming from out here," he called back softly to his friends.

"From the armory," said Raistlin. "I know where I am now. This was the library. What a pity it did not survive!"

He bent down to pick up the remnants of a book. The pages fell out in a shower of ash. The leather cover was all that remained and it was scorched, the corners blackened and curled.

"What a pity," Raistlin repeated softly.

He dropped the book and looked up to find Sturm staring at him. "Armory? Library? How do you know so much about this accursed place?" asked the knight.

"Caramon and I lived here once upon a time," Raistlin said sarcastically. "Didn't we, my brother? I'm sure we must have told you."

"C'mon, Raist," Caramon mumbled. "Don't do this."

Sturm continued to regard the mage with suspicion; he might almost have believed him.

"Oh, for mercy's sake!" Raistlin snapped. "How gullible can you be, Sturm Brightblade? There is a perfectly logical explanation. I have seen maps of Zhaman. There. End of mystery."

Raistlin knelt down to pick up another book, only to feel it crumble at his touch. He let the ashes sift through his fingers. Sturm and Caramon had walked over to the door, taking the torch with them. Crouching on the floor, clutching his staff, Raistlin was glad for the darkness, which concealed his shaking hands, the chill sweat beading on his face and trickling down his neck. He was almost sick with terror and wished with all his soul that he had listened to those who warned him not to come to this place. He had lied to Sturm, lied to his brother. Raistlin had never seen a map of Zhaman. He was not even certain such a map existed. He had no idea how he knew where to find the rune on the mountain side. He had never heard of anyone called Pheragas. He did not know how he knew the sounds were coming from the armory or how he knew this room was the library. He had no idea how he knew that far below this level of the fortress was a laboratory . . .

Raistlin shuddered and clutched at his head with his hand, as though he could reach inside and tear out memories of things he'd never seen, places he'd never been.

"Stop it!" he whispered frantically, "Leave me alone! Why do you torment me?"

"Raist?" Caramon called. "Are you all right?"

Raistlin grit his teeth. He dug his nails into his palms, forcing his hands to quit shaking. He drew in a deep, shivering breath and held tightly to the staff, pressing the cool wood against his burning skin, and closed his eyes. The feeling of dread slowly seeped out of him and he was able to stand.

"I am fine, my brother," he said, knowing that if he did not answer Caramon would come looking for him. He moved slowly across the debris-strewn room to join Sturm and his twin, who were standing by the door, listening to the sounds of battle and arguing about whether they should go investigate or not.

"Some innocent person could be in trouble," Sturm maintained. "We should go see if we can help them."

"What would an innocent person be doing wandering about this place?" Caramon demanded. "It's not our fight, Sturm. We shouldn't go sticking our heads in a goblin's lair. Wait here until it's over, then let's go see what's left."

Sturm frowned. "You stay with your brother. I'm going to at least see—"

A bestial roar of pain, anguish, and bellowing fury shook the floor, sending dust and debris raining down from the ceiling, drowning out the rest of Sturm's words. The roaring ceased suddenly in an agonized gurgle. The harsh voices shouted in triumph, and the sounds of clashing swords grew louder. The three friends stared at each other in alarm.

"That sounded like a dragon!" Caramon said.

"I told you, someone is in danger!" Sturm flung down the sack containing his armor, useless to him now, for there was no time to put it on. Caramon opened his mouth to remonstrate, but before he could say a word, his friend had dashed into the darkness.

Caramon looked pleadingly at his twin. "We can't let him go off alone, Raist! We have to help him."

Raistlin's mouth twisted. "I suppose we must, though how we are supposed to fight a dragon with nothing but swords and rose petals is beyond me!"

"It sounds like it's wounded. Those warriors probably have it cornered," Caramon said hopefully, and he dashed off after Sturm.

"What a relief! A cornered, wounded dragon," Raistlin muttered.

He ran through the mental catalog of his spells, searching for one that would do more than irritate the dragon—or give it a good laugh. Choosing one he thought might be suitable, Raistlin hastened after his brother, hoping, at least, to stop Caramon from getting himself slaughtered in some grand and noble last stand of the Brightblades.

Caramon followed Sturm out of the ruined library and found himself in a wide corridor. This part of the fortress had escaped the worst effects of the blast. The only damages were cracks in the walls and floors and some chunks of the ceiling that had crashed down into the corridor. The dragon's roars sounded as though they were coming from the far end. The bellowings grew louder and more terrifying.

The voices of those battling the beast were growing louder as well. Caramon could not make out the words, but it sounded as if they were jeering their foe and spurring each other on. Sturm was running forward. He had not looked back; he had no idea if Caramon was coming or not.

Caramon advanced more cautiously. Something about this battle struck him as odd. He wished his twin would join him.

Half-turning, Caramon called softly, "Raist, hurry up!"

A hand closed over Caramon's arm, and a voice whispered from the darkness, "I am here, my brother."

Caramon gave a violent start.

"Damn, Raist! Don't creep up on me like that!"

"We must make haste," Raistlin said grimly, "prevent the knight from getting himself burnt to a cinder."

The two of them hurried forward, following the light of Sturm's torch and the bright gleam of his sword.

"I don't like this," Caramon said.

"I can't think why," Raistlin returned caustically. "The three of us marching boldly to our deaths . . ."

Caramon shook his head. "It's not that. Listen to those voices, Raist. I've heard them or something like them before."

Raistlin glanced at his twin and saw that Caramon was serious. The two had served together as mercenaries for years, and Raistlin had come to respect his brother's skill and his warrior instincts. Raistlin drew back the folds of his cowl in order to better hear the voices. He looked at Caramon and gave a nod.

"You're right. We have heard those voices before. Fool knight!" Raistlin added bitterly. "We have to stop him before he gets himself killed! You go on. I'll catch up."

Caramon dashed on ahead.

"*Shirak*," Raistlin spoke the word of magic, and the light of his staff flared. He noted in passing the remnants of a gigantic iron stair rail spiraling downward.

"That leads to my chambers," he said to himself.

Focused on his spellcasting, he did not realize what he was saying.

"Sturm! Wait up!" Caramon called out when he thought the knight could hear him over the clash of arms.

Sturm halted and turned around. "Well, what is it?" he said impatiently.

"Those voices!" Caramon gasped, huffing from the exertion. "They're draconian. No, listen!" He gripped his friend's arm.

Sturm did listen, his brow furrowing. He lowered his sword. "Why would draconians attack a dragon?"

"Maybe they had a falling out," Caramon said, trying to catch his breath. "Evil turns on its own."

"I am not so certain," said Raistlin, coming up to them. He looked from the knight to his twin. "Do either of you sense the debilitating fear that we have felt before around these beasts?"

"No," Sturm replied, "but the dragon cannot see us."

"That shouldn't make a difference. Back in camp, we felt the terror of the red dragon long before it came into view."

"It's all very strange," Sturm muttered, frowning.

"The one thing we do know is this," said Raistlin. "'The enemy of my enemy is my friend'."

"True," said Sturm, smiling slightly. "In that case, we should help the dragon."

"Help the dragon!" Caramon goggled. "Have you both gone crazy?"

Both had, apparently, for Sturm was once more running toward the fight and Raistlin was hastening alongside. Shaking his head, Caramon dashed after his brother and the knight.

The sounds of battle intensified. The draconians' hissing and their guttural voices, could be heard clearly now. They spoke their own language but with a mixture of Common thrown in, so that Caramon could understand about every fourth word. The dragon's roaring diminished, growing weaker. Light flared from the armory, shining into the corridor.

Sturm had flattened himself against a wall. Edging near the door, he risked a glance into the chamber. What he saw amazed him so he could not move but stood transfixed, staring. Caramon yanked him back.

"Well?" he demanded.

"There is a dragon," said Sturm, awed, "like none I have ever seen or heard of. It is beautiful." He shook himself, came back to reality. "And it is badly hurt."

Caramon went to see for himself.

Sturm was right. The dragon was not like any other dragon Caramon had ever encountered. He had seen dragons with scales that were black as the Dark Queen's heart, dragons with scales red as searing flame, dragons with scales the color of a cobolt sky. This one was different. It was smaller than most and it was beautiful, as Sturm has said. Its scales gleamed like polished brass.

"What sort of dragon is it?" Caramon turned back to his twin.

"That's what we must find out," said Raistlin, "which means we can't let it die."

"There are four draconians," Sturm reported. "One is badly wounded. The other three are on their feet. They have their backs to us. They're concentrating on finishing off the dragon. They are armed with bows. They've been loosing arrows at it. We can take them from behind."

"Let me see what I can do," said Raistlin. "Perhaps I can save us time and trouble."

Raistlin drew something from his pouch, crushed it beneath his fingers, spoke the words of magic, and made a motion with his hand.

A ball of blazing fire flew from his fingertips, hurtled across the room, and struck one of the draconians in the back. The magical fire burst on the draconian's scaly skin. The draconian gave a hideous yell and collapsed onto the floor, rolling about in agony as the flames blackened his scales and charred his flesh. His companions scrambled to get away from him, for the flames were spreading, licking at their heels.

"Remember, you two!" Raistlin warned, as Sturm and Caramon charged inside. "Draconians are as dangerous dead as they are alive!"

Sturm shouted his battle-cry, *"Arras, Solamni*! Arise, Solamnia!"

The draconian started at the yell and was about to turn to face this new foe, just as Sturm's sword slid through its entrails. Sturm yanked his blade out swiftly, before the draconian's corpse could freeze into stone, trapping his weapon. Caramon was taking no chances. Wrapping his fist around his sword's hilt, he bashed his draconian on the back of the neck. The draconian's neck cracked and it fell to the floor, stiff as marble.

"Three dead!" Caramon reported, sucking on bruised knuckles. He hurried over to finish off the wounded draconian, only to find that it had died. The body crumbled to dust as he approached it. "Four dead," he amended.

The battle ended, Sturm hastened over to the dragon. The great beast lay sprawled on the floor, its shining brass scales smeared with blood. Raistlin walked over to the dragon as fast as he was able. The magic always took its toll on his body. He felt as weary as though he'd been in battle for three days, instead of three minutes.

"Keep watch on the corridor," he ordered Caramon, as he passed his twin. "There were other draconians in this room. These four were left to finish the job."

Caramon looked about at the vast number of spent arrows lying on the floor and nodded his head in grim agreement. He glanced back at the dragon and his heart smote him. The beast was so beautiful, so magnificent. No matter that it was a dragon, it should not be suffering like this. He left to keep a lookout at the door.

Sturm crouched beside the dragon's head. The dragon's eyes were open but fast dimming. His breathing was labored. He gazed at Sturm in wonder.

"A Solamnic knight . . . Why are you here? Do you . . . fight with the dwarves?" The dragon roused himself with an effort. "You must slay the foul wizard!"

Sturm glanced up at Raistlin.

"Not me," Raistlin snapped. "The dragon speaks of dwarves fighting . . . He must mean Fistandantilus!"

"He found me sleeping," the dragon murmured. "He cast a spell on me, made me a prisoner . . . Now he has sent his demons to slay me . . ."

The dragon coughed, blood spewing from his mouth.

"What kind of dragon are you?" Raistlin asked. "We have never seen your like."

The gleaming body shuddered. The dragon's massive tail thumped the floor, his legs convulsed, wings twitched. He gave a final shiver. Blood poured out of his mouth. The dragon's head lolled. The eyes stared, unseeing.

Raistlin gave an annoyed sigh.

Sturm cast him a reproachful glance, then bowed his head. "Paladine, God of Light and Mercy, Wisdom and Truth," he prayed, "take the soul of this noble beast to your blessed realm—"

"Sturm, I heard something!" Caramon came running into the room. He stopped, abashed, when he saw the knight was praying, and looked at his twin. "I heard voices coming from the library."

"Sir Knight," Raistlin said sharply, "leave off your prayer. Paladine knows what to do with a soul. He does not need you to tell him."

Sturm ignored him. He finished his prayer then rose to his feet.

"I heard voices," said Caramon, apologetic, "coming from the corridor. Maybe draconian. I can't tell."

"Go with my brother," said Raistlin. "The magic has drained me. I must rest."

He sank down onto the floor, leaning his back against the wall.

Caramon was alarmed. "Raist, you shouldn't stay here alone."

"Just go, Caramon," Raistlin said, closing his eyes. "Sturm needs your help. Besides, you worry me to death with your fussing!"

The light glimmering from the crystal shone on his golden skin. His face was drawn. He began to cough and fumbled for his handkerchief.

"I don't know," Caramon hesitated.

"He will be safe enough here," said Sturm. "The draconians have moved on."

Caramon cast his twin an uncertain glance. "You should douse the light, Raist."

Raistlin waited to hear the running footfalls of Sturm and his brother fade away. When he was certain they were gone, hoping his brother would not take it into his head to come back, Raistlin rose to his feet.

The room had been an armory, as he had said. The stands of old-fashioned plate armor lay dismembered on the floor. The draconians had overturned them, probably searching for loot. Weapons of various types littered the blood-covered floor, most of them either broken or rusted beyond repair. Raistlin cast a cursory glance at them but saw nothing of interest. Draconians were intelligent creatures who knew something of value when they saw it. They would have already appropriated anything worth while.

Raistlin walked over to the object that had caught his interest—a large burlap sack near the pile of dust that had once been a draconian. He laid his staff on the floor and knelt beside the sack, taking care to keep his robes out of the blood.

He poked one of the lumps inside the sack with his finger and felt something hard and solid. The sack was soaked with blood. Raistlin's deft fingers pulled and tugged at the knot of the drawstring that closed the top. He finally pried it loose and opened the sack.

The light from the crystal atop his staff shone on a helm and no ordinary helm at that. The draconian had recognized its value beneath the dust and grime that covered it, and though Raistlin was not one to judge the finer points of armor, even he could see that the helm had been crafted by an expert, designed to both protect the wearer and adorn him.

Raistlin rubbed of some of the dirt from the helm with the hem of his sleeve. Three large red rubies sparkled in the light.

Raistlin glanced inside the sack, saw nothing more of interest, and turned his attention back to the helm. Passing his hand over it, he murmured a few words. The helm began to give off a soft, pale glow.

"Ah, so you *are* magic . . . I wonder . . ."

The hair prickled on the back of his neck. A shiver crept up from the base of his spine. Someone was in the room with him. Someone was creeping up on him from behind. Moving slowly, Raistlin set down the helm. In the same motion, he took hold of his staff, and twisting to his feet, turned around.

Eyes, pale and cold, surrounded by shadow, gazed out of the darkness. The eyes had no substance, no head, no body. The eyes were not the eyes of the living. Raistlin recognized in that fell gaze the hatred and pain of a soul constrained to dwell in the Abyss, a prisoner of the God of Death, unable to find rest or relief from the gnawing torment of its terrible existence.

The eyes drifted nearer, abyssal darkness stirring about it, trailing after it.

Raistlin raised his staff, holding it in front of him. The staff was his only protection. He was too weak to cast another spell, even if he could think of any spell that would work against this dread specter. He considered shouting for help, but he feared that this might cause the wraith to attack. Above all, he had to keep the specter from touching him, for the touch of death would drain warmth, drain strength, and drain away his life.

The wraith drifted nearer, and suddenly the staff's light flared in a blaze of dazzling white, nearly blinding Raistlin, who was forced to shield his eyes with his hand. The wraith halted.

A voice spoke. The voice was dry as bone and soft as ash, and it came from an unseen mouth.

"The Master bids me give you this message, Raistlin Majere. You have found what you seek."

Raistlin was so astonished he nearly dropped the staff. His hand shook, and the light wavered. The wraith moved closer, and Raistlin tightened his grip, thrusting out the staff. The light shone steadily, and the wraith retreated.

"I don't . . . understand." Raistlin's mouth was dry. He had to try twice to speak and then the words came out in a croak.

"Nor will you. Nor are you meant to. Not for a long time. Know that you are in the Master's care."

The spectral eyes closed. The darkness dissipated. Raistlin's arm began to shake uncontrollably and he was forced to lower the staff. He was completely unnerved, and when a voice spoke behind him, he nearly crawled out of his skin.

The voice was Sturm's. "Who were you talking to?" The knight's tone was ugly and suspicious. "I heard you talking to someone."

"I was talking to myself," said Raistlin. He thrust the helm into the sack, hoping the knight had not caught sight of it. He asked sharply, "What of those voices my brother heard? Where is Caramon?"

Sturm was not going to be distracted. His eye had caught sight of the gleaming metal.

"What is that you hold?" he demanded. "Why are you trying to hide it? Let me see it!'

Raistlin sighed. "I am not trying to hide anything. I found an ancient dwarven helm inside this sack. I know little about armor, but it looks to be of some value. You can judge for yourself." He handed over the sack. "Where is Caramon?"

"Entertaining guests," said Sturm.

He opened the sack, pulled out the helm, and held it to the light. He breathed a soft sigh.

"Beautiful workmanship. I've never seen the like." He glowered at Raistlin. "Of 'some' value! This is worth a king's ransom. Such a helm would be worn only by one of royal blood, a prince or perhaps the king himself."

"That would explain it . . ." Raistlin murmured. He added off-handedly, "You should handle it carefully. I think it might be enchanted."

He was thinking of the wraith's words. *You have found what you seek.* What had he come here seeking? Raistlin hardly knew. He had told Tanis he was searching for the key to the Thorbardin. Was that true? Or had it been an excuse? Or did the truth lie somewhere in between . . .

"Entertaining guests?" Raistlin repeated, the knight's strange remark having suddenly penetrated the fog of his thought. "What do you mean? He's not in trouble."

"That depends on what you mean by trouble," Sturm replied, and he gave a low chuckle.

Concerned, Raistlin started to go to his twin's aid, only to find Caramon standing in the doorway. His brother's face was flushed red.

"Hey, Raist," he said, with a sheepish grin, "look who's here."

Tika appeared at Caramon's side. She gave Raistlin a smile that quickly evaporated beneath the mage's cold stare.

He opened his mouth but was interrupted by Tasslehoff bounding into the room, his words tumbling over each other in his excitement.

"Hullo, Raistlin! We came to rescue you, but I guess you don't need rescuing. Caramon thought we were draconians and nearly skewered us. Wow, is that a dragon? Is it dead? Poor thing! Can I touch it?"

Raistlin fixed his brother with a piercing glare.

"Caramon," he said in frozen tones, "we need to talk."

13

A royal guest. The way out.
A dread discovery.

turm ran his hands over the helm, marveling at the crafts-manship. He was vaguely aware of the tension in the room, of Raistlin berating his brother in low and angry tones, of Caramon's feet shuffling and his aggrieved replies that it wasn't his fault, of Tika grabbing Tasslehoff by the collar and yanking him out of the room, muttering something about searching for the way out of this horrible place. Sturm was conscious of all that was going on, but he paid no attention to any of it. He could not take his eyes and his thoughts from the helm.

His fingertips carefully brushed the grime off the gemstones so that they gleamed more brightly. One in particular caught his eye—a ruby as large a child's fist, set in the center of the helm. Sturm pictured what the helm would look like polished, shining. He was tempted, suddenly, to try it on.

He did not know where this notion came from. He would not, of course, have traded his own helm that had been his father's and his grandfather's before him for all the steel coins in Krynn, and this helm would not fit him anyway. It had been made for a dwarf and was therefore too large for a human. His head would rattle around inside like a pea in a walnut shell, yet Sturm wanted to put it on. Perhaps he wanted to see what it felt like to wear a king's ransom, perhaps he wanted to judge the quality of the craftsmanship, or perhaps the helm was speaking to him, urging him to place it over his head, draw it down over his long fair hair that was already starting to gray, though he was not more than twenty-nine years old.

He took off his father's helm and rested it on floor at his feet. Holding the helm, admiring it, Sturm seemed to recall Raistlin saying something to the effect that the helm was magical. The knight discounted that notion. No true warrior such as this dwarven warrior must have been would have ever allowed a wizard anywhere near his armor. Raistlin was just trying to ward Sturm off. Raistlin wanted the helm for himself.

Sturm put the helm over his head. To his amazement and gratification, it fit him as if it had been made for him and him alone.

* * *

"So, Raist, what kind of dragon do you think that is?" Caramon asked, with a desperate attempt to change the subject he knew was coming. "It's a strange color. Maybe it's a mute dragon."

"You mean mutant dragon, you dolt," Raistlin said coldly. "The beast was perfectly capable of speech, and right at the moment I don't give a damn what it was!" He drew in a seething breath.

"I think we'll go look for a way out, Caramon," said Tika, speaking the first desperate thought that came into her mind. "C'mon, Tas. Let's go find an exit." She collared the kender.

"But we know how to get out!" Tas argued. "The same way we got in!"

"We're going to find a different way," said Tika grimly, and she hauled him out of the room.

Raistlin fixed Caramon with a withering stare. Caramon wilted beneath it, seeming to shrivel to half his size.

"What is *she* doing here?" Raistlin demanded. "Did you tell her to come? You did, didn't you?"

"No, Raist, I swear it!" Caramon stood with his head hanging, his unhappy gaze on his boots. "I had no idea."

"Of all the stupid stunts you have pulled, this takes the biscuit. Do you realize what danger you have put her in? And the kender. Ye gods, the kender!"

Raistlin was forced to pause to draw in air enough to continue speaking and that made him cough. He could not speak for long moments and fumbled for his handkerchief.

Caramon regarded his twin in anguish, but he dared not say a word of sympathy or try to help him. He was in trouble enough already, trouble that was not in any way, shape, or form his fault. Though some part of him was secretly thrilled that Tika had thought enough of him to come after him, another part wished her on the other side of the continent.

"She won't be a problem, Raist," said Caramon, "or Tas either. Sturm can take them back to camp. You and me—we'll go on to Thorbardin or wherever you want to go."

Raistlin finally caught his breath. He dabbed his lips and eyed his brother with grudging approval. Caramon's plan would not only rid him of Tika and Tasslehoff, it would also rid of him of the knight.

"They leave immediately," Raistlin said, his words rasping in his throat.

"Sure, Raist," said Caramon, relief washing over him. "I'll go talk to Sturm—Sturm? Oh, here you are."

He turned to find Sturm right behind him. Caramon gave his friend a puzzled look. The knight had removed his own helm, a helm that he valued above his life, and in its place he wore a helm that was dirty, stained with blood, and far too big for him. The visor came to his throat. His eyes were barely visible through the top portion of the eye slits.

"Uh, that's a nice helm you found, Sturm," Caramon said.

"I am properly addressed as 'Your Highness'," Sturm intoned, his voice sounding odd coming from inside the helm. "I would ask your names and where you are from, but we have no time to waste on pleasantries. We must ride immediately for Thorbardin!"

Caramon flashed his brother a startled glance. He had no idea what Sturm was doing. It was not like the serious-minded knight to play the fool.

Raistlin was regarding Sturm with narrow, glittering eyes. "I warned him the helm was magical," he said softly.

"Come on, Sturm," said Caramon, now frightened. "Quit horsing around. I've been talking to Raist, and we've decided that you should escort Tas and Tika back to camp."

"I do not know this Sturm person of whom you keep speaking,"

Sturm interrupted impatiently. "I am Grallen, son of Duncan, King Beneath the Mountain. We must return to Thorbardin at once." His voice grew sad. "My brothers are dead. I fear all is lost. The king must be informed."

Caramon's jaw dropped. "Grallen? Son of Duncan? Huh? Raist, do you know what he's talking about?"

"How very interesting," murmured Raistlin, regarding Sturm as though he were some sort of experiment inside a laboratory jar. "I warned him. He would not listen."

"What's happened to him?" Caramon demanded.

"The helm has seized hold of him. Such magic is not uncommon. There is the famous elven Brooch of Adoration, crafted by a wizard to hold the spirit of his dead wife. Then there was Leonora's Singing Flute, which—"

"Raist!" said Caramon. "Stop the history lessons! What about Sturm?"

"Apparently the helm belonged to a dwarven prince named Grallen," Raistlin explained. "He died, either on the field of battle or here in the fortress. I'm not sure of the nature of the enchantment, but my guess is that the prince's soul had some strong reason to remain in this world, a reason so important he refused to relinquish it, even unto death. His soul became part of the helm, hoping that someone would be fool enough to pick it up and put it on. Enter Sturm Brightblade."

"So this dwarven prince is now Sturm?" Caramon asked, dazed.

"The other way around. Sturm is now the dwarven prince, Grallen."

Caramon cast a stricken glance at his friend. "Will he ever go back to being Sturm?"

"Probably," said Raistlin, "if the helm is removed."

"Well, then, we'll remove it!"

"I wouldn't—" Raistlin began, but Caramon had already taken hold of the helm and started jerking on it, trying to drag it off Sturm's head.

Sturm gave a cry of pain and outrage and shoved Caramon away. "How dare you lay rough hands on me, human!" He reached for his sword.

"We beg your pardon, Your Highness," said Raistlin, hurriedly intervening. "My brother is not himself. The heat of battle has left him confused . . ."

Sturm sheathed his sword.

"The helm's stuck tight, Raist," Caramon reported. "I couldn't budge it!"

"I am not surprised," said Raistlin. "I wonder . . ." He lapsed into thought.

"What do we mean you're not surprised? This is Sturm! You have to break this enchantment, lift it, or do something to it!"

Raistlin shook his head. "The spell cannot be broken until the soul of Prince Grallen frees him."

"When will that be? Will Sturm be a dwarf forever?"

"Unlikely," Raistlin said, adding irritably, "Stop shouting! You'll have every draconian in the place down on us! The prince's soul is intent upon completing some mission. Perhaps something as simple as returning to give news of the death of his brothers."

Raistlin paused. He stared at the helm in thoughtful silence.

"Perhaps this is what the messenger meant . . ." he murmured.

Caramon ran his ran through his hair. He looked desperately unhappy. "Sturm thinking he's a dwarf! This is terrible! What are we going to do?"

"Your Highness," said Raistlin, ignoring his brother and addressing Sturm, "we would be glad to escort you back to Thorbardin, but as you see, we are humans. We do not know the way."

"I will guide you, of course," Sturm said at once. "There will be rich reward for you in return for your service to me. The king must hear this terrible news!"

Caramon turned to face his brother, who was looking inordinately pleased with himself.

"You wouldn't use him like this!" Caramon growled.

"Why not? We have found what we sought." Raistlin pointed to Sturm. "Behold the key to Thorbardin."

———————

Tika sat on a broken column and heaved a mournful sigh.

"I wish this whole fortress would just crash down on my head. Bury me in the rubble and have done with it."

"I think you're too late," said Tas, wandering around the debris-strewn corridor, shining the light of his torch and poking his hoopak into murky corners in the hopes of finding something interesting. "The fortress has crashed down as much as it's going to."

"Well then, maybe I'll fall into a pit," said Tika. "Tumble down the stairs and break my neck. Anything so I don't have to face Caramon again. Why, why, why did I ever come?" She buried her head in her hands.

"He didn't look very pleased to see us, did he?" Tas admitted. "Which is strange, considering all the trouble we went to just to rescue him from that man-eating Stalig Mite."

Tika had told a small lie when she said that she and Tas were going to search for the way out. The fortress was dark and eerie, and though Tas would have been happy to explore, Tika was not feeling all that adventurous. She had only wanted to get away from Caramon. She and Tas remained in the corridor, not far from the room where Caramon was arguing with this twin. The light from their torches and Raistlin's staff filtered out into the hallway. Tika could hear their angry voices, especially Raistlin's, but she couldn't make out what he was saying. Undoubtedly bad things about her. Her cheeks burned. Sick at heart, she rocked back and forth and groaned.

Tasslehoff was patting her soothingly on her shoulder, when suddenly he gave a great sniff.

"I smell fresh air," he said, and he wrinkled his nose. "Well, maybe not *fresh* air, but at least it smells like air that's outside, not inside."

"So what?" Tika returned in muffled tones.

"You told Caramon we were going to find the way out. I think we have. Let's go see!"

"I didn't mean a way out," said Tika, sighing. "I meant a way out—of this stupid situation."

"But if we did find a way out that was better than the way in, then you could tell Caramon and he could tell Raistlin and he wouldn't be mad at us anymore. We'd be making ourselves useful."

Tika lifted her head. That was true. If they proved they could be useful, Raistlin couldn't stay mad at them. Caramon would be glad that she'd come. She sniffed the air. At first, all she could smell was the musty, dank smell of some place that has been deep underground for a long, long time. Then she knew what Tas meant. The whiff of air was damp and tinged with decay, but at least, as Tas said, it smelled different from the air trapped down here.

"I think it's coming from up there," Tika said, peering up overhead. "I can't see. Hold the torch higher."

Tas climbed nimbly on top of the fallen column, and from there clamored onto another part of the fallen column that lay on the column beneath it. He now stood head and shoulders above Tika. He held his torch as high as he could, stretching his arm nearly out of the socket. The light revealed the underside of a rickety-looking cat walk constructed of iron.

"The fresh air smell is definitely coming from up there," Tas announced, though, in truth, he couldn't really tell much difference. He wanted to take Tika's mind off her troubles. "Maybe if we climbed onto that cat walk, we'd find a door or something. Do you have any rope?"

"You know perfectly well I don't have any rope," returned Tika, and she sighed again. "It's hopeless."

"No, it's not!" Tas cried. He peered overhead, twisting his neck to see. "I think that if you stood on this column then hoisted me onto your shoulders, I could reach the bottom of the cat walk. You know what I mean?" He looked back at Tika. "Like those tumblers we saw at the faire last year. There was the guy who tied himself in a knot and—"

"We're not tumblers," Tika pointed out. "We'd likely break our necks."

"You were just saying you wanted to break your neck," Tas said. "Come on, Tika, we can at least try!"

Tika shook her head.

Tas shrugged. "I guess we'll just have to go back and tell Caramon we failed."

Tika mulled things over. "Do you really think we could do it?"

"Of course, we can!" Tas balanced the torch on the rock, carefully, so as not to put it out. "You stand here. Brace your feet. Hold very still. I'm going to climb up your back onto your shoulders. Oops, wait! You should take off your sword. . . ."

Tika unbuckled her sword belt and set it down on the rock beside the torch. She and Tas tried several different ways of hoisting the kender onto her shoulders, but climbing a person turned out not to be as easy as the tumblers had made it look. After a few failed attempts, Tas finally figured out how to do it.

"Fortunately you've got big hips," he told Tika.

"Thanks a bunch," she said bitterly.

Planting one foot on her hip, Tas hoisted himself up. He put his other foot on her shoulder, brought up his other foot, then he had both feet on both of Tika's shoulders. Slowly, teetering a little, keeping his hands on the top of Tika's head, he straightened.

"I didn't think you were this heavy!" Tika gasped. "You'd better . . . hurry!"

"Hold onto my ankles!" Tas instructed. He reached up and grasped two of the iron railings.

"You can let loose now!"

Tas swung his right leg up, trying to connect with the balcony. After two tries, he finally made it. He slid one leg through the railings then didn't know what to do with the other leg. He hung there for a moment in an extremely awkward, uncomfortable, and precarious position.

Tika, looking up, put her hands over her mouth, terrified Tas would fall.

Fortunately he came from a long line of kender who climbed up onto balconies or shinnied out onto ledges or walked the ridgepoles of roofs. A wriggle, a few grunts, a readjustment of his leg so that he wasn't about to dislocate a hip, another wriggle and a squeeze, and he was through the iron railings and lying flat on his stomach on the cat walk.

"You did it!" Tika cried, impressed. "What's up there? Is there a way out?"

She could hear Tas rummaging around in the dark, but she couldn't see what he was doing. Once he seemed to trip over something, for he said, "Ouch!" in irritated tones. Then he came back, leaned over the edge of the rail, and called down, "Say, Tika, why do you suppose they call it a cat walk? Do cats walk on these things a lot?"

"How should I know? What difference does that make?" she returned irritably.

"I was just wondering. I think it's because they have nine lives."

Before Tika could point out that this made no sense, Tas added, "There's lots of rope up here, coils and coils of it, and some torches and a sack that has something squishy inside that smells bad. I'll keep looking."

He was off again. Tika picked up the torch and looked around nervously, not liking being left alone. Then she reflected she wasn't truly alone. Caramon was not far away. He would come if she called.

Tas came back. "I found it! There's a hole in the ceiling that I think leads up into a shaft that I'm pretty sure goes outside. I'll bet we could climb up the shaft. Do you want to try?"

"Yes," Tika said, thinking that wherever the shaft led was better than where she was now. Anything was better than going back to Caramon and his brother. "How do I get up onto the cat walk?"

"I'll send down some rope. Hold that torch where I can see what I'm doing."

Tika raised the torch. Working by its flickering light, Tas tied one end of the rope to an iron railing. He tugged on it to make sure it was good and tight, then he flung the rope down to Tika.

"You'd better douse the torch," he advised, "so no draconians come after us. I'll light one up here."

Tika extinguished the light then took hold of the rope and began to pull herself up, hand over hand. She'd been quite adept at rope climbing when she was a girl; the children of the tree-top town of Solace could clamor up and down ropes like spiders. She hadn't done much rope climbing since those days, but the skill came back to her.

"You have strong arms," Tas remarked admiringly.

"And big hips," Tika muttered. She pulled herself up and over the railing.

"The air shaft's over here." Tas and his torch led the way to a wide hole in the ceiling. Though Tika couldn't see sunlight, she could feel and smell the fresh air flowing down from above, gently brushing her face. She drew in a deep breath.

"This is definitely the way out," she said.

"I think it's also the way in," said Tas. "The draconians used this route to enter the fortress. You can tell because they left their stuff lying around."

"That means they'll be back to collect it!" Tika said, alarmed.

"Any minute now probably," said Tas in cheerful tones, "so if we're going to explore the shaft, we should do it pretty quickly."

"What if there are draconian guards inside there?" Tika faltered.

Tas peered up the shaft, his face screwed up into thought wrinkles.

"I don't think so," he said at last. "If the draconianss had gone back up the shaft, they would have taken their stuff with them. No. They're somewhere else. Probably exploring the ruins down below."

"Then let's go up there," said Tika, shivering at the thought.

The two climbed a pile of rubble that lay beneath the shaft and from there into the shaft itself. Dim gray light filtered down from above, so they could leave the torch behind. The shaft did not go straight up, like a chimney, but sloped gradually, and the climb was an easy one. The breeze wafting down the shaft grew stronger and colder, and they soon came in sight of heavy gray clouds that looked so close it seemed they could grab a handful. The opening was a large oval hole in the rock; the edges glistened wetly in the gray light.

Tas poked his head out of the hole and immediately ducked down again.

"Draconians!" Tas whispered. "Lots of them, standing on the ground below us."

They both held very still, then Tas started to raise himself up again.

"What are you doing!" Tika gasped, tugging on his breeches. "They'll see you!"

"No, they won't," Tas said. "We're up above them. Come on. You can look."

Tika didn't like it, but she had to see for herself. She edged her head cautiously out of the hole.

The draconians were gathered at the base of the ruined fortress on one of the few dry patches of ground available. A foul-smelling, evil-looking swamp surrounded them. The gray clouds roiling above turned out not to be clouds at all, but a thick mist rising from dark and putrid waters. The draconians stood in a group around a draconian who appeared to be their leader. He was larger than the others, his scales were a different color, and he was issuing orders. His voice was deep and loud, and they could hear him quite clearly.

"Tika!' said Tas, excited. "I can speak draconian! I know what he's saying."

"I know what he's saying, too," said Tika. "He's speaking Common."

The two listened and watched. Then Tika said softly, "Come on! We have to go tell the others!"

"Shouldn't we wait to hear more?"

"We've heard enough." Tika said.

She began to scrabble back down the shaft. Tas listened a moment longer, then he followed.

"You know, Tika," said Tas, when they reached the cat walk. "It's good we came, after all."

"I was thinking the same thing," Tika said.

14

Baò news. Who's going to go back?

aistlin! Caramon! Sturm! There's a draconian army right outside!" Tas announced, bursting into the armory.

"The draconians are planning to attack our people in the valley!" Tika was saying at the same time. "We heard the big one telling his soldiers! The attack is coming from Pax Tharkas."

"We found out because I can understand draconian now." Tas raised his voice to be heard above Tika. "Say, why is Sturm wearing that funny-looking helm?"

Raistlin glared at them. "I can't understand a word either of you is saying. One person talks at a time!"

"Tas," Tika ordered, "go keep watch in the corridor."

"But Tika—"

She glared at him, and Tasslehoff departed.

Tika repeated what they'd overheard, adding, "These draconians are part of a larger force. They've been posted here to make sure that our people don't come this way. It's a good thing Tas and I came," she said, with a defiant glance at Raistlin, "otherwise we wouldn't have found out about the danger the refugees are in."

Raistlin looked at Caramon, who sighed and shook his head.

"This makes things difficult," said Raistlin.

"What? How? I don't understand," Tika said.

This was not the reception she had been expecting.

She had hoped that Caramon would be pleased with her. Well, maybe not pleased, because her news was very bad, the worst news possible, but he could at least be pleased that she and Tas had found out about the attack in time to prevent it.

Caramon only stood there looking troubled and unhappy. Raistlin's lips were tightly compressed. She couldn't tell how Sturm looked because he was wearing some sort of odd-looking helm that covered his face. All in all, Tika realized, everyone was acting very strangely.

"What's the matter with you? We should get started right away. Right now. And why *is* Sturm wearing that funny looking helm?"

"She's right, Raist," said Caramon. "We should go back."

"What will the refugees do once we have warned them?" Raistlin demanded. "Where can they go that is safe?" He glanced at Sturm. "Thorbardin."

"Of course, we must go to Thorbardin," Sturm said, and he sounded impatient. "We have delayed long enough. I'm leaving. If you're coming with me, humans, then come."

He started to walk out the door. Raistlin hurriedly intervened, stepping in front of him, and laying his hand on the knight's arm. "We plan to go with you, Your Highness, but there is an emergency we must deal with first. If you will just be patient a moment longer . . ."

"Your Highness!" Tika stared at Sturm, then she said in a low voice to Caramon, "Did he get hit on the head again?"

"It's a long story," said Caramon bleakly.

"Let me put it this way," said Raistlin dryly. "Sturm is not himself."

He looked back at his brother. "We must go with the knight to Thorbardin. We may never have another chance to find the dwarven kingdom."

"No, we have to go back to camp," Tika insisted.

"Riverwind is aware that an attack is possible," Raistlin said. "He will be ready for it, if it comes."

"Why can't we do both?" Caramon asked. "We take Prince Grallen here with us back to camp. Then the prince can lead the refugees to Thorbardin. Problem solved."

"Prince Grallen? Who's Prince Grallen?" Tika asked, but no one answered her.

"An excellent idea, but it won't work," Raistlin said flatly.

"Sure it will," said Caramon.

"Try and see," said Raistlin, shrugging. "Tell Prince Grallen."

Caramon, looking extremely uncomfortable, walked over to where Sturm stood by the door, tapping his foot restlessly on the floor. "Your Highness, we are planning to go to Thorbardin, but first we're going to make a little side trip. We have some friends who are trapped in a valley to the north—"

Sturm drew back. He glared at Caramon from out of the helm's eye slits. "North! We do not travel north. Our way lies east across the Dergoth Plains. I would have been grateful to have your company, human, but if you go north, you go alone."

"I told you so," said Raistlin.

Caramon sighed deeply.

"What's wrong with Sturm?" Tika asked, frightened. "Why is he talking like that?"

"The helm's possessed him," said Caramon. "He thinks he's a dwarven prince who lived three hundred years ago. He's dead set on going to Thorbardin."

"The helm will not let him do anything else," said Raistlin. "There is no reasoning with the enchantment."

"What if we knocked him out, tied him up and dragged him?" Tika asked.

Caramon was horrified. "Tika, this is Sturm we're talking about."

"Well, apparently it isn't," Tika snapped. "It's Prince Something-or-other." She didn't understand any of this, but she was understanding enough to see where this conversation was headed, and she didn't like it. "Caramon Majere, our friends are in danger! We can't just abandon them!"

"I know," he replied unhappily. "I know."

"I doubt if we *could* knock him out," Raistlin observed. "The helm will act to protect him from harm. If we tried to attack him, he would fight us and someone would get hurt. Just because Sturm thinks he is a dwarf prince doesn't mean he has lost the ability to use his sword."

Tika interposed herself between Raistlin and Caramon. She

turned her back on Raistlin, faced Caramon, her arms akimbo, her red curls quivering, her green eyes glittering.

"Thorbardin or no Thorbardin, prince or no prince, someone *has* to warn Riverwind and the others! You and I should go back, Caramon. Your brother and Sturm can travel to Thorbardin."

"Yes, Caramon," said Raistlin in dulcet tones. "Run along with your girlfriend. Leave me to make my way across the accursed Plains of Dergoth in company with a knight who thinks he's a dwarf. We will both die, of course, and our mission will fail, but you two will undoubtedly enjoy yourselves."

Tika was so furious she was tempted to turn around and slap Raistlin across his golden-skinned face. She knew that would only make matters worse, however. Digging her nails into her flesh to keep control of herself, she kept facing Caramon, forcing him to look at her, talk to her, think about her and what she was saying.

"Raistlin exaggerates," Tika told him. "He's trying to make you feel guilty. He's a wizard! He has his magic, and like he said, the helm will protect Sturm and Sturm can still use his sword. You have to come with me!"

Caramon was in agony. His face had gone an ugly, blotchy red, mottled with pale white splotches. He looked at his twin and he looked at Tika, then he looked away from both of them.

"I don't know," he mumbled.

Tasslehoff poked his head in the door. "You people are being awfully loud," he said sternly. "I can hear you yelling clear down at the end of the corridor!"

Tika lapsed into irate silence. Caramon still didn't say anything and Sturm began to pace, marching back and forth, impatient to be on his way.

"Whatever *you* decide, my brother," said Raistlin.

Tika eyed Caramon. "Well?"

Caramon cast an uneasy glance at Tika.

"I've got an idea," he said. "We're all tired and hungry. It's been a long day. Let's go back into the tunnel, get something to eat, and talk about this in the morning."

"You're going with your brother," said Tika in frozen tones.

"I don't know," Caramon said, hedging. "I haven't decided. I need to think."

Tika cast him a look—a green-eyed baleful look that skewered

Caramon like a spear. She stalked angrily out of the room.

"Tika! Wait . . ." Caramon started after her.

"Where do you think you are going?" Raistlin demanded. "You must help me persuade the prince to stay. He will not be pleased at the delay."

Caramon watched Tika walking down the corridor, heading back toward the library. She looked angry clear through to her bones.

"Tas, go with her," Caramon said in low tones, so his brother couldn't hear.

Tas obligingly ran off. Caramon could hear the two talking.

"Tika, what's wrong?" Tas called out, racing to catch up with her.

"Caramon's a blithering idiot," Tika answered, choking on her rage, "and I hate him!"

"Caramon!" Raistlin said sharply. "I need you!"

Sighing deeply, Caramon went back to his twin.

<hr/>

After a great deal of talking and reasoning, Raistlin finally persuaded Prince Grallen to stay overnight in Skullcap. He told the prince he and his brother needed to rest before they could undertake the journey, and at last the Prince grudgingly agreed.

They returned to the library and from there went back into the tunnel. Caramon, fearing draconians might find them, wanted to shut the stone door. Raistlin pointed out that the draconians did not know about the tunnel and they should be safe enough here. Shutting the stone door would make a lot of noise. The only reason the draconians hadn't heard the clamor the first time was due to the dragon's roaring. Of course, after this, there was no argument. The door remained open.

They ate sparingly, for they had a long journey ahead of them—no matter which way they decided to go. Sturm ate what was given him then fell immediately into a deep slumber from which he could not be wakened.

Caramon was so unhappy he almost couldn't eat. Tika wouldn't talk to him or even look at him. She sat with her back against the stone wall, moodily chewing on dried meat. Raistlin ate very little, as always, then went to study his spells, ordering everyone to leave him in peace. He sat on the floor, his robes wrapped around him for warmth, bathed in the pale glow of the staff, his book propped on his knees.

Tasslehoff was fascinated by Sturm-turned-dwarf. The kender sat talking to the prince as long as the prince would talk to him, and when Sturm fell asleep, Tasslehoff continued to sit beside him, watching him.

"He even snores different from Sturm!" Tas reported, when Caramon walked over to see how the knight was faring.

Caramon glanced at his brother, then bent down to take hold of the helm.

"Are you going to yank it off? Here, let me help!" Tas offered, adding excitedly, "Can I put it on next? Can I be the prince?"

Caramon only grunted. He tugged on the helm, twisted it, and when that wouldn't work, he gave it a thump to see if he could loosen it.

The helm was stuck fast.

"The only way you're going to get it off is to take Sturm's head with it," Tas said. "I guess that's not an option, huh?"

"No, it isn't," said Caramon.

"That's too bad," said Tas, disappointed but philosophical. "Oh, well, if I can't be a dwarf, at least I have the fun of watching Sturm be a dwarf."

"Fun!" Caramon snorted.

He slumped back against the wall, folded his arms over his chest, and settled himself comfortably on the floor. He had offered to take the first watch. Tika stood up, wiped off her hands, and started to walk toward him. Caramon groaned inwardly and braced himself.

"Did you enjoy your dinner?" he asked, rising nervously to his feet.

Tika glanced over her shoulder at Raistlin. Seeing him absorbed in his reading, she said softly, "You've made up your mind. You're going with your brother, aren't you?"

"Look, Tika, I've been thinking," said Caramon. "What if we all go to Thorbardin tomorrow? We'll meet up with Flint and Tanis, then Raistlin can stay with them, and you and I will go back to warn the others—"

"We'll go back to bury them, you mean," said Tika. She turned on her heel and returned to her place by the wall.

"She doesn't understand," Caramon said to himself. "She doesn't understand how weak Raistlin is, how sick he gets. He needs me. I can't leave him. The refugees will be all right. Riverwind is smart. He'll know what to do."

Raistlin, who had been only pretending to study his spells, smiled to himself in satisfaction when he saw Tika walk off. He shut the spellbook, put it back in his pack that his brother always carried for him, and feeling suddenly weary from the day's exertions, he doused the light of his staff and went to sleep.

———————————————

The night deepened. The darkness in the tunnel was impenetrable. Tika sat awake, listening to the various sounds: Sturm's rumbling snore, Caramon's shuffling, Tasslehoff's twitches and whiffles, and other noises that were maybe rats and maybe not.

Tika knew what she had to do. She just had to find the courage to do it.

Caramon gave a jaw-cracking yawn. Fumbling about in the dark, he located Tas and shook him.

"I can't stay awake any longer," he said softly. "You take over."

"Sure, Caramon," said Tas sleepily. "Is it all right if I sit by Sturm? He might wake up and then I can ask the prince if I could wear the helm, just for a little while."

Caramon muttered something to the effect that the prince and the helm could all go straight to the Abyss as far as he was concerned. Tika heard him walking over by her, and she swiftly lay down and closed her eyes, though he probably couldn't see her in the darkness.

He called out her name.

"Tika," he whispered loudly, hesitantly.

She didn't answer.

"Tika, try to understand," he said plaintively. "I have to go with Raist. He needs me."

She kept quiet. Caramon heaved a huge sigh then, tripping over Sturm's feet, he groped about until he found his blanket and lay down. When he was snoring, Tika rose to her feet. She found her pack and a torch and crept over to where Tasslehoff was keeping himself entertained by poking at Sturm with his hoopak in an effort to make him wake up.

"Tas," said Tika in a smothered voice. "I need you to light this torch for me."

Always glad to oblige, Tas fumbled about in one of his pouches. He produced flint and a tinderbox and soon the torch was burning brightly. Tika held her breath, waiting for the light to wake the sleepers. Raistlin muttered something and pulled his cowl over his eyes and rolled over. Sturm did not so much as twitch. Caramon, who had overslept through an ogre attack and kept on snoring.

Tika gave a little sigh. She hadn't wanted to wake him, but a part of her was disappointed.

"Do you remember what I did with my sword?" she asked Tas.

The kender gave the matter some thought. "You took it off when we climbed up to the cat walk. I guess you forgot it in all the excitement. It's probably still lying on that rock back in the fortress."

Tika gave an inward sigh. No true warrior was likely to forgot where she'd put her sword.

"Should I go back to get it?" Tas asked eagerly.

"No, of course not!" Tika returned. "Who knows what awful things are lurking about there at night? Look what happened to Sturm."

Now it was Tas who gave the inward sigh. Some people had all the luck. It wasn't fair.

"Let me borrow Rabbitslayer then," said Tika.

Tas gave his knife a fond pat and handed it over.

"Don't lose it. Where are you going?" Tas asked.

"Back to camp, to warn the others."

"I'll come with you!" Tas jumped up.

"No." Tika shook her red curls. "You're on watch, remember? You can't leave."

"Oh, yeah. I guess you're right," Tas agreed, more easily than Tika had expected. She'd feared she would have an argument on this point.

"I'll go if you really need me," Tas told her. "But if you don't, I'd rather stay here. I don't want to miss out on Sturm being a dwarf. That's something you just don't see every day. I'll wake up Caramon."

"No, you won't," Tika said grimly. "He'll try to stop me."

She thrust Tas's knife in her belt and slung her pack over shoulder.

"Are you really going by yourself?" Tas asked, impressed.

"Yes," said Tika, "and don't you say a word to anyone. Understand? Not until morning. Promise?"

"I promise," Tas said glibly.

Tika knew Tas, and she also knew that promises were like lint to kender—easily brushed off. She eyed him sternly.

"You must swear to me by every object you have in your pouches," she said. "May they all change into roaches and crawl off in the night if you break your vow."

Tas's eyes went round at this terrible prospect. "Do I have to?" he asked, squirming. "I already promised—"

"Swear!" said Tika in a terrible voice.

"I swear." Tas gulped.

Fairly certain this fearful oath would be good for at least a few hours, long enough for her to get a good start, Tika walked off down the tunnel. She'd gone only a short distance, however, before she remembered something and turned around.

"Tas, give Caramon a message for me, will you?"

Tasslehoff nodded.

"Tell him I do understand. I do."

"I'll tell him. Bye, Tika," Tas said, waving.

He had the feeling this wasn't right, her going off by herself like this. He should wake up someone, but then he thought of all the wonderful things he had in his pouches changing into roaches and skittering off, and he didn't know what to do. He sat back down beside Sturm and tried to come up with some way around the promise. The light Tika carried grew smaller and smaller in the distance until he couldn't see it anymore, and he still hadn't thought of any way out of his predicament.

He continued to think, and he thought so hard that hours passed without him noticing.

As it turns out, Raistlin was wrong when he stated that the draconians did not know about the tunnel. A baaz draconian, wandering into the library in search of loot, had discovered the secret tunnel. He was inside it when he heard the humans returning. They were on him before he realized it, and he was trapped. The baaz considered attacking them, for there were only five of them, and one was a sniveling runt of a kender and the other a female.

Seeing the female, the baaz had a better idea. He would kill the others, capture her alive, have his fun with her, then drag her back to his comrades and trade her for dwarf spirits. The baaz retreated a safe distance down the dark tunnel and spied on the group.

Two of them were warriors who wore their swords with assurance. One was a loathsome wizard carrying a staff with a light that hurt the baaz's eyes. The baaz hated and distrusted all magic-users, and disappointed, he decided to leave the group alone, at least for the time being. Maybe one would fall asleep on watch, then he could sneak up on them and butcher them in their sleep.

The baaz was doomed to disappointment, it seemed, for the big warrior took first watch and he remained alert the entire time. The draconian was afraid to shift a claw for fear he'd hear him. The big man then woke up the kender and the draconian's hopes rose, for even a draconian new to Krynn had come to know that kender, while delicious, are not to be trusted. He also knew that kender had sharp ears and sharper eyes, and this one appeared more alert than usual. The kender was also wide awake.

The draconian had settled himself for a long night of boredom when his luck took a sudden change. The human female lit a torch, had a short talk with the kender, then walked off down the tunnel by herself. She passed right in front of the draconian, who lurked in the shadows, doing his utmost to keep quiet. If she had turned her head, she would have seen the torch light gleam in his brass scales and his lust-filled eyes. She walked with her head down, her gaze fixed on her feet. She did not notice him.

The baaz waited tensely for the kender or someone to come after her, but no one did.

Moving slowly and quietly to keep his claws from clicking on the stone floor, the baaz crept down the tunnel after the female.

He would have to let her get far enough away from the others before accosting her, so that no one would hear her scream.

15

Caramon's choice. Tika misses her skillet. Raistlin misses a spell.

he did what?" Caramon towered over Tasslehoff. The big man's face was red, his eyes flashed. The kender had never seen him so angry. "Why didn't you wake me?"

"She made me promise!" Tas wailed.

"Since when in your life have you ever kept a promise?" Caramon roared. "Light that torch for me, and be quick about it!'

"She said that if I told you, everything in my pouch would change into roaches," Tas returned.

Light flared. Raistlin sat up, rubbing his eyes.

"What is the matter with you two? Stop bellowing, Caramon. You're making noise enough to wake the dead!"

"Tika's gone," said Caramon, buckling on his sword belt. "She left in the middle of the night. She went back to warn the others."

"Well . . . good for her," Raistlin said. He watched his brother for a few moments in silence, then said, "Where do you think you're going?"

"After her."

"Don't be a fool," Raistlin said coldly. "She's been gone for hours. You'll never catch up with her."

"She might have stopped to rest." Caramon grabbed hold of the torch. "You wait here. Go back to sleep. I won't be gone long . . ." He paused then said in altered tones, "Where's Sturm?"

"Oh for the love of—" Raistlin scrambled to his feet. "*Shirak*!" he said, and the staff's light began to glow. "This is what comes of leaving a kender on watch!"

"He went in there." Tas pointed at the library. "I thought he was going to go pee."

"Did he say anything?" Raistlin's eyes glittered feverishly.

"I asked him if I could wear the helm and he said 'no'," Tas reported sulkily.

Raistlin began to gather up his things. "We have to go after Sturm. He has no idea what he is doing. He could walk straight into the draconian army!"

"It isn't fair," Tasslehoff said, gathering up his pouches. "Sturm got to wear the helm all night. I told him it was my turn."

"What about Tika?" Caramon demanded. "She's by herself."

"She is going back to camp. She is not in any danger. Sturm is."

Caramon agonized. "I don't know . . ."

Raistlin picked up his pack. "You do what you want. I am going after Sturm." He stalked off.

"Me too," Tas said. "Maybe it will be my turn to wear the helm tonight. I gave Tika Rabbitslayer, Caramon," he added, feeling sorry for his friend. "She left her sword in the corridor. Oh, and she gave me a message for you! I almost forgot. She said to tell you she understands."

Caramon groaned softly and shook his head.

"I'd stay and talk some more, but I've got to be going," said Tas. "Raistlin might need me."

Tas waited a moment to see if Caramon would come, but the big man did not stir. Fearful that the other two would leave him behind, Tas turned and ran off. Caramon heard the kender's voice coming from the library.

"I can carry your pack for you, Raistlin!"

He heard his brother's voice in answer, "Touch it, and I will slice off your hand."

Caramon made up his mind. Tika understood. She'd said so.

He caught up with his twin at the door leading into the fortress.

"Let me carry that. It's too heavy for you," Caramon said, and he shouldered Raistlin's pack.

* * *

Tika walked for hours, anger and frustration and love blazing like embers inside her. First love would flare up, then die down, only to have anger burst into flame. The fire fed her energy, and she made good time, or thought she did. It was hard to tell how far she'd come; the tunnel seemed unending. She talked to herself as she walked, holding imaginary conversations with Caramon and telling Raistlin exactly what she thought of him.

Once she thought she heard something behind her and she stopped, her heart pounding—not with fear, but with hope.

"Caramon!" she called eagerly. "You came after me! I'm so glad . . ."

She waited, but there was no answer. She didn't hear the sound anymore and decided she must have imagined it.

"Wishful thinking," she muttered to herself and kicked angrily at a loose rock, sending it rolling across the floor. "He's not coming."

In that moment, she faced up to the truth. All the fires in her died.

Caramon was not coming. She'd given him an ultimatum: her or his brother. He had chosen Raistlin.

"He will always choose Raistlin," Tika said to herself. "I know he loves me, but he will always choose Raistlin."

She had no idea why this was so. She only knew it would be so until something happened to separate the two, and maybe not even then.

There was the sound again. This time Tika knew she hadn't imagined it.

"Tasslehoff? Is that you?"

It would be just like the kender to abandon his post and chase after her. He was probably planning to sneak up on her, jump at her out of the shadows, then collapse with laughter at her fright.

If it was Tas, he didn't answer her shout.

She heard the noise again. It sounded like harsh breathing and scraping footfalls, and whoever it was, it wasn't bothering to hide anymore.

"Tasslehoff," Tika faltered. "This isn't funny . . ."

Even as she said the words, she knew it wasn't Tas. Fear twisted into a cold, hard knot in her belly. Her throat constricted. She couldn't breathe or swallow. She shifted the torch to her left hand, almost dropping it. Her right hand closed spasmodically over the dagger in her belt. She didn't want to die, not alone, in the darkness, and at the thought, a little whimper of terror escaped her.

She couldn't see, but she could hear the sound made by claws scraping across the stone floor, and she knew immediately her pursuer was a draconian. Her first panicked instinct was to run, but though her brain was screaming at her to flee, her legs refused to budge. Besides, there was nowhere to go. Nowhere to run. Nowhere to hide.

The harsh panting and grunting came closer and closer. The draconian was finished sneaking about.

He emerged into the torchlight right in front of her, racing straight at her. At the sight of her, his hideous scaly face contorted in a slavering grin. He gurgled, saliva flicked from his jaws. He wore a curve-bladed sword, but he had not drawn it. He did not want to kill his prey; he wanted to enjoy it first.

Tika let the beast-man draw close to her—not from any planned strategy, but because she was too terrified to move. The draconian's red eyes gleamed; his clawed hands opened. He spread his wings and leaped at her, planning to drag her to the stone floor with him on top of her.

Determination hardened in Tika. Determination steadied her hand, turned her terror to strength. Swinging the torch in a wild, backhand stroke, she bashed the draconian in his leering face. Her hit was perfectly if accidentally timed and caught the draconian in mid-flight.

The blow knocked the baaz's head one way and his momentum carried his feet in the opposite direction, upending him. He landed with a heavy thud on the stone floor, his wings crumpled beneath him. Tika flung aside the torch, and holding the dagger in both hands, she was on the baaz in an instant. Screaming in fury, she slashed and stabbed.

The draconian howled and tried to grab hold of her. She didn't know what part of the draconian she was striking; she couldn't see all that well, for a red rage dimmed her vision. She struck at anything that moved. She kicked, stomped, stabbed and slashed, knowing only that she had to keep fighting until the thing stopped moving.

Then her blade struck rock, jarring her arms painfully. The dagger slid out of her blood-slick hands. Panicked, Tika scrabbled to find her weapon. She caught hold of it, picked it up, whirled around, and saw her foe dead at her feet. The rock she had hit was the draconian, turned to stone.

Sobbing for breath, shaking all over, Tika tasted a horrid, bitter liquid in her mouth. She retched and felt better. Her frantic heartbeat slowed. She breathed a little easier, and only then felt the burning pain of the scratches on her arms and legs. She picked up the torch, held it over the draconian and waited for the corpse to turn to ashes. Only when it finally disintegrated did she believe it was dead.

Tika shuddered and was about to slump down on the stone floor, when the thought came to her that there might be more of the monsters out there. She hurriedly wiped the blood from her hand to get a better grip on the knife and waited. The pain burned in her arms and her legs and she began to shiver.

Her thinking cleared. If there had been any others, they would have attacked her by now. This one had acted alone, hoping to have his prize all to himself.

Tika took stock of her wounds. Long jagged scratches crisscrossed her arms and her legs, but that was the extent of the damage. Her violent attack had taken the draconian completely by surprise. The scratches burned horribly and bled freely, but that was good. The bleeding would keep the wounds from putrefying.

Tika cleaned out the scratches with water from the water skin, rinsed the draconian's blood from her face and hands, and swished the water around in her mouth to rid herself of the horrid taste. She spit the water out. She was afraid to swallow, afraid she'd throw up again.

She was bone-tired, sick and shaking. She longed to curl up in a ball and have a good cry, but she couldn't bear the thought of spending another moment in this horrid tunnel. Besides, she had to reach Riverwind and there was no time to waste.

Gritting her teeth, Tika thrust Rabbitslayer in her belt and walked determinedly on.

Tasslehoff led Caramon, Raistlin, and Prince Sturm, as the kender was now calling him, up the airshaft. Reaching the top, they peered out cautiously and hopefully. They had not heard any sounds of draconians during the night and had hoped that, having slain the dragon and looted the place, they would have moved on. Instead, they found the draconians camped out underneath the way out.

The draconians slept on the ground, curled up, their tails wrapped around their feet and their wings folded. Most of them slept with their heads on lumpy sacks filled with whatever treasure they'd found in the fortress. One draconian had been left on watch. He sat up with his back against a rock. Every so often, his head would nod and he would slump forward, only to jerk awake again.

"I thought you said it was an army," said Caramon dourly. "I count fifteen."

"That's almost an army," Tas returned.

"Not even close," said Caramon.

"Fifteen or fifteen hundred, it makes little difference," Raistlin said. "We still have to get past them."

"Unless there's another way out." Caramon looked at Sturm, who shook his helmed head.

"Thorbardin lies that way." He pointed to the south. "Across the Plains of Dergoth."

"Yeah, I know," Caramon said. "You've told us that three times in the last five minutes. Is there another way out of this fortress? A secret way?"

"Our army stormed the gates of the fortress. We came in through the front and swept aside the defenders."

"This is the only way," said Raistlin.

"You can't know for sure. We could do some exploring."

"Trust me," Raistlin said flatly. "I know."

Caramon shook his head, but he did not continue to argue.

"We will simply wait for the draconians to leave," Raistlin decided. "They will not hang about all day. They will likely return to the fortress to continue searching for loot. Once they have gone inside, we can depart."

"We should just kill them now," Sturm said. "They are merely goblins. Four of us can handle such vermin with ease."

Caramon looked at Sturm in astonishment. "Goblins? Those aren't goblins." Puzzled, he looked at Raistlin. "Why does he think they're goblins?"

"Remarkable," said Raistlin, intrigued. "I can only speculate, but since draconians did not exist during the time in which the prince lived, the helm does not know what to make of the monsters. Thus the prince sees what he expects to see—goblins."

"Great," Caramon muttered. "Just bloody great."

He peered over the edge down a sheer wall, black and smooth, that extended for about thirty feet, ending in a massive pile of rubble—chunks of the fortress, boulders, and rocks all jumbled together. At the foot of the rubble heap was the large patch of dry ground on which the draconians were camped and beyond that the mists and miasma of a swamp.

"I suppose we could climb down the wall," said Caramon dubiously. "Looks kind of slick though."

Caramon waited until he saw the draconian's head slump, then he pulled himself out over the ledge for a better look. The moment his hand touched the smooth, black rock, he gave a curse and snatched his hand back.

"Damn!" he said, rubbing his palm that was bright red. "That blasted rock is cold as ice! Like sticking your hand in a frozen lake!" He sucked on his fingers.

"Let me feel!" said Tas eagerly.

The guard's head jerked up. He yawned and looked about. Caramon grabbed the kender and dragged him back.

"At least *you* can use your magic to float down," Caramon grumbled to his brother. "The rest of us will have to use the ropes to push ourselves off the rock. It will be slow going, and we'll be sitting ducks on the way down."

Raistlin glanced sidelong at his twin. "You are in a very bad mood this morning, my brother."

"Yeah, well . . ." Caramon rubbed his stubbled jaw. He had not shaved in a couple of days, and his beard was starting to itch. "I'm worried about Tika, that's all."

"You blame me for the fact that the girl ran off by herself."

"No, Raist, I don't blame you," Caramon said with a sigh. "If you must know, I blame myself."

"You can blame me, too," Tas offered remorsefully. "I should have gone with her."

The kender took hold of his topknot and gave it a painful tug as punishment.

"If anyone is to blame, it is Tika herself. Her foolishness prompted her to leave," said Raistlin. "Suffice it to say, she's in far less danger returning to camp than she would be now if she were here with us."

Caramon stirred and seemed about to say something, but Raistlin cut him off.

"We had best prepare for our departure. Caramon, you and Tas go back and bring up the extra rope and anything else you can find that you think we might be able to use. I will remain here with His Highness."

The moment Caramon and Tasslehoff were on their feet, Sturm thought they were leaving, and only Raistlin's most persuasive arguments could prevent the knight from rushing off.

"I hope those draconians go inside soon," said Caramon. "We're not going to be able to keep Sturm here much longer."

Caramon and Tasslehoff returned with the rope and started to secure it for the trip down the mountainside. Once Sturm was aware of what they were doing, he offered his assistance. Sturm knew nothing about mountain climbing, but Prince Grallen, having lived all his life beneath the mountain in the subterranean halls of the dwarves, was skilled in the subject. His advice proved invaluable. He showed Caramon how to tie strong knots and how to best anchor the ropes.

As they were working, the draconian camp below woke up. Raistlin, keeping watch, noted the bozak draconian as being the one in charge. Larger and presumably smarter than the baaz, the bronze-scaled bozak was not so much commander as he was bully and slave driver.

Once he woke up, he went about kicking and hitting the baaz until, grumping and grousing, they stumbled to their feet. The bozak doled out hunks of maggot-ridden meat to the baaz, keeping the largest share for himself and five baaz, who were apparently his bodyguards.

From what Raistlin could gather from listening to the mixture of Common, military argot, and draconian, the bozak was ordering his men back inside the fortress to continue searching for anything valuable. He reminded them that he would be taking his cut, and nobody had better try to keep anything from him, or he'd slice off their wings.

Led by the bozak, the draconians trooped inside the fortress, and soon Raistlin could hear the bozak's guttural shouts echoing along the corridors far below the airshaft.

Caramon waited tensely, rope in hand, until the draconian voices and the sounds of tromping feet faded away. Then he looked at his brother and nodded.

"We're ready."

Raistlin climbed up onto the lip of the hole. Gripping the Staff of Magius, he positioned himself, looked down at the ground some eighty feet beneath him, and raised his arms.

"Don't, Raist!" said Caramon suddenly. "I can carry you down on my back."

Raistlin glanced around. "You've seen me do this countless times, my brother."

"Yeah, I know," Caramon returned. "It's just . . . your magic doesn't work *all* the time."

"My magic does not work all the time because I am human and fallible," Raistlin said irritably, for he never liked to be reminded of that fact. "The magic of the staff, however, can never fail."

Despite his confident words, Raistlin felt the same flutter of uncertainty in the pit of his stomach he always felt whenever he gave himself completely into the hands of the magic. He told himself, as he always did, that he was being foolish. Spreading his arms, he spoke the word of command and leaped into the air.

The Staff of Magius did not fail him. The staff's magic enveloped him, carried him downward, and set him drifting gently upon the currents of magic as though he were light as thistledown.

"I wish I could do that," said Tasslehoff wistfully, peering over the edge. "Do you think I could try, Caramon? Maybe there's a little magic left over . . ."

"And miss the fun of scaling this sheer rock wall that's so cold it'll burn off your skin if you touch it?" Caramon grunted. "Why would you want to do that?"

He looked down. Raistlin waved up at him to let him know he was safe, then hurried over to the fortress entrance. Raistlin stayed there, looking and listening for a long while, then he waved his arm again to indicate that all was safe. Caramon lowered down their packs, including the kender's hoopak and Sturm's armor, which Raistlin wanted to leave behind, but Caramon insisted that they bring with them.

Raistlin untied the packs, set them to one side, then took up a position near the entrance, hiding himself behind a boulder so that if the draconians came out, he could take them by surprise. Caramon, Tas and Sturm began their descent.

Sturm climbed down hand over hand with practiced ease. Tasslehoff found out that scaling rock walls was, indeed, fun. Shoving off the rock wall with his feet sent him flying out into the air, then he'd come sailing back. He did this with great glee, bouncing over the rock face, until Caramon ordered him gruffly to cut out the nonsense and get himself to solid ground. Caramon moved slowly, nervous about trusting his weight to the rope and clumsy with the placement of his feet. He was the last one down and landed with a heartfelt sigh of relief. Compared to that, the climb down the pile of rubble was relatively simple. They were gathering up their possessions when Raistlin rose up from his hiding place and hissed at them to be quiet.

"Someone's coming!"

Caramon looked up in alarm at the three ropes dangling from the opening. Seen from this vantage point, he understood how the fortress had come by its name. It bore an uncanny resemblance to a skull. The air shaft formed one of the eyes. Another air shaft opposite formed the other eye. The entrance to the fortress was the skull's mouth, with rows of jagged stalagmite and stalactite teeth. The ropes, trailing down from an eye socket, told all the world they were here. Caramon considered hiding in the thick vapors of the swamp, but the draconians would come after them, and if that happened, he'd rather fight them on dry land.

Caramon drew his sword. Tasslehoff, mourning the absence of Rabbitslayer, hefted his hoopak. Sturm drew his sword as well. Caramon hoped that Prince Grallen was as a skilled a warrior as Sturm Brightblade. Raistlin, hidden behind the boulder, readied his magic spells.

The bozak and his five baaz bodyguards walked out of the fortress entrance, intending to have a private search through the loot the baaz had left behind to see if any of them had been holding out on him. Planning to loot the looters, the bozak was not prepared for a fight. He and the others were extremely startled to find themselves facing armed foes.

Draconians were born and bred to battle, however, and the bozak was quick to recover from the shock. He used his magic first, casting a spell on the warrior who appeared to be the greatest threat. A beam of blinding light shot from the bozak's clawed hand and struck Sturm, who cried out, clutched his chest, and crumpled to the ground, groaning.

Seeing the knight down, the bozak turned to Caramon. The creature extended his huge wings, making the bozak seem even bigger, and charged, snarling and swinging his sword in powerful, slashing arcs. Caramon parried the first blow with his sword; the force of the attack jarring his arm to the elbow.

Before Caramon could recover, the bozak flipped around and struck Caramon with his massive tail, knocking his feet out from under him and sending Caramon to his knees. As he tried frantically to scramble to his feet, he looked up to see the bozak rounding on him, sword raised. Caramon raised his own sword and the two came together with a crash.

Raistlin crouched unseen in his hiding place near the entrance. Scattering his rose petals, he cast a spell of enchanted sleep on the three baaz who were nearest. He was not particularly confident of the results, for he'd tried this and other spells on draconians before and they had been able to resist the magic's influence.

Two of the baaz stumbled, and one gaped and lowered his sword, but only for a moment. He managed to shake off sleep and charged into the fray. The other two remained on their feet, and worse, they realized a wizard had tried to spellbind them. They turned around, swords in hand, and saw Raistlin.

Raistlin was about to hurl fiery death at them when he found, to his horror, that the magical words to the spell eluded him. Frantically, he searched his memory, but the words were not there. He bitterly cursed his own folly. He had been more intent on watching Tika and his brother last night than he had been on studying his spells.

By now, one of the draconians was on him, swinging his sword in a vicious attack. Raistlin, desperate, lifted his staff to block the blow, praying that the staff did not shatter.

As the sword hit the staff, there came a flash, a crackling sound, and a howl. The baaz dropped his sword and danced about, snarling and wringing his hand in pain. Seeing the fate that had befallen his comrade, the other baaz approached Raistlin and the staff with caution, but he kept on coming. Raistlin put his back against the rocks and held his staff before him.

None of the draconians had bothered with the kender, thinking he was not a threat and they could leave him for last. One of the baaz ran over to Sturm, either to finish him off, or to loot the body, or both.

"Hey, lizard-lips!" yelled Tasslehoff, and, dashing up, he struck the baaz in the back of the head with his hoopak.

The blow did little to the thick-skulled draconian except annoy him. Sword in hand, he turned around to gut the kender, but he couldn't seem to catch him. Tasslehoff leaped first here, then there, taunting the baaz, and daring him to try to hit him.

The baaz swung his sword time and again, but wherever he was, the kender was always somewhere else, calling him names and thwacking him with the hoopak. Between the jumping and the ducking, and name-calling that included "scaly butt" and "dragon turd," the baaz lost all reason and gave chase.

Tasslehoff led the draconian away from Sturm, but unfortunately, in his excitement, the kender did not watch where he was going and found himself perilously near the swamp. Making one last jump to avoid being sliced in half by the enraged baaz, Tas slipped on a rock, and after much arm-flailing and flapping, he toppled with a cry and a splash into the swamp water.

The baaz was about to wade in after him, when a sharp command from the bozak recalled the draconian to his senses. After a moment's hesitation, the baaz left the kender, who had disappeared in the murk, and ran to help his comrade finish the magic-user.

Caramon and the bozak exchanged a series of furious blows that caused sparks to fly from their blades. The two were evenly matched, and Caramon might have prevailed in the end, for the bozak had been up carousing all night and was in sorry shape. Fear for his brother and his desperate need to finish this battle made Caramon reckless. He thought he saw an opening and charged in, only to realize too late that it had been a feint. His sword went flying and landed in the water behind him with a heart-rending splash. Caramon cast an anguished glance at his twin and then leaped to one side and went rolling on the ground as the bozak came at him.

Caramon kicked out with his boot and caught the bozak in the knee. The bozak gave a pain-filled grunt and kicked Caramon in turn, right in the gut, driving the air out of Caramon's lungs and leaving him momentarily helpless. The bozak raised his sword and was about to deal the death blow when a hideous, agonized scream coming from behind him caused the bozak to check his swing and look around.

Caramon lifted his head to see. Both he and the bozak stared in horror.

Pale, cold eyes cloaked in the shredded tatters of night hovered near Raistlin. One draconian lay on the ground, already crumbling to ashes. The other baaz was screaming horribly as a hand as pale and cold as the disembodied eyes twisted the creature's arm. The baaz shriveled beneath the wraith's fell touch and then toppled over in its stony death throes.

Caramon struggled to try to regain his feet, certain that his brother would be the next victim of the wraiths. To his astonishment, the wraiths paid no attention to Raistlin, who was flattened against the rocks, his staff held out before him. The lifeless eyes and the trailing darkness dropped like an awful cloud over the bozak. Shrieking in agony, the bozak writhed in the deadly grasp. He twisted and fought to escape but was held fast.

As the bozak's body began to stiffen, Caramon remembered what happened to bozaks when they died, and he crawled, slipped and slid in his scramble to put as much ground between him and the corpse as possible. The bones of the bozak exploded. The foul heat and shock of the blast struck Caramon, knocking him flat and momentarily stunning him.

He shook his head to clear it and rose hastily to his feet, only to find the battle had ended. Two of the surviving draconians were fleeing back into the fortress, running for their lives. The wraiths flowed in after them and Caramon heard their death shrieks. He gave a sigh of relief, then froze.

Two of the pale eyes hovered near Raistlin.

Caramon ran toward his twin, though he had no idea how to save him.

Then he saw the eyes lower, almost as if the undead was bowing to his brother. The eyes disappeared, leaving behind a bone-numbing chill and the dust of their victims.

"Are you hurt?" Caramon gasped.

"No. You?" Raistlin asked tersely.

He gave his brother a quick glance that apparently answered his question, for he shifted his gaze to Sturm. "What about him?"

"I don't know. He was hit by some sort of magic spell. Raist, those wraiths—"

"Forget the wraiths. Is he hurt badly?" Raistlin asked, shoving past his brother.

"I don't know," Caramon said, limping after him. "I was kind of busy."

He reached out and took hold of his brother's arm, dragging Raistlin to a stop.

"That thing bowed to you. Did you summon it?"

Raistlin regarded his brother with a cold stare, a slight sardonic smile on his lips. "You have an inflated notion of my powers, my brother, to think that I could command the undead. Such a spell is far beyond my capabilities, I assure you."

"But Raist, I saw it—"

"Bah! You were imagining things." Raistlin glowered. "How many times must I tell you that I do not like to be touched!"

Caramon released his grip on his twin.

Raistlin hurried off to check on Sturm. Caramon could not remember his brother having ever been this worried about the knight before. Caramon had a feeling that Raistlin was more worried about Prince Grallen than Sturm. Caramon trailed after him, just as Tasslehoff, sputtering and spitting out muck, pulled himself up out of the water.

"Ugh!" said the kender, dragging sopping wet hair out of his eyes. "What a stupid place to put a swamp! How's Sturm? What did I miss?"

Raistlin had his hand on the knight's pulse. His breastplate was scorched, but it had protected him from the worst of the blast. At Raistlin's touch, Sturm moved his hands and his eyes opened. He tried to stand up.

"Raist," said Caramon, helping Sturm to his feet, "if you didn't summon them, then why didn't the wraiths attack us? Why just attack the draconians?"

"I don't know, Caramon," Raistlin said in exasperation. "I am not an expert on the undead."

Seeing his brother still expected an answer, Raistlin sighed. "There are many explanations. You know as well as I do that undead are often left behind as guardians. Perhaps the draconians took some sort of sacred artifact, or perhaps, as the knight is so fond of saying, evil turned upon itself."

Caramon seemed unconvinced. "Yeah, maybe." He eyed his brother, then said abruptly, "We should clear out of here, before the rest of those baaz come back."

Raistlin looked at the cave's opening, which resembled the grinning jaw of a skull, and he fancied for a moment that the ruins were laughing. "I do not think the others will be coming back, but you are right. We should leave." He glanced around at the bundles of loot lying on the ground, and shook his head. "A pity we do not have time to go through this. Who knows what valuable objects they found down there?"

"I wouldn't touch it if you paid me," said Caramon, giving the bundles a dark glance. "All right, Your Highness. Lead the way."

Sturm was groggy but appeared to be uninjured, except for some superficial burns on his hands and arms. He plunged into the swamp, wading ankle-deep through the water. The mists rolled and twined about him.

"I just came out of there," Tas protested. "It's not as much fun as you might imagine." He shrugged his shoulders and picked up his hoopak. "Oh well. I guess I can't get any wetter." He jumped in and went floundering after Sturm.

Raistlin grimaced. Kilting up his robes around his knees, he thrust his staff into the murk to test the bottom and then stepped gingerly into the dark water.

Caramon came after him, his hand ready to steady his brother. "It's just that I thought I heard that wraith say something to you, Raist. I thought I heard it call you 'Master'."

"What a vivid imagination you have, my brother," Raistlin returned caustically. "Perhaps, when this is over, you should write a book."

16

Tika's warning. Riverwind's dilemma. The refugees decide.

aurana was in the cavern she shared with Tika, lying on the bed. She had been up a day and a night, out searching for her missing friend and the kender, and she was exhausted. Still, she couldn't sleep. She kept thinking back over everything Tika had said, everything she'd done the last time they'd been together. The clues were there, right in front of her. Laurana should have known immediately that Tika meant to go off after Caramon and that Tas would go with her. She should have done something to stop them.

"If I hadn't been so preoccupied, thinking about . . . other things . . ."

Other things such as Tanis. Laurana had just shut her eyes and was starting to drift off, when Goldmoon's voice brought her wide awake. "Laurana! They've found her!"

Two Plainsmen carried Tika on a make-shift litter into the cave where the sick and injured were tended. People gathered to see, and murmurs of pity and concern rose from the women, while the men shook their heads. They rested the litter gently on the floor.

Riverwind built up the fire, as his wife brought cool water. Laurana hovered over Tika.

"Where did they find her?"

"Lying on the bank of the stream," said Goldmoon.

"Was Tas with her?"

"She was alone. No sign of the kender."

Tika moaned in pain and stirred restlessly. Her eyes were wide open and hectically brilliant, but she saw only her feverish world. When Goldmoon bent over her, Tika screamed and began to strike her savagely with her fists. It took Riverwind and the two Plainsmen to hold her down, and even then she tried to struggle to free herself.

"What's the matter with her?" Laurana asked, alarmed.

"Look at those scratches. She's been attacked by some sort of wild animal," Goldmoon answered, bathing Tika's forehead in cool water. "A bear or a mountain lion, maybe."

"No," said Riverwind. "Draconian."

His wife raised her head, looking at him in consternation. "How can you tell?"

Riverwind pointed to several smears of gray ash on Tika's leather armor. "The claw marks are only on her arms and legs, whereas a wild beast would have left its marks all over her body. The draconian was trying to subdue her, to rape her . . . "

Laurana shuddered. Riverwind looked very grim and his wife deeply troubled.

"What's the matter?" Laurana asked. "She'll be all right, won't she? You can heal her . . ."

"Yes, Laurana, yes," said Goldmoon, reassuringly. "Leave her with me, all of you." She smoothed Tika's red curls, damp with sweat, and placed her hand on the medallion of Mishakal she wore around her neck. "You should call a meeting of the Council, husband."

"I need to talk to Tika first."

Goldmoon hesitated, then said, "Very well. I will summon you when she is awake, but only talk to her for a little while. She is in need of food and rest."

"Let me stay," Laurana pleaded. "This is my fault."

Goldmoon shook her head. "You need to go find Elistan."

Laurana didn't understand, but she could see that both were worried over something. Laurana accompanied the chieftain out of the shelter.

"What is it? What's wrong?"

"Tika was attacked by a draconian," Riverwind said. "The attack must have occurred here. Or near here."

Laurana suddenly understood the terrible implications. "The gods have mercy on us! That means our enemies have found a way into the valley! Goldmoon was right—I must tell Elistan—"

"Do so quietly," Riverwind cautioned "Bring him back with you. Say nothing to anyone else, not yet. We don't want to start a panic."

"No, of course not," Laurana said, and hastened off.

People were gathered at a respectful distance outside the cave, waiting for news. Tika, with her ready laughter and her cheerful disposition, was a favorite of nearly everyone in the camp, not counting the High Theocrat.

Maritta stopped Laurana as she left the cave, asking in concern how Tika was doing. Laurana saw that it would be easier to make a general announcement.

"She is very sick right now, but Goldmoon is with her and she will recover," Laurana told the crowd. "She needs rest and quiet."

"What happened to her?" asked Maritta.

"We won't know until she wakes up," Laurana hedged, and, managing to extricate herself, she went off in search of Elistan.

She met him on his way to Goldmoon.

"I heard about Tika," he said. "How is she?"

"She will be well, thank the gods," said Laurana. "Riverwind asks to speak to you."

Elistan looked at her searchingly. He saw the worry and fear in her face, and he was about to ask her what was wrong, then thought better of it. "I will come at once."

They returned to find a few people still lingering outside the cave. Laurana assured them once more that Tika was going to be fine and added that the best thing they could do to help her was to include her in their prayers.

Riverwind stood at the cave entrance. As Laurana and Elistan came up to speak to him, Goldmoon drew aside the blanket and bade them come in.

"Her fever has broken and her wounds are healing, but she is still shaken from her ordeal. She wants to speak to you, though. She insists on it."

Tika lay wrapped in blankets near the fire. She was still so pale that her freckles, which were the bane of her existence, stood out in stark contrast to her white skin. Yet she tried to sit up when the others entered.

"Riverwind! I have to talk to you!" she said urgently, reaching out a trembling hand. "Please, listen to me—"

"So I shall," said Riverwind, kneeling beside her, "but you must drink some of this broth first and then lie down, or my wife will throw us both out into the cold."

Tika drank the broth, and some color came back to her face. Laurana knelt down beside her.

"I was so worried about you."

"I'm sorry," Tika said remorsefully. "Goldmoon tells me that every-one was out looking for Tas and me. I never meant . . . I didn't think . . ." She gave a deep sigh and set the bowl down. Her face took on a look of resolve. "As it turned out, it was a good thing that we went."

"Wait a moment," said Riverwind. "Before you tell your tale, where is the kender? Is Tasslehoff safe?"

"As safe as can be, I suppose," said Tika bleakly. "He's with Raistlin, Caramon, and Sturm. If you can call him Sturm anymore . . ."

Seeing their look of concern, Tika sighed. "I'll start from the beginning."

She told her story, how she'd decided to go after Caramon to try to talk some sense into him.

"It was stupid; I know that now," she added ruefully.

How she and Tas entered the tunnel that went underneath the mountain, how they came out at the other end of the tunnel to find themselves in Skullcap with a dead dragon, hordes of draconians, and Grallen, prince of Thorbardin, formerly Sturm Brightblade.

"The helm he put on was cursed, or enchanted, or something. I didn't understand, and Raistlin wouldn't talk about it," Tika said.

Elistan looked grave, Riverwind doubtful, and Goldmoon anxious. She placed a cool cloth on Tika's forehead and said she should rest.

Tika took away the cloth. "I know you don't believe me. I wouldn't believe me either except I saw it for myself. I even talked to this . . . this Prince Grallen. Caramon said the helm was waiting for someone to come along and put it on so that it could force the person go to Thorbardin, to tell the king that the battle was lost."

"Three hundred years too late," said Laurana softly.

"But now, you see, they've found the way to get inside Thorbardin," said Tika. "This Prince Grallen is going to lead them there."

All of them exchanged glances. Riverwind shook his head. The Plainsman had an inherent distrust of magic, and this sounded too bizarre to be believed. He fixed on the more immediate threat.

"You heard the draconians say that an army was coming. Coming here. To the valley."

"Yes. That's why I came back. To warn you."

"Why didn't Caramon come with you?" Riverwind asked in stern disapproval. "Why did he send you back alone?"

"Caramon wanted to come," Tika said, stoutly defending him. "I told him not to. I told him he should stay with Sturm, his brother and Tas, what with Sturm thinking he's a dwarf and all. I told him I could manage fine on my own, and I did."

Her eyes hardened. Her fists clenched. "I killed that monster when it attacked me. I killed it dead!"

She saw their troubled expressions, and she burst into tears. "Caramon didn't know there was a draconian hiding in that passage! No one knew!" She collapsed back onto her pallet, sobbing.

"She must rest now," said Goldmoon firmly. "I think you know all you need to know, husband."

She ushered them outside and returned to hold Tika in her arms, letting her have her cry out.

"What do we do, Revered Son?" Riverwind asked.

"The decision is yours," Elistan replied. "Tanis placed you in charge."

Riverwind sighed deeply and gazed moodily to the south. "If you believe Tika's story—"

"Of course, we believe her!" Laurana interjected angrily. "She risked her life to carry us this warning."

"Hederick and the others won't," Riverwind observed.

Laurana fell silent. He was right, of course. The High Theocrat and his cronies didn't want to leave, and they would find any excuse to remain. She could almost hear Hederick telling the people how Tika was not to be trusted. A former thief, now a barmaid (and the gods knew what else), she had run off to be with her lover and made up this tale to cover her sins.

"Few people like Hederick," Laurana pointed out, "and they *do* like Tika."

"What is more important," added Elistan, "is that they like and admire you, Riverwind. If you tell the people danger is coming and they must leave, they will listen."

"Do you think we should leave?" Laurana asked.

"Yes," Riverwind said readily. "I have thought that since the day the dragon flew over us. We should travel south before the heavy snows block the mountain passes. This valley is no longer a safe haven. Tika's story simply confirms what I have long feared."

He paused then said quietly, "But what if I am wrong? Such a journey is fraught with uncertainty and danger. What if we reach Thorbardin and find the gates closed? Worse still, what if we never find Thorbardin at all? We could wander about the mountains until we drop from hunger and perish from the cold. I'm asking the people to leave a place of safety and walk headlong into danger. That makes no sense."

"You just said that this wasn't a place of safety," Elistan observed. "Ever since the dragon came, the people have been uneasy, afraid. They know that dragons keep watch on us, though we can't see them."

"The burden is a heavy one," Riverwind said. "The lives of hundreds are in my care."

"Not in your care alone, my friend," Elistan told him gently. "Paladine is with you. Take your fears and worries to the god."

"Will he give me a sign, Revered Son? Will the god tell me what to do?"

"The god will never tell you what to do," Elistan said. "The god will grant you the wisdom to make the right decision and the strength to carry it through."

"Wisdom." Riverwind smiled and shook his head. "I am not one of the wise. I was a shepherd . . ."

"As a shepherd, you used your skills and instincts to keep your flock safe from the wolf. That is the wisdom Paladine has given you, the wisdom on which you must rely."

Riverwind thought this over.

"Summon the people for a meeting at noontime," he said at last. "I will announce my decision then."

As they were leaving, Laurana glanced back at Riverwind over her shoulder. He was walking toward the grotto where they had built a small altar to honor the gods.

"He is a good man. His faith is strong and steadfast," she said. "Tanis chose wisely. I wish he . . ."

She stopped talking. She hadn't meant to speak her thoughts aloud.

"You wish what, my dear?" Elistan asked.

"I wish Tanis could find the same faith," Laurana said at last. "He does not believe in the gods."

"Tanis will not find faith," said Elistan, smiling. "I think it more likely that faith will find him, much as faith found me."

"I don't understand."

"I'm not sure I do either," Elistan admitted. "My heart is troubled about Tanis, yet Paladine assures me that I may safely rest those troubles in his hands."

"I hope his hands are very large," said Laurana, sighing.

"As large as heaven," said Elistan.

━━━━━━━━━━━━━━━━━━

If Riverwind spoke to Paladine, he did not seem to have found much ease or solace in his communion with the god. His face was dark and grim as he took his place at the front of the multitude. His words were not comforting or reassuring. He told the people of Tika's journey. He said the knight, Sturm Brightblade, had discovered the way to Thorbardin (he was vague as to details). Riverwind told them Tika had overheard draconians talking about an army preparing for an assault on the valley and how she had been attacked by a draconian on her way back to warn them.

Hederick pursed his lips and rolled his eyes and gave a snort. "Tika Waylan is a nice girl, but as some of you will recall, she used to be a barmaid—"

"I believe her," Riverwind said, and his firm tones silenced even Hederick, at least temporarily. "I believe that this valley, once a haven of peace, may soon become a battle ground. If we are attacked here, we have no place to run to, no refuge. We will be trapped like rats to be captured or slaughtered. The gods have sent us this warning. We do wrong to ignore it. I propose that we leave in the next few days, travel south to Thorbardin, there to meet our friends."

"Come now, be reasonable," said Hederick. He turned to the crowd, raising his hands for silence. "Don't you people find it strange that the gods chose to deliver this warning to a barmaid instead of someone honored and respected—"

"Such as yourself?" Riverwind said.

"I was going to say, such as Revered Son Elistan," said Hederick humbly, "but yes, I think the gods might also use me as their vessel."

"If they wanted to store ale, perhaps," said Gilthanas in Laurana's ear.

"Hush, brother!" she scolded him. "This is serious!"

"Of course it is, but they won't listen to Riverwind. He is an outsider, as are we." He glanced at Laurana. "You know, for the first time in my life, I begin to understand how alone and isolated Tanis must have felt when he lived among us."

"I don't feel alone among these people," Laurana protested.

"Of course not," Gilthanas answered, frowning. "You have Elistan."

"Oh, Gil, not you too," began Laurana, but he had walked off, going over to stand with the Plainsmen. They said nothing to the elf, but silently and respectfully moved to make room for him among their ranks.

Outsiders together.

Laurana should have gone after him, but she was angry at him, at Tanis, at Tika, at everyone who seemed willfully determined to misconstrue her relationship with Elistan. She worked for Elistan much as she had worked for her father: acting as a diplomat and intermediary. She had a gift for talking to people, a gift for soothing people, helping them work through anger and fear to see reason. She and Elistan were a good team. There was nothing romantic about it! He was, if anything, like a father to her.

Or a brother.

She looked at Gilthanas, and her anger softened to remorse. The two of them had once been very close. She had barely spoken to Gilthanas since she had started working with Elistan. No, it went back further than that. Since Tanis had once more entered her life.

Maybe it wasn't even Tanis, she reflected. Her brother did not approve of her relationship with the half-elf any more now than he'd done in the past. But it was her relationship with all humans that stuck in his craw. She should keep herself aloof from them, hold herself apart.

Like their father, Gilthanas was angry over the fact that the gods had seen fit to use humans to herald their return. The gods should have come to the elves, who were, after all, the chosen people. It was the humans whose transgressions had called down the wrath of the gods on the world.

"We are the good children," said Laurana to herself. "We should not have been punished. But were we really good? Or were we just never caught?"

Elves had no such doubts. Elves were certain of their place in the universe. Humans, on the other hand, were always doubting, always seeking, always questioning. Laurana liked that about humans. She did not feel so alone with her doubts.

The thought occurred to her that she'd never tried to explain this to Gilthanas. She resolved to do so. Help him understand. She looked over at him and smiled to show that she wasn't angry. He saw her but deliberately avoided meeting her eyes. Laurana sighed and brought her attention back to the meeting.

The arguing continued. Elistan supported Riverwind, as did Maritta.

"We all of us saw the dragon," Maritta told them, "with that fiend, Verminaard, on its back. Now one of our own has been attacked here in this valley, or as near this valley as makes no difference. If that isn't a sign that we are no longer safe, I don't know what is."

Yet Hederick's arguments were also persuasive, weighted with the fact that the people were in no danger now, but would be if they left the safety and shelter of caves to venture into the wilds, as was proven by the attack on Tika.

Riverwind could not argue against any of this. The burden lay on his heart, and he acknowledged it simply and openly.

"If we go, some or all of us may die," he said, "but I believe that if we stay and do nothing, if we ignore Tika's warning, we will fall victim to a cruel and brutal enemy."

He was certain, at least, of his own people joining him. The Plainsmen were united in their belief that trouble was coming and they had at last agreed, even the Que Kiri, to accept Riverwind as their chief. Their quiet confidence gave him confidence, as did his time spent with the god. During his prayers, Riverwind had heard no immortal voice making promises, he'd felt no soothing touch of an immortal hand, but he had come away from the altar with the comforting knowledge that he did not walk alone.

He was about to say more when there was a stir at the entryway. Goldmoon appeared, guiding Tika's faltering steps.

"She insisted on coming," Goldmoon said. "I urged her to rest, but she said she had to speak for herself."

People murmured softly in sympathy. The scratches on her arm had healed, but they were still visible. Pale and weak from the effects of the fever, Tika put aside Goldmoon's hand and stood on her own to have her say.

"I just want to remind all of you who it was who freed you from Pax Tharkas," Tika told them, "who saved you from slavery and death. It wasn't him, the High Theocrat." She cast a scathing glance at Hederick. "It was Tanis Half-Elven and Flint Fireforge, and they've gone to try to find Thorbardin. It was Sturm Brightblade, Caramon Majere, and Raistlin Majere, and they've gone, at great peril, to Skullcap, where they've found a way to enter Thorbardin. It was Riverwind and Goldmoon, who showed you how to survive and healed your hurts.

"They didn't have to do this, any of them. They could have gone off long ago, returned to their homeland, but they didn't. They stayed here and risked their lives to help you. I know it will be hard to leave, but . . . but I just want you to think about that."

Many did think about it and made their arguments accordingly, speaking out in favor of departing. Others were not so certain. Riverwind allowed the discussion to flow freely, but when the same arguments were being presented time and again, he called a halt.

"My mind is made up. Each of you must do the same. My wife and I and those who are going with us should be ready to depart the day after tomorrow with the first light."

He paused a moment, then added, "The way will be difficult and dangerous, and I cannot promise you that we will find safe haven in Thorbardin or anywhere in this world, for that matter. I can promise you one thing: I pledge my life to you. I will do all I can to stand between you and darkness. I will fight to defend you until the last breath leaves my body."

He left the meeting hall amid silence. His people and Gilthanas accompanied him. Tika insisted on going back to her own cave, saying she would rest better in her bed.

The people gathered around Elistan, seeking his advice and reassurance. Many wanted him to make their decisions for them—should they stay or go? This he would not do, but he insisted that each person must make up his or her own mind. He advised them repeatedly to take their cares and concerns to the gods, and he was gratified to see some go to the altar. Others, however, stalked off in a huff, demanding to know what good were gods who could not tell them what to do?

Laurana remained by his side, patiently assisting him, offering her own reassurances and advice. When the last person left, she felt utterly drained and dejected.

"I never understood before how anyone could knowingly worship an evil god. Now I do," she said to Elistan. "If you were a cleric of Takhisis, you would promise these people everything they ever wanted. Your promises would come at a terrible price and they would not be kept, but that wouldn't matter. People refuse to take responsibility for their own lives. They want someone to tell them what to do, and they want someone to blame when it all goes wrong."

"We are in the early days yet of the gods' return, Laurana," said Elistan. "Our people are like blind men who can suddenly see again. The light blinds them as much or more than the darkness. Give them time."

"Time—the one thing we don't have," Laurana said with a sigh.

In the end, most of the people decided to go with Riverwind. The terror of the dragons flying over their camp did as much to convince them to leave as any of his arguments. Hederick and his followers, however, let it be known that they planned to stay.

"We will be here waiting to welcome those who turn back," Hederick announced, adding in ominous tones, "Those who survive . . ."

Riverwind worked tirelessly that day and long into the night and all the next day, answering questions, assisting people to decide what to take, helping them pack. The refugees had made the hard journey from Pax Tharkas to the valley, and they knew already what they would need for the road. Even little children made up their small bundles.

Riverwind could not sleep the night before the departure. He lay awake, staring into the darkness, doubting himself, doubting his decision, until Goldmoon took him in her arms. He kissed her and held her, and matching his breathing to hers, he fell asleep.

Riverwind was up before dawn. The people emerged from their caves in the half-darkness, greeting friends or scolding children, who viewed this departure as a holiday and were behaving with untoward exuberance. Hederick made an appearance, sighing a great deal and bidding people farewell with a mournful air, as though he could already see them dead on the trail.

Riverwind could sense a few people starting to waver in their decisions, and he was determined to set off the moment there was the faintest light in the sky, before they had a chance to change their minds. His scouts had picked up Tanis's blazed trail, and they reported that the first part of the journey would be easy; that would help boost people's spirits and give them confidence.

The day dawned bright and sunny. Just before they started, scouts returned with news that the dwarf's trail led to a hitherto unnoticed pass between the mountains. Riverwind studied the crude map Flint had drawn up for him and the scouts agreed that his map matched with what they had found. Looking at the map, Riverwind recalled the dwarf's last enigmatic command—bring along pick-axes. Though this meant an added burden for some, he followed the dwarf's order.

The people cheered at news that a pass had been discovered, taking it for a good omen for the future. The refugees set forth quietly, without undue fuss or bother. Their harsh lives had innured them to hardship. They were accustomed to physical exertion; they had walked miles to reach this place, and they were prepared to walk many more miles. They were in good health. Mishakal had healed their sick. Even Tika was almost back to normal. Laurana noted that her friend was unusually somber and silent and chose to walk by herself, eschewing any offer of company. The wounds of the body had healed; the wounds of the heart were deeper, and not even a goddess could remedy those.

The sun shone. The day grew warm, with just enough chill in the air to keep the exertion of hiking from overheating anyone. Maritta started singing a marching song, and soon everyone joined in. The refugees made good time, trudging along the trail at a steady pace.

Riverwind felt his burden ease.

———————————

That night, after the refugees' departure, Hederick the High Theoocrat sat alone in his cave. He had spent the day regaling those of his followers who had chosen to stay with some of his best speeches. Fewer had chosen to stay han he'd expected, and they had heard all Hederick's harangues before. As darkness fell, they made some excuse to slip away, either going to their beds or gathering by the firelight to play black dots—a gambling game in which white tiles marked with black dots are arranged in various number patterns. Since the High Theocrat had laid down a strict injunction against wagering, the men thought it best to keep their game secret.

Hederick found himself alone without an audience. The night was quiet, unbelievably quiet. He was accustomed to the noise and bustle of the campsite, accustomed to walking around the camp being important. All that was gone now. Though he had taken care not to show it, he was irate that so few people had trusted him enough to stay, choosing instead to go off into the unknown with a crude, uneducated savage. Hederick told himself they would be sorry.

Now that he was alone with time to think, he was the one who was sorry. He sat in the darkness and wondered uneasily what would happen to him if that silly barmaid should turn out to be right.

17

No shadows. Too many shadows.
A dwarf's dreams.

he same sunshine that warmed the hearts and spirits of the refugees shone in the sky above Caramon, Raistlin, Sturm, and Tas. The sun brought no warmth or cheer to any of these four, however. They walked a land barren and wasted, a devastated land, bleak, empty, and desolate. They walked the Plains of Dergoth.

They had all thought nothing could be worse than wading through the swamp surrounding Skullcap. The water stank of rot and decay. They had no idea what sort of creatures could live beneath the slime-covered water, but something did. They could tell by the ripples on the surface, or sudden dartings around their feet, that they had disturbed some species of swampy denizen. They had to keep close together or lose sight of each other in the thick mists. They were forced to move slowly, with a shuffling gait, to avoid snags and dead branches hidden beneath the water.

Fortunately, the swamp was not large, and they soon left it, emerging from the murk onto ground that was dry, flat, and hard. The mists grasped at them with wispy fingers, but a cold wind soon blew them apart. They could see the sun again, and they thought well of themselves, believing they'd survived the worst. Sturm pointed to a distant mountain range.

"Beneath that peak known as Cloudseeker lies Thorbardin," Prince Grallen told them, and Raistlin cast Caramon a triumphant look.

After a short rest, they continued on, entering the Plains of Dergoth. Soon each one of them began to wish he was somewhere else, even back in the foul miasma they had just left. At least the swamp was alive. The life within was green and slimy, scaly and sinuous, creepy and slithering, but it was life.

Death ruled the Plains of Dergoth. Nothing lived here anymore. Once there had been grasslands and forest, populated by birds and animals. Three hundred years ago, this had been a battlefield, with dwarf battling dwarf in bitter contest. The field had been soaked in blood, the deer slaughtered, the birds fled. The grass was trampled and trees cut down to make funeral biers on which to burn the corpses. Still, life remained. The trees would have grown back. The grass would have flourished, the birds and animals returned.

Then came the horrific blast that brought down a mighty fortress and killed all those on both sides. The blast destroyed all living things, tearing life apart with such fury that no little bit of it survived. No trees, no grass, no beasts, no bugs. No lichen, no moss. Nothing but death. Grotesque piles of twisted, blackened, melted armor and mounds of ash littered the fire-swept ground—all that was left of two great armies whose struggles had ended in a single terrible moment, as the fire devoured their flesh, boiled their blood, and consumed them utterly.

The Plains of Dergoth, standing between Skullcap and Thorbardin, were plains of despair. The sun shone in the blue sky, but its light was cold, like the light of the faraway stars, and held no warmth for any of those forced to cross this dread place that was so horrible it even quenched the spirits of the kender.

Tasslehoff was marching along, staring down at his ash-covered boots, for staring at his boots was better than looking ahead and seeing nothing except nothing, when he noticed something odd. He looked up at the sky and back down at the ground and then said in a tense voice, "Caramon, I've lost my shadow."

Caramon heard the kender, but he pretended he hadn't. He had enough to do worrying about his brother. Raistlin was having a difficult time of it. Whatever strange energy had sustained and strengthened him on the trip to Skullcap appeared to have deserted him at their departure. The trip through the swamp had left him exhausted. He walked slowly, leaning on his staff, every step seeming to cost him an effort.

He refused to stop to rest, however. He insisted that they continue their journey, pointing out that Prince Grallen would not allow them to stop, which was probably true. Caramon was constantly having to reign in Sturm, who marched along at a rapid pace, his gaze fixed on the mountains, or he would have left the slow-moving mage far behind.

"Look, Caramon, you've lost yours, too," said Tas, relieved. "I don't feel so bad."

"Lost what?" Caramon asked, only half-listening.

"Your shadow," Tas said, pointing.

"It is probably near noon time," returned Caramon wearily. "You can't see your shadow when the sun's directly over head."

"That's what I thought," said Tas, "but look at the sun. It's almost on the horizon. Only a couple of hours 'til dark. Nope." He sighed. "Our shadows are gone."

Caramon, feeling silly, actually turned to look for his shadow. Tas was right. The sun was before him, but no shadow stretched out behind him. He could not even see his footprints, which should have shown up clearly in the fine, gray ash. He had the terrible feeling suddenly that he'd ceased to exist.

"We walk a land of death. The living do not belong here," Raistlin said, his voice barely above a whisper. "We cast no shadows. We leave no marks."

Caramon shuddered. "I hate this place."

He balefully eyed Sturm, who had stopped to wait for them and was tapping his foot impatiently. "Raist, what if that accursed helm he's wearing is leading us into a death trap? Maybe we should turn back."

Raistlin thought longingly of returning to Skullcap. He could not account for it, but while he'd been there he'd felt strong and healthy, almost whole again. Out here, he had to force himself to take each step, when what he longed to do was to drop down to the ash-gray ground and sleep in the dust of the dead. He coughed, shook his head, and made a feeble gesture toward the knight.

Caramon understood. Sturm, under the influence of the helm, was bound to go to Thorbardin. If they turned back, he would go on without them.

Raistlin plucked at Caramon's sleeve.

"We must keep moving!" he gasped. "We must not find ourselves benighted in this terrible place!"

"Amen to that, brother!" said Caramon feelingly. He placed his strong arm supportively under his twin's arm, aiding his faltering footsteps, and caught up with Sturm.

"I hope I get my shadow back," said Tasslehoff, trailing behind. "I was fond of it. It used to go everywhere with me."

They slogged on.

Tanis could see his shadow lengthening, sliding across the trail. Only a few hours of daylight left. They had descended the mountain, moving rapidly on the old dwarven road that led down among the pine trees. A few more miles and they would reach the forest. A bed of pine needles sounded very good after the uncomfortable and cheerless nights on the mountain, with rock for a mattress and a boulder for a pillow.

"I smell smoke," said Flint, coming to a sudden halt.

Tanis sniffed the air. He, too, smelled smoke. He had not noticed it particularly. Back in camp, the smell of smoke from the cook fires had been pervasive. He was tired from walking all day and didn't fully appreciate what this might mean. When he did, he lifted his head and searched the sky.

"There it is," he said, spotting a few tendrils of black drifting up out of the pine trees not far from them. He eyed the smoke. "Maybe it's a forest fire."

Flint shook his head. "It smells like burnt meat."

He scowled and cast the smoke a gloom-ridden glance from beneath his heavy brows. "Naw, it's no forest fire." He jabbed the pick-axe into the ground and stated dourly, "It's gully dwarf. That's the village I was telling you about." He glanced about. "I should have recognized where we were, but I've not come at it from this direction before."

"I've been wondering, is this the village where you were held prisoner?"

Flint gave an explosive snort. His face went very red. "As if I would go near that place in a hundred thousand years!"

"No, of course not," said Tanis, hiding his smile. He changed the subject. "We've always encountered gully dwarves in cities before. Seems strange to find them living out here in the wilds."

"They're waiting for the gates to open," said Flint.

Tanis stared at the dwarf in perplexity. "How long have they been here?"

"Three hundred years." Flint waved his hand. "You'll find nests of them all over these parts. The day the gates closed, shutting them out, the gully dwarfs squatted in front of the mountain and waited, certain the gate would open again. They're still waiting."

"At least this proves gully dwarves are optimists," Tanis remarked. He turned from the road onto a trail that veered off in the direction of the smoke.

"Where do you think you're going?" Flint demanded, standing stock still.

"To talk to them," Tanis replied.

Flint grunted. "The kender's not about, so you're missing your daily dose of foolishness for the week."

"Gully dwarves have a knack for locating that which is hidden," Tanis returned. "As we saw in Xak Tsaroth, they worm their way into secret passages and tunnels. Who knows? They may have discovered some way inside the mountain."

"If so, why are they living outside it?" Flint asked, but he trudged along after his friend.

"Maybe they don't know what they've found."

Flint shook his head. "Even if they have found the way into Thorbardin, you'll never make sense of what they tell you, and don't let the wretches talk you into staying for supper." He wrinkled his nose. "Phew! What a stink! Not even roast rat smells as bad as this!"

The smoke was thick here and the stench particularly foul. If it was a cook fire, Tanis couldn't imagine what it was the gully dwarves were cooking.

"Don't worry," he said, and covered his nose and mouth with his hand, trying to breathe as little as possible.

The trail brought them to a break in the trees. Here Flint and Tanis stopped abruptly, gazing in grim silence at the terrible scene. Every building had been set ablaze, every gully dwarf slaughtered, their bodies burned. All that was left were charred skeletons and smoldering lumps of blackened flesh.

"Not roasted rat," said Flint gruffly. "Roasted gully dwarf."

Tying rags over their noses and mouths, their eyes stinging from the smoke, Tanis and Flint walked through the destroyed village, searching for any who might still be alive. Their search proved hopeless.

Whoever had done this had struck swiftly and ruthlessly. Gully dwarves—noted cowards—had been caught flat-footed apparently, without any time to flee. They had been cut down where they stood. Some of the bodies had gaping holes in them; some were hacked to pieces. Others had half-burned arrow shafts sticking out from between their ribs. Some bore no wounds at all, but were dead just the same.

"Foul magic was at work here," said Tanis grimly.

"That's not all that was at work."

Flint reached down and gingerly picked up the hilt of a broken sword lying beside the body of gully dwarf who had been wearing an overturned soup kettle on his head. The improvised helm had saved his life for a short while perhaps, long enough for him to have made it to the very edge of camp before his attacker caught him and made him pay for breaking the sword. The gully dwarf, the kettle still on his head, lay in a twisted heap, his neck broken.

"Draconian," said Flint, eyeing the sword.

Though he had only half of it, he could easily identify the strange, serrated blades used by the servants of the Queen of Darkness.

"So they're on this side of the mountain," said Tanis grimly.

"Maybe they're out there watching us right now," said Flint and he dropped the broken sword and drew his battle axe.

Tanis drew his sword from its sheathe, and both of them stared hard into the shadows.

The sun's last rays were sinking behind the mountains. Already it was dark beneath the pine trees. The shadows of coming night mingled with the smoke, made seeing anything difficult.

"There's nothing more we can do for these poor wretches," said Tanis. "Let's get out of here."

"Agreed," said Flint, but then both froze.

"Did you hear that?" Tanis asked softly.

He could barely see Flint in the gloom.

The dwarf moved closer, put his back to Tanis's back, and whispered, "Sounds like armor rattling, something big sneaking through the trees."

Tanis recalled the enormous draconians with their large wing span, their heavy limbs encased in plate armor and chain mail. He could picture the monsters trying to slink through the pines, rustling the undergrowth, stepping on dry leaves and breaking branches—exactly the sounds they were hearing. Suddenly the noise ceased.

"They've seen us!" Flint hissed.

Feeling vulnerable and exposed out in the open, Tanis was tempted to tell Flint to make a run for the trees. He restrained himself. With the dusk and the smoke, whatever was out there might have heard them, but not yet seen them. If they ran, they would draw attention to themselves, give away their location.

"Don't move," Tanis cautioned. "Wait!"

The enemy in the forest had the same idea apparently. They heard no more sounds of movement, but they knew it was still out there, also waiting.

"Bugger this!" muttered Flint. "We can't stand here all night." Before Tanis could stop him, the dwarf raised his voice. "Lizard-slime! Quit skulking about and come out and fight!"

They heard a yelp, quickly stifled. Then a voice said cautiously, "Flint? Is that you?"

Flint lowered his sword. "Caramon?" he called out.

"And me, Flint!" cried a voice. "Tasslehoff!"

Flint groaned and shook his head.

There was a great crashing noise in the forest. Torches flared and Caramon emerged from the trees, half-carrying Raistlin, who could barely walk. Tasslehoff came running toward them, leading Sturm by the hand, tugging him along.

"Wait until you see who I found!" Tas cried.

Tanis and Flint stared at the knight, wearing the strange helm that was much too big for him. Tanis walked over to embrace Sturm. The knight drew back, bowed, then stood aloof. His gaze fixed on Flint, and it was not friendly.

"He doesn't know you, Tanis," said Tasslehoff, barely able to contain his excitement. "He doesn't know any of us!"

"He didn't get hit on the head again, did he?" Tanis asked, turning to Caramon.

"Naw. He's enchanted."

Tanis glanced at Raistlin.

"Not me," said the mage, sinking down wearily onto a tree stump that had escaped the fire. "It was the knight's own doing."

"It's a long story, Tanis. What happened here?" Caramon asked, looking grimly at the destruction of the village.

"Draconians," said Tanis. "The monsters have crossed the mountain apparently."

"Yeah, we ran into some draconians ourselves," said Caramon. "Back in Skullcap. Do you think they're still around?"

"We haven't seen any. So you managed to reach the fortress?" Tanis asked.

"Yeah, and are we ever glad to be out of that horrible place and off those accursed plains." He gave a jerk of his head in the direction from which they'd come.

"How did you find us?"

Raistlin coughed and glanced at his brother. Caramon's face flushed red. He shuffled his big feet.

"He thought he smelled food," Raistlin said caustically.

Caramon gave a sheepish grin and shrugged.

———

Flint, meanwhile, had been staring at Sturm and at Tasslehoff, who was wriggling with suppressed delight."What's wrong with Sturm?" Flint asked. "Why is he glaring at me like that? Where'd he get that helm? And why's he wearing it? It doesn't fit him. The helm is—" Flint drew closer, squinting to see the helm in the twilight— "it's dwarven!"

"He's not Sturm!" Tasslehoff burst out. "He's Prince Grallen from under the mountain! Isn't it wonderful, Flint? Sturm thinks he's a dwarf. Just ask him!"

Flint's mouth gaped. Then his jaw shut with a snap. "I don't believe it." He walked up to the knight. "Here now, Sturm. I won't be made sport of—"

Sturm clapped his hand to the hilt of his sword. His blue eyes, beneath the helm, were cold and hard. He said something in dwarven, stumbling over the words, as though his tongue had trouble forming them, but there was no mistaking the language.

Flint stood staring, dumbfounded.

"What'd he say?" Tas asked.

"'Keep your distance, hill dwarf scum,'" Flint translated, "or words to that effect." The dwarf glowered around at Caramon and particularly Raistlin. "Someone had better tell me what's going on!"

"It was the knight's own fault," Raistlin repeated, giving Flint a cold look. "I had nothing to do with it. I warned him the helm was magical, and he should leave it alone. He refused to listen. He put the helm on, and this is the result. He believes he is Prince Grallen, whoever that is."

"A prince of Thorbardin," said Flint. "One of the three sons of King Duncan. Grallen lived over three hundred years ago." Not entirely trusting Raistlin, he drew near to inspect the helm.

"Truly it is a helm fit for royalty," he admitted. "I've never seen the like!" He reached out his hand. "If I could just—"

Sturm drew his sword and held it to Flint's breast.

"Do not go nearer!" Raistlin cautioned. "You must understand, Flint. You are a hill dwarf. Prince Grallen takes you for the enemy he died fighting."

"Understand!" Flint repeated angrily. Keeping a wary eye on Sturm, he raised his hands and backed away. "I don't understand any of this." He glowered at Raistlin. "I agree with Tanis. This smacks of mage-work!"

"So it is," said Raistlin coolly, "but not mine."

He explained that he had come across the helm quite by accident and how Sturm had seen him holding it and become enamored of it.

"The helm's enchantment was undoubtedly searching for a warrior, and when Sturm picked it up, the spell took hold of him. The magic is not evil. It will do him no harm, beyond borrowing his body for a short time. When we reach Thorbardin, the prince's soul will be home. The magic will probably release the knight, and he will go back to being the same grim and dour Sturm Brightblade we have always known."

Tanis looked back at Sturm, who still had his sword drawn, still keeping a baleful eye on Flint.

"You say the magic will 'probably' release him," he said to Raistlin.

"I did not cast the spell, Tanis. I have no way of knowing for certain." He coughed again, paused, then said, "Perhaps you don't understand the significance of this. Prince Grallen knows where to find the gates of Thorbardin."

"Great Reorx's beard!" Flint exclaimed. "The mage is right!"

"I told you the key to Thorbardin lay in Skullcap."

"I never doubted you," said Tanis, "though I have to admit I was thinking more along the lines of a map." He scratched his beard. "The problem as I see it is how we keep the prince from killing Flint before we get there."

"The prince thinks we're mercenaries. We could tell the prince that Flint is our prisoner," Caramon suggested.

"You will do no such thing!" Flint roared.

"What about an emissary coming to talk peace terms?" Raistlin said.

Tanis looked at Flint, who felt called upon to argue, saying that no one in his right mind would believe it. At last, however, he gave a grudging nod. "Tell him I'm a prince too, a prince of the Neidar."

Tanis hid a smile and went to explain matters to Prince Grallen, who apparently found this acceptable, for Sturm slid his sword back into its sheathe and gave Flint a stiff bow.

"Now that that's settled," said Caramon, "do you two have anything to eat? We ran out of everything we brought."

"I don't see how you can be hungry," said Raistlin. He pressed his sleeve over his nose and mouth. "The stench is appalling! We should at least move up wind."

Tanis looked again around the ruined village, the pathetic, crumpled, and smoldering little bodies. "Why would draconians do this? Why go to the trouble to slaughter gully dwarves?"

"To silence them, of course," said Raistlin. "They stumbled across something they should not have—some secret of the draconians or some secret the draconians were charged with protecting. Thus they had to die."

"I wonder what that secret is," Tanis mused, troubled.

"I doubt we will ever know," Raistlin said, shrugging.

━━━━━━◆◆◆━━━━━━

They left the village, returning to the road that led up the mountain to Thorbardin.

"I spoke a prayer over the poor gully dwarves," said Tasslehoff solemnly, coming up to walk beside Tanis. "A prayer Elistan taught me. I commenced their souls to Paladine."

"Commended," Tanis corrected. "Commended their souls."

"That too," said Tas, sighing.

"It was good of you to think of that," said Tanis. "None of the rest of us did."

"You're busy thinking big things," said Tas. "I keep track of the small stuff."

"By the way," said Tanis, a sudden thought striking him, "I left you back in camp! How did you come to be with Raistlin, Sturm and Caramon? I thought I told you to keep watch over Tika."

"Oh, I did!" said Tas. "Wait until you hear!"

He launched into the tale, to which Tanis listened with increasing grimness.

"Where's Tika? Why isn't she with you?"

"She went back to warn Riverwind," said Tasslehoff cheerfully.

"Alone?" Tanis turned to look at Caramon, who was trying, unsuccessfully, to hide his big body behind that of his twin.

"She sneaked off in the night, Tanis," Caramon said defensively. "Didn't she, Raist? We didn't know she left."

"You could have gone after her," Tanis said sternly.

"Yes, we could have," said Raistlin smoothly, "and then where would you be, Half-Elven? Wandering about the mountain searching for the way inside Thorbardin. Tika was in no danger. The route we traveled was one known only to us."

"I hope so," said Tanis grimly.

He walked on ahead, biting back the angry words that would have done no good. He had known Raistlin and Caramon for many years, and he knew the twins had a bond that could not be broken. An unhealthy bond, or so he had always considered it, but it was not his place to say anything. He had been hoping that the romance blossoming between Tika and Caramon would give the big man strength enough to break free of his brother's death grip. Apparently not.

Tanis had no idea of what had happened back in Skullcap, but he guessed from the unhappy look Caramon had given his twin that Tika had tried to persuade Caramon to go with her and Raistlin had prevented it.

"If anything happens to her, I will take it out of Raistlin's hide," Tanis muttered to himself.

At least Tika'd had sense enough to carry the warning to Riverwind. He hoped she had reached the refugees in time and that they would heed the warning and escape. He could not go back there now, much as he would have liked to. His mission to Thorbardin had just become eight hundred times more urgent.

Flint marched along at the rear, following after Sturm, unable to take his eyes from the knight and the marvelous helm he wore—or rather, according to Raistlin, the helm that wore him. The dwarf did not trust magic of any kind, especially magic that had anything to do with Raistlin, and no one would ever persuade him that this was not somehow Raistlin's doing.

Flint was forced to admit that something had happened to change Sturm. The knight could speak a few words of dwarven learned from Flint over time but not many. He certainly could not speak the language of Thorbardin, that was slightly different from the language of the hill dwarves.

After they made camp, Tanis asked the prince to describe the route to Thorbardin. Prince Grallen readily did so, speaking of a ridge line they would follow up the mountain. He told them how far they would travel and how to locate the secret gate, though he would not tell them what to do to open it when they found it.

Tanis looked to Flint for verification. Flint did not know specifically which ridge the prince meant, but it did sound plausible, though he didn't say as much.

All the dwarf would say, grumbling, was that he supposed they'd find out the truth of the matter tomorrow and he wished Tanis would let them get some rest.

As Flint lay down, he looked into the sky, searching the heavens until he found the red star that was the fire of Reorx, Forger of the World.

Flint found he liked the idea of being an emissary. He had protested, of course, when Raistlin first proposed it, simply because it was Raistlin, but the dwarf had not protested too strongly. He'd given in without much of a fuss.

The thought came to him: What if I am truly an emissary? What if I am the dwarf to bring the warring clans together at last?

He lay awake a long time, watching the sparks fly across the sky as the god went about his eternal task of forging creation, and he saw himself as one of those sparks, only his light would shine forever.

Leaving the valley. Treacherous trail.
The keystone.

The first day's travel for the refugees had been relatively easy. They had not gone far on the second day before traveling grew more difficult. The trail wended its way upward, and as it did so, it grew steeper, more narrow, until at last it devolved into a ribbon-thin path with sheer wall on one side and a terrifying drop of hundreds of feet onto the rocks on the other. Beyond lay the pass. They were almost there, but they had to cross this first.

They would have to walk this perilous part of the trail single-file, and Riverwind called a halt. Many were already terrified at just the sight of the precipice and the fall so close to their feet. Among these, as Tanis had foreseen, was Goldmoon.

She had been born and raised on the Plains of Dust, a flat and featureless land stretching endlessly for miles with nothing between her and the glorious sky. This world of mountains and valleys was new to Goldmoon and she had not grown used to it. Riverwind had been up and down the line, encouraging the others, when one of the Plainsmen came running for him.

"It is Goldmoon," the man said. "You had better come."

The Plainsman found his wife with her back pressed against the side of the cliff, her face deathly pale, trembling in terror. He approached her, and the hand that seized hold of him and gripped him like death was freezing cold.

She was at the head of the line. He had not forgotten her terror of high places, and he had tried to persuade to walk at the end, but she would have none of it. She was cured of that, she said, and she had walked forward confidently. She might have made it, for the distance was not far, but she committed the fatal error of looking down. She could see herself plunging through the air, landing on the rock-strewn ground, bones breaking, skull crushed, blood spattering the stones and pooling beneath her broken body.

"I am sorry, but I cannot do this, husband," she said in a low voice. When he urged her gently forward, she went stiff. "Give me a few moments."

"Goldmoon," he said softly, looking back down the trail, where the line of refugees stood waiting. "Others are watching you, looking to you for courage."

She stared at him pleadingly. "I want to go. I know I must go, but I can't move!"

She glanced over the edge at the sheer side of the cliff face, the rocks, trees, and the valley that seemed so far, far below her feet, and she shuddered and shut her eyes again.

"Don't look down," he counseled. "Look up. Look ahead. See that V-shape cut up there. That is the pass through the mountain. We have only to cross that and we are on the other side!"

Goldmoon looked, shook her head and pressed her back against the wall.

"Have you prayed to the gods for courage?" Riverwind asked his wife.

Goldmoon gave him a tremulous smile. "The courage of Mishakal is in my heart, husband, but it has yet to make its way to my feet."

He loved her very much at that moment, and he kissed her cheek. She flung her arms around him, clasping him so tightly that she nearly cut off his breathing. He led her back off the trail onto solid ground and wondered what he was going to do.

There would be others like his wife who would find this trail difficult, if not impossible, to walk. He had to think how to help them.

He told the people to stop to rest while he considered this problem. As he was pondering, one of the advance scouts came hastening back down the trail. He motioned to Riverwind.

"We have found something strange," the Plainsman reported. "Up ahead, at the opening to the pass, the dwarf's pick-axe lies on the ground."

"Perhaps it grew too heavy for him to carry," he suggested.

The scout smiled and shook his head. "I have no great love for dwarves as you know, Chieftain, but I never yet met the dwarf who could not carry the weight of this mountain on his back, if he were so minded. It is not likely that he would leave behind a pick-axe."

"Unless there was some good cause," Riverwind said thoughtfully. "There is nothing else? Nothing to suggest he and Tanis were attacked or met with some other terrible fate?"

"If there had been fighting, we would see signs of a battle, but there is no blood on the stones, no gouges in the dirt, and no packs or other pieces of equipment left behind. To my mind, the pick-axe was left deliberately, as some sort of sign, but what it means, none of us can say."

"Leave it where it is," said Riverwind. "Let no man touch it. I'll come look at it. Perhaps I can read this puzzle."

The Plainsman nodded and returned to his fellows. The scout, whose name was Eagle Talon, walked the trail with the sure-footed ease of a mountain lion. Riverwind watched him go and eyed the trail ahead. It widened in some places, enough for two or even three people to walk abreast. He could post men like Eagle Talon, who had no problem with the heights, at each of those places, prepared to offer a strong arm and reassuring hand to those who made their way along the path.

Riverwind explained his plan, and called for volunteers, choosing men who were stout, sturdy, and had no fear of the dizzying heights, posting them at various points along the trail. He went to Goldmoon, told her what she should do, and indicated the first man, who stood on a ledge only a few feet away, his hand outstretched.

"You just have to cross a short distance on your own," he said to her. "Don't look down. Keep your back to the wall and look only at Nighthawk."

Goldmoon gave a tremulous nod. She had to do this. Her husband was counting on her. She whispered the name of the goddess, then, shivering, she edged her way along the trail, moving her feet an inch at a time. Her heart pounded in her chest, her mouth was dry as stone. She made it and clasped Nighthawk's hand with convulsive strength. He helped her sidle past him, holding onto her firmly and speaking to her encouragingly. The next man was farther away, but she looked back at Riverwind and smiled a triumphant, though shaky smile and crept on.

Riverwind was proud of her. His plan seemed to be working, but it was slow going, so very slow. Some of the people would have no difficulty, of course. Maritta, coming after Goldmoon, traveled the trail with confidence, waving away Nighthawk's helping hand. Others, like Goldmoon, hung on for dear life. Some could not stand but were forced to crawl along on their hands and knees.

At this rate, it would take all day or longer for the people to reach the pass. Leaving Elistan in charge, Riverwind went on ahead to see for himself the pick-axe the dwarf had unaccountably left behind.

―――――――――――

Riverwind agreed with Eagle Talon. The axe had been left here deliberately. He wondered why. Not to mark the trail, which was obvious at this point. He noticed the striped rock, different from the others around it, and he saw how the point of the axe rested on the rock.

Not just on the rock, he realized, squatting down to look at it more closely. The point was actually wedged in gently beneath the rock.

He stood up, arms folded across his chest, looking intently all around, up and down the mountainside. His scouts had traversed the cut and returned to say that it did indeed cross the mountain. They had found Tanis's markers on the other side.

What, then, did this sign mean? That it was important, he had no doubt.

At least, he thought, watching the slow progress of the refugees up the trail, I have time to figure it out.

He was not to have as much time as he thought.

―――――――――――

Late in the afternoon, when the sun began to sink, blanketing the trail in shadow, Riverwind called a halt to the ascent. He was pleased with the progress they had made. Only about a hundred more people had yet to make the treacherous walk up the trail to the pass. They had not lost a single person, though there had been heart-stopping moments as feet slipped and hands lost their grip. Or when a boy froze on the trail, unable to move, and one of the men had to edge his way down to rescue him.

Those who had crossed were now preparing to spend the night in the pass, relieved that this part of the trip was over and speaking hopefully that the worst was behind them. Riverwind's scouts reported that they had found what appeared to be an ancient dwarven road. The going would be easier from now on.

Riverwind calculated that they would be through the pass by midmorning. Some of those who had not yet dared the trail would require more time, for among them were several who had not found the courage to even make the attempt. They had taken some comfort in the fact that their fellows had managed to cross without incident and told Riverwind they thought they could do so themselves after a night's rest. Everyone was in good spirits, preparing to make camp for the night. Laurana and Elistan had both offered to remain with this group and Riverwind left them, confident that the people were in good hands.

The evening was cold, and camping among the rocks was far from comfortable. Riverwind discouraged the refugees from building fires. Light on the mountain would show up like a beacon in the darkness. The people wrapped themselves in cloaks and blankets and huddled together for warmth, wedging themselves in among the rocks and boulders as best they could, prepared to spend an uncomfortable and cheerless night. Riverwind walked the rounds, spoke with those on guard duty, made certain they were awake and alert. All the while, he kept wondering about the pick-axe.

The last thing he did, before going to bed, was to stand over the pick-axe, pondering it by the cold light of the stars, wondering what it meant.

———————◆———————

Riverwind was wakened by a frightened cry from his wife. He woke to find Goldmoon clutching him by the shoulder.

"Something is out there!"

He felt it too, and so did many others, for he heard people crying out and stirring restlessly around him. Riverwind was on his feet, when one of the guards came running.

"Dragons!" he said softly, urgently, keeping his voice down. "Flying over the mountains!"

"What is it?" people asked fearfully, as Riverwind accompanied the guard out of the pass and into an open area where he could see. He looked to the north. A shudder went through him.

Dark wings obliterated the stars. Dragons at the far end of the valley. They flew slowly, their wings making wide, sweeping motions, as though the beasts carried a burden and were struggling to remain airborne. Riverwind was reminded of the struggles made by a hawk trying to carry off a prairie rabbit.

Dragonfear crept over him, but he recognized it now and refused to give in to it. He was about to summon his warriors when he heard footfalls, and turning, he found his people gathered around him, silent and expectant, awaiting his orders.

"This is the attack on our camp Tika warned us about," he said, marveling at his own calm. "I do not think the dragons know we have left. Tell the people they *must* remain quiet, and they must keep hidden! Their lives depend on it. A baby's wail could give us away."

Goldmoon hastened away, in company with some of the other Plainsmen, and began explaining the danger.

Here and there, a child whimpered, there were moans and stifled cries as the dragonfear spread, but Goldmoon and others were on hand to provide comfort with prayers to the gods. Soon silence, like a heavy, smothering blanket, settled over the camp. People crouched among the rocks and boulders in the shadow of the pass and clasped their children to their hearts, waiting.

The dragons reached a point in the sky above the burned-out grove. Lunitari was half-full this night, and her light shone on red scales and on a helmed figure riding the lead dragon. Riverwind recognized the horned helm of Lord Verminaard. Behind him flew four more red dragons. As Riverwind watched, the flight of the dragons slowed. They began to perform slow and laborious turns in mid-air, their flight now taking them over the caves where the refugees had made their home.

These were not the graceful, wheeling red dragons Riverwind had seen battling in the skies over Pax Tharkas. These dragons flew ponderously, and he once again had the impression they carried a heavy load.

Gilthanas appeared at his elbow.

"What of Laurana and the people on the other side of the trail?" he asked.

Riverwind had been thinking of Hederick and those who had remained behind, and he could only shake his head, meaning that for them there was no hope. Then he realized this was not what Gilthanas meant. He meant those who had not yet ventured along the trail. They were camped out in the open, exposed on the side of the mountain with no shelter, nowhere to conceal themselves.

"We have to get them across," Gilthanas urged.

"In the darkness? It's too risky." Riverwind shook his head. "We must hope the dragons will be content to attack the caves and not think to come this way."

He braced himself, prepared to watch the dragons breathe fire on the caves, but that did not happen. Instead, the dragons continued to circle the valley, flying lower and lower, spiraling down in formation. The dragon bearing Verminaard remained hovering overhead, watching from above. Riverwind was puzzled by this, and then he saw something even more puzzling.

Bundles were falling off the backs of the dragons; at least, that's how it appeared. Riverwind could not imagine what the dragons were dropping and then he sucked in his breath in horror.

These were not bundles. They were draconians and they were leaping off the dragons' backs! He could see the monster's wings spread as they jumped, see the moonlight glint on their scaly hides and gleam off the tips of their swords.

The draconians' wings slowed their descent, giving them the ability to glide to a landing once they reached the ground. The draconians were not adept at dragon-jumping, or so it appeared. Some fell headlong into the thick stands of trees and many plunged, kicking and flailing, into the stream. Howls of rage split the frosty air. He could hear orders being shouted by those on the ground, as officers tried to sort through the confusion, find their men, and form them into ranks.

That would happen soon enough. The draconians would march up to the caves and find their prey was gone. They would come searching for them.

"You're right," he said to Gilthanas. "We must get the others across." He shook his head softly. "The gods help us!"

Walking the steep and narrow path had been difficult and frightening by day. Now he was going to ask these people to walk it by night, and they must do so in the darkness. And in silence.

Riverwind made his way back across the treacherous trail and found Elistan and Laurana waiting for him.

Elistan forestalled him. "We have already roused everyone and they are ready."

"Poor Hederick," Laurana said quietly, watching the draconians start to swarm into the hills.

Riverwind found it difficult to dredge up any pity for that man or those deluded enough to trust him. Nor did he have time to waste thinking about him. He looked at the assembled group. Their pale faces glimmered white in the darkness, but all were quiet, prepared. Riverwind hated to do what he had to do next, but there was no choice.

"We must bind cloths around their mouths."

Elistan and Laurana both stared at him, perhaps wondering if he'd gone mad.

"I don't understand—" Laurana began.

"Silence is our only hope of escaping," Riverwind explained. "If someone should fall, the draconians might hear his screams."

Laurana blanched, covering her mouth with her hand.

"Of course," Elistan said quietly, and hurried off.

"Are you all right?" he asked Laurana.

"Yes," she managed faintly.

"Good." Riverwind was brisk, matter-of-fact. "We have to get them started now. No time to waste. The draconians will attack the caves, but it won't take them long to figure out we're gone. Then they'll come looking for us."

"Will we be safe in the pass?" Laurana asked.

"I hope so," Riverwind replied, trying to reassure himself as much as her. "We did not know the pass was there, and we have lived here for months. With luck and help from the gods, the draconians will not find us. If they do, we can defend ourselves against attack."

He stopped talking, sucked in a breath. He saw in dazzling brilliance, as though lightning had streaked across his mind, the pick-axe lying beneath the striped rock that did not belong there.

"Make haste!" he told Laurana. "Keep them moving. Don't let anyone stop." He turned away, then turned back. "If anyone balks, he must remain behind. We don't have time to mollycoddle people. Keep everyone moving!"

He made his own way back across the treacherous trail, thinking, as he did so, that it was actually easier to cross in the darkness. He couldn't see how far he had to fall or the sharp rocks waiting to break his body. The men who had done this same task today took up their places again, standing at intervals, ready to assist those who were already beginning to cross. Elistan remained at the start, saying reassuring words and giving Paladine's blessing to all. Gags bound around their mouths, the people began to edge their way along the path.

Riverwind paused to glance back in the direction of the camp. Some of the draconians were now running toward the caves. Once they reached the living area, they would be thrown into confusion when they found their victims were gone. They would think the people had retreated deeper into the caves, and they would search the tunnels and passages. Eventually, the draconians would realize the truth. The caves had been abandoned. Verminaard knew the refugees could not go north. The most logical route lay to the south. That's where he would look first.

Riverwind glanced to the east, wondering how many hours they had until daylight.

He did not think he had many . . .

"Come with me," he said to his warriors. "You won't need your weapons. You need pick-axes! And bring me some of the men who worked in the mines!"

●━━━━━━━━➤━━━━

The first wave of draconians broke on the cliffs where the refugees had once dwelt. Howls meant to strike fear into the hearts of their victims changed to curses as they entered cave after cave and found crude furniture, toys, and clothes, and stores of food and water the refugees had been forced to leave behind.

Riverwind took the miners to where Flint had left the pick-axe. He showed them the axe and the striped rock, explaining to them what he thought the dwarf was trying to tell them.

The miners examined the area as best they could by moonlight and starlight, agreeing that this rock was a keystone. But whether it would work or not, they could not say.

The crossing proceeded, though with agonizing slowness. Riverwind kept watch on the sky. There was as yet no light visible, but the stars were starting to fade.

The last few people were creeping across. One, a young woman, staggered and fell to the ground. Tears streamed down her cheeks and she was shaking, but she had not made a sound. Goldmoon took hold of her and led her away.

Laurana came next to last. Gilthanas, one of those doing duty on the cliff face, spoke to her in elven as he helped her across. She clasped his hand and kissed him.

Elistan came across last. He carried a child on his back, the little boy's hands clasped around his neck. The cleric's steps were firm. He did not falter. The little boy's mother, waiting on the other side, hid her face in her hands, unable to watch.

"That was fun, Elistan," said the little boy, pulling the gag off his mouth when they reached safety. "Can we do it again?"

People laughed, though their laughter was shaky. The men left the trail, and everyone started to move into the pass.

Back in the camp, the draconians emerged from the caves. The sky was light enough now that Riverwind could easily see what was transpiring. Verminaard's dragon landed on the ground. Draconians swarmed around the Highlord. He leaned over the neck, conferring with his officers. At his command, the other three red dragons flew across the valley. One headed east. One flew west.

One flew south, straight toward them.

The dragon was not looking in their direction, however. The beast stared down below, searching the floor of the valley.

"Quickly, quickly!" Riverwind urged in soft tones, herding the people as he had once herded his sheep. "Take shelter in the pass. Move as far back as you can."

The people hurried. There was no panic, and Riverwind was just thinking they might actually succeed in escaping, when a cry pierced the air, "Wait! Don't leave me! Don't leave me!"

The dragon heard the voice. The beast lifted its head, shifted its gaze.

Cursing, Riverwind turned around.

Hederick was running along the trail, his flabby gut bobbing up and down as he ran, his face blotchy, his mouth gaping wide. His cronies trailed behind him, pushing and shoving each other in their panicked haste.

Hederick came to the precipice. He looked at Riverwind, looked down, and his face paled.

"I can't cross that!"

"The rest of us did," said Riverwind coldly, and he pointed at the dragon, who had changed direction and was now flying toward them.

Hederick's friends shoved him aside, stepped onto the trail, and hurried across. Hederick, quivering in fear, crept along after them.

He made it safely, and once on the other side, he came storming up to Riverwind, about to launch into demands. Riverwind seized hold of the man and gave him a shove into the arms of several Plainsmen, who caught hold of the High Theocrat and hustled him off into the pass.

The dragon lifted its head and gave a great bellow.

Riverwind ran for the place where the dwarf had left the pick-axe. Glancing over his shoulder, he saw the dragon's call had alerted Lord Verminaard. His dragon leapt off the ground and took to the skies. The draconians were starting to run in this direction as well. They could move faster over the ground than humans, for they used their wings to aid them. Hopping and leaping, they flowed over the trail like a scaly river.

Verminaard's dragon bore him swiftly toward the pass. The draconians were closing on the pass much faster than Riverwind could have believed possible.

Riverwind seized hold of the pick-axe He looked to see that the last few stragglers were safely inside the pass.

"Paladine, be with us!" Riverwind prayed then, in a nod to Flint, he added, "Reorx, guide my hand."

Riverwind struck the striped rock with the pick-axe, hitting it at the place where the point had rested. The rock went bounding down the mountainside, and Riverwind scrambled backward. At first, nothing happened, and his heart sank. He looked to see the dragon swooping toward them. Verminaard had his hand outstretched, pointing at the pass, guiding the beast.

Then the earth shuddered. There was a rending, grinding sound and it seemed to Riverwind's astonished gaze as if the side of the mountain was on the move, rushing down on top of him.

He turned and ran for the safety of the pass. Boulders bounded off other boulders and went sailing over his head. With a sound like rumbling thunder, the rock slide cascaded down the mountain side, taking with it the trail the refugees had just walked. The opening to the pass began to fill with chunks of stone.

Riverwind flattened himself on the ground, his arms protecting his head. He could not see the dragon, but he could hear its frustrated roars. The rock slide continued for several more moments, then ended in sudden silence, broken only by a few rocks shifting or settling into place.

Riverwind cautiously raised up to look. The face of the landscape had changed. The entrance to the pass was choked with enormous boulders. He heard the dragon's wings flapping on the other side of the newly made stone wall. The dragon could not land. The rock slide had taken what level ground there was down the mountainside. He heard sounds as though the beast was making some attempt to claw its way through the debris into the pass. This must have proven ineffectual, for the dragon soon ceased its efforts.

Riverwind looked skyward. Snow capped peaks soared high above him on either side. He wondered fearfully if the dragon would attempt to fly over the pass. The cleft in the mountain was steep and narrow; he doubted if the dragon would be able to fit inside. It would certainly risk injury to its wings. The dragon might still be able to deal destruction from far above.

Riverwind waited tensely for the shadow of the massive red body and wings to blot out the dawn, but the dragon did not appear. Riverwind realized it had flown off only when he no longer felt the dragonfear. For the moment, they were safe.

For the moment.

Riverwind wended his way among the rocks to join the others. They were hugging each other and laughing, weeping and praying in thankfulness. Riverwind could not join in their celebration. He knew full well why Verminaard had not attacked. There was no need to risk his dragon in the pass when all he had to do was wait for them to come out the other side. As Tika had told them, there were draconians on the opposite side of the mountain. The refugees could not stay holed up in this pass forever. They must eventually come out, and the Highlord's forces would undoubtedly be waiting for them.

Their one hope was that Tanis, Flint, and the others could find the Gates to Thorbardin.

Otherwise, the refugees would be at a literal dead end.

BOOK TWO

I

Prince Grallen returns. The Gates of Thorbardin. Now what?

ed by Sturm under the magical influence of the enchanted helm, the companions wended their way up Cloudseeker, climbing along a steep defile that cut into the side of the mountain wall. The defile was one among many, and without the prince to guide them, they would have either never found it or would have chosen it by merest accident.

Tanis continued to mark the trail for the refugees, wondering more than once as he did so if he was wasting his time. He often looked back the way they had come, hoping to see some sign that they were safe, but the pass was often shrouded in fog or low hanging clouds, and he could see nothing.

The climb proved to be relatively easy. Whenever they came to a part of the defile that was steep and could have been hard to traverse, crude stairs carved into the rock wall provided safe passage. Not even Raistlin found the going difficult. A night's rest had allowed him to recover his strength. He said that the pure, chill mountain air opened his lungs. He coughed less and was actually in a relatively good mood.

The sun was bright, the sky cloudless. They could see the desolate plains spread out beneath them and far off in the distance the ruined fortress, looking, as Caramon said, like a skull on a platter. They made good time, at least as far as Tanis was able to judge, considering he had no idea where they were going. He asked Sturm more than once to point out their destination, but the knight only shook his helmed head, refusing to answer, and continued to climb. Tanis looked to Flint, but the dwarf shrugged. He was obviously highly skeptical about all this.

"If there is a gate in the side of the mountain, I don't see it," he huffed.

As they climbed higher, the air grew colder and thinner. The humans, the half-elf, and the kender began to feel dizzy. Their breathing grew labored.

"I hope we don't have much further to go," Tanis said, catching up to Sturm. "If we do, I'm afraid some of us aren't going to make it."

He looked back at Raistlin, who had slumped down to the ground. So much for pure mountain air. Caramon leaned against a boulder. Tasslehoff was wobbly on his feet. Even Flint was breathing hard, though he refused to admit anything was wrong.

Sturm raised his head and peered through the helm's eyeslits. "Almost there."

He pointed to a stone ledge about five feet wide jutting out from the side of the mountain. The defile ended here. Tanis looked back at Flint, and to his surprise, the old dwarf's eyes were bright, his face flushed. He stood smoothing his beard with his hand.

"I think this is it, lad," he said softly. "I think we're close!"

"Why? Do you see something?" Tanis asked.

"Just a feeling I have," said Flint. "It feels right to me."

Tanis looked around. "I feel nothing. I see nothing, no sign of any gate."

"You won't," Flint said proudly, "not with those half-elf, half-human eyes of yours. Admit it, my friend. You would have never found the way."

"I readily admit it," said Tanis, adding with a smile, "Would you?"

"I would have," Flint insisted, "if I'd been interested in finding it, which I wasn't up until now."

Tanis's gaze scanned the vast gray expanse of rock before them. "If we do find the gate, will the mountain dwarves let us in?"

"That's not what I'm asking myself," Flint returned.

Tanis gave him a questioning glance.

"What I'm asking is if there are any dwarves beneath the mountain to say 'yeah' or 'nay' to the matter. Perhaps the reason the gate has remained shut for three hundred years is that there is no one left alive to open it."

Sturm was already on the move, and Flint hiked after him. Tanis looked back at the others.

"We're coming," said Caramon.

Raistlin nodded, and aided by his staff and his brother, he began to climb. Tasslehoff trailed along after.

They left the defile and walked onto the rock ledge.

"Dwarves built this," said Flint, stamping on the ledge. "We're here, Half-Elven. We're here!"

The ledge was smooth and level. It had once been much wider, but parts of it had either fallen off or crumbled away over time. They had not gone far along the ledge, perhaps thirty feet, when Sturm came a halt and turned to face the rock wall. Flint eagerly scanned the stone. The dwarf's eyes grew moist. He gave a long, tremulous sigh. When he spoke, his voice was husky.

"We have found it, Tanis. The Gate to Thorbardin."

"We have?" Tanis looked up and he looked down and saw nothing but smooth rock.

Sturm approached the wall, his hand outstretched.

"Watch this!" Flint said softly.

Raistlin elbowed Tanis out of his way in his eagerness to see what was about to happen. Tasslehoff hurried to Sturm's side and stared expectantly at the blank wall.

"I would not stand there if I were you," Sturm warned.

"I don't want to miss anything," Tas protested.

Sturm shrugged and turned to face the mountain. Raising his hands, he cried out words in dwarven.

"I am Grallen, son of Duncan, King Beneath the Mountain. My spirit returns to the halls of my fathers. In the name of Reorx, I call upon the gate to open."

At the mention of the god's name, Flint snatched off his helm and held it close to his chest. He bowed his head.

A beam of light blazed from the ruby in the center of Sturm's helm. Red and bright as the flame of Reorx's fire, the light illuminated the side of the mountain.

The ground rumbled, knocking Tanis to his hands and knees. The mountain shook and trembled. Raistlin balanced himself with his staff. Caramon lost his footing and slid part way down the trail. An enormous gate some sixty feet in height and thirty feet wide appeared in the side of the mountain. A grinding, screeching sound came from somewhere inside.

"Get out of the way!" Flint roared. He seized hold of Tasslehoff by the scuff of his neck and dragged him to one side.

Like a cork in an ale barrel, the gigantic block of stone burst out of the side of the mountain and went rumbling over the ledge right where the kender had been standing.

Now that the gate was open, they could see the enormous screw mechanism that was shoving the huge block of granite forward. The gate grated along the ledge and continued on, past the edge. The mechanism that operated the gate whined and groaned, pushing the gate farther and farther until the heavy stone block hung out over the side of the mountain.

The shaft that propelled the gate was made of oak, massive and strong, but it could not withstand the strain and snapped. The stone block broke off and went plunging down the side of the mountain, landing with a crash on the rocks below. They stared at the ruins in shocked silence. Then Raistlin spoke.

"The Gate to Thorbardin is open," he said, "and it cannot now be closed."

———————————◆◆◆———————————

Tanis checked to see that everyone was all right. Caramon was making his way back up the defile. Flint was fending off Tasslehoff, who was trying to give the dwarf a hug, claiming that he'd saved his life.

"Where's Sturm?" Tanis asked in alarm, fearing he'd been crushed.

"He went inside," said Raistlin, "shortly after the gate opened."

"Damn and blast it!" muttered Tanis.

They peered inside, but they could see nothing, hear nothing. Warm air with a strong earthy smell to it wafted out of the cavern.

"It smells of darkness," Caramon muttered.

Tanis drew his sword, as did Caramon. Raistlin reached into his pouch. Flint, his expression grave, hefted his battle-axe. They started to move inside slowly and cautiously.

All except Tasslehoff.

"I'll bet I'm the first kender to set foot in Thorbardin in three hundred years!" he cried, and waving his hoopak, he dashed inside shouting, "Hello, dwarves! I'm here!"

"Three hundred centuries is more like it," said Flint irately. "No kender were ever permitted underneath the mountain. With good reason, I might add!"

The dwarf went lumbering after Tas. Tanis and the others were hurrying after him when, from out of the darkness, came Tasslehoff's voice, making the most dreaded sound anyone can hear when dealing with kender.

"Oops!"

"Tas!" Tanis yelled, but there was no answer.

———————◆——◆◆——————

Pale sunlight streamed inside the gate, lighting their way for a short distance. The companions soon left the light behind, however, and were swallowed up in impenetrable and endless night.

"I can't see my nose in front of my face," Caramon grumbled. "Raist, light your staff."

"No, don't!" Tanis cautioned "Not yet. We don't want to give ourselves away. And keep your voices down."

"The dwarves already know we're here," Caramon pointed out irritably, "unless they're deaf."

"Maybe so," said Tanis, "but let's err on the side of caution."

"The dwarves can see us in the dark," Caramon muttered to his twin. "Tanis can see in the dark! *We're* the ones left blind."

From out of the darkness came the sound of running footfalls and the clanking and rattling of armor. Caramon raised his sword, but Tanis shook his head.

"It's Flint," he told them. "Did you find Tas?" he called to the dwarf as Flint came up to them.

"*And* Sturm," Flint reported grimly. "Look! There. See for yourselves. The fool kender's got himself in a fix this time. They've been captured by Theiwar!"

"I can't see a thing!" Caramon muttered.

"Hush, my brother," said Raistlin softly.

Tanis with his elven sight saw Sturm lying on the floor, either dead or unconscious. Tasslehoff was crouched at the knight's side, holding the helm of Prince Grallen in his hands. By the looks of it, he had been about to put the helm on, when he was interrupted.

Six dwarves, clad in chain mail that came to their knees and armed with swords, stood around the kender. At least, Tanis assumed they were dwarves. He wasn't certain, for he'd never seen any dwarves quite like them. They were thin and looked undernourished, with long unkempt black hair and scraggly black beards. Their skin was not the nut-brown complexion of most dwarves but was a sickly white, pale as a fish's underbelly. He could smell the stench of their unwashed bodies. Three of the dwarves were pointing their swords at Tasslehoff. The other three had gathered around Sturm with the apparent intent of stealing his armor.

"What's happening?" Caramon demanded in a loud whisper. "What's going on? I can't see!"

"*Shirak*," said Raistlin, and the crystal on his staff burst into bright white light.

Tanis rounded him angrily. "I thought I told you—"

Piercing shrieks interrupted him. He turned in astonishment to see the dwarves fling their swords to the ground in order to shield their eyes with their hands. They moaned in pain and cursed in rage.

Flint looked back at Raistlin. The dwarf's eyes narrowed.

"Why do you stare at me?" the mage demanded. "You said these were Theiwar dwarves. Theiwar are known to be extremely sensitive to light."

"Known by dwarves, maybe," Flint countered, glowering. "I never met the human who ever heard of Theiwar."

"Well, now you have," Raistlin returned coldly.

Flint glanced sidelong at Tanis, who shook his head. The half-elf had never heard of Theiwar dwarves, and he'd been friends with Flint for years. Raistlin was certainly acting strangely this trip—even for Raistlin.

"Be gone, Theiwar scum!" Flint commanded in Dwarvish. He strode forward, his axe raised menacingly.

"Hill dwarf dung!" snarled one of the Theiwar, and he began to mumble to himself and wiggle his fingers.

"Stop him!" Raistlin warned. "He's casting a magic spell!"

Flint skidded to a halt. "You're the mage!" he bellowed at Raistlin. "You stop him!"

"Then get out of my way."

Flint flung himself flat on the floor as lightning bolts streaked overhead. The bolts struck the Theiwar in the chest, and a shattering concussion shook the chamber. The Theiwar's smoldering body crumpled. His fellows quit trying to rob Sturm and ran off down the corridor. The rattling of their chain mail and their pounding boots could be heard for a short time, then abruptly stopped.

"They haven't gone far," Tanis warned.

"Filthy Theiwar!" Flint fumed. He glared at Tanis. "I said it was a mistake to come back! I'll go on down the corridor and keep watch. You see to the knight." He started off, then added in a roar, "And take that helm away from the kender!"

———————————

Raistlin stood over Sturm, shining his light on the knight, as Caramon examined him. "He's alive. His life-beat is strong. I don't know what's wrong with him. I can't find any wounds . . ."

Tanis looked sternly at Tas.

"I didn't do it!" Tas said immediately. "I found him on the floor, unconscious. The helm was next to him. I think he must have dropped it."

"The helm dropped him, so to speak," said Raistlin. "Since Prince Grallen is once more in the hall of his fathers, the magic of the helm has released the knight. When Sturm wakes, he will be himself—more's the pity."

Tanis held out his hand to the kender. "I think you'd better give me the helm."

Tasslehoff clutched the helm to his chest. "Those ugly dwarves were going to steal it! I saved it! Couldn't I try it on just once? I'd love to be a dwarf—"

"Over my dead body!" Flint hollered from out of the darkness.

"Sturm!" Caramon was shaking his friend by the shoulder. "Sturm! Wake up!"

The knight groaned and opened his eyes. He stared at Caramon in confusion for a moment, then he recognized his friend.

"Why did you let me sleep so long? You should have wakened me. It must be well past my turn to stand watch." Sturm sat up and then put his hand to his head, assailed by a sudden dizziness. "I was having the strangest dream . . ."

Tanis motioned Raistlin off to one side. "Will he remember anything of this?"

"I doubt it," said Raistlin. "In fact, he may have difficulty believing us when we tell him what happened to him."

———

"Sturm, I swear it's true!" Caramon was saying. "You put the helm on your head and suddenly you weren't you. You were a dwarf, Prince Grallen. We're not in Skullcap anymore. You brought us here to Thorbardin. No, really, Sturm. I'm not lying. It happened, I swear it. If you don't believe me, ask Tanis."

Sturm turned to Tanis, recoiled from him in shock. "What are you doing here in Skullcap? You went with Flint."

He paused, stared about in confusion. "Is it true then, what Caramon tells me? That I was under . . . some sort of enchantment? That we are here, inside Thorbardin? And that I led you?" He looked truly perplexed. "I don't know how that can be! I have no idea where we are, or how we came here!"

"Perhaps next time I warn you to leave an object alone, you will heed my advice," Raistlin remarked.

Sturm looked at Raistlin, and his face flushed in anger. Then his gaze went to the helm, which Tasslehoff had reluctantly and with much protesting handed over to Tanis. Sturm looked at the helm for a long time. His anger faded. He glanced again at Raistlin and said gruffly, "Perhaps I will." Shaking his head, he turned and walked off, out of the light and into the darkness.

"He needs time alone," Raistlin said, stopping Tanis, who would have gone to speak to him. "Sturm has to come to terms with this himself. You have other matters to think about, Half-Elven."

"Yeah," said Caramon. "Here we are. In Thorbardin." He looked at Tanis. "Now what?"

Good question.

* * *

The gate opened into a hallway littered with bits and pieces of armor, broken weapons, remnants of some past battle. Tanis, looking about, guessed by the accumulated dust and cobwebs that no one had been here since the end of the war three hundred years ago. Tasslehoff, to console himself over the matter of the helm, was rummaging through the debris and Raistlin was poking at some of it with his staff, when Flint came running out of the darkness.

"Someone's coming! Hylar dwarves, by the looks of them," he added. "They're tangling with the Theiwar."

Light shone in the distance. They could not yet see the dwarves, but they could hear the sounds of heavy boots clomping on stone, the clank of armor, the jingle of chain mail, and the rattle of weapons. A deep voice spoke in a commanding tone. The voice was answered with curses, and there was the sound of running feet.

The tromp of boots continued, heading their way.

"Stand your ground," Flint told them, "and let me do the talking." He glared very hard at Tasslehoff as he said this.

"What are Hylar dwarves?" Caramon asked in an undertone. "What's the difference between them and the Theiwar?"

"Theiwar are known as dark dwarves, for they hate the light. They're not to be trusted. They have long wanted to rule beneath the mountain, and for all I know, perhaps they do now."

"Theiwar are also the only dwarves who know how to use magic," said Raistlin.

Flint cast a baleful glance at the mage. "Like I said, the Theiwar are not to be trusted."

"The Hylar used to be the rulers in Thorbardin," Flint continued. "It was their king, Duncan, who shut the gates against us and left us to starve."

"That was long ago, my friend," said Tanis quietly. "Time to let bygones be bygones."

Flint said nothing. The tromping boots came closer. Sturm had put on his own helm, which Caramon had brought with them, and he had drawn his sword. Raistlin was readying another spell. Tasslehoff twirled his hoopak in his hands. Tanis looked around at all of them.

"We are here to ask the dwarves for a favor," he reminded them. "Remember those who are counting on us."

"You had best give me the Helm of Grallen," Flint said.

Tanis handed the helm to him. Flint took it, brushed off some of the grime, and polished the rubies with his shirt sleeve. Then he tucked it under his arm and stood waiting.

"Are these Hylar dwarves afraid of light?" Caramon asked.

"No," said Flint. "The Hylar are not afraid of anything."

2

HERO REBORN. AN UNFORESEEN COMPLICATION.

contingent of twelve Hylar dwarves walked abreast down the corridor. All but one were clad in chain mail and wore heavy plate armor over that. The exception was a dwarf who was filthy and sickly looking and wore manacles on his wrists. While the Hylar dwarves confronted the strangers, this dwarf sank down onto the floor as though worn out. One of the dwarves paused to put his hand on this dwarf's shoulder, saying something to him. The sickly dwarf nodded, as though assuring his companion that he was all right.

Some of the Hylar held swords; other carried spears in addition to war hammers slung in harnesses on their backs. Several held lanterns that shone with an odd greenish light that illuminated a vast area. The dwarves walked slowly but steadily down the corridor.

As they came near, one dwarf moved out ahead. He was accoutered in armor as were his fellows, but unlike them, he wore a tabard over his armor. The tabard bore a hammer on it, and he carried a hammer in his hand—an extremely large war hammer—far larger than a hammer a dwarf would normally carry. Runes praising Reorx,

God of the Forge Fire, Creator of the World, were etched up and down the handle and even extended onto the hammer's head.

Sturm stared at the hammer and drew near Tanis.

"That is the Hammer of Kharas!" Sturm said in a low voice. "I recognize it from the old paintings!"

"You have a good eye, human," said the dwarf, speaking Common. He lifted the hammer, regarding it fondly. "This is not the true hammer. It is a replica. I had the hammer made when I took my name, for I am Kharas," he said proudly, "Arman Kharas. The lesser Kharas. Kharas reborn. One day, I will be given the knowledge of how to find the true hammer. Until that day, I carry this with me as a reminder to all that I am destined for greatness."

"Good gods!" Sturm muttered. He did not dare catch Tanis's eye.

Arman Kharas was taller than the other dwarves. He was the tallest dwarf Tanis had ever seen and his physique and stature rivaled Caramon's. His shoulders were massive, his chest broad, his legs thick and well-muscled. Long black hair streamed down his shoulders. His plaited black beard extended past his waist. He wore a helm studded with jewels and marked with the symbol of the hammer.

Arman and his soldiers halted about twenty paces from the companions. The other Hylar were staring at the companions in astonishment mingled with suspicion. Arman regarded them calmly. He motioned to some of his men.

"Go see what that noise was."

The soldiers departed, running past the companions, casting them distrustful looks.

"That noise you heard was the opening of Northgate," said Flint, shifting to Dwarvish.

Arman cast him a brief glance then looked away, waiting for his men to return. They came hastening back, reporting that the Northgate was open and could not be closed; the gate lay in ruins at the base of the mountain.

"You did this?" Arman asked, frowning.

"We didn't break the gate, if that's what you mean," Flint stated.

Tasslehoff, who had been staring hard at the lanterns carried by the dwarves, said suddenly, "There are worms inside there! Worms that glow! Caramon, look—"

"Four humans, a Neidar, and a *kender*." Arman spoke the last word as though it tasted bad.

"Tasslehoff Burrfoot," said Tasslehoff, starting forward, his hand outstretched.

Caramon caught hold of the kender and yanked him back. He kept a firm hold on Tas's shoulder, and Raistlin assisted by planting his staff in front of the kender.

"I was only being polite," Tas said, aggrieved.

"How did four humans, a Neidar, and a kender enter the sealed gate?" Arman demanded.

Flint opened his mouth to answer, but Arman raised his hand in a commanding gesture. "Where did you come by this helm you hold? It is of ancient Hylar design and worth a king's ransom by the looks of it. How did a Neidar come into possession of such a helm?"

"We found it," Tas answered, reciting the kender mantra. "I think you must have dropped it."

Caramon sighed and clapped his large hand over the kender's mouth.

Flint had been slowly seething ever since Arman Kharas spoke. He could stand it no longer. His rage boiled over.

"I see the dwarves beneath the mountain have learned no manners in three hundred years!" Flint said angrily. "You stand in the presence of an elder, young man, yet you do not have the courtesy to ask my name, or why we are here, before you start in with your accusations."

Arman's face flushed. "I am a Hylar prince. I ask the questions, and I give the commands. Still," he said, after a pause which indicated that perhaps he was not quite as confident of himself as he let on, "I will permit you to explain, if you can. Introduce yourselves."

"I am Flint, son of Durgar, son of Reghar Fireforge. A hill dwarf," Flint added, almost shouting the words, "as were my father and grandfather before me. Who is your father, Arman Kharas, that you claim to be a prince?"

"I am, as I said, Arman Kharas, the son of Hornfel, Thane of the Hylar. I am the hero of the dwarves reborn. When I was given this name, a hallowed light surrounded me—the spirit of Kharas entered my body. I am the living embodiment of him, and as such, I am destined to find the Hammer, unify the dwarven nations, and make my father, Hornfel, king."

As Arman was proclaiming his grand legacy, Tanis noticed some of his men roll their eyes. Several appeared embarrassed. One muttered something in a low voice and those near him grinned. Their amusement vanished swiftly when Arman happened to glance their way.

Flint stroked his beard. He did not know what to say to this and at last decided to return to the subject of the gate.

"As I told you, Arman Kharas, the gate opened for us. We had no part in its destruction. The ledge on which the block should have come to rest has crumbled with time. The mechanism pushed the gate out beyond the end. The shaft could not bear the heavy weight of the stone block, and it broke off and fell into the ravine below."

"How did you find the gate that has been concealed for three hundred years, Flint Fireforge?" Arman Kharas demanded, frowning. He continued to use Common, so that they could all understand. "And by what means did you enter, you and your human companions?"

"And kender," Tasslehoff mumbled behind Caramon's hand. "He keeps leaving me out!"

"Wishful thinking," Caramon muttered.

"We were guided by this," Flint replied, and he held up the Helm of Grallen. "My friends found the helm in Skullcap—"

"*I* found the helm in Skullcap," Raistlin corrected. He gave a slight bow to Arman Kharas. "I am Raistlin Majere, and this is my brother, Caramon."

Caramon made an awkward, bobbing bow.

"I knew immediately the helm was magical," Raistlin continued. "It was possessed by the spirit of its late owner, who died in that battle. His name was Grallen, son of Duncan—

Arman gave a cry, and placing his hand on his sword, he took a step backward. His men crowded around him, shouting and clamoring, their deep voices booming.

Caramon clapped his hand to his sword, as did Sturm. They looked at Flint, who appeared as confused as any of them. This was not the reaction they had expected. They had assumed that they would be lauded as heroes for returning the helm of the dead prince. Instead it seemed more likely that they were going to be forced to fight for their lives.

Arman silenced the tumult with a commanding gesture. He stared at the helm, his expression dark and grim, then looked back at Raistlin.

"A human wizard. I might have known. Was it you who brought the helm here?" he demanded.

"I found it," said Raistlin. "This noble knight"—he indicated Sturm—"volunteered to wear the helm, thus permitting the spirit of the dwarven prince to take control of his body. Under the helm's enchantment, Prince Grallen asked us to accompany him to the hall of his fathers. The spirit of the prince opened the gate. We are glad to have been able to fulfill his soul's request, aren't we, Sturm?" Raistlin said pointedly.

"I am Sturm, son of Angor Brightblade," Sturm said, not moving his hand from his sword. "I am honored to have been able to serve the fallen prince."

Arman gazed at each of them, his dark eyes glinting beneath lowering brows.

"Your turn, Tanis," said Raistlin softly.

Tanis glanced at Flint, who shrugged. He was as confused as the rest.

"Your Highness," Tanis said, addressing Arman Kharas, "Raistlin is being diplomatic when he says that we came here with the helm voluntarily. The truth is that we had no choice in the matter. The helm took our friend, Sturm Brightblade, hostage, as it were, and forced him to come to Thorbardin. He did not know what he was doing. He was held in thrall by a prince who died three hundred years ago. We had no idea who this prince was. None of us have ever heard of him, except Flint, who knows the history of your people."

"I know it well. I know how King Duncan shut us out of the mountain, left us to starve—"

"You're not helping," Tanis murmured.

Flint muttered something into his beard.

Kharas shook his head.

"If I believe your tale, and you did bring the helm back to us in all innocence, that is worse." He gazed at the helm, and his expression darkened. "The helm of Prince Grallen is cursed, and, if this is the helm of the prince, you have brought the curse on us. You bring the doom of the dwarves upon us!"

Tanis sighed. "I'm sorry. We had no way of knowing." His apology was lame, but he didn't know what else to say.

"Perhaps you did, perhaps you did not," said Arman Kharas. "I must report this matter of the destruction of the gate to the Council of Thanes. You will have a chance to tell your story to them. If they believe it—"

"What do you mean 'if'?" Flint said, bristling. "Do you have the nerve to tell me to my beard that my friends and I are lying?"

"We have only your word that this helm is what you claim it to be. It might be a fraud, a fake."

Flint seemed to swell in rage. Before he could, speak, Raistlin said coldly, "There is a simple way to find out if we are telling the truth, Your Highness."

"What would that be?" Kharas demanded, suspicious.

"Put the helm on your head," said Raistlin.

Kharas cast the helm an appalled glance. "No dwarf would dare! The Council will judge how best to proceed."

"I'll put it on!" Tasslehoff offered, but no one took him up on it.

"I have no need to prove to this Council or anyone that I am not a liar!" Flint was so angry he could barely speak. He whipped around to face his friends. "I told all of you it was a mistake to come here! I don't know what the rest of you plan to do, but I'm leaving! And seeing as how this helm is not wanted here, I'm taking it with me!"

Flint tucked the helm under his arm and stalked off down the corridor, heading toward the ruined gate.

"Stop him!" ordered Arman Kharas. He made a commanding gesture. "Seize them!"

His soldiers were already on the move. Sturm looked down at a dwarven spear tickling his throat. Tanis felt something sharp jab him in the back. Caramon raised his fists. Raistlin said something to him, and Caramon, glowering at the dwarves, let his arms fall to his sides. Tasslehoff made a swipe with his hoopak, but a dwarf kicked the weapon out of the kender's hand, and grasping Tas by the hair, put his knife to Tas's neck.

Hearing the commotion behind him, Flint turned around. He was red-faced with fury, the veins in his head popping. Placing the Helm of Grallen at his feet, he stood over it protectively, and raised his battle axe.

"I'll send the soul of the first dwarf who comes near me to the hall of his fathers, Reorx take me if I don't!"

Arman Kharas spoke a sharp command, and four dwarves went after Flint, weapons drawn.

"He's going to get us all killed, Tanis!" Raistlin warned.

Tanis shouted for Flint to stop, but the outraged hill dwarf was cursing, swearing, and swinging his axe in vicious arcs, and either he could not hear or he was ignoring Tanis's command. The dwarf soldiers prodded at him with their spears. Flint struck at them with his axe. All the while, another solider had slipped up behind him. The soldier thrust out his foot, tripping Flint, who went over backward. The other soldiers jumped on him. One snatched away his axe. The others pinned his hand and feet.

"Thorbardin treachery! I expected it! I warned you of this, Tanis!" Flint bellowed, struggling to free himself, to no avail. "I told you they would treat us this way!"

Once Flint's hands were bound, the soldiers hoisted him to his feet, still cursing and raving. All of them, Kharas included, eyed the Helm of Grallen that stood on the floor where Flint had placed it. None of them made any move to go near it, much less touch it.

"I will carry it," Raistlin offered.

Kharas appeared tempted to accept, but he shook his head.

"No," he said. "If this curse is come to Thorbardin, let it fall on me."

He reached down for the helm. The other dwarves backed away from him, watching in dread anticipation, certain something dire was about to happen.

Kharas clasped the helm, involuntarily wincing as he touched it.

Nothing happened.

He lifted the helm, placed it under his arm, wiped the sweat from his face. He gestured to the companions. "Take their weapons and tie them up securely."

Dwarves bound their hands, all except Raistlin, who forbade them to touch him. They glanced at him askance, glanced at each other, and let him be. Arman stopped to gently assist the sickly dwarf to his feet then led the way through the darkened hall.

Tanis, prodded from behind by a spear, followed.

"I don't suppose this would be a good time to ask them to provide shelter for eight hundred humans," Raistlin murmured, coming up behind him.

Tanis flashed him a grim glance.

The dwarf behind Tanis prodded him again in the back. "Keep moving, scum!" he ordered in Dwarvish.

They kept moving deeper into the mountain, bearing the doom of the dwarves—and most likely their own—along with them.

3

Faith. Hope. And Hederick.

he refugees trekked through the narrow pass. The going was slow and wearisome, for they had to pick their way among the rocks and crags, always keeping one eye on the gray and cloud-choked sky above them. They could see no dragons, but they could feel their constant presence. The dragonfear that radiated from the beasts was not strong, for the dragons flew high overhead, hidden by the clouds, but the fear was an added weight on their hearts, an added burden on their souls and slowed the people down.

"The pass is too dangerous for the dragons to enter. Why should they bother?" Riverwind said to Elistan, "They have only to wait for us to emerge from this pass, which we must do sooner or later, for we do not have the supplies to remain here long. Once we move out into the open, they will attack us, and we have no idea how far we are from Thorbardin, or even if there will be a refuge for us when we get there."

"I feel the fear," Elistan replied, "like a shadow over my heart, yet, my friend, shadows are caused by sunlight behind them. Other eyes look down on us and watch over us. It might be well to remind the people of that."

"Then you'd first better remind me," Riverwind said. "My faith in the gods is being sorely tested. I admit it."

"Mine, as well," said Elistan calmly, and Riverwind regarded the cleric in astonishment.

Elistan smiled. "You seem surprised to hear me say that. Faith in the gods does not come easily, my friend. We cannot see them or hear them. They do not walk beside us, like overprotective parents, coddling and cosseting us, holding us by the hand lest we trip and fall. I think we would soon grow angry and rebellious if they did."

"Isn't it wrong to doubt them?"

"Doubt is natural. We are mortal. Our minds are the size of this small pebble compared to the minds of the gods that are as large as all heaven. The gods know that we have no way to comprehend their vision. They are patient with us and forbearing."

"Yet they hurled a fiery mountain down on the world as punishment," said Riverwind. "Thousands died and thousands more suffered as a result. How are we to account for that?"

"We cannot," said Elistan simply. "We can feel sorrow and anger. That is perfectly natural. I am angry when I think back on it. I do not understand why the gods did this. I question them constantly."

"Yet you remain faithful to them." Riverwind marveled. "You love them."

"When you have children, will they never grow angry at you? Never doubt you or defy you? Do you want your children to be meek and submissive, always look to you for answers, obey you without question?"

"Of course not," said Riverwind. "Such weak children would never be able to make their own way in the world."

"Would you love your children if they defied you, rebelled against you?"

"I would be angry with them, but I would love them," said Riverwind quietly, and his gaze went to Goldmoon, moving among the people, speaking to them softly, bringing them comfort and ease, "for they are my children."

"So do the gods of light love us."

One of the Plainsmen was hovering near, not wanting to break in on their conversation, yet obviously the bearer of important news. Riverwind turned to him, signing to Elistan that he was to remain.

"Yes, Nighthawk, what is it?"

"The trail marked by the half-elf and the dwarf continues down this mountain into a pine forest, then ascends into the mountain along a narrow defile. The elf, Gilthanas, who has the eyes of the eagle, can see a gaping hole in the side of the mountain. He believes this could be the fabled gate of Thorbardin."

"Or a cave . . . or a dragon's lair," said Riverwind.

Even as he spoke his doubts, he smiled ruefully at Elistan.

Nighthawk shook his head. "According to Gilthanas, the hole is rectangular with squared-off edges. Nature did not form it, nor a dragon."

"What kind of terrain lies between us and this gate, should it prove to be a gate?" Riverwind asked.

"Open to the wind and sky," Nighthawk replied.

"And to the eyes of dragons," said Riverwind, "and the eyes of a draconian army."

"Yes, Chieftain," Nighthawk replied. "The enemy is out there and on the move. We saw what looked to be draconian troops leaving the foothills and heading into the mountains."

"They know we are here. The dragons have told them."

"We can defend this pass," suggested Nighthawk.

"We cannot stay here forever, though. We have supplies enough for a few days, and soon the snows will start. What is this ancient road like?"

"Well built. Two can walk side-by-side with room to spare, but there is no cover until we reach the tree line at the bottom, nor is there cover when we start back up the mountain. Not a tree or a bush in sight."

Riverwind shook his head gloomily.

"Return and keep watch on the enemy and on that hole in the side of the mountain. Let me know if anyone comes out, or goes in. This might tell us if we have truly found the gate.

Riverwind turned back to Elistan.

"Now what do I do, Revered Son? It looks as though we may have found the Gate of Thorbardin, but we cannot reach it. The gods give us their blessing with one hand and smack us in the face with the other."

Elistan was about to say something in response, when Goldmoon walked up.

"My turn," she said. She looked angry clear through. Her lips were compressed, her blue eyes glinting

Riverwind sighed. "What new problem do you bring me, wife?"

"An old problem—Hederick. Why Mishakal didn't yank his feet out from under him while he was crossing that cliff face—" Goldmoon saw Elistan standing there, and she flushed. "I'm sorry, Revered Son. I know such thoughts are wicked. . . "

"Hederick is enough to try even a god's patience," Elistan said dryly. "I'm sure Mishakal must have been tempted to do just that. What mischief is he causing now?"

"He's going among the people saying that Riverwind has led us to our deaths. Riverwind caused the rockslide, and now we cannot return to the caves. We are trapped in this pass, where we will die of cold and hunger."

"What else?" Riverwind asked, for Goldmoon had hesitated. "Tell me the worst."

"Hederick is advocating that we should surrender, give ourselves up to Verminaard."

"Hederick was the one who led the dragons to us!" Riverwind said angrily. "I was forced to start the rock slide because he put us in danger! I should have left him to his fate!"

"Are the people listening to him?" Elistan asked, his expression grave.

"I'm afraid so, Revered Son." Goldmoon rested her hand on her husband's arm in sympathy. "It is not your fault. The people know that, but they are cold, tired, and weighed down by the dragon-fear. They can't go back to the caves, and they are terrified of going forward."

"They know what Verminaard will do to them! He'll send them back to the mines."

"I very much doubt it," said Elistan. "He came to the caves with the intention of killing, not capturing."

"The people won't believe that. A man lost and wandering in the wilderness sees even a prison cell as a refuge," Goldmoon said. "You must talk to them, husband. Reassure them. Nighthawk told me that the scouts may have found the gate—"

"For all the good it will do us," Riverwind muttered. "There is a draconian army between us and the gate, and we're not even sure this hole in the mountain is the gate. It might just be a hole in the mountain. If it is the gate, there may be a dwarven army massed inside waiting to slaughter us!"

Riverwind sat down dejectedly on a boulder. His shoulders slumped. "Tanis chose the wrong man. I do not know what to do."

"At least you know what *not* to do," said Goldmoon spiritedly. "Don't pay attention to Hederick!"

Riverwind smiled at this and even gave a low chuckle, though his laughter faded away. He put his arm around Goldmoon and drew her close.

"What do you advise me to do, wife?"

"Tell the people the truth." She put her hands on his face, looked lovingly into his eyes. "Be honest with them. That's all they ask. We will give our prayers to the gods, ask them to help us through the long night. The dawn brings a new day and fresh hope."

Riverwind kissed her. "You are my joy and my salvation. The gods know what I would do without you."

"And there *is* a small blessing," said Goldmoon, nestling in her husband's arms. "The dragons know we are here. There is no longer any need to hide from them. We can light fires for warmth."

"Indeed, we can," said Riverwind. "We will light the fires not only for warmth but for defiance, and instead of begging the gods to save us, we will offer them our grateful thanks for our deliverance. We will not even think of surrendering!"

The refugees lit the fires in defiance of the dragons, and when the fires were burning brightly, bringing warmth and cheer, the people sent their prayers to the gods in thanksgiving. The dragonfear seemed to melt and spirits lifted. Everyone spoke hopefully of the dawn of a new tomorrow.

Hederick saw that he had lost his audience, and he ceased talking of surrender and gave his prayers of thanks piously with the rest. He had no faith at all in these new gods, though he pretended he did because it was politically expedient. He had unbounded faith in himself, however, and he truly believed that if they surrendered to Verminaard, as he advocated, he could worm his way into the Highlord's good graces. To give Hederick credit, he did not believe they had any chance at all of escape. He was convinced that Riverwind was an ignorant brute who would rather see them all perish than bow to his enemy.

Hederick was not dismayed. As a politician, he knew the masses were fickle. All he had to do was bide his time, and they would come around to his point of view. He went to sleep that night thinking complacently of tomorrow when Riverwind, Elistan and their cohorts must finally admit defeat.

The next day dawned and brought change. Unfortunately the change was not for the good. The dragons flew nearer, the dragonfear was stronger, the air was colder, and the day bleaker.

Hederick walked up to Riverwind and spoke loudly, so that as many as possible could hear him.

"What will you do now, Chieftain? Our people are starting to sicken, and soon they will begin to die. You know as well as I do that we cannot stay here. Your gods have failed you. Admit that this venture was foolishly undertaken. Our only hope is to surrender to the Dragon Highlord—an unpleasant and dangerous task, but one I offer to undertake."

"And you will receive Verminaard's reward for handing us over to him," said Riverwind.

"Unlike you, I am thinking of the people's welfare," said Hederick. "You would see all us all perish rather than admit you were wrong!"

Riverwind could have cheerfully seen at least one of them perish, but he kept silent.

"Perhaps you are waiting for the gods to perform a miracle?" Hederick said, scoffing.

"Perhaps I am," Riverwind muttered, and he turned on his heel and walked off.

"The people will no longer follow you!" Hederick warned. "You will see."

Riverwind thought this very likely. As he walked among the refugees, he saw them huddled together for warmth, their faces pale and pinched. The fire's glow that had warmed hearts last night was cold ash this morning. They had food and water enough for a few days more, and they were at least that far from the gate—if gate it was and if the dwarves would let them in.

If, if, if. So many ifs.

"We could use a miracle," Riverwind said somberly, lifting his gaze to the heavens. "I'm not asking for a big one, not like moving the mountain—just a small one."

Something cold and wet stung Riverwind's skin. He put his hand to his cheek and felt a snowflake melting on his skin. Another snowflake landed in his eye; another splattered on his nose. He gazed up into the gray clouds, into masses of white flakes drifting lazily from the sky.

Instead of a miracle, the gods had sent yet more to test them. The snow would clog the pass. They would have to leave or risk becoming trapped here for good.

Even as despair settled over Riverwind, he felt his heart lift. He did not understand why at first, then the reason came to him. The dragonfear was gone. The dragons were no longer in the skies.

He stared at the snow falling thick around him and he would have fallen to his knees to give thanks, but he had no time to waste.

Riverwind had been given his miracle. It was up to him to make use of it.

4

Arman's Destiny. Anvil's Echo.
Murder Holes and Worm Meat.

lint had described the wonders of the dwarven realm of Thorbardin many times to Tanis, always with a touch of bitterness, for although no hill dwarf would ever trade his place in the world "above" to live beneath the mountain, every hill dwarf was deeply offended that the choice had been taken away from him.

Tanis had always secretly believed that Flint had exaggerated his tales of the amazing sights to be found in mountain kingdom. Flint actually had never seen any of these sights. He was merely recounting tales that had been told him by his father, who had heard them from his grandfather, and so on back several generations. Flint was convinced that there was immense wealth in Thorbardin that was being denied him and his people, so when he told the tale of a city built entirely inside a gigantic stalactite, Tanis was always careful to hide his smile.

Now, walking the roads beneath the mountain, Tanis was starting to think he'd done his old friend an injustice. Whereas humans constructed buildings out of stone by mounting blocks one atop the other, the dwarves had carved their buildings out of the mountain's interior, taking away rock rather than adding it, so that all the structures seemed to flow together in beautiful and entrancing formations.

Leaving the gate, they entered an immense hall supported by round pillars. The light of the strange green glowing worms and the gleaming crystal atop Raistlin's staff shone on wonderfully carved stone work portraying scenes from dwarven life.

Although now the hall was deserted, it had apparently been constructed so as to take advantage of the traffic that had once moved in and out of the great gate. Wagons with iron wheels once ran along rails embedded in the floor, ferrying goods and visitors deeper into the mountain's interior.

Looking around in awe, Tanis imagined the vast hall bustling with dwarves and people of other races who came to Thorbardin. Elves had once walked here, as had humans, for dwarven goods and dwarven craftsmanship were much in demand. Gold and silver had flowed into Thorbardin then. Iron, steel, and rare and precious gems dug from the mountain had flowed out.

Now the iron rails were rusted. The wagons lay on their sides, their wheels frozen in time. The shops that had once sold pots and kettles, rims for wagon wheels, wooden toys, swords, armor and glittering jewels now catered only to the sad and empty dreams of ghosts.

Houses had been boarded up, their shutters falling off; wooden doors hung on rusted hinges.

"Tanis," said Caramon quietly. "Take a look at Flint. Something's wrong."

Tanis looked back at the dwarf in concern. Caramon was right. Flint did not look well. He had ceased to swear at his captors and quit struggling, all of which was a bad sign. His face was mottled, ashen gray with red spots. His breathing seemed labored. Their guards were urging them on a rapid pace. The dwarven soldiers held their weapons at the ready, keeping a keen watch.

"Your Highness," Tanis called out, "would it be possible for us to stop to rest or at least slow down?"

"Not here," Arman replied. "We have already been in this part of the realm too long. We came here to free my brother, Pick," he added, gesturing to the sickly dwarf, who walked along at his side. "We heard the noise of the gate and came to investigate, and now we must leave before more Theiwar come."

"So this part of the realm is ruled by the Theiwar?" Tanis asked, glancing at Flint. The dwarf barely seemed to be listening. "Are the Theiwar and the Hylar at war?"

"Not yet," Arman said grimly, "but it is only a matter of time."

"Just our luck," Sturm muttered. "War *beneath* the ground as well as above."

Tanis was thinking the same and wondering how this fighting among the dwarves would affect his own cause, when he became aware, with a start, that Raistlin was walking quite close beside him. Tanis could smell the disquieting odor of rose petal and decay, and he drew back slightly.

"A word with you, Half-Elven," Raistlin said. "Speaking of the Theiwar, don't you find it odd that they did not appear surprised to see us? Compare their reaction to that of Arman Kharas and his soldiers."

"To be honest, I don't recall the Theiwar's reaction," Tanis said, "other than the swords in their hands, of course."

"This is not a matter for levity," said Raistlin reprovingly, and before Tanis could say anything else the mage left in a huff, going back to walk alongside his brother.

Tanis sighed. He had some idea what Raistlin was getting at, but it was one more worry he didn't need and he put it out of his mind. He looked again at Flint. His jaw was clenched, perhaps in anger, or perhaps against pain—with the stubborn old dwarf, it was hard to tell.

Caramon asked him if he was hurt or ill, but Flint paid him no heed. He stomped along, deaf to his friends' concerns.

To Tanis's surprise, Arman Kharas left his place in the lead and dropped back to walk beside his prisoners. Arman seemed to find them fascinating, for he kept staring at them, especially at Tanis.

"You are not a human," he said at last.

"I have elven blood," Tanis acknowledged.

Arman nodded, as if he had guessed as much.

"This hall once must have been very beautiful," said Tanis. "Perhaps now that the gate is open, this deserted part of Thorbardin can be rebuilt. Bring back the old prosperity."

"This now belongs to the Theiwar and they have small interest in building, being more concerned with their own dark plots and schemes. And this part of the realm is not deserted," Arman said, adding ominously, "The Theiwar are out there, watching us from the shadows, making certain that we do not linger in their kingdom."

"Why don't they attack us?" Tanis asked, pleased that the Hylar prince was at least talking to him.

"The Theiwar prefer opponents who travel alone and are not armed, like my half-brother. He accidentally stumbled into Theiwar holdings and was taken prisoner. They made a ransom demand, but my father rightly refused to pay off thugs and murderers. Our spies informed me where Pick was being held, and my father sent his troops under my command to free him."

They left the hall and entered an area that appeared to be an ancient temple, for there were symbols for the various gods carved on the walls.

"A great many people must have come to Thorbardin in the old days," Tanis remarked.

"They came from all over Ansalon," said Arman proudly, "even from as far away as Istar. They came to buy or barter. They came to hire our iron workers and our stone masons. They brought wealth and prosperity to our people." His voice grew hard, his words bitter. "They brought the Cataclysm, and after that the war, and all our prosperity ended."

"It need not have ended if those beneath the mountain had not closed the gate, keeping out their cousins who had a right to enter," Flint stated, the first words he'd spoken in a long while.

Tanis was relieved to see some color starting to return to Flint's face. That and the fact that he was bringing up this old argument was an indication the dwarf was recovering from whatever had ailed him.

"We don't need to go into all that now," Tanis admonished, but he might have saved his breath.

"King Duncan—or Derkin as you Neidar named him—had no choice in the matter," Arman stated. "We were also affected by the Cataclysm. Many of our farming warrens were destroyed. Our food supplies were limited. If we had allowed your people to come inside, we would not have saved you. We would have all starved to death together."

"So you say." Flint snorted, but he didn't speak with his usual outrage and conviction.

He kept darting glances about at the ruins of the once great city, and though he was trying his best to hide it, he was obviously shocked and depressed by what he saw. The wonders of Thorbardin were wrecked wagons and rusted door hinges.

Tanis decided to change the subject before Flint started some new tirade.

"If Northgate remains open, the Theiwar will control it. How will that affect the Hylar?"

"The gate will not remain open," Kharas said flatly. "Unless something happens to prevent it, the Council of Thanes will send soldiers to guard the gate and keep out intruders until it can be closed and sealed once more."

"You think the gate should be remain open, don't you?" Tanis said, hoping he had found an ally.

"I believe it is my destiny, once I have obtained the Hammer of Kharas, to rule the united Dwarven Nations," said Arman. "To do that, the gate must remain open."

"Why are you so sure you're the one who will find the hammer?" Flint asked.

Arman lifted his head and raised his voice. His words reverberated throughout the cavern. "Thus spake Kharas: 'Only when a good and honorable dwarf comes to unite the nations shall the Hammer of Kharas return. It will be his badge of righteousness.'" He placed his hand on his chest. "I am that dwarf."

A rude noise came out of the darkness. Some of the soldiers were sniggering into their beards. If Kharas heard, he pretended he hadn't.

"Ask him more about the Hammer of Kharas," Sturm urged Tanis, who shook his head.

Flint had once more lapsed into silence. The old dwarf would never admit to being tired, but Tanis noted that walking was costing him an effort.

"How much farther do we have to go until we are out of Theiwar territory?" Tanis asked.

"We have to cross that bridge," Arman replied, gesturing ahead. "Once we are on the other side, in the West Warrens, we will be safe. Then we can stop to rest."

A vast cavern opened up before them, spanned by a stone bridge of curious make. Small figures of dwarves carved out of stone lined the bridge on either side. The stone dwarves stood about three feet in height, forming a barricade to keep people crossing the bridge from tumbling off. Iron tracks ran down the middle of the bridge, with walkways for pedestrians on either side. The bridge, like everything else in this part of Thorbardin, showed signs of neglect. Some of the dwarven statues were missing heads or arms, while others had been destroyed completely, leaving gaps in their ranks.

"This cave is known as Anvil's Echo, for it is said that the sound of a dwarven hammer striking an anvil in this cave will echo for all eternity," Arman Kharas told them.

"An excellent defensive measure," said Sturm, looking on the bridge with approval. He stared overhead, but could see nothing for the darkness. "I take it there are murder holes in the ceiling?"

Arman Kharas was pleased by the knight's praise. "The enemy never made it past this bridge. The defenders of Northgate dropped down boulders, molten lead, and boiling oil on those who tried to cross. Few did, and their skeletons still lie at the bottom of the cave."

Flint glowered at the mention of this. He halted, frowning. "I won't cross," he stated.

Arman misunderstood. "No one ever goes up there now. You need have no fear—" he began in patronizing tones.

"Fear?" Flint went red in the face. "It's not fear! It's respect. My people died on this bridge and you tell me they lie there unburied, their souls lost and wandering."

"My people lie there, as well," said Arman. "When the blessed day comes when I unify the kingdoms, I will give orders that the dead of both sides are given proper respect."

Flint was considerably taken aback by this statement, which appeared to leave him at a loss for words. He muttered something to the effect that he guessed he would cross, but he kept giving Arman strange looks.

Arman sent some of his soldiers on ahead, to make certain the bridge was secure. He followed with the prisoners, and the rest of his soldiers closed in behind, as they began the long trek from one side of Anvil's Echo to the other.

"Mad as a marmot," muttered Flint.

* * *

"This is certainly a long bridge," stated Tasslehoff, with a gusty sigh.

Caramon grunted in agreement.

Tasslehoff had been keeping out of mischief mainly due to the fact that the dwarves had trussed up the kender so efficiently he had not been able to slip free. Every time Tas saw something interesting and started to wander off, the soldier would poke him in the back with a spear. Caramon wondered how long this would go on before either the kender found some way to escape, or the dwarf grew so frustrated he skewered him.

"I thought crossing a bridge with murder holes would be extremely interesting, but it isn't. It's boring."

"And never a mention of dinner," Caramon grumbled. "My stomach's so empty it's flapping around my backbone. What do Thorbardin dwarves eat anyway?"

"Worms," said Tasslehoff. "Like the ones inside the lanterns."

"No!" Caramon said, shocked.

"Oh, yes," said Tas. "The dwarves have huge farms where they raise these gigantic worms, and butcher shops where they cut them into worm steak and worm stew and worm chops—"

Caramon was appalled. "Raist, Tas says that dwarves eat worms. Is that true?"

Raistlin was eavesdropping on Tanis's conversation with Arman, and he cast Caramon a look that said plain as words that he was not to be bothered with stupid questions.

Caramon suddenly found he wasn't as hungry as he had been. The kender was leaning over the barricade, trying to see the bottom.

"If I fell off, would I keep falling until I came out on the other side of the world?" Tas asked.

"If you fell, you'd fall until you hit bottom and ended up splattered all over the rocks," said Caramon.

"I guess you're right," said Tas. He looked up ahead to where Flint, Tanis, and Arman Kharas were walking together. "Can you hear what they're saying?"

"Naw," said Caramon. "I can't hear anything over all the tromping, rattling, and clanging. These dwarves make noise enough for an ogre feast day!"

"Not to mention the thunder," said Tas.

Caramon glanced at him, puzzled. "What thunder?"

"A moment ago I heard thunder," said the kender. "Must be a storm coming."

"If there was, you couldn't hear thunder down here." Caramon's brow crinkled. "Are you making this up?"

"No, Caramon," said Tas. "Why should I do that? I heard thunder, and I felt it in my feet like you do when the thunder falls out of the sky . . ."

Caramon heard it too now. He stared up into the darkness. "That's not thunder . . . Raistlin! Look out!"

Hurling himself forward, Caramon knocked his brother down and flung his body across him protectively just as an enormous boulder struck the bridge where Raistlin had been standing. The boulder crushed two of the dwarven statues and opened a large hole in the barricade before it went bounding off into the darkness.

The Hylar scattered as another boulder came hurtling after the first. This one missed its mark, going wide of the bridge. They heard the first boulder land down below, smashing into pieces.

"Raistlin! Douse that light!" Tanis shouted. "Everyone get down, hug the floor!"

"*Dulak*!" Raistlin gasped, and the light atop his staff went out. The dwarves shuttered their lanterns, and they were plunged into darkness.

"Not that this will do much good," Flint growled. "The Theiwar can see in the darkness better than they can in the light. It is only a matter of finding their aim."

"I thought you said the way to the murder holes was impassable," Tanis said to Arman.

"It used to be." The dwarf leader alone remained on his feet, staring upward in astonished outrage. "The Theiwar must have repaired it, though that is odd . . ."

His voice broke off as another boulder came down, striking the bridge some distance ahead of him, cracking the stone and causing the bridge to shake alarmingly.

"Caramon," said Raistlin testily, "move your great bulk off me! I can't breathe."

"Sorry, Raist," said Caramon, shifting his weight. "Are you all right?"

"I am lying on my back on a bridge in pitch darkness with someone hurling boulders at me. No, I am not all right," Raistlin retorted.

Another boulder smashed into the railing, crumbling more dwarven statues and causing everyone to flinch.

"That one just missed me!" Sturm reported grimly. "We can't stay here and wait to be smashed into jelly!"

"How far to go until we reach cover?" Tanis asked Arman in a low voice.

"Not far. Only about another forty feet."

"We should run for it," Tanis urged.

"Some of us can't see in the dark like you can, Half-elf," Caramon pointed out. "I think I'd rather get flattened by boulders than fall off this bridge."

They all ducked as another boulder thudded somewhere nearby.

Arman gestured to his men. "Unshutter the lanterns!"

The soldiers did as they were ordered, working quickly, and everyone started running.

"This bridge didn't turn out to be as boring as I thought," said Tasslehoff cheerfully. "Do you think they'll pour boiling oil on us next?"

"Just run, damn it!" Tanis ordered.

Tasslehoff ran, and being extremely nimble and accustomed to fleeing all sorts of dangers, from irate sheriffs to angry housewives, the kender soon outdistanced everyone. Caramon lumbered along, keeping near his brother. Raistlin hiked up the skirts of his robes, and staff in hand, ran swiftly. Sturm brought up the rear. It was awkward going, trying to run with their hands bound, but the hurtling boulders gave them an excellent incentive to keep moving.

Suddenly, a cry sounded behind them. Pick, the sickly dwarf, had stumbled and fallen to his knees. Arman turned around. Seeing his brother's plight, he started to hand the Helm of Grallen to one of his soldiers. The soldier cringed, shook his head, and kept running.

"I'll take it!" offered Flint. "You'll have to cut my hands loose."

Another boulder whistled past, and they all ducked involuntarily. Pick cried out in terror as the boulder struck the bridge close to him, showering him with stone fragments. Kharas hesitated only a moment then whipped out a knife, sliced Flint's bonds, and tossed him the helm. Arman dashed back along the bridge, dodging a boulder as it struck the rail and bounded off. Clasping his brother's hands, Arman lifted him up, and slung him over his back.

They continued to run across the bridge. The green light from the worm-lanterns flared first in one place, then another, as the lanterns swung back and forth. The wildly flashing lights made the dwarven statues appear to be capering in some sort of mad dance that added to the macabre terror of their race against death.

Tanis kept near Flint, who was now encumbered with the helm, thinking he might need help. The old dwarf ran strongly, however, his head down, legs pumping. He held the Helm of Grallen clasped fast in his arms and even running for his life, he wore a grim smile of satisfaction that boded ill for anyone who might try to take the helm from him again.

More boulders sailed down through the green-lit darkness, whistling past so close they could feel the rush of air on their cheeks. Tanis could see the end of the span now, sheltered beneath a large entry way. The light shone on the bars and the wicked points of a portcullis that, fortunately, was raised.

The sight spurred them on, giving those who were flagging their second wind. Tasslehoff reached the entrance first, followed by the dwarven soldiers in a thundering rush. The rest of the companions came after. Raistlin collapsed just short of the opening and had to be dragged inside by his brother. Arman Kharas, carrying Pick on his back, came last. Once they were off the bridge, the boulders ceased to fall.

"The Theiwar targeted us," said Sturm, gasping for breath.

"They targeted Raistlin," Tanis pointed out.

Flint snorted. "I said the Theiwar were evil. I never said they didn't have good sense."

5

ll of them, even the stalwart dwarves, who generally make light of any physical exertion, sank to the floor and lay there gasping for air. Tanis had a great many questions, but he lacked the breath to ask them.

Raistlin leaned back against the wall of the gatehouse. His golden skin took on an odd greenish cast in the lantern light. His eyes were closed. Every so often, his breath rasped.

"He's not hurt, just exhausted," Caramon informed them.

"We are all exhausted, not just your brother," Sturm said testily, trying to rub a cramp out of his leg. "We spent the first half the day climbing a mountain. My throat is parched. We need water and rest—"

"—and food," said Caramon, then added hurriedly, "vegetables or something."

"This area is still inside Theiwar territory and is not safe. A short distance ahead is a temple to Reorx," Arman told them. "We can rest there in safety."

"Raist, can you make it?" Caramon eyed his twin dubiously.

Raistlin, eyes closed, grimaced. "I suppose I will have to."

"I am afraid I must ask you to continue to carry the helm," Arman said to Flint. "Poor Pick cannot go on without my aid, and none of my men wants anything to do with it."

"If they think this helm's that terrible, why don't they just toss it off that bridge and have done with it?" Caramon asked Flint.

"Would you toss your dead father's bones off that bridge?" Flint asked, glaring at him. "Cursed or no, the spirit of the prince has come back to his people and must be laid to rest."

Arman insisted they leave, and groaning and grunting, they started off, crossing a drawbridge that did not appear to have been raised in years. Fearing pursuit from behind, Sturm suggested they might attempt to raise this bridge, but Arman said that the mechanism was rusted and would not work.

"The Theiwar will not pursue us," he added.

"You said they wouldn't attack us either," Flint remarked.

"My father will be angry to hear of this assault on me and my men," Arman stated. "This might lead to war."

Leaving the gatehouse, they emerged onto a main road lined with more abandoned buildings and shops. Streets and alleys led off the road in various directions. There were no lights, no sounds, no signs of habitation.

Raistlin was limping. He was being helped by his brother. Flint marched with his head down, holding fast to the helm. Tasslehoff's footsteps were starting to flag. Arman left the main street, and taking a turn to the left, he led them down a side road.

A large building rose in front of them. Doors of bronze, marked with the sign of a hammer, stood open.

"The Temple of Reorx," said Arman.

The Hylar soldiers removed their helms as they went, but they seemed to do this more out of habit than true reverence or respect. Once inside, the dwarves relaxed and felt free to make themselves at home, stretching out on the floor where the altar had once stood, taking long pulls from their ale skins, and rummaging in their knapsacks for food.

Arman conferred with his soldiers, then sent one on ahead to carry news to his father. He detailed another to keep watch at the door and ordered two more to stand guard on the companions.

Tanis could have pointed out that they weren't likely to try to escape, since none of them had any desire to cross Anvil's Echo a second time. He was too weary to argue, however.

"We will spend the night here," Arman announced. "Pick is not strong enough to travel. We will be safe enough, I think. The Theiwar don't usually venture this far, but just in case, I have sent one of my men to bring up reinforcements from the West Warrens."

Tanis considered this an excellent idea.

"Could you at least untie us?" he asked Arman. "You have our weapons. We have no intention of attacking you. We want to have our say before the Council."

Arman eyed him speculatively, then gave a nod. "Untie them," he ordered his soldiers.

The Hylar did not appear happy about this, but they did as he said. Arman fussed over his brother, making sure he had something to eat and was resting comfortably. Tanis gazed curiously around the temple. He wondered if Reorx had made himself known to the dwarves, as the other gods had made themselves known. Judging by the dilapidated state of the temple and the casual attitude of the dwarves as they set up housekeeping for the night, Tanis assumed the god, for whatever reasons, had not yet informed the dwarves of his return.

According to the wise, the creation of the world began when Reorx, a friend of the God of Balance, Gilean, struck his hammer on the Anvil of Time, forcing Chaos to slow his cycle of destruction. The sparks that flew from the god's hammer became the stars. The light from these stars was transformed into spirits, who were given mortal bodies by the gods, and the world of Krynn, in which they could dwell. Although the creation of the dwarves had always been in dispute (dwarves believing they were formed by Reorx in his image, while others maintain dwarves were brought into being by the passing of the chaotic Graygem of Gargath), dwarves were firm in their belief that they were the chosen people of Reorx.

The dwarves were devastated when Reorx departed along with the other gods after the Cataclysm. Most refused to believe it and clung to their faith in the god, even though their prayers were answered with silence. Thus while most other people on Krynn forgot the old gods, the dwarves still remembered and revered Reorx, telling the old tales about him, confident that someday he would return to his people.

The Thorbardin dwarves still swore oaths in Reorx's name; Tanis had heard swearing enough on the bridge to know that. Flint had done the same all the years Tanis had known him, though Reorx had been absent for hundreds of years. According to Flint, the clerics of Reorx vanished from the world just prior to the Cataclysm, leaving the same time the other clerics of the true gods mysteriously departed. But were there now any new clerics beneath the mountain?

His friends were also looking around the temple, and Tanis guessed they were thinking along the same lines, some of them, at least. Caramon was staring wistfully at the food, as Arman came by, offering everyone a share.

The dwarves were munching on hunks of some sort of salted meat. Caramon eyed it hungrily then glanced at Tasslehoff, thinking of worms, and with a deep sigh, shook his head. Arman shrugged and gave some to Flint, who accepted a large portion with muttered thanks.

Raistlin had refused any nourishment and gone straight to his bed. Tasslehoff sat cross-legged in front of one of the lanterns, munching on his meal and watching the worm inside. Flint had told him the worm was the larva of gigantic worms that chewed through solid stone. Tas was fascinated, and he kept tapping on the glass panel to see the larva wriggle.

"Should we say anything about the return of the gods?" Sturm asked, coming to sit down beside Tanis.

Tanis shook his head emphatically. "We're in enough trouble as it is."

"We will have to bring up the gods," Sturm insisted, "when we ask about the Hammer of Kharas."

"We're not going to talk about the hammer," said Tanis shortly. "We're going to try to keep out of a dwarven dungeon!"

Sturm considered this. "You're right. Speaking of the gods would be awkward, especially if Reorx has *not* returned to them. Still, I don't see why we should not ask Arman about the hammer. It shows we have a knowledge of their history."

"Just drop it, Sturm," Tanis said sharply, and he went over to have a talk with Flint.

He sat down beside the dwarf and accepted some of the food. "What's wrong with Caramon? I never before saw him turn down a meal."

"The kender told him it was worm meat."

Tanis spit the meat out his mouth.

"It's dried beef," said Flint with a low chuckle.

"Did you tell Caramon?"

"No," the dwarf returned with a sly grin. "Do him good to lose some weight."

Tanis went over to assuage Caramon's fears. He left the big man chewing voraciously on the tough and stringy beef, swearing he would tear off the kender's pointy ears and stuff them into his boots. The half-elf went back to finish his talk with Flint.

"Have you heard these dwarves mention Reorx, other than swearing by him?" Tanis asked.

"No." Flint held the Helm of Grallen in his lap, his hands resting protectively on top of it. "You won't either."

"Then you don't think Reorx has returned to them?"

"As if he would!" Flint snorted. "The mountain dwarves shut Reorx out of the mountain when they sealed the doors on us."

"Sturm was asking me . . . do you think we should tell the dwarves about the gods' return?"

"I wouldn't tell a mountain dwarf how to find his beard in a snowstorm!" Flint said scornfully.

His hands on the helm, Flint propped himself up against a wall and settled himself for sleep.

"Keep one eye open, my friend," said Tanis softly.

Flint grunted and nodded.

———————————

Tanis made the rounds. Sturm lay on the floor, staring up into the darkness. Tasslehoff had fallen asleep beside the worm lantern.

"Drat all kender anyway," Caramon said, pulling a blanket over Tas. "I could have starved to death!" He glanced surreptitiously around. "I don't trust these dwarves, Tanis," he said quietly. "Should one of us stand watch?"

Tanis shook his head. "We're all exhausted and we have to appear before this Council tomorrow. We need to have our wits about us."

He stretched out on the cold stone floor of the abandoned temple and thought he had never been so tired in his life, yet he couldn't sleep. He had visions of them all being cast into the dwarven dungeons, never to see the light of day again. Already he was starting to feel closed in; the stone walls pressed down on him. As large as this temple was, it was not large enough to hold all the air Tanis needed. He felt himself being smothered, and he tried to shake off the panicked feeling that came over him whenever he was in dark and closed-up places.

His body ached with fatigue, and he was starting to relax and drift off when Sturm's voice jolted him wide awake.

"Your hero, Kharas, was present at the final battle, was he not?"

Tanis swore softly and sat up.

Sturm and Arman were seated together on the opposite side of the chamber. The dwarven soldiers were making the walls shake with their snoring, but Tanis could hear their conversation quite clearly.

"The knights of Solamnia gave Kharas his name," Sturm was saying, "*Kharas* being the word in my language for 'knight'."

Arman nodded several times and stroked his beard proudly, as though Sturm were speaking of him, not his famous ancestor.

"That is true," Arman stated. "The Solamnic knights were much impressed with his honor and courage."

"Did he carry the legendary Hammer with him during the final battle?" Sturm asked.

Tanis gave an inward groan. He would have intervened, for he did not want the dwarves to begin to suspect they had come here to steal the Hammer, but it was too late. It would do more harm than good. He kept silent.

"Kharas fought courageously," Arman told the story, enjoying himself immensely, "even though he was bitterly opposed to the war, for he said brother should not be slaying brother. Kharas even went so far as to shave off his beard to mark his opposition to the war, shocking the people. A clean-shaven chin is the mark of a coward.

"And so some called Kharas, for when he saw that dwarves on both sides had lost all reason and were killing each other out of hatred and vengeance, he left the field of battle, bearing with him the bodies of two of King Duncan's sons, who had died fighting side-by-side. Thus Kharas survived the terrible explosion that took the lives of thousands of dwarves and men.

"King Duncan saw the bodies of his sons, and when word came to him of the blast and he knew that countless dwarves lay dead on the Plains of Dergoth, he ordered the gates of Thorbardin sealed. He vowed in his grief that no more would die in this dreadful war."

"You say Duncan had two sons and they died on the field of battle and Kharas returned their bodies. What, then, of Prince Grallen?" Sturm paled; he seemed troubled. "I do not know how I know this, but the prince did not die on the field of battle. His body was never found."

Arman cast a dark glance at the helm. Flint had fallen asleep, but even in sleep he kept fast hold of the relict.

"The Council will decide if that story will be told," Arman said sternly. "For now, we will not speak of it."

"Then let us talk of more pleasant subjects," said Sturm. His voice grew husky with reverence. "All my life, I have heard the stories of the fabled Hammer of Kharas, the sacred hammer wielded by Huma Dragonbane himself. I would like very much be able to see the Hammer and do it honor."

"So would we all," said Arman.

Sturm frowned, as if he thought the dwarf was making fun of him. "I do not understand," he said stiffly.

"The Hammer of Kharas is lost. We have spent three hundred years searching for it. Without the sacred Hammer, no dwarf can be named High King, and without a High King, the dwarven people will never be unified."

"Lost?" Sturm repeated, shocked. "How could the dwarves misplace such a valuable artifact?"

"It was *not* misplaced," Arman Kharas returned angrily. "After the gates were sealed, the clans began to plot to overthrow King Duncan, whom they now deemed to be weak. Each thane came to Kharas seeking support for his claim to the throne. Kharas wanted nothing to do with any of them, so he left Thorbardin by secret means and went into self-imposed exile. He stayed away many years. Finally, growing weary of his travels and longing for his home and his people, Kharas returned to Thorbardin, only to find the situation had worsened.

"The kingdoms were embroiled in civil war. Kharas was able to talk with Duncan one final time before he died. Grief-stricken, Kharas carried the king's body to the magnificent tomb Duncan had built for himself. Kharas took with him the famous hammer. I told you what he said," Arman added. "The prophecy that I will fulfill."

Sturm gave a polite nod, but he was not interested in prophecies. "So the Hammer is in King Duncan's Tomb."

"We can only assume so. Kharas never returned to tell us. None know his fate."

"Where is the tomb located?"

"In the final resting place of all dwarves, the Valley of Thanes."

Sturm tugged on his long mustache, a sign that he was disturbed. Tanis could guess the cause. No true knight would ever disturb the sacred sleep of the noble dead, yet his desire for the Hammer was great.

"Perhaps," he said after a moment, "I might be permitted to enter the tomb. I would do so with reverence and respect, of course. Why do you shake your head? Is this forbidden?"

"So it would seem," said Arman. "When Kharas did not return, the thanes and their followers raced to the tomb, each hoping to be the one to lay claim to the hammer. Fighting broke out in the sacred valley and it was then, when the battle was at its height, that a powerful force ripped the tomb from the ground and carried it into the sky."

"The tomb vanished?" Sturm was dismayed.

"It did not vanish. We can see it, but we cannot reach it. Duncan's Tomb floats hundreds of feet above the Valley of the Thanes."

Sturm's brow darkened.

"Do not look so downhearted, Sir Knight," said Arman complacently. "You will yet have a chance to see the wondrous Hammer."

"What do you mean?" Sturm asked.

"As I said, I am the dwarf of whom the prophecy speaks. I am the one destined to find the Hammer of Kharas. When the time is right, Kharas himself will guide me to it, and I am certain the time is almost upon us."

"How can you tell?"

Arman would not say. Stating that he was tired, he went over to check on his brother then took himself to his bed.

Deeply disappointed, Sturm lapsed into gloomy silence. Tanis stared into the impenetrable darkness. The Hammer they needed to forge the dragonlances was lost, or if not lost, out of reach.

Nothing was going right it seemed.

***

Flint was doing as Tanis suggested, sleeping with one eye open, and that eye opened wide when he saw a strange dwarf come strolling into the temple as nonchalantly and confidently as if he owned the place. The dwarf was like no dwarf Flint had ever seen in his life. The stranger had a magnificent beard, glossy and luxuriant, and long curling hair that flowed down his back. He wore a blue coat with golden buttons, high boots that came to his thighs, a ruffled shirt, and a wide brimmed hat topped by a red plume. At this astonishing sight, Flint he sat bolt upright.

He was about to shout a warning, but something in the cocky attitude of the dwarf stopped him, that and the fact that the dwarf walked right up to Flint and stared at him rudely.

"Here now," said Flint, frowning. "Who are you?"

"You know my name," said the dwarf, continuing to stare down at him, "just as I know yours. I'm an old friend of yours, Flint Fireforge."

Flint sputtered in protest. "You're no such thing! I never in my life had a friend who wore such frippery. Feathers and ruffles! You put a Palanthas dandy to shame!"

"Still, you know me. You call on me often. You swear by my beard and you ask me to take your soul if you're lying." The dwarf reached into the darkness and pulled out a jug. Removing the stopper, he sniffed at it and smiled expansively and offered it to Flint.

The redolent odor of the potent liquor known as dwarf spirits filled the air.

"Care for a swallow?" the stranger asked.

A terrible suspicion entered Flint's mind. He felt in need of support. Taking the jug, he put it to his mouth and took a gulp. The fiery liquor burned his tongue, took him by the throat, wrung his neck, then sizzled down his gullet to his stomach where it exploded.

Flint gave a moist sigh and wiped tears from his eyes.

"Good, eh? It's my own home brew," said the dwarf, adding proudly, "I'll wager you've never tasted anything like it."

Flint nodded and coughed.

The dwarf snatched back the jug, took a pull himself, then corked it up and tossed it back into the air where it vanished. He squatted down on his haunches in front of Flint, who squirmed under the intense gaze of the stranger's black eyes.

"Figured out my name yet?" the dwarf asked.

Flint knew the dwarf's name as well as he knew his own, but the realization was so stupefying that he didn't want to believe it, and so he shook his head.

"I won't make an issue of it," the dwarf said with a shrug and a good natured grin. "Suffice it to say, I know you, Flint Fireforge. I know you very well. I knew your father and your grandfather, too, and they knew me, just like you know me, even if you're too stubborn to admit it. That gratifies me. It gratifies me highly.

"Therefore," said the dwarf, and he leaned forward and jabbed Flint rudely in the breastbone. "I'm going to do something for you. I'm going to give you the chance to be a hero. I'm going to give you the chance to find the Hammer of Kharas and save the world by forging the dragonlances. Your name, Flint Fireforge, will echo in halls and palaces throughout Ansalon."

Flint was suspicious. "What's the catch?"

The dwarf guffawed, doubling over with laughter. Oddly, no one else in the temple seemed to hear him. No one else stirred.

"You don't have much time left, Flint Fireforge. You know that, don't you? You have trouble catching your breath sometimes, pain in your jaw and your left arm . . . same symptoms your father had right near the end."

"I do not!" Flint stated indignantly. "I'm fit as you or any dwarf here. Fitter, if I say so myself!"

The stranger shrugged. "All I'm saying is that you need to think of the legacy you will leave behind. Will your name be sung by the bards after you are gone, or will you die an ignominious death, alone and forgotten?"

"Like I said, what's the catch?" Flint asked, frowning.

"All you have to do is put on the Helm of Grallen," said the dwarf.

"Hah!" Flint said loudly. He thumped his knuckles on the helm that rested beneath his hands. "I knew it! A trap!"

"It's not a trap," said the dwarf, and he smoothed his beard complacently. "Prince Grallen knows where the Hammer can be found. He knows how to reach it."

"What of the curse?" Flint challenged.

The dwarf shrugged. "There is danger. I don't deny it, but then, life is a gamble, Flint Fireforge. You have to risk all to gain all."

Flint mulled this over, absently rubbing his left arm. Then he caught the dwarf regarding him with a sly smile and stopped.

"I'll think about it," Flint said.

"You do that," said the dwarf, and he rose to his feet and stretched and yawned.

Flint rose, too, out of respect. "Have you . . . uh . . . have you made this offer to anyone else?"

The dwarf winked slyly. "That's for me to know."

Flint grunted. "Do they . . . these dwarves . . . know you're here?"

The dwarf glared about the temple. "Does it look like they know? Spoiled brats! 'Do this! Do that! Give me this. Give me that. Favor me over him. Heed my prayers; don't listen to his. I'm worthy. He's not.' Bah!"

The dwarf gave a great roar. He raised his hands to heaven and shook his fists and roared again and again. The mountain trembled and Flint fell, cowering, to his knees.

The dwarf lowered his arms. He smoothed out his coat, settled his lace, and retrieved his plumed hat.

"I may come back to Thorbardin," he said with a wink and a sly smile. "I may not. It all depends."

He put his hat on his head, cast Flint a piercing glance, and strolled out of the temple, whistling a jaunty tune as he went.

Flint remained on his knees.

Arman Kharas, waking, saw him crouched on the floor.

"Ah, you felt the quake," he said. "Don't be alarmed. It was a small one. A rattler we call it—rattles a few dishes. Nothing more. Go back to sleep."

Arman lay back down and rolled over and was soon snoring again.

Flint stood up shakily and wiped the sweat from his brow. He eyed the Helm of Grallen and thought—not for the first time—of what it would be like to be a hero. He thought of the pain in his arm, and he thought of death, and he thought of no one remembering. He thought of dishes rattling in Thorbardin.

Flint lay back down, but he did not go to sleep. He put the helm to one side and took care not to touch it.

6

FROZEN AMBITIONS. PLANS FOR A THAW.

Dray-yan paced the room, waiting for Grag to come with his report. Pacing, like shrugging, was another mannerism the aurak had picked up from humans. When he'd first witnessed Dragon Highlord Verminaard think out problems by walking the length of the room, Dray-yan had viewed the practice with disdain, a lamentable waste of physical energy. That was before Dray-yan had been faced with problems of his own. Now the aurak paced.

When the knock came at his door, Dray-yan recognized Grag's rapping and barked out a command to enter using Verminaard's voice.

Grag came inside and swiftly shut the door behind him.

"Well?" Dray-yan demanded, seeing the glum look on Grag's face. "What news?"

"The gate to Thorbardin is open, and it is snowing in the mountains. We had to give up our pursuit of the slaves."

"A pity," said Dray-yan.

"The snow is heavy and wet, and it blots out everything!" Grag said in his defense. "The dragons, both red and blue, refuse to fly in the stuff. They say that it builds up on their wings. They can't see in it, they become disoriented, and they're afraid of blundering into the side of the mountain. If we want dragons who are accustomed to snow, we should send for the white dragons who are in the south."

"They are being used in the Ice Wall campaign. Even if they agreed to come, it would take weeks of negotiation with Dragon Highlord Feal-Thas, and I don't have the time to spare."

"You don't appear much interested in the slaves," Grag observed, "after going to all that trouble to attack them."

"I'm not. The slaves can go to the Abyss." Dray-yan scowled, gesturing at a scroll bound by a black ribbon that lay on his desk. "I have received a commendation from Ariakas for doubling the iron output."

"You should be pleased, Dray-yan," Grag said, wondering why the aurak wasn't.

"Let me put it another way. *Lord Verminaard* has received the commendation," said Dray-yan, grinding his teeth on the name, then spitting it out.

"Ah," said Grag, understanding.

"Entering Thorbardin was *my* doing!" Dray-yan raved. "*My* idea! *My* time spent dealing with those hairy, squinty-eyed Theiwar rodents! And who gets the credit? Verminaard! *He* has received a summons from the emperor inviting him to Neraka to receive Ariakas's grateful thanks and a promotion! What am I to do, Grag? I cannot walk into Her Dark Majesty's temple wearing this illusion, nor do I want to! I—Dray-yan! I deserve that commendation, the thanks, the promotion!"

"You could always send a message to Ariakas to say that Verminaard was killed."

"Ariakas would dispatch another human Highlord here so fast my scales would fly off, that female they call the Blue Lady. She'd like nothing better than to take command of the Red Army, and from what I've heard, she despises draconians. You and I would both end up working in the iron mines if she took over!"

Dray-yan began to pace the floor again. His claws had torn large holes in the carpeting and he was now leaving scratch marks on the tiles beneath.

"The emperor is asking again about the escaped slaves and about that artifact, that dwarf hammer. He seems obsessed over it. He wants me, or rather Verminaard, to find it and bring it to

Neraka when I come. How am I supposed to unearth some moldy old hammer? The emperor also wants assurances the slaves have all been killed. There are dangerous people hiding among them, elf assassins or some such thing."

Grag watched the aurak pace in silence. He really didn't give a damn about the aurak's personal ambitions to become Dragon Highlord, but Dray-yan did have a point. Grag had heard a few rumors about the Blue Lady himself. Grag had a good life here, and he knew it.

"What are we going to do about these slaves?" Grag asked. "They will likely take advantage of the snow to try sneak past us and gain entrance to Thorbardin."

Dray-yan turned to face him. "Do we have troops in the area?"

"Some, but most of them are being positioned around the southern part of Thorbardin. They couldn't reach the north in time. It's too bad Lord Verminaard bungled that attack in the valley."

Dray-yan swore beneath his breath. His plan of attack — bringing in draconian troops on the back of dragons — had been a brilliant one. He'd supervised the battle himself in the guise of Dragon Highlord Verminaard. He didn't like to be reminded that his plan had failed. He wasn't pleased with Grag for bringing it up.

"The humans knew we were coming!" he snarled. "It's the only explanation. I'd like to know how they found out."

"Don't you understand, Dray-yan? The fault is *Lord Verminaard's,*" said Grag, laying emphasis on the name. "The Highlord could not keep his mouth shut. He blabbed about his brilliant idea of putting draconians on dragons and sending them after the humans. Their spies heard about it and managed to warn the humans, so that they had time to escape. At least, that is what you will tell the emperor, if he should ask."

Dray-yan caught the glint in the bozak's eye.

"You are right, Grag!" Dray-yan said, intrigued. "The fault was Lord Verminaard's. Go on. You were speaking of our troops in the area. What about the forces at Skullcap?"

"They failed to show up at the rendezvous site. Either they deserted, or they're dead."

"So," said Dray-yan, "because of Lord Verminaard's bungling, we don't have enough men in the area to stop these humans from reaching Thorbardin."

"Lord Verminaard has really managed this very badly. It is a shame," Grag continued, "because Her Dark Majesty knows that it was *your* idea to put draconian troops on the backs of dragons. Her Dark Majesty is pleased with you."

"Is she?" Dray-yan asked skeptically. "Then why is she making my life difficult? Why not clear the skies of snowclouds so that her dragons can fly?"

"The lesser gods do what they can to fight her," Grag said dismissively. "Her Dark Majesty pays them small heed. She is giving you a chance to prove yourself, Dray-yan, and while I still don't like you—"

"So you keep telling me," Dray-yan sneered.

"—your success bodes well for all draconians. If you were to become a Dragon Highlord, all of us would benefit."

"Yes, go on," said Dray-yan.

"Lord Verminaard is already in trouble for having let the refugees escape in the first place. He is now in trouble for failing to recapture them."

"But Verminaard is being commended by Emperor Ariakas for negotiating with the dwarves."

"Negotiations he turned over to you, while he went chasing after the slaves."

"Brilliant . . ." murmured Dray-yan.

"If Lord Verminaard were to fail yet again and then follow up that failure by dying an ignoble and ignominious death, and if you were to spring to the fore and save the day, the emperor could hardly fail to reward you. Her Dark Majesty would see to that."

Dray-yan was silent, mulling this over. The more he thought about this scheme, the more he liked it. All his mistakes could be attributed to Lord Verminaard. The triumphs would be his own. Grinning broadly, he clapped the bozak on his scaly shoulder.

"Well, done, Grag! We make a good team!"

"I hope you will keep that in mind when you are a Dragon Highlord," Grag said stiffly, his scales clicking in irritation. He disliked being touched.

"I will! I will. What do you want in reward, Grag?" Dray-yan asked magnanimously.

"Command of a regiment," said Grag at once, "a regiment of humans."

Dray-yan grinned. "I think that could be arranged. Now, in regard to these slaves—"

"We could attack them with the forces we have," Grag said. "The troops who wiped out that nest of gully dwarves are still in the area."

"Gully dwarves?" Dray-yan had forgotten.

"The ones who discovered our secret tunnels."

"Ah, those. No," Dray-yan replied after a moment's thought. "Lord Verminaard is going to botch this yet again. He's going to allow the humans to reach Thorbardin." The aurak shook his head in sorrow. "A fatal error on his lordship's part, don't you agree, Grag?"

"Fatal," said Grag, with a snap of his teeth.

"Fortunately for Her Dark Majesty," Dray-yan continued, reaching for pen and ink and parchment, "the brilliant aurak draconian who is Verminaard's second-in-command will be on hand to save the day."

7

Bad dreams. Giant mushrooms.
Private thoughts.

lint woke up to find his hand resting on the Helm of Grallen. He snatched his hand off, eyeing the helm uneasily. He remembered last night's dream vividly, so vividly that it seemed almost real. Ridiculous, of course. Oh, it was all very well for Goldmoon and Elistan to have encounters with gods. They were human, after all, and humans were forever speaking about their gods in familiar terms, almost if they were buddies, then going about proselytizing, sharing their religious beliefs with everyone they met.

Not so Flint Fireforge. Religion was a deep and private matter for the dwarf. Oh, he might swear by Reorx's beard on occasion, but that was out of respect, and Flint did not go around extolling the god's virtues to perfect strangers. Why, if he did that, the kender might decide to worship Reorx!

Reorx wasn't a god to go poking his nose into a dwarf's own private affairs. Likewise, a dwarf shouldn't go about badgering the god to intervene. Those were Flint's feelings on the subject. It sounded to him as if some of his fellow dwarves didn't agree with that notion. All that talk about dwarves demanding Reorx do this for them and fix that . . .

If he believed some fancy-pants stranger who had nothing better to do than disturb a fellow's sleep.

Flint eyed the helm. He'd taken it from Arman because he'd been furious that Arman had taken it away from him. Otherwise, Flint was forced to admit, he wouldn't have touched the accursed thing. That it *was* cursed, he had no doubt.

The helm was magic, which meant that it must have been made by Theiwar, the only dwarves who were skilled in magic. True, the helm was of ancient make, and by all accounts, the Theiwar had not always been as devious and dark-souled in the old days as they were now. The helm had brought him and his friends here and showed them how to enter the gate, though whether that was a good thing or not remained to be seen. The helm hadn't done anything bad to Sturm. As far as Flint was concerned, being transformed from a human into a dwarf was a step up.

Still, the helm was magic, and to Flint's mind there was no such thing as good magic. He had no intention of putting it on.

Flint looked over at Tanis, still sleeping, though not soundly or peacefully to judge by his sighs and mutterings.

"I wonder if I should tell him about my dream."

Of all of his friends, Tanis was the only one the dwarf would even consider telling. He knew what the others would say if they found out that Reorx had promised him a chance to find the Hammer of Kharas. Once they heard that all he had to do was put on the helm, Raistlin and Sturm would be dragging it down around his ears. Telling Caramon was out of the question. He'd just tell his twin. Flint didn't even consider Tasslehoff.

"No," Flint decided. "I can't tell Tanis, either. He's got all those refugees on his hands. He'd never do anything to cause me harm, but if it came right down to it and he had to make a choice, he'd ask me to put on the helm . . ."

Flint sighed, then said gruffly to himself. "It was a dream! A stupid dream. As if I could ever be a hero . . . or even *want* to be!"

───────────◆───◆───

Arman woke them for an early start the next morning—at least, they assumed it was morning; there was no way to tell what time it was. They continued walking through the dwarven realm, the vastness of which amazed them, for it seemed to go on and on, and as Tasslehoff said, "went up and down and sideways."

"Thorbardin encompasses three hundred square miles beneath the mountain," Arman bragged. "We have built dwellings, shops, and businesses on every level, level upon level, all of them laid out in orderly fashion. You can go into any city in any part of Thorbardin, and you will always know exactly what to find where."

You could not have proven that by Tanis. He was lost in the maze; all the streets, shops, and dwellings looked alike to him, until they came to what Arman termed "transport shafts"—large holes bored in the rock that connected all the levels. Buckets attached to huge chains clanked up and down between the levels. Those wanting to go from one level to another (and not wanting to climb the chain ladders suspended between levels) could enter one of the buckets and ride to their destination.

Tanis peered over the edge of one of these shafts, and he was astounded to see how many levels there were. Arman Kharas considered these buckets a marvel of dwarven engineering, and he expected the companions to be impressed. He was disappointed to find that they'd seen a similar device at use in the ruined city of Xak Tsaroth, and said dismissively that dwarven engineers must have designed it.

They did not ride in the buckets, for which Caramon was grateful; his last experience with dwarven transportation having been one he'd just as soon forget. They continued walking on what Arman called the Road of the Thanes. Their journey took them from the abandoned city delvings of the Theiwar to a forest—a strange and wondrous forest located in a large natural cavern dubbed the "West Warrens." Here the companions were impressed enough to suit even Arman Kharas.

"The trees are all mushrooms!" cried Tasslehoff.

The kender clapped his hands in delight and inadvertently let fall a small knife which Tanis recognized as belonging to Arman Kharas. Tanis swiftly retrieved the knife, and when the dwarf was busy showing off the wonders of the mushroom forest, he slipped it deftly into the top of the dwarf's boot.

Raistlin, who had long made a study of herbs and plants, was eager to inspect the gigantic mushrooms towering over their heads. The mushrooms, other fungi, and strange darkness-thriving plants sprouted up out of rich loam that filled the area with an earthy, pungent odor. The smell was not unpleasant, but served to remind Tanis that he was deep underground, buried alive.

He suddenly had the terrible feeling that if he didn't get out of here, he was going to smother to death. His chest constricted. Sweat broke out on his forehead. He was strongly tempted to break away and run back to the gate. Even the thought of boulders raining down on him didn't deter him. He licked dry lips and looked about for an escape route.

Then there was Flint, solid and reassuring beside him.

"The old trouble?" asked the dwarf softly.

"Yes!" Tanis tugged on the collar of his tunic that, though loose, wasn't loose enough.

Flint brought out a water skin he had filled from a public well near the temple. "Here, take a drink. Try to think of something else."

"Something other than being sealed up in a tomb!" Tanis said, swallowing the cool water and laving it on his forehead and neck.

"I had a dream last night," Flint said gruffly. "Reorx came to me and offered to give me the Hammer of Kharas. All I have to do is put on this helm."

"Then put it on," said Sturm. "Why do you hesitate?"

Flint scowled and glanced around behind him to see the knight breathing down his neck. "I wasn't talking to you, Sturm Brightblade. I was talking to Tanis."

"The god of the dwarves comes to you and tells you to put on the helm and in return he will guide you to the Hammer of Kharas, and you weren't going to tell me!"

"It was a dream!" Flint said loudly.

"What was a dream?" Caramon asked, coming up.

Sturm explained.

"Hey, Raist," Caramon called. "You'd better come hear this."

"Come hear what?" cried Tasslehoff, dashing over.

Raistlin reluctantly pulled himself away from studying the fungi and joined them. Sturm told the story, and Flint again stated testily that it was nothing but a dream and he was sorry he'd ever brought it up.

"Are you sure about it being a dream?" Tanis asked. "We were in Reorx's temple, after all."

"So you're saying that now you believe in the gods?" Flint demanded.

"No," said Tanis.

Sturm gave him a reproachful look.

"But I do think . . ." Tanis stopped.

"You think I should put on the helm?" Flint said.

"Yes!" Sturm said firmly, and Raistlin echoed him.

Tanis did not answer.

"The helm didn't tell Sturm where the Hammer was," Flint pointed out.

"Sturm isn't a dwarf," Caramon said.

Flint glowered at him. "Would you put on this helm, you big lummox?"

"I will!' Tasslehoff cried.

Caramon shook his head.

"I thought not," Flint grunted. "Well, Half-Elven?"

"If you found the Hammer of Kharas and returned it to the dwarves, you would be a hero," Tanis said. "The Thanes would be willing to grant you anything you asked for, maybe even open up their kingdom to the refugees."

"Oh, bosh!" said Flint, and he stomped off in high dudgeon.

"You have to make him put on that helm, Tanis," Sturm said. "One of the soldiers speaks Common, and I asked him about the Hammer. He told me outright that it never existed; it is only a myth. According to him, Arman Kharas has been up and down the Valley of the Thanes for years searching for the way inside the tomb. But if Flint knows how to find the hammer . . ."

"He's right, Tanis," said Raistlin. "You have to convince Flint to put on the helm. It won't hurt him. It didn't hurt Sturm."

"Just enslaved him, taking over his body," Tanis returned, "changing him into another person and forcing him to come here."

"But it brought him back," said Raistlin, spreading his hands, as though he couldn't understand the fuss.

"You know Flint. You know how stubborn he can be. How do you suggest we get the helm on him if he refuses to even consider it? Tie him up and hold him down and jam it on his head?"

"I have rope in my pouch!" Tas offered helpfully.

"It has to be his choice," Tanis stated. "You know that the more you badger him, the more he'll get his back up and the less likely he'll be to do anything. I suggest you two leave him alone. Let him make his own decisions."

Raistlin and Sturm exchanged glances. Both did know Flint, and they both knew Tanis was right. Raistlin inclined his head and went back to his fungus. Sturm stalked off, tugging on his mustaches.

Tanis wished the dwarf had kept his mouth shut."Damn it to the Abyss," he muttered.

Arman came up. "We have spent enough time here. I have received word that the Council of Thanes will meet with you."

"That's big of them," said Caramon. "I'll go pry Raistlin loose."

Caramon went off to find his brother, locating him at last down on his hands and knees studying a grotesque looking plant that had black leaves and a purple stem which gave off an odor like cow dung. They eventually persuaded Raistlin to leave, but only by promising that he could return at some point to continue his studies.

Raistlin waxed voluble over the wonders he'd seen and endeared himself to Arman by asking the dwarf countless questions about the cultivation process of the mushrooms, the type of soil they preferred, how the dwarven farmers kept the ground moist, and so on, as they proceeded along the Road of the Thanes.

At least, thought Tanis, the dwarf's startling revelation had taken his own mind off the notion that he was trapped miles beneath ground.

Tanis supposed he should be grateful.

* * *

The mushroom forest gave way to fields of tended mushrooms, other fungi and more odd-looking plants. Arman hurried them along now, not allowing time for any more stops. The dwarves in the fields halted their work to stare at them. Even the small ponies who pulled the plows lifted their heads to take a look. More than one dwarf threw down his rake or hoe and went racing off over the fields, presumably to spread the news that for the first time in three hundred years "Talls" had found their way beneath the mountain.

In the more populated parts of Thorbardin, the wagon and rail system still worked. Arman's guards commandeered several wagons, ordering out the dwarves who had been riding in them and telling them to wait for another. None of these dwarves had ever seen a human and probably thought them myths, like the Hammer. They stood rooted to the spot, staring. Children burst into wails of terror.

For the most part, no one said anything but were simply content to gape. Here and there, however, a few dwarves had comments to make and these were all directed at Flint, who, by his clothes and the manner in which he wore his beard, was clearly a hill dwarf. He obviously did not belong beneath the mountain and soon the word went around that he was a Neidar, one of the enemy.

Tanis was well aware that Flint and all his people had nursed a three-hundred-year-old grudge against Thorbardin. He'd been hoping that the dwarves of Thorbardin would be more generous. After all, they'd won the war—if one could call it winning—when thousands on both sides had perished. But by the dark looks and muttered remarks, neither side was prepared to forget, much less forgive.

Not all the insults were aimed at the outsiders, nor were the rocks, one of which struck one of the soldier's shoulders between his shoulder blades. The rock wasn't very big, and it bounced harmlessly off the soldier's breastplate. The Hylar soldiers were irate, however, and wanted to chase after the malefactors, who had vanished into the throng.

Arman reminded his men sternly that the Council would be in session that afternoon, and they must not arrive late. The soldiers grumbled but did as they were ordered. Tanis had the feeling this was just an excuse. Looking around at the gathering crowd of dwarves and seeing the grim expressions on their faces, he saw what Arman Kharas was seeing—his forces were outnumbered, and the crowd was in an ugly mood. What was astonishing and troubling was that these dwarves were not Theiwar.

"Trouble beneath the mountain," said Flint, and he couldn't help but look a bit smug.

"Find out what's going on," Tanis said. "It might affect what the Council decides to do with us."

Flint didn't feel all that inclined to have a conversation with Arman Kharas, but he conceded that Tanis was right. They needed to know something of the political situation of Thorbardin before they faced the Council. He waited to speak to Arman until they were all inside the wagon and it was trundling along the tracks, heading still deeper into the mountain's interior. Flint was not used to prying information out of people. He was uncomfortable and didn't know where to start. Fortunately, Arman was given to conversation, and he turned to Flint.

"For some the war has not ended," he stated, and Flint could not tell whether the dwarf meant this as some sort of apology or an accusation.

"For some it will never end," Flint replied dourly, "not so long as those beneath the mountain live in safety and comfort, while my people work the land and fight off goblins and ogres to defend it."

Arman snorted. "Do you think we live well here?"

"Don't you?" Flint challenged, and he gestured at the farm fields, snug homes and businesses gliding past them.

"This looks prosperous," said Arman, "but what you do not see are the hundreds of miners who have no work because the iron mines have closed, or rather," he added, "you saw them—those who threw the rocks at us."

"The mines closed!" Flint was astonished. "Why? Are they played out?"

"Oh, we have iron ore aplenty," said Arman, "just no one to buy it. If every dwarf who lived in Thorbardin needed ten swords or fourteen kettles or thirty-six stew pots our iron mongers would have business enough, but no one does. The owners of the mines could not pay the miners. Dwarves who have no work cannot pay their butchers, who in turn cannot pay their landlords, who cannot pay the farmers . . ."

"Our children are being killed by dragons, goblins, and lizard-men," Flint said heatedly. "War rages above, and you complain about not being able to pay a butcher's bill! But there, I've said more than I should. The half-elf will tell our tale when he's before the Council."

Arman's eyes flickered. "Tell me more about what is happening on the surface."

Flint shook his head.

"There will be war down here as well," Arman said, when it was apparent the dwarf would not elaborate. "You saw those dwarves back there. You heard the names they called us. The Council still rules in Thorbardin, but the people are growing more and more discontented. A year ago, no Theiwar would have dared attack a Hylar. Now with the increasing unrest among the population, our enemies, the Theiwar *and* the Daegar, view us as weak and vulnerable."

Arman was silent, then he said abruptly. "You asked me what sign I was given that my destiny is near. I will tell you. I believe it was the opening of Northgate."

"What about the Helm of Grallen?" Flint asked.

Arman's face darkened. "I don't know. I don't quite understand that part." He shrugged, and his expression cleared. "Still, I have faith in Kharas. He will guide me. My time is at hand."

Flint squirmed in his seat. He felt unaccountably guilty about his dream, as though he and Reorx were somehow plotting behind Arman's back.

"Don't be an old fool," Flint scolded himself.

Arman Kharas fell silent. He wore a rapt look, dreaming of his destiny.

The companions continued the journey along the Road of the Thanes, all of them absorbed in their own thoughts and dreams.

Caramon hung on to the side of the wagon that was swaying perilously back and forth along the track, thinking of Tika, berating himself for letting her go off alone, praying she was all right, and knowing he would blame himself if anything had happened to her. He hoped she would forgive him, hoped she did understand, as she had told him.

"Raistlin needs me, Tika," Caramon said silently over and over, his big hand gripping the side of the wagon. "I can't leave him."

Raistlin was thinking over the strange events that had happened to him in Skullcap. How had he known his way around a place he'd never been? Why had he called Caramon by a strange name that wasn't entirely strange? Why had the wraiths protected him? He had no idea, yet there was the nagging feeling deep within him that he did know why. The feeling was unpleasant and uncomfortable, and it irritated him, like the feeling you have when you need to recall something vitally important, and it is on the tip of your mind, yet you cannot remember.

"The Master bids us . . ." the wraiths had said to him. What Master?

"Not *my* master," Raistlin said firmly. "No matter what he does for me, no one will ever be *my* master!"

Sturm was thinking of the Hammer of Kharas and its long and glorious history. Originally known as the Hammer of Honor, it had been forged centuries ago in memory of the hammer of Reorx and had been given by the dwarves to the humans of Ergoth as a sign of peace. At one point, the great elven ruler, Kith-Kanan, was said to have had the Hammer in his possession. Always it had been used for peaceful and honorable purposes, never to shed blood.

Thus it was that Huma Dragonbane had sought out the Hammer, giving it into the hands of a famous dwarf smith and bidding him forge the first dragonlances. Armed with these, blessed by the gods,

Huma had been able to drive the Queen of Darkness and her evil dragons back into the Abyss.

After that, the Hammer had disappeared, only to reappear again in the hands of a hero worthy of it—Kharas, who had used the Hammer to try to forge peace, but had failed and now the Hammer was lost.

"If only I could be the one to bring it back to the knights!" said Sturm to himself. "I would stand before the Lord of the Rose and I would say, 'Take this, my lord, and use it to forge the blessed dragon-lances!' The Hammer would help the knights defeat evil, and it would absolve me of my guilt, making up for all the evil that I have done."

Tasslehoff's thoughts were less easy to relate, being rather like a tipsy bee buzzing erratically from one flower to another. They went something like this:

"Caramon needn't hang on to me so tightly. (Indignant) I'm not to going to fall out. Oh! Look at that! (Excited) I'll have a closer look. No, I guess I won't. (Wistful) There it goes. See there! More dwarves! Hullo dwarves! My name is Tasslehoff Burrfoot. Was that a turnip? (Thrilled) Arman, was that a turnip they chunked at you? It certainly is a funny color for a turnip. (Intrigued) I never saw a black one before. Mind if I look at it? Well, you needn't be so cross. (Hurt) It didn't hit you that hard. Whew, boy! Would you look at *that*! (Excited) . . ."

Tanis's thoughts were on Riverwind and the refugees, wondering if they had survived the draconian attack, wondering if they were on their way to Thorbardin. If they were, they were counting on him to find them a safe haven here in the dwarven kingdom.

Tanis looked back on the moment last autumn when he'd met Flint on the hilltop near Solace and he wondered, not for the first time, how he'd come from that point to this—riding along in a dwarf-made wagon over rusted wheels miles beneath the surface of the earth, carrying eight hundred men, women, and children on his back. How he had found himself embroiled in a war he'd never meant to fight. How he had helped bring back gods he didn't believe in.

"When all I ever did was go into the bar to have a drink with old friends," he said with a smile and a sigh.

Flint sat in the wagon, holding onto the Helm of Grallen, and he heard the wheels clicking out the words, "Not much time. Not much time. Not much time . . ."

8

The old dwarven road. Tracks in the snow.

he refugees trudged through the snow, which Riverwind considered a blessing from the gods. The snow fell in huge flakes that came drifting straight down from the gray sky. The air was calm, the wind still. All was silence, for the snow muffled every sound.

He feared that the snow, though a blessing, would also be a curse, for it would make the road slippery and dangerous to travel. Hederick, finding the gods had once again outfoxed him, spoke ominously of compound fractures and people slipping on the ice and falling to their deaths, for of course this ancient road would be in bad repair, cracked and broken.

Hederick did not know dwarves. When dwarves build a road, they build it to last. Though narrow, the road was intact and safe to walk, for the dwarves had taken into account the fact that those traveling the road would be doing so in bad weather and good, in winter and summer, through rain and snow, hail and fog, sleet and wind. They had carved grooves in the stone where the road was steepest, to prevent slipping, and they had built walls to prevent people from falling off the mountain side.

While the snow hid them from their enemies, it also hid them from each other. The people stayed close together, not daring to lose sight of those ahead of them for fear they would end up lost. At times, when the snow fell so thickly that no one could see anything except the woolly flakes, they were forced to halt to wait until the flurries passed and they could once again move on.

Still, they were making good time and Riverwind was hopeful that everyone would be off the mountain by nightfall.

Thus far, they had not been attacked, and Riverwind couldn't help but wonder why. He feared his enemy would be waiting for them in the forest, but his scouts had thus far found no trace of draconians, whose tracks would have been easy to spot in the snow.

"Perhaps, like lizards, draconian blood runs sluggish in the cold," he suggested to Gilthanas.

The two walked near the front of the line. The pine forest was directly ahead of them; they could see the trees, so dark green as to be almost blue, through the breaks in the snow. Some of the refugees had already reached the forest and were setting up camp. Riverwind's plan was that they would remain here, sheltered beneath the trees, while he ventured up the mountain to investigate the opening to find out if it was the gate to the dwarven kingdom.

"Or else our enemy is waiting until night falls," Gilthanas remarked.

"You're such a comfort," said Riverwind.

"You are the one who insists on looking the gods' blessing in the mouth," Gilthanas returned.

"This is too easy," Riverwind muttered.

At that moment, Gilthanas lost his footing in a slushy mix of snow and ice and would have taken a nasty fall if Riverwind hadn't caught hold of him.

"If this is easy, I would hate to see what you consider hard, Plainsman," Gilthanas grumbled. "My clothes are soaked through. My feet are so cold I can no longer feel them. I'd almost welcome a dragon for his fire."

Riverwind shivered suddenly, not from cold but from some unnamed foreboding. He turned to look back up the mountain, blinking away the snow that settled on his eyelashes. When the snow lifted for a moment, he could see the people spread out along the trail, slogging along the road.

"The snow will be ending soon," Gilthanas predicted.

Riverwind agreed. He could feel change coming. The wind was picking up, blowing the snow in swirling circles. The air was growing warmer. The snow would end, and dragons could fly once more.

By the time he and Gilthanas reached the pines, some of the refugees had built a large bonfire in a cleared area. Riverwind was pleased with the location his scouts had chosen for their campsite. The pine branches were thickly intertwined, forming a canopy that even dragon eyes would have a difficult time penetrating. Women were hanging wet blankets and clothes from the branches near the fire to dry, and some, led by Tika, were considering what they might cook for supper. Gilthanas forget his complaints about the cold and spoke of forming a hunting party. He went off to find men to join him.

Tika had recovered from her wounds, but Riverwind was still concerned about her. She stood among the group of women talking of stews, soups, and roast venison. Ordinarily, her infectious laughter would have shaken the snow from the tree limbs and caused all around to smile or join in her merriment. She still spoke her piece, giving her opinion, but she was subdued and quiet. Goldmoon came up to stand beside her husband. She clasped her hands over his arm, leaning her head against his shoulder. Her gaze, too, was fixed on Tika.

"She is not herself," he said. "Perhaps she is not fully healed. You should speak to Mishakal about her."

Goldmoon shook her head. "The gods can heal wounds made to flesh and bone. They cannot heal those of the heart. She is in love with Caramon. He loves her, or rather he would if he if were free to love her."

"He is free," said Riverwind grimly. "All he has to do is tell that brother of his to let him live his own life for a change."

"Caramon can't do that."

"He could if he wanted. Raistlin is powerful in magic, more powerful than he lets on. He's clever and intelligent. He can make his way in this world. He doesn't need his brother."

"You don't understand. Caramon knows all that. It is his greatest fear," said Goldmoon softly, "the day his brother does not need him."

Riverwind snorted. His wife was right; he didn't understand. He turned to Eagle Talon, who had been standing patiently at his elbow.

"We have found something you should come see," said the scout in quiet tones. "Just you," he added with a glance at Goldmoon.

Riverwind followed. The snow had fallen more lightly in this area, barely covering the ground with a white feathery powder. After walking about two miles deeper among the trees, they came to the ruin of the village and the charred bodies of the gully dwarves.

"Poor, miserable wretches," Riverwind said, his brow furrowed in anger.

"They tried to flee. They had no thought of fighting," Eagle Talon said.

"No, gully dwarves would not," Riverwind agreed.

"They were cut down trying to run from their attackers. Look at this—arrows in the back, heads sliced off. Children hacked to bits. And here." He pointed to clawed footprints in the frozen mud. "Draconians did this."

"Any recent signs of them?"

"No. The attack took place days ago," Eagle Talon said. "The ashes are cold. The attackers are long gone. But come see what else we have found."

"Here," he said, indicating footprints. "And here. And here and here. And this."

He pointed to a bent pewter spoon that had been gently laid upon the body of a gully dwarf child, along with a little sprig of pine and a white feather.

"A gift to the dead," he said quietly. "These footprints are those of the kender."

Riverwind looked from the spoon to the small body and shook his head. "I recognize the spoon. It belongs to Hederick."

"He must have dropped it," said Eagle Talon, and they both smiled.

"You can see Tasslehoff's footprints are all over the place, and there is more—two sets of prints that keep together—large feet and small. Here the butt of a staff has left its mark."

"Caramon and Raistlin. So they made it this far," said Riverwind.

"Here the half-elf has left his customary trail marker, and there are the tracks of hob-nailed boots for the dwarf and these for the knight, Sturm Brightblade. As you can see, they stood here for some time talking. Their tracks sank deep in the mud. Then they went off together in that direction, heading up the mountain."

"Our friends are alive and they are together, unless," Riverwind said, his expression darkening, "they were here when the draconians attacked."

"I think not. They came after. You can see where their feet trod in the ashes. Whatever reasons the draconians had for committing this slaughter, it was not because of our friends. My guess is they did it for the love of killing."

"Perhaps," said Riverwind, unconvinced. He did not want to speak his thoughts aloud, for though he did not know it, they tended along the same line as Raistlin's speculations—the gully dwarves had died for a reason. "Keep this to ourselves, no need to worry the others. As you say, whoever did this is long gone."

Eagle Talon agreed, and he and the other scouts returned to camp, there to eat and rest. They would head out early in the morning, making their way up the mountain.

The snow quit during the night. The air grew warmer as the wind shifted, blowing from the ocean waters to the west. The snow began to melt and Riverwind, before he fell asleep, worried that on the morrow the sun would shine and the dragons would return.

The gods had not forgotten them. When dawn came, the sun was not to be seen. A thick layer of fog rolled off the snow and over the pine trees. Wrapped in the gray blanket, the people waited in the forest as Gilthanas and Riverwind, and two of the scouts climbed the face of the mountain, heading for the gaping hole that might or might not be the Gates of Thorbardin.

9

The Life Tree. The Council of Thanes. Bad to worse.

he rattling wagon on wheels rocked along the metal tracks, carrying the companions to the heart of Thorbardin—an enormous cavern. Before them was a gigantic underground lake, and rising out of the lake was one of the wonders of the world.

So astonishing was the sight that for long moments no one could neither move nor speak. Caramon gulped. Raistlin breathed a soft sigh. Tasslehoff was struck dumb, an amazing occurrence in itself. Tanis could only stare. Flint was moved to the depths of his soul. He had heard stories of this all his life and the thought that he was here, the first of his people in three hundred years to view this fabled place, stirred him profoundly.

Arman Kharas stepped out of the wagon.

"The Life Tree of the Hylar," he said, gesturing like a showman. "Impressive, isn't it?"

"I've never seen the like," said Tanis, awed.

"Nor ever will," Flint said huskily, his heart swelling with pride. "Only dwarves could have built this."

The Life Tree of the Hylar was a gigantic stalactite rising up out of the lake known as the Urkhan Sea. Narrow at the bottom, the stalactite widened gradually as it soared upward to the ceiling so far above them they had to crane their necks to see the upper levels. A strange sort of iridescent coral found in the sea had grown up the outside of the stalactite, and the warm glow pulsing from its myriad branches lit the vast cavern almost as bright as day. In addition, lights twinkled from all parts of the Life Tree, for the dwarves had built an enormous city complex in the stalactite. This was the fabled Life Tree, home of the Hylar dwarves for many centuries.

Boats drawn by cables crossed the lake at different points, carrying dwarves of all the clans back and forth from the Life Tree, for as implied by its name, it was the beating heart of Thorbardin. The Hylar dwarves might claim it as their city, but dwarves from all the other clans did business here and took advantage of the inns, taverns, and ale houses that could be found on every level.

The boat docks were busy places. Dock workers tromped about loading and unloading cargo from the boats, while the boat passengers stood patiently in long lines, waiting their turn to cross.

Word had spread from the West Warrens that the gate had been opened, and the Talls who had entered were prisoners and were going to be taken before the Council of Thanes. A large crowd of dwarves had gathered on the docks to see the strangers. There were no disturbances here as there had been in the outlying district. A few dwarves scowled at the sight, with Flint, the kender, and the wizard coming in for the majority of their enmity. Flint noted, however, that many dwarven eyes were fixed on what he carried—the Helm of Grallen. Word of that had spread, too. The looks were dark, bitter, and accusing. Many dwarves made the ancient sign to ward off evil.

Flint juggled the helm nervously. Whatever curse this helm carried must be a potent one. These dwarves were not the ignorant, superstitious Theiwar or the wild-eyed Klar. They were Hylar for the most part, well educated and practical-minded. Flint would have chosen shouted insults over the heavy, ominous silence that lay like on a pall on the crowd.

As Arman Kharas sent soldiers ahead to commandeer a cable boat, Caramon cast Tanis a troubled glance.

"What are we going to do about the dwarf?" he said.

"What about him?" Tanis asked, not understanding.

Caramon jerked a thumb at the boat. "He swore he'd never set foot in one again."

Tanis remembered. Flint was terrified of boats. He claimed it was because Caramon had once nearly drowned him during a fishing expedition. Tanis glanced with trepidation at his friend, expecting a scene. To his surprise, Flint regarded the boats with quiet equanimity and did not seem in the least bothered. After a moment, Tanis realized why.

The dwarf has not been born who can swim. A dwarf in the water sinks like a rock—like a whole sack of rocks. No dwarf feels comfortable on the water, and they had designed their boats with this in mind. The boats were flat-bottomed, long, wide, and solidly built, with never a thought of rocking, swaying, or bobbing in the water. Low seats lined high, windowless, wooden sides that blocked out all sight of the water gurgling beneath.

Arman hustled the companions into the boat, saying they had a long way to go yet before they reached the Court of Thanes, which was located on one of the upper levels. The dwarves on the docks continued to stare after them as they departed. Then one voice called out.

"Throw the cursed helm in the lake and Marman Arman along with it."

Marman Arman. "Marman" was Dwarvish slang for "crazy." Flint glanced at Arman, curious to see what he would do. All he could see was his back. Arman stood in the prow, staring straight ahead. His back was rigid, his shoulders braced, his chin jutting in the air. He acted as if he hadn't heard the insulting play on words.

Flint shifted slightly so that he could see Arman's face. The young dwarf was flushed, his jaw set. His fists were clenched, nails digging into his palms.

"I will find it," he swore. His eyes blinked rapidly, and tears glittered on his lashes. "I will!"

Flint looked away in embarrassment, wishing he hadn't seen. He did not like Arman, considering him a boaster and a braggart, but he found himself feeling sorry for him, as he had once felt sorry for a half-elf who could not find a home among either elves or humans, as he'd felt sorry for orphaned twins left to fend for themselves at an early age, and for a young Solamnic boy separated from his father and forced to live in exile.

Flint did not consciously equate Arman with the others. He certainly had no intention of coming to the aid of this young dwarf who had put them under arrest, but by the same token, Flint had never intended to come to the aid of Tanis, Sturm, Raistlin, or Caramon. If anyone had accused him of such a thing, he would have vehemently denied it. The twins happened to be neighbors; Tanis happened to need a business partner. That was all.

Still, at that moment, Flint felt extremely sorry for Arman Kharas. If the old dwarf could have found who shouted out the insult, he would have slugged him.

The cable boat landed on the Life Tree dock. There were larger crowds here, a mixture of all the clans. Soldiers had cordoned off an area and were holding back the gawkers. The companions met with the same scowls, the same dark looks, the same ominous silence that was broken only by the cheerful voice of the kender, who was constantly trying to stop to introduce himself and shake hands, only to be dragged away by a grim-faced Caramon.

Then, from somewhere in the crowd's midst, a low rumbling sound started, like the growl of a gigantic beast with many throats. The growling grew louder and more menacing and suddenly the mob surged forward, straining against the soldiers, who held them in place with by locking arms and bracing their feet firmly on the stone floor.

"You'd better get them out of here, Your Highness!" a captain cried in dwarven to Arman. "Some are Klar dock workers, and you know the Klar, crazy as rabid bats. I can't hold them back for long."

Arman pointed to a transport shaft that carried the dwarves up and down the levels of the Life Tree. The companions raced for it, with Hylar soldiers closing in behind them, prodding those who came too close with the ends of the spears.

They scrambled into the large bucket-like carriers, which, Caramon was thankful to see, were far more stable than the crude kettle-turned-bucket-turned-carrier they'd encountered at Xak Tsaroth. Crammed inside the bucket along with Arman Kharas, the companions stared out at the thwarted mob. The car gave a lurch and began to clank upward, jolting everyone.

They made the clanking, clattering, jerking ascent in tense silence. The strange world in which they found themselves, the oppressive darkness, the dangers they had already faced, and the hostile reception were beginning to tell on all of them.

"I wish you'd never found this helm," Flint said suddenly, glaring at Raistlin. "Always sticking your nose where it doesn't belong!"

"Do not blame me," Raistlin retorted. "If the fool knight had heeded my warning and not stuck *his* nose in the helm—"

"—we wouldn't be here in Thorbardin now," Sturm countered in icy tones.

"No," Flint returned caustically, "we'd be someplace else, someplace where people didn't want to slit our throats!"

"Just get off Raistlin's back, will you, Flint?" Caramon said heatedly. "He didn't do anything wrong!"

"I do not need you to defend me, Caramon," Raistlin said, adding bitterly, "You can all go to the Abyss for all I care."

"I've always wanted to go to the Abyss," Tasslehoff said. "Wouldn't you like to go there, Raistlin? It must horrible! Wonderfully horrible, that is."

"Oh, just shut up, you doorknob!" Flint thundered.

"Good advice for us all," said Tanis quietly.

He stood braced against the side of the lurching carrier, his arms crossed, his head bowed. Everyone knew immediately what he was thinking—of the refugees who were their responsibility, and of the people counting on them to find safety. Perhaps the refugees were fleeing for their lives this moment, running from their enemies, putting all their hopes for survival on them, and this would be their welcome: angry mobs, swords and spears, boulders hurled at them from the darkness.

Sturm, frustrated, twisted his mustache. Caramon flushed guiltily. Tasslehoff opened his mouth, only to shut it again when Raistlin rested his hand in gentle remonstrance on the kender's shoulder. Flint kept his glowering gaze fixed on the floor of the bucket, refusing to look at any of them, for he guessed rightly that they were all looking at him.

And the Helm of Grallen. The cursed Helm of Grallen.

The bucket clanked its way up the transport, rising higher and higher inside the shaft. When the bucket finally shuddered to a stop, they found themselves on one of the very top levels of the stalactite. Here, according to Arman, was the Court of Thanes, where the Council of Thanes would be meeting this day to consider the destruction of the gate and the return of a ghost.

10

The Thanes of Thorbardin. Dark allies.

anis and the others had no way of knowing that by walking into the Court of Thanes, they were walking into a trap. For unbeknownst to any of them, including the other Thanes, Queen Takhisis had seduced one of their number and convinced him to join her evil cause.

The Council of Thanes ruled Thorbardin and had done so for centuries. Each of the eight dwarven kingdoms had a seat on the Council: Hylar, Theiwar, Neidar, Klar, Daewar, Daergar, and Aghar.

The Hylar, due to their education and innate skills in diplomacy and leadership, had long been the dominant clan of Thorbardin. Although there was currently no High King, the Hylar, under the leadership of their Thane, Hornfel, maintained nominal control over the kingdoms and were working hard to keep civil war from breaking out beneath the mountain. With the closing of the mines, Hornfel understood that the dwarves' only salvation was to rejoin the world, unseal the gates. Unfortunately, the Hylar themselves were divided on this, with some wanting to venture into the world and others maintaining that the world was a dangerous place, best to keep the gates shut.

The Neidar were the only clan who might have, long ago, challenged the Hylar for ascendancy in Thorbardin, but the Neidar's restless nature found the caverns beneath the mountain too cramped and small for their liking. Long before the Cataclysm, the Neidar had left Thorbardin to travel the world, hiring out as craftsmen, farming the land, raising crops, and tending the beasts that could not live in the perpetual darkness beneath the mountain. The Neidar and the other clans had remained on good terms with each other, until the Cataclysm struck and the world changed forever.

As famine and plague stalked the mountain kingdom, the High King, Duncan, believed the Neidar could survive on their own, and he made the agonizing decision to shut the gates. The Neidar were furious. They, too, faced starvation and sickness, and worse, they were being attacked by goblins, ogres and desperate humans. They broke with the dwarves beneath the mountain and went to war against them with disastrous results. The Neidar still claimed a seat on the Council, though the seat has been empty for centuries.

The Klar were an afflicted people, whispered by some to have been cursed by Reorx when a Klar was caught trying to cheat the god at a game of bones. A streak of madness ran through the clan. Every Klar family had at least one member who was either wholly or partially insane. The Klar tended to keep to themselves, therefore, and this suited them well, for they were skilled in handling the tunnel-digging Urkhan worms and in tending the farms and herding beasts. The Hylar considered themselves protectors of the Klar, who in turn pledged to support the Hylar in everything they did.

If the Klar were cursed by Reorx, the Daewar were the beloved of Reorx—or so the Daewar maintained. With a tendency to fanaticism in any of their chosen pursuits, the Daewar saw themselves as the chosen of the god and many of their clan became clerics dedicated to Reorx. They built grand temples with rich furnishings. Daewar priests charged high fees for their services and used this money to build even grander temples.

When the gods left the world, the Daewar were crushed and bewildered. Some of their people, true clerics, vanished at this time. Those who remained no longer had any power to heal the plagues that swept through the realm or cast nurturing spells on the crops. The other dwarves began to blame their misery on the Daewar and attacked their temples. Fearing their beautiful temples would be destroyed, the Daewar desperately maintained that Reorx and the other gods were still around; they were just keeping to themselves.

The Daewar priests went about their daily routines, keeping the fires burning in the temples of Reorx, begging for him to hear their prayers and in some instances, creating their own "miracles" to try to prove he had answered. The fierce Daewar soldiers—as fanatical in battle as their clerics were in their beliefs—saw to it that other clans kept out of their kingdom.

As time passed, all but the most fanatical ceased to believe in the gods. Some turned to cults that worshipped everything from a sacred albino rat to an unusual rock formation. Many Daewar went in for soldiering, and the Daewar had the best-trained, fiercest, and most dedicated fighting force beneath the mountain.

Though superb warriors, the Daewar were not particularly intelligent or creative. "Their beards grew into their brains," as the saying went.

The Daergar were an offshoot of the Theiwar clan and were still considered "dark" dwarves by their cousins. The Daergar were accused of having conspired against the Hylar during the Dwarfgate Wars and were banished by King Duncan to the deepest parts of the mountain. This was not a great hardship on the Daergar, for they had long been miners by trade, skilled at finding and digging out the valuable ore, be it iron, gold, or silver.

The loss of the mining revenues hit the Daergar hard, and the Daergar had sunk into squalor and degradation. Thugs and gangs ruled the streets of their realm, as the poverty-stricken dwarves scrounged a living by any means they could, most often dishonest.

The Daergar blamed the Hylar for their trouble, believing the closing of the mines was a plot to destroy them. The Hylar Thane, Hornfel, feared the Daergar and Theiwar were planning to join together with the intent of overthrowing the Council and seizing control of Thorbardin. Hornfel was doing his best to try to be conciliatory to both, with the unfortunate result that he had made himself appear weak.

As it turned out, Hornfel was already too late. The Theiwar and the Daergar weren't planning to ally. They had already done so, and they'd found powerful new friends to assist them in their cause.

The Aghar, known as gully dwarves, also held a seat on the Council, to the general mystification of the rest of Krynn. Universally reviled, woefully ignorant, and notorious cowards, gully dwarves were not even true dwarves—at least so the dwarves had always claimed. Gully dwarves were said to have gnome blood in them. (Gnomes, of course, dispute this.) As to the reason why the Aghar had been given a seat on the Council, this dates back to the very early days when Thorbardin was in the process of being built.

At that time, the Theiwar were the leading clan of mountain dwarves. They could see, however, that the Hylar were gaining in power and the Theiwar wanted to insure they would maintain a majority on the Council. Having long terrorized and intimidated the gully dwarves, the Theiwar believed they could continue to coerce them and force them to support any measure they proposed. The Theiwar insisted that the Aghar be given a seat and full voting privileges on the Council.

The Hylar saw through the Theiwar's scheme and tried to prevent it, but the Theiwar cleverly put it out that if the Aghar were banned from the Council, other clans would be next to go. This enraged the hot-headed Daergar and frightened the insecure Klar. The Hylar had no choice but to give in and thus, though the gully dwarves had no city beneath the mountain, but infested all parts of it like the rats that were the staple of their diet, they were awarded a seat on the Council. Unfortunately for the Theiwar, the gully dwarves ended up supporting the Hylar cause more often than not, simply because the Hylar felt sorry for them and were good to them (at least by gully dwarf standards).

The eighth seat was held by the Kingdom of the Dead. The dwarves revered their ancestors, and although this seat was always vacant, the dwarves felt strongly that their dead were an integral part of dwarven life and should not be forgotten.

The ninth seat was for the High King, one of their own as chosen by the Council. This seat was also vacant and had been so for three hundred years. According to Arman Kharas, there could be no High King unless the Hammer of Kharas was found. This, perhaps, was just an excuse. There had been High Kings in times before the Hammer. Given the current state of unrest, no clan was currently strong enough to claim the kingship. One Thane was positioning himself to remedy this situation.

Realgar of the Theiwar was an extremely dangerous dwarf, far more dangerous than anyone suspected. This had partly to do with his appearance, for he was scrawny and under-sized. His family had been among the poorest of the poor, to the point where they envied gully dwarves. Hunger had stunted his growth, but it had also sharpened his mind.

He had escaped poverty by selling himself to a Theiwar warlock, performing various degrading acts for the warlock, including robbery and murder. In between beatings, Realgar eagerly picked up what scraps of spell-casting knowledge the warlock let fall. Clever and cunning, Realgar soon became more skilled in dark magic than his master. He took his revenge upon the warlock, moved into his late master's dwelling, and worked hard to become the most feared and consequently the most powerful dwarf in the Theiwar realm. He declared himself Thane, but he was not content with that. Realgar was determined to be crowned High King. Once more, the Theiwar would rule beneath the mountain.

He had no way to accomplish this lofty goal, however. The Theiwar were not skilled warriors. They knew nothing of discipline and could never be made to band together in a cohesive fighting unit. Nor could the self-serving Theiwar fathom the concept of sacrificing one's life for a cause. The Theiwar were further handicapped by their inability to tolerate light. Shine a light in their eyes, and they were essentially blind.

The Theiwar were good at stabbing people in the back, using their dark magic against enemies, kidnapping, and thieving. While such skills were useful in helping the Theiwar survive and maintain control over their own realm, they would never defeat the powerful Hylar or the fierce Daewar. It seemed that the Theiwar must live beneath the boot heel of the detested Hornfel forever.

Realgar brooded over the ruin of his ambition for years, until at last his whining reached the ears of one who was seeking out dark and discontented souls. Takhisis, Queen of Darkness, came to Realgar and he prostrated himself before her. Takhisis offered to help Realgar achieve his goal in return for a few favors. The favors were not difficult to perform and actually benefited the Theiwar. Realgar had no problems keeping his end of the bargain, and thus far Takhisis had kept hers.

Realgar had approached the Thane of the Daergar, a dwarf known as Rance, and made him a proposition. Realgar had found a buyer for the iron ore in the closed Daergar mines. He wanted a few of mines, those that were hidden deep within the labyrinthine caverns of the Daergar realm, to reopen. The miners would go back to work, but they would do so in secret.

In return for this and for a promised share in the power when Realgar should become High King, Rance promised to build a secret tunnel through the mountains leading to Pax Tharkas, currently under the rulership of the Dragon Highlord, Verminaard. All this had to be done without the knowledge of any of the other Thanes.

Rance was a large dwarf of no particular intelligence who had become Thane because his gang of thugs was currently the gang in power. He didn't care much who was High King, so long as he received a cut of the profits. Accordingly, he built the secret tunnels that led to Pax Tharkas. Unknown to Hornfel, Realgar and Rance were the first to open the gates of Thorbardin, and the first person to enter was the Dragon Highlord Verminaard.

The deal was finalized. In return for sending in an army of draconians to help defeat the Hylar, the Theiwar and Daergar agreed to sell iron ore to Pax Tharkas, along with swords and maces, battle hammers and axes, steel arrow- and spear-heads. All this came at a fortunate time for Lord Verminaard, though he did not live to realize it.

As it was, Dray-yan was able to keep the iron ore flowing, and provided the Dragonarmies with excellent weapons.

The draconian army had already entered the secret tunnel. Realgar had been about ready to launch his attack when the opening of Northgate and the arrival of outsiders derailed his plot. He had tried to kill the Talls himself, hoping to get rid of them before anyone else found out. Draconian engineers had repaired and rebuilt the murder holes above Anvil's Echo. Their work was supposed to be secret, for the draconian commander intended to use the murder holes in case the Hylar army invaded.

Realgar had no time for secrets. He sent his Theiwar up there with orders to roll the boulders down on the bridge.

This turned out to be not nearly as easy as Realgar had imagined. The Theiwar are not physically strong, and they had difficulty wrestling the boulders into position. They could not see their targets—the magical light of the wizard's staff blinded them whenever they peered over the edge of the murder holes—and they let the boulders fall rather than trying to aim them. The Talls escaped, and Realgar found himself in trouble with the draconian commander, a detestable lizard named Grag, who railed at him that he had given away one of their best strategic advantages.

"You may have cost us the war," Grag said to him coldly. "Why did you not summon me and my men? We would have dealt swiftly with this scum. In fact, you would have been rewarded. These criminals were the instigators in the revolt of the human slaves. There is a bounty on their heads. Because of your bungling, they are now deep in the heart of Thorbardin, beyond our reach. Who knows what mischief they will cause?"

Realgar cursed himself for not having summoned the draconians to help him kill the Talls. He had not known that there was money to be made out of these Talls or he most certainly would have.

"These slaves are coming to Thorbardin," Grag had gone on, fuming. "They plan to seek a way inside. There are eight hundred humans out there, practically on your doorstep!"

"Not eight hundred warriors?" Realgar asked in alarm.

"No. About half are children and old people, but the men and some of the women are stout fighters, and they have a god or two on their side. Weak gods, of course, but they have proven a nuisance to us in the past."

"I hope you are not saying you are afraid of a few hundred human slaves and their puny gods?" Realgar asked with a sneer.

"I can deal with them," Grag returned grimly, "but it will mean dividing my forces, fighting a battle on two fronts with the possibility of being flanked on both."

"They have not yet entered the mountain," Realgar said. "They would need the permission of the Council to do so, and that will not be easily granted. I have heard it said that they have brought with them a cursed artifact known as the Helm of Grallen. Not even Hornfel is so soft or so stupid as to permit eight hundred humans to come traipsing inside Thorbardin, especially when they're cursed! Do not worry, Grag. I will be in attendance at the Council meeting. I will do what must be done to insure that our plans go forward."

Realgar had sent out his informants to spread the word that the strangers brought with them the cursed helm of a dead prince. Everyone knew the dark tale, though speaking about it in public had been outlawed by the Hylar for three centuries. Having done what he could to turn the people against these strangers, Realgar went to the meeting of the Council.

293

The Theiwar wizard did not wear robes. Realgar was a renegade, as were most dwarven wizards. He knew nothing of the Orders of High Sorcery. He did not even know that his magic came to him as a gift of the dark god, Nuitari, who had taken a liking to these dwarven savants. Realgar had no spellbook, for he could neither read nor write. He cast the spells his master had cast before him, having learned them from his master before him, and so on back through time.

Realgar wore armor to the Council meeting, and his was excellent armor, for the Theiwar had a gift for crafting steel. His helm was made of leather specially fitted with smoked glass over the eyeslits to protect his light-sensitive eyes. The mask had the additional advantage of preventing anyone from seeing his face, which resembled that of a weasel, for he had a long narrow nose, small squinty eyes, and a weak chin covered with a scraggly beard.

Realgar had not even entered the Court of Thanes before Rance accosted him.

"What do you know about these Talls?" Rance demanded.

"Not so loud!" Realgar hissed, and he drew Rance off to one side.

"I hear that these Talls entered the Northgate and came through your realm! They have with them the accursed helm. There is a wizard among them *and* a Neidar! Why did you let them in the gate? Why did you allow them to get this far? What will this do to our plans?"

"If you'll shut up for a moment, I'll tell you," said Realgar. "I didn't 'let' them in. They destroyed the gate, which already marks them as criminals. As for the helm, it may be a curse for the Hylar and a blessing for us. Keep your mouth shut, and follow my lead."

Rance did not like this, for he did not trust his Theiwar brother in the slightest. Had they been alone, he would have hounded Realgar until he had answers, but Hornfel had arrived and he was casting suspicious glances in their direction. They could not be seen to be too cozy. Muttering beneath his breath, Rance stomped into the Court and went to take his seat on the Throne of the Daergar. Realgar went to take his place on his throne.

The Council of Thanes was about to convene.

II

The Helm of Grallen speaks.
Flint makes a wager.

he Court of Thanes was an imposing structure located on an outer wall of the Life Tree. Hylar soldiers in full regalia marched the companions through double doors of bronze and into a long, imposing hallway lined with columns. At the end of the hall was a curved dais on which stood nine thrones. The thrones were carved of striated marble, each a different color, ranging from white to gray, red- dish brown to green. The throne belonging to the Dead was carved of black obsidian. The ninth throne, standing in the center, was larger than the rest, and it was carved of pure white marble and adorned with gold and silver.

The soldiers formed two rows along the line of columns. Arman Kharas brought the companions forward to stand beneath a rotunda in front of the thrones. So placed, a person addressing the Council would address the High King, whose throne stood in front, with the other Thanes looking on from either side. Since there was no High King, the speaker was relegated to the middle of the hall in order to face all the Thanes at once or he had to constantly turn this way and that to talk to all the Thanes, thus putting the speaker at a considerable disadvantage.

Flint walked in front of his comrades. He carried the Helm of Grallen in his hands. There had been a brief altercation between him and Arman outside the Court as to which of them should carry the Helm. Truthfully, Flint didn't want anything to do with the cursed thing and he would have been glad to relinquish it, but his pride had been hurt and he wasn't about to let the Hylar have it. Then, too, the promise of Reorx was always at the back of Flint's mind.

Arman Kharas did not want the helm either. He had asked to carry it because he felt honor bound to do so and he graciously did not press the issue, stating that he feared an altercation might lead to bloodshed.

Tanis came behind Flint with Sturm at his side. Raistlin and Caramon followed, keeping Tasslehoff between them. Raistlin had threatened to cast a sleep spell on the kender if he opened his mouth, and while ordinarily Tasslehoff would have found being "magicked" quite a charming prospect, he didn't want to miss anything that might happen with the dwarves and thus he was torn. He eventually decided that he could be magicked any day, while appearing before the Council of Thanes was a once-in-a-lifetime opportunity, so he determined to make a heroic effort to keep his mouth shut.

The Thanes sat on their thrones, maintaining an outwardly calm demeanor, though the unsealing of the gate and the arrival of the accursed helm had been a shock. The only one who was truly unfazed was the Thane of the Aghar, Highbluph Bluph of the Bluph clan, who was sound asleep. He continued to sleep through most of the proceedings, rousing only a when a particularly prodigious snore shook him awake. When that happened, he blinked, yawned, scratched himself, and went back to sleep.

Flint took note of the Thanes, as Arman Kharas introduced them, marking which might be friendly and which were dangerous. Hornfel of the Hylar was a dwarf of stately mien and noble bearing, grave and dignified. His intelligent gaze fixed intently upon each one of the companions. His expression grew troubled as he looked at Flint and went grim at the sight of the helm.

The Theiwar, Realgar, whose throne stood in the darkest of the dark shadows, eyed them with frowning dislike, as did the Daergar Thane, Rance. Flint was not surprised by this—dark dwarves hate everyone. What made him uneasy was an air of smugness about the Theiwar. Flint could not see Realgar's eyes behind the smoked glass of his helm, but there was a sneering curl to the lips which Flint found unsettling, as though Realgar knew something others did not. Flint determined to keep his own eyes on the Theiwar.

The leader of the Daewar, Gneiss, was a very imposing figure, decked out in his war panoply, but that seemed about all that could be said for him. Tufa, of the Klar, had the same wild-eyed look that characterized all the Klar, even those who were sane. Tufa kept flicking uncertain glances at Hornfel, as though waiting to be told what to think. Rance of the Daergar would be the Neidar's enemy just because that was how it had always been and always would be. The question was whether the Daergar were allied with the Theiwar in whatever mischief they were plotting.

When all the Thanes had been introduced, Flint made a respectful bow to the empty throne of the Kingdom of the Dead, and he bowed defiantly before the other empty throne, that belonging to the Neidar. Hornfel looked grave at this. Realgar snorted loudly, waking the Highbluph and causing him to grumble before curling back on his throne and dozing off again.

Flint began his own introductions. "I am Flint Fireforge." He turned to Tanis. "This is—"

Realgar rudely interrupted. "Why aren't these criminals in chains and leg irons? They destroyed the Northgate. They are assassins and spies. Why aren't they in the dungeon?"

"We are not spies," said Flint angrily. "We bring urgent news and a warning from the world beyond the mountain. Queen Takhisis, whom we dwarves know as False Metal, has returned from the Abyss and brought her evil dragons with her. She has created dragon-men, fearsome warriors led by Dragon Highlords, who are waging war on the world. Many realms have already fallen to the darkness, including Qualinesti. Thorbardin may be next."

All the Thanes began talking at once, shouting and gesticulating, jabbing fingers at each other and at Flint, who shouted and jabbed right back.

"Our priests would have certainly known if False Metal had returned," Gneiss said scornfully. "We have seen no signs."

"As for this claim of dragons and dragon-men, are we children to believe such tales?" Rance cried.

The Highbluph, jolted out of his nap, looked around in bewilderment.

"What's going on?" Sturm asked Tanis, who was the only one beside Flint who spoke Dwarvish. The knight was accustomed to the stately formalities of the Solamnics, and he was shocked at the turmoil. "This is a drunken brawl, not a meeting of kings!"

"Dwarves do not stand on ceremony," said Tanis. "Flint told them that Takhisis has returned. They're disputing his claim."

"I will prove they are spies!" Realgar's voice was thin and rasping and had a whining quality to it, as though he considered himself perpetually ill-used. "My people tried to arrest this lot, but they were driven off by Arman Kharas and his thugs, who had no right to be in our realm."

"I had every right to deliver my brother from your dungeons," Arman countered hotly.

"He broke our laws," Realgar said sullenly.

"He broke no law. You kidnapped him in order to try to extort ransom—"

"That is a lie!" Realgar jumped to his feet.

"Is it also a lie that we had to run for our lives across Anvil's Echo?" Arman Kharas thundered. "Your people dropped boulders down through the murder holes in an effort to crush us to death!"

"What is this?" Hornfel also rose from his throne. He fixed a baleful gaze on the Theiwar Thane. "I had not heard of this until now!"

Tanis translated the Dwarvish for his friends. Flint did not take his attention from the Theiwar. He had been trying to steer the conversation back to the reason why he and his friends had come but was not making much headway. Suddenly Flint knew what the Theiwar was going to say and he realized in dismay that he and Arman had both been cleverly manipulated.

"I admit that we did attack our Hylar cousins," said Realgar. "My people were trying to stop these criminals from entering our realm. The Talls are spies. They tried to sneak into Thorbardin unseen, bringing with them the accursed helm in order to destroy us. They would have succeeded, but their crime was foiled by my people."

"Spies? Criminals?" Hornfel repeated, exasperated. "You keep saying this, Realgar, but what basis do you have for such accusations?" His voice took on an edge. "That also does not explain why you tried to kill my son and Hylar soldiers."

Flint knew what was coming. He saw the pit before him, but by the time he saw it, he was already lying helpless at the bottom.

"Yes, we tried to kill them, in order to protect Thorbardin. These Talls"—Realgar jabbed a finger at Tanis and the others—"and their Neidar toady opened the gate in order that an army of humans, which now lies hidden in the foothills, can launch at attack against us!"

The Thanes were stunned into silence. All of them, Hornfel included, cast dark, suspicious glances at Flint and his friends.

Realgar sat back on his throne. "I hate to tell you this, Hornfel, but your son is part of the plot. My people were going to place the Talls under arrest. Your son rescued them. He has revealed our defenses to them." Realgar paused, then said smoothly, "Or perhaps you already know all this, Hornfel. Perhaps you are in on the plot as well."

"That's a lie!" Arman shouted angrily. He lunged at Realgar. The soldiers, weapons drawn, quickly surrounded him and, for good measure, also surrounded the companions.

"This is how Hornfel plans to become High King," Realgar cried, "by selling Thorbardin to the humans!"

The Highbluph was now adding to the confusion by standing on his throne and shrieking at the top of his lungs that they were all about to murdered by the Talls. Geniss, the Daewar thane, was on his feet, pompously declaiming rules of order to which no one was listening. The Klar Thane was on his feet, too, with a knife in his hand.

Tanis gave up translating. He simply told everyone what was going on.

"This is terrible!" Sturm said grimly. "Now they will never let the refugees inside!"

"The question is: how did he know about the refugees?" Raistlin hissed. "Tell Flint to ask him that."

"I don't see how that matters?" Sturm said impatiently.

"Of course, *you* don't," Raistlin returned caustically "Ask him, Flint."

The dwarf shook his head.

"They won't listen," he said grimly. "We walked into Realgar's trap. Not much I can do about it now."

Hornfel was forced to defend himself, strenuously denying the charges leveled at him by Realgar. Arman Kharas denied them, too, stating that he had come upon the companions by accident, adding that he himself had placed them under arrest and brought them before the council.

"Along with the curse of Grallen," Realgar shouted.

"Silence, all of you," Hornfel roared and, finally, the other Thanes ceased arguing. He glared at them until they all resumed their seats. The soldiers released Arman, who smoothed his beard and glowered at Realgar, who regarded the young dwarf with a leer.

Turning to Flint, Hornfel said in grim tones, "Answer me, Flint Fireforge of the Neidar. Are these charges true?"

"No, the charges are not true, great Thane."

"Ask him about the humans hiding in the valley!" Realgar snarled.

"We *do* come in the name of a group of humans," Flint said.

"He admits it!" Realgar cried in triumph.

"But they are not soldiers. They are refugees!" Flint countered angrily. "Men, women, and children. Not an army! And we did *not* try to sneak into Thorbardin. The Northgate opened for us."

"How?" Hornfel asked. "How did you find the gate that has been hidden these three hundred years?"

Flint answered reluctantly, knowing this was exactly the wrong thing to say, for it played right into the Theiwar's hands, yet there was no other explanation he could offer. "The Helm of Grallen led us here and opened the gate for us."

Raistlin was at Tanis's side, his hand closed over Tanis's arm.

"Tell Flint to ask the Theiwar how he knew about the refugees," Raistlin urged.

"What does it matter?" Tanis shrugged. "Once the gate was open, his people probably went to investigate."

"Impossible," Raistlin countered. "The Theiwar cannot abide sunlight!"

Tanis stared at him. "That's true . . ."

"Hush, both of you!" Sturm cautioned.

Hornfel had taken a step forward. He raised his hand for silence.

"The charges made against you and your friends are very serious, Flint Fireforge," he stated. "You have entered our realm without permission. You have destroyed the gate."

"That wasn't our fault," cried Tasslehoff, and he was immediately half-smothered by Caramon's large hand.

"You bring among us the accursed helm—"

"The Helm of Grallen is not cursed," Flint said wrathfully, "and I can prove it."

Lifting the helm, he jammed it onto his head.

The Thanes, one and all, leapt to their feet, even the Aghar, who mistakenly thought that since everyone was standing it was time to adjourn.

Raistlin dug his nails into Tanis's arm. "This could be very bad, my friend."

"You were the one who wanted him to put the damn thing on!" Tanis said.

"This is not the time or the place I would have chosen," Raistlin returned.

Sturm instinctively put his hand to his scabbard, forgetting the dwarves had taken his sword. The dwarves had deposited the confiscated weapons near the entrance. Sturm calculated the distance, wondering if he could reach his sword before the soldiers reached him. Tanis saw the knight's look and knew what he was thinking. He cast Sturm a warning glance. The knight gave an oblique nod, but he also edged a couple of steps nearer the door.

Flint stood in the middle of the Court, the helm on his head, and for long, tense moments, nothing happened. Tanis started to breathe easier, then the gem on the helm flared red, flooding the court with bright red-orange light—a holy fire blazing in their midst. The helm covered Flint's face; only his beard showed, flowing from beneath, and his eyes.

Tanis did not recognize Flint in those eyes, nor, it seemed, did Flint recognize him or anyone else. He stared around as if he had walked into a room filled with strangers.

The Thanes were silent, their silence grim and foreboding. All laid hand to hammer, sword, or both. The soldiers held their weapons ready.

Flint paid no attention to the Thanes or the soldiers. He studied his surroundings; his gaze, filtered through the helm's eyeslits, taking in everything, like someone returning to a loved place after a long journey.

"I am home . . ." Flint said in a voice that was not his.

Hornfel's angry expression softened to doubt, uncertainty. He looked at his son, who shook his head and shrugged. Realgar smirked, as though he'd expected nothing less.

"He's play-acting," he muttered.

Flint walked over to the dais, climbed the stairs, and sat down on an empty throne—the black throne, the throne sacred to the Kingdom of the Dead. He gazed defiantly upon the Thanes as though daring them to do anything about it.

The Thanes one and all stared at him in paralyzing shock.

"No one sits on the Throne of the Dead!" cried Gneiss. Grabbing hold of Flint's arm, he tried to drag him bodily from the sacred throne.

Flint did not stir hand or foot, but suddenly the Daewar Thane reeled backward, as though he'd been struck a blow by an unseen hammer. He fell off the dais and lay, trembling with fear and astonishment, on the floor.

Flint, seated on the Throne of the Kingdom of the Dead, wearing the helm of a dead man, spoke.

"I am Prince Grallen," he said, and his voice was stern and cold and not Flint's own. "I have returned to the hall of my fathers. Is this how I am welcomed?"

The other Thanes were eyeing the Daewar, who was still on the floor. No one went to help him. No one was leering or scoffing now.

Rance turned to Hornfel and said nervously, "You are his descendant. Your family brought the curse upon us. You are the one who should speak to him."

Hornfel removed his helm, a mark of respect, and approached the throne with dignity. Arman would have gone with his father, but Hornfel made a sign with his hand, indicating his son was to remain behind.

"You are welcome to the hall of your fathers, Prince Grallen," Hornfel said, and he was polite but proud and unafraid, as became a Thane of the Hylar. "We ask your forgiveness for the wrong that was done you."

"We Daergar had nothing to do with it, Prince Grallen," Rance said in a loud voice. "Just so you know."

"It is not fair that we should be cursed," added Gneiss, heaving himself to his feet. "Our father's fathers knew nothing about the plot against you."

"Your curse should fall on the Hylar alone," said Rance.

"What a farce!" said Realgar.

"Peace, all of you," said Hornfel, glowering around at them. "Let us hear what the prince has to say."

Tanis understood. Hornfel was clever. He was testing Flint, trying to discover if he was acting all this out, or if he really had been taken over by the spirit of Prince Grallen.

"There was a time when I would have cursed you," Flint told them. His voice grew hard and terrible. "There was a time when my rage would have brought down this mountain." His anger flared. "How dare you bandy words with me, Hornfel of the Hylar? How dare you further affront my ghost, untimely murdered, my life cut off by my own kin!"

Flint brought his fist down, hard, on the arm of the throne.

The mountain shivered. The Life Tree shuddered. The floor shook, and the thrones of the Thanes rattled on the dais. A crack appeared in the ceiling. Columns creaked and groaned. The Aghar Highbluph let out a piercing shriek and fell over in a dead faint.

Hornfel sank to his knees. He was afraid now. They were all afraid. One by one, the soldiers in the hall went down on their knees onto the stone floor. The Thanes followed, until only Realgar was standing, and at last, even he knelt, though it was obvious he hated every moment of it.

The tremor ceased. The mountain was still.

Tanis glanced around swiftly to make sure everyone was all right. Sturm knelt on one knee, his arm raised in salute, as knight to royalty. Raistlin remained standing, balancing on his staff, his face and his thoughts hidden in the shadows of his cowl. Caramon had whipped off his helm. He was still keeping hold of Tasslehoff, who was saying wistfully, "I wish Fizban was here to see this!" Tanis shifted his attention back to Flint, wondering what was going to come of this.

Nothing good, he thought grimly.

The silence was so absolute it seemed that Tanis could hear the sound of the rock dust sifting to the floor.

Hornfel spoke again, his voice unsteady. "Your brothers confessed their crime before they died, Prince Grallen. Though they did not kill you, they held themselves responsible for your death."

"And so they were," said the prince balefully. "I was the youngest, my father's favorite. They feared he would overlook them, leaving the rulership of Thorbardin to me. While it is true their hands did not deal my death blow, yet by their hands I died.

"I was young. I was fighting in my first battle. My elder brothers vowed to watch over and protect me. Instead they sent me to my doom. They ordered me to march with a small force on the fortress of Zhaman, the evil wizard's stronghold. I did what they told me. How not? I loved them and admired them. I longed to impress them. My own men tried to warn me. They told me the mission was suicidal, but I would not heed them. I trusted my brothers, who said that my men lied, the battle was as good as won. I was to have the honor of capturing the wizard and bringing him back in chains.

"They gifted me with this helm, saying that it would make me invincible. They knew the truth—the helm would not make me invincible. Crafted by the Theiwar, the magic of the gem would capture my soul and keep it imprisoned so that even my vengeful ghost would not return to tell the truth of what happened."

"Your brothers were ashamed of what they had done, noble prince," said Hornfel. "They admitted their guilt to Kharas and then hurled themselves to their death in battle. Your father grieved when the bitter news was brought to him. He did what he could to make amends. He raised a statue in your honor and built a tomb for you. He buried your brothers in an unmarked grave."

"And yet, my father never again spoke my name," said Prince Grallen.

"Your noble father blamed himself, Your Highness. He could not bear to be reminded of the tragedy. 'Three sons I lost,' he said. 'One in battle and two to darkness.'

"In truth, you have no need to curse us, great prince," Hornfel added bitterly. "The throne where once your father sat as High King has been empty since his death. The Hammer of Kharas is lost to us. We do not even have the solace of paying homage at your father's tomb, for some terrible force wrenched it out of the earth, and now it hangs suspended high above the Valley of the Thanes. There the tomb of our High King floats, out of reach, forever a punishment and a reproach to us.

"Our nation is divided and soon, I fear, we must end up in a civil war. I do not know what more harm you can do to us, Prince Grallen," Hornfel said, "unless you bring the mountain down on top of us."

"Whew, boy!" Tasslehoff whistled. "Could Flint really do that? Bring down the mountain?"

"Shush!" Tanis ordered, and his expression was so very fierce that Tasslehoff shushed.

"There was a time when I would have taken out my vengeance upon you, but my soul has learned much over the centuries."

Flint's voice softened. He gave a sigh, and the hand that was clenched in a fist relaxed. "I have learned to forgive."

Flint rose slowly to his feet.

"My brothers' spirits have gone on to the next part of their life's journey. My father's soul has done the same, and with him traveled the soul of the noble Kharas. Soon I will join them, for I am now free of the cruel enchantment that bound me.

"Before I leave, I give you a gift—a warning. False Metal has returned, but so have Reorx and the other gods. The gate of Thorbardin is once more open. The light of the sun shines into the mountain. Shut the gate again, shut out the light, and the darkness will consume you."

"This is an act," Realgar muttered. "Can't you fools see that?"

"Shut your mouth, or I will shut it for you!" said Tufa. The Klar still held his knife in his hand.

"We thank you, Prince Grallen," Hornfel said respectfully. "We will take heed of your words."

Arman Kharas rose to his feet. "Is this all you have to tell us, Prince Grallen? Do you not have some word for me?"

"My son, be silent!" Hornfel admonished.

"The prince has said the gods are with us again! This is the time of which Kharas spoke: 'When the power of the gods returns, then shall the Hammer go forth to forge once again the freedom of Krynn.'"

Arman Kharas came to stand before the Throne of the Kingdom of the Dead. "Tell me how to enter Duncan's Tomb. Tell me where to the Hammer of Kharas, noble prince, for such is my destiny!"

The gem's light dwindled and diminished, flickered and died out.

"Wait, Prince Grallen!" Arman shouted. "You cannot leave without telling me!"

Slowly Flint lifted his hands and slowly removed the helm from his head. He didn't look triumphant or elated. He looked tired. His face was drawn and pale. He seemed to have aged as many years as the prince had been dead.

"*You* know!" Arman cried suddenly, pointing at Flint. The young dwarf's voice burned with fury. "He told *you*!"

Flint walked away from the throne of the Dead, holding the Helm of Grallen underneath one arm.

Realgar laughed. "This is sham, a fraud! He is lying. He has been lying all along. He has no idea where to find the Hammer!"

"He knew the details of Prince Grallen's life and death," Hornfel said. "The mountain shook when we doubted him. Perhaps Reorx and the other gods *have* returned."

"I agree with Realgar," said Rance. "Cloudseeker has shaken before now, and none of us claimed it was anything more than the way of the mountain. Why should this time be different?"

Flint pushed past the Thanes, only to be confronted by Arman.

"Tell me where to find the Hammer! I am a prince. It is my destiny!"

"Why should I?" Flint flared. "So you can take the Hammer, and throw my friends and me in your dungeons?"

"Hold his friends as hostage for the Hammer's return," the Daewar suggested.

"Do that and the Hammer can stay lost for another three hundred years!" Flint said angrily.

Realgar's squinting eyes had been observing Flint narrowly. He smiled, then said, "I propose a wager."

The other Thanes looked intrigued. Like their god, dwarves loved to gamble.

"What wager?" asked Hornfel.

"If this Neidar finds the Hammer of Kharas and returns it to us, then we will consider permitting these humans safe entry into our realm—provided they are not an army, of course. If he fails, then he and his friends remain our prisoners, and we seal up the gate."

Hornfel stroked his beard and eyed Flint speculatively. The Daewar nodded in satisfaction and the Klar gave a low chuckle and scratched his chin with the knife blade.

"You can't mean they are actually considering doing this!" Sturm said, when Tanis translated. "I cannot believe they would gamble on something this serious! Of course, Flint will have no part of it."

"I agree with the knight," Raistlin said. "Something's not right about this."

"Maybe so," Flint muttered, "but sometimes you have to risk all to gain all. I'll take that bet," he called out loudly, "on one condition. You can do what you like with me, but if I lose, my friends go free."

"He can't do this, Tanis!" Sturm protested, shocked and outraged. "Flint cannot gamble with the sacred Hammer of Kharas!"

"Calm down, Sturm," Tanis said testily. "The Hammer is not anybody's to do anything with yet."

"I won't stand for this!" Sturm stated. "If you will do nothing, then I must. This is sacrilege!"

"Let Flint handle this his way, Sturm," Tanis warned. He gripped the knight's arm as he would have turned away, forced him to listen. "We're not in Solamnia. We're in the realm of the dwarves. We know nothing about their rules, their laws and their customs. Flint does. He took an enormous risk, putting on that helm. We owe him our trust."

Sturm hesitated. For a moment, he seemed prepared to defy Tanis. Then he thought better of it and gave a grudging nod.

"We will make the wager," Hornfel said, speaking for the rest of the Thanes, "with these conditions: We make no terms regarding your friends, Flint Fireforge of the Neidar. Their fate is bound up in yours. If you do indeed find the Hammer of Kharas and return it to us, we will consider allowing the humans you represent to enter Thorbardin, based on our assessment of them. If they are, as you claim, families and not soldiers, they will be welcome. Is this agreeable?"

"The gods help us!" Sturm murmured.

Flint spit into his palm and extended his hand. Hornfel spit into his palm. The two shook on it, and the wager was done.

Hornfel turned to Tanis.

"You will be our guests in your friend's absence. You will stay in guest quarters in the Life Tree. We will provide guards for your safety."

"Thank you," said Tanis, "but we're going with our friend. He can't undertake what may be a dangerous quest alone."

"Your friend will not go alone," Hornfel replied with a slight smile. "My son, Arman, will accompany him."

"This is madness, Flint!" Raistlin said in his soft voice. "Let us say you find the Hammer. What is to prevent this dwarf from turning on you and murdering you and stealing it?"

"*I'm* there to prevent it," stated Flint, glowering.

'You are not so young as you once were," Raistlin countered, "nor as strong, whereas Arman is both."

"My son would never do such a thing," said Hornfel angrily.

"Indeed, I would not," said Arman, insulted. "You have my word as my father's son and as a Hylar that I will consider the life of your friend as a sacred charge."

"For that matter, Flint could murder Kharas and steal the Hammer," Tasslehoff piped up cheerfully. "Couldn't you, Flint?"

Flint went red in the face. Caramon, heaving a sigh, put his hand the kender's shoulder and marched him toward the door.

"Flint, don't agree to this!" Sturm urged.

"There is no agreement to be made," said Hornfel in tones of finality. "No human or half-human, and certainly no kender, will defile the sacred tomb of our High King. The Council of the Thanes is ended. My son will escort you to your quarters." Hornfel turned on his heel and left.

The soldiers closed in around the companions. They had no choice but to go along.

Flint walked at Tanis's side. The old dwarf's head was bowed, his shoulders slumped. He held tightly to the Helm of Grallen.

"Do you really know where to find the Hammer?" Tanis asked in a low undertone.

"Maybe," Flint muttered.

Tanis scratched his beard. "You realize you agreed to gamble the lives of eight hundred people on that 'maybe?'"

Flint cocked an eye at his friend. "You got a better idea?"

Tanis shook his head.

"I didn't think so," Flint grunted.

12

The Inn of the Talls. Sturm argues. Flint whittles.

he quarters provided the companions by the dwarves were located on the ground floor of the Life Tree in a part of the city that was older than the rest and little used. All the buildings were abandoned and boarded up. Flint pointed out why.

"Everything is human height—the doors and the windows. This part of the Life Tree was built to house humans."

"It used to be known as Tall Town," Arman informed them. "This was the area set aside for the human and elven merchants who once lived and worked here. We are giving you quarters in one of the inns built specially for your race."

Caramon in particular was relieved. He had already squeezed his big body into dwarf-size wagons and buckets, and he'd been worried about having to spend the night in a bed built for short dwarven legs.

The inn was in better repair than most of the buildings, for some enterprising dwarf was currently using it as a warehouse. It was two stories tall with lead-paned glass windows and a solid oak door.

"Before the Cataclysm, this inn was filled every night," said Arman, ushering his "guests" inside. "Merchants came from all over Ansalon, from Istar, Solamnia, and Ergoth. Once this common room rang with the sounds of laughter and the clink of gold. Now you hear nothing."

"Except the screeching of rats." Raistlin drew his robes close to him in disgust as several rodents, startled by the sudden light shed by a larva lantern, went racing across the floor.

"At least the beds are our size," Caramon said thankfully, "and so are the tables and chairs. Now if we just had something to eat and drink . . ."

"My men will bring you meat, ale, and clean bedding," Arman said, then turned to Flint. "I suggest we both get a good night's sleep. We set out for the Valley of the Thanes first thing on the morrow." Arman hesitated, then said, "I assume that is where we will be going?"

Flint's only response was a grunt. He walked over to a chair, plunked himself down, and took out a stick of wood and his whittling knife. Arman Kharas remained standing in the doorway, his gaze fixed on Flint, apparently hoping the dwarf would reveal more.

Flint obviously had nothing to say. Tanis and the rest stood looking around the dark and gloomy inn, not knowing what to do with themselves.

Arman frowned. He clearly wanted to order Flint to talk, but he was hardly in a position to do so. At last he said, "I will post guards outside so that your rest is not disturbed."

Raistlin gave a sardonic laugh. Tanis flashed him a warning glance, and he turned away. Sturm stalked off and went to work dragging down some wood bed frame that had been stacked together in a corner along with barrels, boxes, and crates. Caramon offered to help, as did Tasslehoff, though the first thing the kender did was to start poking holes in a crate to see if he could tell what was inside. Arman stood watching them. Flint continued to whittle.

At length, Arman tugged on his beard and asked if they had questions.

"Yeah," said Caramon, holding one of the heavy bed frames above his head, preparatory to placing it on the floor. "When's dinner?"

✦ ✦

The food they were given was plain and simple, washed down with ale from one of the casks. Arman Kharas finally wrenched himself away. Tanis felt sorry for the young dwarf, and he was annoyed at Flint, who could have at least been nice to Arman, whose life-long dreams had just been shattered. Flint was in a dark mood, however, and Tanis kept quiet, figuring anything he said would only make matters worse. Flint ate in silence, shoveling his food in his mouth rapidly, and when he was finished, he walked away from the table and went back to his whittling.

Sturm sat bolt upright all through dinner, disapproval evident in his bristling mustaches and the ice blue glint in his eyes. Raistlin picked at his food, eating little, his gaze abstracted, his thoughts turned inward. Caramon drank more ale than was good for him and fell asleep with his head on the table. The only person talking was Tasslehoff, who prattled away happily about the exciting events of the day, never seeming to mind that no one was listening to him.

Raistlin suddenly shoved his plate aside and rose to his feet. "I am going to study my spells. I do not want to be disturbed." He appropriated the only comfortable chair and dragged it near the large stone fireplace, where Tanis had managed to coax a small fire into burning.

Raistlin cast a disgusted glance at his twin, who lay sprawled on the table, exhaling beery breath.

"I trust someone will put that great lump to bed," Raistlin said. He took out his spellbook and was soon absorbed in his reading.

Sturm and Tanis hauled the sodden Caramon to the stoutest bed and dumped him down onto the mattress. Sturm then walked over and stood beside Flint, staring down at him.

"Flint, you can't do this," said Sturm.

Flint's knife scraped against the wood, and a particularly large chip flew off, nearly hitting Tasslehoff, who was engaged in attempting to pick a lock on a large chest.

"You can't go off on a quest of this importance with that Arman Kharas. In the first place, I'm none too certain of his sanity. In the second, it is too dangerous. You should refuse to go unless one of us goes with you."

Small curls of wood flowed out from under Flint's knife, landing at his feet.

Sturm's face reddened. "The Thanes cannot refuse you, Flint. Simply tell them that you will not fetch the hammer without proper protection! I myself would be glad to serve as your escort."

Flint looked up. "Bah!" he said, and looked back down. Another chip flew. "You'd escort the hammer right out of Thorbardin and back to Solamnia!"

Sturm smashed his fist on the table, setting the pewter plates dancing, and startling Tas, who dropped his lock pick. "Hey!" the kender said sternly. "Be quiet. Raistlin and I are trying to concentrate."

"The hammer is vital to our cause!" Sturm said angrily.

"Keep your voice down, Sturm," Tanis cautioned. "The walls are thick, but that door is not, and the guards are right outside."

"They speak nothing but Dwarvish," Sturm said, but he did lower his voice. He walked a couple of times around the room, trying to calm himself, then went back to confront Flint.

"I apologize for shouting, but I do not think you understand the importance of your undertaking. The dragonlance is the only weapon known to us that can slay these evil dragons, and the Hammer of Kharas is the only hammer that can be used in the making of the dragonlances. If you bring the hammer to the knights you will be a hero, Flint. You will be honored in legend and song for all time. Most important, you will save thousands of lives!"

Flint did not look at him, though he appeared to be interested in what the knight had to say. His whittling slowed. Only very small shavings fell now. Tanis didn't like the way the conversation was tending.

"Have you forgotten the reason we came here, Sturm?" Tanis asked. "We came seeking a safe haven for eight hundred men, women, and children. Flint has promised to give the dwarves the hammer if he finds it. In return, Hornfel has promised that the refugees can enter Thorbardin. He won't do that if we try to walk off with the dwarves' sacred hammer. In fact, we probably wouldn't get out of here alive. Face facts, Sturm. The dragonlance is a dream, a legend, a myth. We are not certain such a weapon even existed."

"Some of us are," Sturm said.

"The refugees are real and their peril is real," Tanis countered. "I agree with Sturm that you should not go alone tomorrow, Flint, but I should be the one to go with you."

"You do not trust me, Half-Elven, is that it?" Sturm's face blanched, his eyes dilated.

"I trust you, Sturm," said Tanis, sighing. "I know that you would give your life for me, or Flint, or any of us. I do not doubt your courage, your honor, or your friendship. It's just . . . I worry that you are being impractical! You have traded common sense for some wishful dream of saving mankind."

Sturm shook his head. "I honor and respect you, Tanis, as I would have honored and respected the father I never knew. In this matter, however, I cannot give way. What if we save eight hundred lives now, only to lose thousands as the evil queen moves to conquer and enslave all of Ansalon? The dragonlance may be a dream now, but we have it in our power to make that dream reality! The gods brought me here to seek the Hammer of Kharas, Tanis. I believe that with all my heart."

"The gods told *me* where to find it, Sturm Brightblade." Flint thrust his knife in his belt, stood up, and tossed the chunk of wood he'd been whittling into the fire. "I'm going to bed."

"Sturm is right about one thing, Flint," said Tanis. "You should tell the Thanes that you want one of us to accompany you. I don't care who it is. Take Sturm, take Caramon. Just take someone! Will you do that?"

"No." Flint stalked off toward a dwarf-size bed he'd found for himself in a distant corner of the room.

"Be logical, my friend." Tanis was growing exasperated at the dwarf's stubbornness. "You can't go off alone with Arman Kharas! You can't trust him."

"Actually, Flint, if you want a companion who will be truly useful, you would choose me," said Raistlin from his place by the fire.

"As if anyone trusts you!" Sturm gave the mage a baleful glance. "I should be the one to go."

Flint halted half-way across the room and turned to face them. His face was livid with rage.

"I'd sooner take the kender than any one of you lot. So there!" He stomped off to bed.

Tasslehoff jumped to his feet. "Me? You're taking me, Flint?" he cried in excitement.

"I'm not taking anyone," Flint growled.

He marched over to his bed, climbed in it, pulled the blanket up over his head, and rolled over, his back to them all.

"But Flint," Tas wailed, "you just said you were—"

"Tas, leave him alone," said Tanis.

"He said he was taking me!" Tas argued.

"Flint's tired. We're all tired. I think we should go to bed. Perhaps matters will look different in the morning."

"Flint said he was taking me," Tasslehoff muttered. "I should sharpen my sword."

He rummaged about in his pouches, searching for his knife. He located Rabbitslayer then began looking in his pouches for a whetstone. He didn't find that, but he did come across several other objects that were so interesting he completely forgot about the knife.

Raistlin closed his book with a snap.

"I hope you two are pleased with yourselves," the mage said, as he walked past Sturm and Tanis on his way to his bed.

"He'll think better of it by morning," said Sturm.

"I'm not so sure." Tanis glanced at the dwarf. "You know how stubborn he can be."

"We'll reason with him," Sturm said.

Tanis, who had tried on occasion to reason with the irascible old dwarf, did not hold out much hope.

———————————

Flint lay staring into the darkness. Sturm was right. Tanis was right. Even Raistlin was right! Logic dictated he should take one of them with him on the morrow. Hornfel would let him if he made an issue of it. The Thanes wouldn't have much choice.

Yet as he continued to think things over, Flint came to realize he'd made the right decision. He'd made it for the wrong reasons, but that didn't make it less right.

"The Hammer of Honor doesn't belong to the knights and their dreams of glory," Flint said to himself. "It doesn't belong to elves. It doesn't belong to humans, no matter how much trouble they're in. The hammer was made by dwarves, and it belongs to dwarves. Dwarves should be the ones who decide what to do with it, and if that means using it to save ourselves, then so be it."

This was a good reason and sounded very fine, but it wasn't the only reason Flint was going off on his own.

"This time, the hero is going to be me."

Of course, there was always the possibility that the hero would be Arman Kharas, but Flint didn't think that likely. Reorx had promised him that if he put on the helm, the hammer would be his reward.

Flint Fireforge, Savior of the People, Unifier of the Dwarven Nations. Perhaps even Flint Fireforge, High King.

Flint smiled to himself. That last wasn't likely to come true, but an old dwarf could dream, couldn't he?

13

False metal. Strange bedfellows.
Flint's promise.

t seemed to the companions that they had only just gone to bed when they were awakened by Arman Kharas banging on the door. Being deep underground, bereft of sunlight, they had no way to tell the time, but Arman assured them that in the world outside, the sun's first rays were gilding the snow on the mountain peaks.

"How do you know?" Caramon grumbled. He was not happy about being wakened "in the middle of the night," as he termed it, especially when suffering from the effects of drinking too much ale.

"There are parts of Thorbardin where one can see the sun, and we regulate our water clocks by it. You will view one of those places today," he added in solemn tones, speaking to Flint. "The light of the sun shines always upon the Kalil S'rith—the Valley of Thanes."

Sturm looked grimly at Tanis, who shook his head and looked at Flint, who very carefully did not look at anyone. The old dwarf clumped about the room, busy over various tasks—putting on his armor, putting on his helm with the "griffin's mane," and strapping the Helm of Grallen to his belt.

315

Tanis saw Sturm's expression alter. He knew what the knight was going to say before he said it, and he tried to stop him, but he was too late.

"Flint," Sturm said sternly, "be reasonable. Take one of us."

Flint turned to Arman.

"I'll need a weapon. I'm not going to face whatever hauled that tomb out of the ground without my battle-axe in my hands."

Arman Kharas removed the ornate hammer from the harness on his back. He looked at it regretfully for a moment then held it out to Flint.

"That's yours," said Flint, "I'll take my battle-axe."

Arman frowned at this refusal. "You have been given the knowledge of how to find the true Hammer. You should be the one to carry the replica. I had it made especially for this moment. It's my homage to Kharas. You will carry it to the Tomb of the King in Kharas's honor."

Flint didn't know what to say. He would have been much more comfortable with his battle-axe, but he didn't want to hurt the young dwarf anymore than he'd already been hurt.

Flint reached out, took hold of the hammer, and nearly dropped it. He suspected he knew now why Arman had given it to him. The hammer was heavy and unwieldy, well-crafted, but not well-designed. He gave it an experimental swing or two, and the thing nearly broke his wrist.

He glanced suspiciously at Arman to see if he was smiling. Arman stood looking grave, however, and Flint realized the young dwarf had meant what he said.

Flint held out his hand to Arman. "I accept this in the name of friendship."

Arman hesitated, then stiffly shook hands.

"Perhaps we misjudged Arman," said Tanis.

Sturm snorted. "He walks around carrying a fake magical hammer. I think that merely confirms the fact that he is crazy."

Raistlin seemed about to say something, then stopped. He regarded Flint and the hammer thoughtfully.

"What?" Tanis asked the mage.

"You should try once more to talk to Flint."

Tanis could have told him it was a waste of time, but he walked over to where Flint was continuing to gather up his gear. Tasslehoff had offered his assistance, with the result that Flint came up missing his favorite knife. He immediately rounded on the kender, seized hold of him and began to shake out his pouches, ignoring Tas's cries of protest.

"Sturm, a word with you," said Raistlin.

Sturm did not trust the strange gleam in Raistlin's hourglass eyes, but he accompanied him to the window.

"Is that hammer an exact replica of the real one?" Raistlin asked softly.

"I have only ever seen the Hammer in paintings," Sturm replied, "but from what I can judge it is identical."

"How can a person distinguish between the real and the false?"

"The Hammer is reputed to be light in weight, yet when it strikes it does so with the force of the god behind it, and when the true Hammer hits the sacred Anvil of Thorbardin, it sounds a note that can be heard throughout the earth and heavens."

Raistlin cast a sharp glance at the false hammer. Folding his hands in his sleeves, he leaned near to whisper, "Flint could switch hammers."

Sturm stared at him, either uncomprehending or refusing to comprehend.

"Flint has the false hammer," Raistlin explained. "He has only to replace the true Hammer with the false. He keeps the true one and gives the dwarves the other."

"They will know the difference," said Sturm.

Raistlin smiled. "I think not. I can cast a spell on the false hammer, recreating the effects you described—or close enough so that the dwarves will not be able to tell the difference for a long time. Once Arman has the hammer in his possession—the hammer he's been searching for all his life—he won't look very hard to find fault with it. I can do this," he added, "but I need your help."

Sturm shook his head. "I won't be a party to this."

"But it solves all our problems!" Raistlin said insistently, placing his hand on Sturm's arm. The knight flinched beneath the touch, but he remained to listen. "We give the dwarves what they want. We have what we want. Once the dragonlances are forged, you can bring the Hammer back to them. No harm done—and much good."

"It is . . . not honorable," said Sturm.

"Oh, well, if honor is what you want, then by all means, say an honorable prayer over the little children as the dragons of the Dark

Queen sear the flesh from their bones." Raistlin's grip on the knight tightened. "*You* may have the right to choose honor over life, but think of those who have no choice, those who will suffer and die under the Dark Queen's rule. And she will rule, Sturm. You know as well as I that the forces of good—what paltry forces of good there are—cannot do anything to stop her."

Sturm was silent. Raistlin could both see and feel the conflict raging inside the knight. Sturm's arm muscles tensed and hardened. His eyes glinted, his fists clenched. He was thinking not only of the innocents, but also of himself. He would bring the Hammer to the knighthood. He would be the one to forge the fabled dragonlances. He would be the savior of the Solamnic people, of all people everywhere.

Raistlin could guess much of what the knight was thinking, and he almost guessed right. Raistlin assumed that Sturm was being seduced by a dream of glory when, in truth, the thought of those innocents who would suffer in the coming war affected the knight profoundly. He could see again the smoldering ruins and the butchered children of Que-shu.

"What do you want me to do?" Sturm asked, the words falling reluctantly from his lips. He had never imagined agreeing to help Raistlin weave one of his webs. Sturm reminded himself, again, of the innocents.

"You must talk to Flint," said Raistlin. "Tell him the plan. He will not listen to me."

"I'm not convinced he will listen to me," Sturm said.

"At least we must try! Put the idea into his head." Raistlin paused, then said softly, "Say nothing to Tanis."

Sturm understood. Tanis would oppose such a scheme. Not only was it dishonest, it was dangerous. If the dwarves found out, it could be the death of them all, yet the dragonlances were their best hope for winning the war—something the half-elf stubbornly refused to understand.

Sturm gave a stiff nod. Raistlin smiled to himself from within the darkness of his cowl. He had won a victory over the virtuous knight, knocking him off his lofty pedestal. In the future, whenever Sturm's lectures on morality grew too tedious, all Raistlin would have to do would be to murmur, "The Hammer of Kharas."

"I will draw Tanis aside. You talk to Flint."

Tanis had recovered Flint's whittling knife and sent Tasslehoff off to investigate a strange sound he claimed to have heard in the back of the building. He and Flint were discussing the journey; that is, Tanis was discussing it, and Flint wasn't saying a word, when Raistlin asked Tanis if he could speak to him.

"I am concerned about Caramon's health," Raistlin said gravely. "He is not well this morning."

"He just drank too much, that's all," said Tanis. "He has a hangover. This isn't the first time. I should think you'd be used to it, by now."

"I think it is more serious than that," Raistlin persisted. "Some sickness. Please come look at him."

"You know more about illness than I do, Raistlin—"

"I would like your opinion, Half-Elven," Raistlin said. "You know how much I respect you."

Tanis didn't, not really, but on the off-chance that Caramon had truly fallen ill, Tanis accompanied Raistlin over to the bed where Caramon lay with a cold rag over his eyes.

Raistlin hovered solicitously near his brother as Tanis looked Caramon over. Raistlin's gaze focused on Sturm and Flint. Raistlin could not hear their conversation, but he did not need to. He knew exactly when Sturm told the dwarf about switching the hammers, for Flint's jaw dropped. He stared at Sturm in astonishment, then, frowning, he gave a violent shake of his head.

Sturm continued to talk, pressing harder. The knight was earnest, serious. He was talking about the innocents. Flint shook his head again, but less forcefully. Sturm kept talking, and now Flint was starting to listen. He was thinking it over. Flint glanced at Arman, then glanced at the false hammer. His brow furrowed. He looked at Raistlin, who regarded him with an unblinking, unwavering stare. Flint averted his gaze. He said something to Sturm, who turned away and walked in studied nonchalance back to Raistlin.

"How is poor Caramon?" Sturm asked in the somber tones of one keeping watch at a deathbed.

Raistlin shook his head and sighed.

"He drank too much, that's all," said Tanis, exasperated.

"Perhaps it was the worm meat," Raistlin suggested.

"Oh, gods!" Caramon groaned. Clutching his gut, he rolled out of bed, dashed over to the corner, and threw up in the slop bucket.

"You see, Tanis," said Raistlin reproachfully. "My brother is gravely ill! I leave him in your care. I must have a word with Flint before he departs."

"And I would like a word with you, Raistlin," said Sturm. "If you could spare me a moment."

The two walked off, leaving Tanis staring after them in wonder, scratching his beard. "What are those two up to? Ganging up on Flint, I suppose. Well, good luck to them."

He went over to assure Caramon that he had not been fed worms.

"Flint has promised to at least consider it," said Sturm.

"He must consider quickly, then," Raistlin said. "I need time to cast the spell, and our young friend grows impatient to be gone."

Arman stood in the doorway, his arms folded across his chest. Every so often he would frown deeply, heave a loud sigh, and tap the toe of his boot on the floor. "Once we send it, we are to take the Hammer to the Temple of the Stars," Arman declared. "I told my father we would be there by sunset, if not before."

Flint stared at him. "What do you think? That we're going to just stroll into the tomb, pick up the Hammer, and stroll back out?"

"I do not know," Arman replied coldly. "You are the one who knows how to find it."

Flint grunted and shook his head. He closed his pack, lifted it off the floor, and slung it over his shoulder. His eyes met Raistlin's. Flint gave a very slight nod.

"He'll do it!" Raistlin said exultantly to Sturm. "There is one problem. The spell I am going to cast is a transmutation spell. It is designed to shrink an object."

"Shrink?" Sturm repeated, aghast. "We don't want to shrink the hammer!"

"I am aware of that," Raistlin said irritably. "I plan to modify the spell so it will reduce the hammer's weight but not the size. There is a small chance that I might make a mistake. If so, our plot will be discovered."

Sturm glowered. "Then we should not proceed."

"A small chance, I said," Raistlin remarked. "Very small."

He went over to Flint, who gave him a dark glance from beneath lowered brows.

"This replica is an object of fine craftsmanship," said Raistlin. "Could I hold it to examine it more closely?"

Flint looked around. Arman had left off haunting the doorway and gone outside to try to walk off his mounting frustration. Tanis was across the room talking to Caramon. Slowly, Flint reached for the hammer. He drew it awkwardly from the harness and handed it over.

"It's heavy," he said pointedly.

Raistlin took the hammer, hefted it to test the weight, then affected to study the runes.

"It would be easier to carry," Flint said, fidgeting nervously with the straps on his armor, "if it was lighter in weight."

"Anyone watching?" Raistlin murmured.

"No," said Sturm, smoothing his mustaches. "Arman is outside. Tanis is with your brother."

Raistlin closed his eyes. He gripped the hammer with one hand, running the other over the rune-etched metal. He drew in a soft breath, then whispered strange words that Flint thought sounded like it feels when a bug crawls up your leg. He regretted his decision and started to reach for the hammer, to take it away.

Then Raistlin gave a sigh and opened his eyes.

"It *is* heavy," he said, as he handed it back. "Remember to be careful when you use it."

Obviously, the spell had failed. Flint was relieved. He grabbed hold of the hammer and nearly went over backward. The hammer was as light as the kender's chicken feather.

Raistlin's eyes glittered. He slid his hands inside the sleeves of his robes.

Flint looked the hammer up and down, but he could not see any change. He started to put it back into the harness, then he caught Raistlin's eye and remembered just in time that the hammer was heavy. Flint wasn't very good at play-acting. He was doubly sorry he'd agreed to go along with this scheme, but it was too late now.

"Well, I'm away," he announced. He stood hunched over, as if bowed down by the weight of the hammer, which was, in truth, weighing on him.

"I wish you would reconsider," said Tanis, walking over to say good-bye. "You still have time to change your mind."

"Yeah, I know." Flint rubbed his nose. He paused, cleared his throat, then said gruffly, "Do this old dwarf a favor, will you, Tanis? Give him a chance to find glory at least once in his dull life. I know it sounds foolish—"

"No," said Tanis, and he laid his hand on Flint's shoulder. "It is far from foolish. Walk with Reorx."

"Don't go praying to gods you don't believe in, half-elf," Flint returned, glowering. "It's bad luck."

Straightening his shoulders, Flint walked out to join Arman Kharas, who told him in no uncertain terms it was time to depart. The two walked off, escorted by Hylar soldiers. Two Hylar guards remained behind, taking up their posts outside the inn's door.

"I hope they haven't forgotten breakfast," said Caramon, sitting up in bed.

"I thought you weren't feeling well," said Raistlin in withering tones.

"I feel better now that I threw up. Hey!" Caramon walked over, opened the door, and stuck his head out. "When do we eat?"

Tasslehoff stared out the window until Flint had disappeared around the corner of a building. Then the kender plunked down on a chair.

"Flint promised me I could go with him to the Floating Tomb," Tas said, kicking the rungs.

Tanis knew it would be hopeless to try to convince the kender that Flint had made no such promise, so Tanis left Tas alone, confident that he would forget all about going in another five minutes, once he found something else of interest.

Sturm was also staring out the window. "We could handle the guards at the door. Tanis. There are only two of them."

"Then what?" Raistlin demanded caustically. "How do we slip through Thorbardin unnoticed? Pass ourselves off as dwarves? The kender might do it, but the rest of us would have to put on false beards and walk on our knees."

Sturm's face flushed at the mage's sarcasm. "We could at least speak to Hornfel. Tell him of our concern for our friend. He might reconsider."

"I suppose we could request an audience," said Tanis, "but I doubt we'd succeed. He made it very clear that only dwarves can enter the sacred tomb."

Sturm continued to stare gloomily out the window.

"Flint is on his way to the Valley of Thanes," said Tanis, "the Kingdom of the Dead, with a mad dwarf to watch his back and the spirit of a dead prince to guide him. Fretting over him won't help."

"Praying for him will," said Sturm, and the knight went down on his knees.

Raistlin shrugged. "I'm going back to bed."

"At least 'til breakfast comes," said Caramon.

There was nothing else to do. Tanis went to his bed, lay down and stared at the ceiling.

Sturm began to pray silently. "I know what I did was wrong, but I did it for the greater good," he told Paladine. He closed his hands and clenched his hands. "As I have always done . . ."

***

Tasslehoff stopped kicking the rungs of the chair. He waited until Sturm was caught up in the rapture of his communion with the god, waited until Tanis's eyes closed and his breathing evened out, waited until he heard Caramon's loud snore and Raistlin's rasping coughing cease.

"Flint promised I could go," Tas muttered. "'I'd sooner take the kender.' That's what he said. Tanis is worried about him, and he wouldn't worry half so much if I was with him."

Tasslehoff divested himself of his pouches. Leaving them behind was a wrench. He felt positively naked without them, but he would make this sacrifice for his friend. Sliding off the chair, moving silently as only a kender can move when he puts his mind to it, Tas opened the door and slipped quietly outside.

The two soldiers had their backs to him. They were talking and didn't hear him.

"Hullo!" Tas said loudly.

The guards drew their swords and whipped around a lot faster than Tas would have given dwarves credit for. He did not know dwarves were so agile, especially decked out in all the metal.

"What do you want?" snarled the soldier.

"Get back in there!" said his friend, and pointed at the inn.

Tas spoke a few words in Dwarvish. He spoke a few words of many languages, since it's always handy to be able to say, "But you dropped it!" to strangers you might meet along the way.

"I want my hoopak," said Tas politely.

The dwarves stared at him and one made a threatening gesture with his blade.

"Not 'sword'," said Tas, misunderstanding the nature of the gesture. "Hoopak. That's spelled 'hoo' and 'pak' and in kender it means 'hoopak'."

The soldiers still didn't get it. They were starting to grow annoyed, but then so was Tasslehoff.

"Hoopak!" he repeated loudly. "That's it, standing there beside you."

He pointed to Sturm's sword. The soldiers turned to look.

"Oops! My mistake," said Tasslehoff. "This is what I meant." A leap, a bound, and a grab, and he had hold of his hoopak. A leap and a thwack, and he'd cracked one of the guards in the face with the butt end of the staff, then used the pronged end to jab the other guard in his gut.

Tas rapped each of them over the head, just to make sure they weren't going to be getting up too soon and be a bother. Choosing the smaller of the two, he plucked the helm off the dwarf.

"That was a good idea Raistlin had. I'll disguise myself as a dwarf!"

The helm was too big and wobbled around on his head. The dwarf's chain mail nearly swallowed the kender, and it weighed at least six tons. He ditched the chain mail and put on the dwarf's leather vest instead. He considered the false beard idea a good one, and he gazed thoughtfully at the dwarf's beard, but he didn't have anything to use to cut it. Tas took off the helm, shook out his top knot, dragged his hair in front of his face, and put on the helm again. His long hair flowed out from underneath.

Unfortunately, all the hair that was bunched up in front of his eyes was a little troublesome because he couldn't see through it all that well, and it kept tickling his nose, so that he had to stop every so often to sneeze. Any sacrifice for a friend, however.

Tasslehoff paused to admire himself in a cracked window. He was quite taken with the results. He didn't see how any one could possibly tell the difference between him and a dwarf. He set off quickly down the street. Flint and Arman Kharas had a pretty good head start, but Tas was confident he'd catch up.

After all, Flint had promised.

14

Three hundred years or half.
The Valley of the Thanes.

lint had hoped to be able to make his way to the Kalil S'rith, the Valley of the Thanes, quietly and quickly, avoiding fuss, bother and gawking crowds. But the Thanes had not kept quiet. Word had spread throughout the dwarven realms that a Neidar was going to seek the Hammer of Kharas.

Flint, Arman, and their escorts left the city of the Talls and walked into a hostile mob. At the sight of Flint, dwarves shook their fists and shouted insults, yelling at him to go back to his hills or take himself off to other places not so nice. Arman came in for his share of abuse, the dwarves calling him traitor and the old insulting nickname, "Mad Arman."

Flint's ears burned, and so did his hatred. He was suddenly glad Raistlin had come up with the idea of sneaking the true Hammer out of Thorbardin and leaving the dwarves the false. He would take the Hammer with him and let his loathsome cousins remained sealed up inside their mountain forever.

The mob was so incensed that Flint and Arman might have ended up in the Valley of the Thanes as permanent residents, but Hornfel, receiving word of the near riot, sent his soldiers out in force. The soldiers ordered the crowds to disperse and used their spears and the flats of their swords to enforce their commands. They closed and sealed off the Eighth Road that led to the Valley. This took some time. Arman and Flint had to wait while the soldiers cleared the road of pedestrians and ordered passengers out of the wagons. If Flint had been paying attention, he would have noticed a very odd-looking dwarf pushing and shoving his way through the crowd: a dwarf of slender (one might say anemic) build, whose helm wobbled about on his head and whose beard poked out of the helm's eye slits. Flint was nearly blind with rage, however. He held the hammer in his hand, longing to use it to bash in a few mountain dwarf heads.

Just when the odd-looking dwarf had almost caught up with them, the soldiers announced that the Eighth Road was clear. Arman Kharas and Flint climbed inside the lead wagon. Flint was taking his seat when he thought he heard a familiar voice cry out in shrill tones, "Hey, Flint! Wait for me!"

Flint's head jerked up. He turned around, but the wagon rattled away before he could see anything.

———————————————

Tasslehoff fought, pushed, shoved, kicked, and slithered his way through the angry crowds of dwarves. He had just managed to get near enough to Flint to yell at him to wait up, when the wagon carrying his friend gave a lurch and began to roll down the rails. Tas thought he'd failed.

Then Tas remembered he was on a Mission. His friends were all worried about Flint going off alone. Sturm was even praying over it. They would be sorely disappointed in him—Tasslehoff—if he let a small thing like a regiment of dwarves armed with spears stop him.

Arman and Flint had entered the first wagon in a series of six wagons hooked together; the soldiers in Arman's escort had been going to accompany him. Arman ordered them to stay behind, however, which left the other five wagons empty.

The wagons were gathering speed. The dwarven soldiers stood arm-in-arm, their feet planted wide apart, forming a human barricade to keep the mob from rushing the mechanism that controlled the wagons. Tas saw an opening. He dropped down on all fours and crawled between the legs of a guard, who was so preoccupied with forcing back the heaving press of bodies that he never noticed the kender.

Tas sprinted down the rail line and caught up with the last wagon. He threw his hoopak inside, then he leapt onto the back of the wagon and clung there as tight as a tick.

After a tense moment when he nearly lost his grip, Tas hoisted one leg up over the side. The rest of him followed, and he tumbled down to join his hoopak at the bottom of the wagon. Tasslehoff lay on his back, admiring the view of passing stalactites on his way to the Valley and thinking how pleased Flint was going to be to see him.

———————————————————

The Seventh, Eighth, and Ninth Roads led to the Kalil S'rith, the Valley of the Thanes. Each road ended at an entrance known as Guardian Hall, though no dwarves ever stood guard there. There was no need. Reverence and respect were the guardians of the Valley. Dwarves coming to bury their dead were the only ones who ever entered, and they stayed only long enough to pay their homage to the fallen.

It was not like that in the old days, at least so Flint had heard. Before the Cataclysm, the priests of Reorx tended the Valley, keeping all neat and trim. Dwarves came to celebrate family anniversaries with their ancestors. Pilgrims came to visit the resting places of ancient Thanes.

After the clerics departed, the dwarves continued to come to the Valley, but without the clerics to tend to it, the grass grew long and wild, the tombs fell into disrepair, and soon the dwarves quit coming. Although dwarves revered their ancestors and thought enough of them to include them in their politics and in their daily lives, asking them for guidance or assistance, the dwarves were now reluctant to disturb the slumbers of the dead. Once a dwarf was laid in tomb or cairn, his family bid farewell and departed, returning to the Valley only when it was time to bury another family member.

The Valley of the Thanes was hallowed ground, blessed centuries ago by Reorx. Once the valley had been a place of quiet and peace. Now it was a place of sorrow. The valley was also a place of sun and wind, cloud and stars, for the valley was the only area in Thorbardin on which the sunlight shone. This was another reason the dwarves rarely went there. They were like babes in the womb, who cry at the light. Living all their lives in the snug darkness beneath the mountain, the dwarves of Thorbardin felt uncomfortable—vulnerable and exposed—when they entered the wind-swept, sun-drenched emptiness of the valley.

The huge bronze doors of the Guardian Hall were marked with the symbol of the Eighth Kingdom—a hammer prone, lying at rest; the warrior's hand having put it down.

———————————————

Neither Flint nor Arman spoke during the journey down the Eighth Road. Neither spoke as they walked toward the bronze doors. The noise of the chaotic scene behind them had faded away in the distance. Each was occupied with his own thoughts, hopes, dreams, desires, and fears.

They came to the double doors, and by unspoken, mutual consent, they put their hands to opposite sides—Flint taking the left and Arman Kharas the right. Removing their helms and bowing their heads, they pushed open the great doors of the Kilil S'rith.

Sunlight—bright, brilliant, blinding—struck them full in the face. Arman Kharas squinted his eyes half-shut and held up his hand to blot out the dazzling light. Flint blinked rapidly, then drew in a huge gulp of crisp mountain air and lifted his face to the warmth of the sunshine.

"By Reorx!" Flint breathed. "I did not know how much I missed this! It is like I have come back to life!"

Ironic, he thought, in a valley of death.

Arman shielded his eyes. He could not look into the wide, blue sky.

"For me it is like death," he said grimly. "No walls, no borders, no boundaries, no beginning, and no end. I see the vast expanse of the universe above me, and I am nothing in it, less than nothing, and I do not like that."

It was then Flint truly understood, for the first time, the vast gulf that lay between his people and those beneath the mountain. Long ago, both clans had been comfortable walking in sunlight and in darkness. Now what was life to one was death to the other.

Flint wondered if his people could ever go back to what had once been, as Arman Kharas dreamed. Hearing again the curses, the insults, the words of hate—sharper, harder, and more lethal than missiles—feeling the burning of anger in his own heart, Flint did not consider it likely, hammer or no hammer. Though his anger burned, he felt a sorrow at that, as though he'd misplaced something treasured.

The two dwarves stood waiting for their eyes to grow accustomed to the bright light before they proceeded. Neither could see very well, thus neither of them noticed Tasslehoff climb out of the wagon. He had thrown off the bulky helm and removed his smelly and itchy leather vest, and he hurried toward the bronze door intending to take Flint by surprise, for it was always fun to see the old dwarf jump into the air and go red in the face.

Tas ran inside the doors, and the sun hit him smack in the face. The sunlight was bright and completely unexpected. Clapping his hands over his eyes, the kender went reeling backward through the bronze doors. The glare jabbed right into his brain, and all he could see was a huge red splash streaked with blue and decorated with little yellow speckles. When this admittedly entertaining and interesting phenomenon had passed, Tas opened his eyes and saw, to his dismay, that the bronze doors had swung shut, leaving him stranded in darkness that was worse than ever.

"I'm going to an awful lot of trouble," Tas grumbled, rubbing his eyes. "I hope Flint appreciates it."

The Valley of the Thanes had been a cavern that had collapsed thousands of years ago, leaving it open to the air. The dead lay in small burial mounds rising up out of the rustling brown grass, or in large cairns marked by stone doors, or in the instances of very wealthy and powerful dwarves, the dead were entombed inside mausoleums. Each site was marked with a stone in which the family name had been carved at the top, with the names of the individual family members added in rows underneath. Some families had several such stones, for their generations extended back through time. Flint kept an eye out for Neidar names as he went, including his own, Fireforge. Another point of contention between the clans when Duncan sealed up the mountain was that the Neidar who came back to Thorbardin to be buried were now barred from their traditional resting place.

No paths or trails circled the mounds. The feet of mortals rarely walked here. Flint and Arman wended their way among the mounds, their destination visible to them the moment their eyes grew accustomed to the light—Duncan's Tomb.

The ornate and elaborate structure, more like a small palace than a tomb, floated majestically many hundred feet above a still blue lake in the center of the valley. The lake had been formed by run-off from the mountain snows flowing into the hole left behind when the tomb was wrenched out of the earth.

Flint could not take his eyes from the marvelous sight. He stared at the tomb in awe. He had seen many dwarven-built monuments before, but none to rival this. Weighing tons upon tons, the tomb floated among the clouds as if it were as light as any of them. Towers and turrets made of white marble adorned with flame red tile shone in the sunlight. Stained glass windows opened onto balconies. Steep stairs led from one level to another, crisscrossing up and down and circling round the edifice.

A deep musical note resonated from the tomb and echoed throughout the valley. The note sounded once, then the music faded away.

"What was that?" Flint asked, astonished.

Arman Kharas gazed up at the miracle of the floating tomb.

"Some say it is Kharas wielding the hammer. None know for sure."

The note sounded again, and Flint was forced to admit, it did sound very much like a hammer striking metal. He thought about what might be waiting for them in that tomb—should they ever manage to reach it—and he wished he had taken Sturm's advice and insisted that Hornfel allow his friends to come with him.

"King Duncan began building his tomb in his lifetime," Arman stated. "It was to be a grand monument where his children and their children and those who would come after him would all be laid to rest. Alas, his vision of a Hylar dynasty was not to be. His two sons he buried in a plain, unmarked cairn. The tomb of his third son will forever remain empty.

"When the king died, Kharas, disgusted by the fighting among the clans, bore the body to the tomb himself. Fearing that the king's funeral would be marred by unseemly behavior on the parts of the feuding Thanes, Kharas banned all of them from attending. It is said that they sought to enter, but the great bronze doors slammed shut upon them. Kharas never returned. The Thanes pounded on the doors, trying to force them open. The earth began to shake with such violence that buildings toppled, the Life Tree cracked, and the lake overflowed and flooded the surrounding land.

"When the mountain ceased trembling, the bronze doors swung

open. Each eager to find the hammer and claim it for his own, the Thanes fought over who would be the first to enter the Valley. Bloody and battered, they surged inside, only to discover, to their horror, that the king's tomb had been torn from the ground by some dread force and set floating in the air far above their heads.

"Down through the years, many have searched for the means that would gain us entry, but to this day, none have found it, and now"— Arman turned his dark gaze from the tomb to Flint—"you, a Neidar, claim to know the secret." Arman stroked his long black beard. "I, for one, doubt it."

Flint took the bait. "Where is Prince Grallen's tomb?" He was suddenly eager to have this over and done with.

"Not far." Arman pointed. "The obelisk of black marble you see by the lake. Once the obelisk stood in front of Duncan's Tomb, but that was before it was torn out of the earth. A statue of the prince stands at the site, and beyond it are the remains of a marble archway that crumbled when the mountain shook."

Arman cast a glance at Flint. "What do we do once we reach the prince's tomb? Unless you would rather not tell me," he added stiffly.

Flint felt he owed the young dwarf something. Arman had given him his hammer, after all.

"I'm to take the helm to his tomb," said Flint.

Arman stared, astonished. "That is all? Nothing about the Hammer?"

"Not in so many words," Flint said evasively.

There had been a feeling, an impression, but nothing specific. That was the main reason he hadn't said more to his friends and yet another reason he had decided to leave them behind.

"But you agreed to make the wager with Realgar—"

"Ah, now," said Flint, walking among the mounds of the dead, "what dwarf who calls himself a dwarf ever turned down a bet?"

———◆——▸◂——

Tasslehoff stared at the bronze doors, then he went over and gave one of the doors a swift kick, not so much because he thought he could kick the door open, but because he was so profoundly annoyed with them. Tas's toes tingled all the way up to his shoulders, and he became more annoyed than ever.

Dropping his hoopak onto the ground, Tas put both hands on one of the doors and pushed. He pushed and pushed, and nothing happened. He paused to wipe the sweat from his face and thought to himself that he wouldn't go to this much trouble for anyone except Flint. He also thought that he'd felt the door give just a little, so he pushed again, this time throwing all his weight into it.

"You know who would come in handy about now?" Tas said to himself, pushing with all his might on the door. "Fizban. If he were here, he would hurl one of his fireballs at this door, and it would just pop open."

Which is exactly what the door did at that moment.

Pop open. With the result that Tas found himself pushing against nothing but air and sunlight, and he landed flat on his face on the ground. Landing flat on his face reminded Tas of something else Fizban would have done—given the absence of flame, smoke, and general destruction that usually accompanied the daft old wizard's spells. Tas spent a moment lying in the grass, sighing over his friend's demise. Then, remembering his Mission, he jumped to his feet and looked about.

It was then he realized that the bronze door was swinging shut behind him. Tas made a leap for his hoopak and managed to haul it inside at the last moment before the door boomed shut. Turning around, he looked up into the sky and saw the floating tomb, and he heard what sounded like a hammer striking a gong. The kender was enthralled.

Tas lost several moments staring at the tomb in dumbfounded wonder. The hammer was up there in that tomb that was floating in the sky, and Flint was going up there to get it. Tas gave a moist sigh.

"I hope I don't hurt your feelings, Queen Takhisis, when I say this," he said solemnly, "and I want to assure you that I still plan to visit the Abyss someday, but right now the place I most want to be in all the world is up there in Duncan's Tomb."

Tasslehoff trudged off in search of his friend.

———————◆———————

The tomb of Prince Grallen was one of many cairns, tombs, and burial mounds that had been constructed around the lake in the center of the valley. Here, around the lake, Thanes and their families had been buried for centuries. Grallen's tomb was the only empty tomb, however; left open to receive the body that would never be found. The tomb was marked by a black obelisk and a life-size statue of the prince. The statue was of the prince in full battle regalia, but it held no weapons. The hands were empty as the tomb, the head bare.

Kharas stood before the statue of the prince, his head bowed in respect, his own helm in his hand. Flint, his mouth dry, walked slowly forward, carrying the Helm of Grallen. He was at loss to know what to do. Was he supposed to place the helm in the empty tomb? He started to turn away, when he felt a chill touch on his flesh. The stone hands of the statue were resting on his own.

Flint's stomach lurched. His hands shook, and he nearly dropped the helm. He tried to move, but the stone hands held him fast. He looked into the statue's face, into the eyes, and they were not empty stone. They shone bright with life.

The stone lips moved. "My head has been bare to the sun and the wind, the rain and the snow these many long years."

Flint shuddered and wished he'd never come. He hesitated, nerving himself, and then, quaking in fear, he placed the helm on the statue's head. Metal scraped against stone. The helm slid over the cold face and covered the eyes. The red gem flared.

"I go to join my brothers. Long have they waited for me that we could make this next journey together."

A feeling of peace flowed through Flint, and he was no longer afraid. He felt overwhelming love, love that forgave all. He let go of the helm almost reluctantly and stepped back and bowed his head. The feeling of peace faded away. He heard Arman gasp, and when he could see through the mist that covered his eyes, Flint saw the prince now wore a helm of stone.

He choked back the lump in his throat, rubbed the moisture from his eyes, and looked about. Finding what he sought, he circled around the obelisk.

"What do we do now?" Arman asked, following after him. "Where are you going?"

"That arch over there," Flint said, pointing.

"The arch was a monument to Kharas," said Arman. "It fell down when the tomb was torn from the earth. It lay in ruins for many years. My father had it rebuilt and rededicated in hopes that it would lead us to the Hammer, but nothing came of it."

Flint nodded. "We have to walk through the arch."

Arman was skeptical. "Bah! I've walked through the arch countless times and nothing happened."

Flint made no reply, saving his breath for walking. As Raistlin had so unkindly reminded him, he was not getting any younger. The fracas with the mob, the hike through the valley, and the encounter with the statue had taken its toll on his strength. For all he knew, he was a long way from the hammer.

The arch was made of the same black marble as the obelisk. It was very plain with nothing carved on it except the words, "I wait and watch. He will not return. Alas, I mourn for Kharas."

Flint halted. He rocked back and forth on his feet, making up his mind, then, sucking in a huge breath and shutting his eyes, he ran through the arch. As he did so, he shouted out loudly, "I mourn for Kharas!"

Flint's run should have taken him to the brown grass on other side of the arch. Instead, his boots clattered on rickety wooden floor boards. Shocked, he opened his eyes and found himself in a shadowy room lit by a single ray of sunlight shining through a narrow arrow slit in a stone wall.

Flint sucked in a breath and let it out in awe. He turned around, and there was the arch, far, far behind him. He heard a distant voice cry, "I mourn for Kharas" and Arman appeared in the archway. He stared around in wonder.

"We are here!" he cried. "Inside the tomb!" He sank to his knees. "My destiny is about to be fulfilled."

Flint stumped over to the arrow slit and peered out. He looked down on brown grass and a sun-lit lake and a small obelisk. His eyes widened. He took a hasty step backward.

"Quick! Block the entrance!" he bellowed, but he was too late.

"I mourn for Kharas," cried a shrill voice.

Tasslehoff Burrfoot, hoopak in hand, burst through the arch.

"You promised you were going to take me, Flint," he said, "but I guess you forgot and I didn't want you to feel bad, so I came along myself."

"A kender!" Arman exclaimed in horror. "In the tomb of the High King! This cannot be permitted! He must go back."

He rushed at Tasslehoff, who was so astonished he forgot to run. Arman grabbed hold of the kender and was about to hurl him back through the arch when he suddenly let go.

"The arch is gone!" Arman gasped.

"Say," said Tas, picking himself up off the floor, "if the arch is gone, how do we get back down on the ground?"

"Maybe we don't," Flint said grimly.

15

Lizards. Fleas. Vermin.

Tell me more about this hammer," said Dray-yan.

"It is a moldy old dwarven relic," Realgar replied. He eyed the lizard-men suspiciously. "Nothing you'd be interested in."

"According to what His Lordship has heard, the dwarf who finds the hammer will determine who is to be High King," said Dray-yan, "and now we have found out that two dwarves have set off in search of it. You failed to mention this to Lord Verminaard."

Realgar scowled. "I did not think his lordship would interested."

"On the contrary," said Dray-yan, his long tongue flicking out from between his teeth. He sucked it back in. "His lordship is interested in everything that happens here in Thorbardin."

The aurak draconian and his commander, Grag, were deep inside Thorbardin meeting with the Thane of the Theiwar. One of Dray-yan's paid informants had taken the information about the hammer to a draconian message bearer, who deemed it important enough to travel swiftly through the secret tunnels and wake Grag in the middle of the night. Grag had deemed it important enough to wake Dray-yan. The same messenger had also brought information about the escaped slaves and the gang of assassins who led them.

Dray-yan and Grag traveled swiftly to Thorbardin to discuss these matters with Realgar. Dray-yan had met with the Theiwar leader before, but then he had been in the guise of Lord Verminaard. Dray-yan decided to appear as his true scaly self when he met with Realgar today. Lord Verminaard was on his way to Thorbardin, Dray-yan told Realgar. His Lordship would be present when the hammer was found.

Realgar sneered. "As for determining who will be High King, axes, swords, and spears will do that, not some rusty hunk of metal." The Thane scratched his neck, plucked off a flea and squeezed it between his fingers. He tossed it aside.

Dray-yan was patient, as he continued his questioning. Emperor Ariakas was vitally interested in obtaining this hammer. Dray-yan doubted very much if the emperor cared who was king of the dwarves. "But the hammer is reputed to possess magical powers."

Realgar gave the draconians a sharp glance. He thought he knew what this was about now. "The dragonlances. That's what you mean, isn't it?" He chuckled. "I can see where that might interest Verminaard."

Dray-yan and Grag exchanged glances. Grag shook his head.

"His Lordship knows nothing about dragonlances," said Dray-yan.

"They're lances used to kill dragons—and other lizards," Realgar added with an ugly grin.

Dray-yan looked grimly at the Theiwar. He would have liked to have throttled the stinking little maggot. He had to be conciliatory, however. Their plans depended on him.

"I will inform His Lordship about these dragonlances," Dray-yan said. "In the meantime, the hammer is said to be located in the . . ." He forgot the name and glanced at Grag for the information.

"Valley of the Thanes," Grag supplied.

"Two dwarves have gone seeking it—"

"Let two hundred go. They won't find it. Even if they do, what will it matter?" Realgar leered at Dray-yan. "Or perhaps you see yourself as King Beneath the Mountain, Lizard?"

The aurak answered in draconian for the benefit of Grag. "Trust me, you filthy little weasel, I have no plans to become High King of a bunch of hairy, vermin-infested rodents. Being slave-master will be punishment enough. Still we all must make sacrifices for the cause."

Grag's tail twitched in agreement.

Realgar, who didn't understand draconian, looked irritably from one to the other. "What did you say to him?"

"I told Grag I dare not dream of rising to such exalted heights, Thane," said Dray-yan. "To serve my Lord Verminaard is the extent of my humble ambitions." He paused, "I cannot say the same for Lord Verminaard, however."

Realgar's bushy brows came together over his squinty eyes, causing them to nearly vanish from sight. "What do you mean?"

Dray-yan looked at Grag. "Should we tell him?"

Grag nodded solemnly. "The Thane has been of great help to us. It is right that he should know."

"Know what?" Realgar demanded.

"Let us consider what might happen if Lord Verminaard obtained the Hammer of Kharas and became High King of Thorbardin. He would control the iron ore production. He would receive the profits."

"No human can be High King!" cried Realgar, swelling with fury. "The hammer is a hunk of metal. Nothing more."

"Her Dark Majesty does not consider the hammer a 'hunk of metal,'" said Dray-yan. "She might also have an interest in these spears."

"Lances," said Grag. "Dragonlances."

Dray-yan shrugged. "If, as you say, the hammer is nothing but a 'hunk of metal,' then you have nothing to fear. If the hammer does truly possess magical powers, then Emperor Ariakas, in the name of Her Dark Majesty, will reward the person who brings it to him and make that person High King of Thorbardin. And that person will be Lord Verminaard."

"Verminaard has no right to rule us!" Realgar declared sulkily.

Dray-yan sighed deeply. "His Lordship's ambition is vast, as are his appetites. Not that this in any way diminishes his greatness," he added hastily.

"I asked for his help in making *me* king," Realgar stated. "If I had known he planned to claim the throne himself, I would have never brought him in on this deal. *I* will be king, no one else, especially no human."

He brooded awhile, then regarded Dray-yan with speculative interest. "You seem to be intelligent—for a lizard, that is."

Dray-yan didn't dare glance at Grag, for fear they'd both burst out laughing.

"I am grateful for your good opinion, Thane," said Dray-yan. He added, with a sigh, "I wish His Lordship shared it."

"You speak as though you were willing to switch allegiance," said Realgar, "serve a new master."

"Grag and I might consider it," said Dray-yan, "depending on what was in it for us."

"Your own share of the profits."

Dray-yan and Grag discussed this proposition.

"The weasel has taken the bait," said the aurak in draconian. "As we discussed, when this hammer is recovered I will keep the Thanes distracted—or rather, 'His Lordship' will keep them distracted. Your troops will enter Thorbardin, take over and occupy key dwarven fortifications."

Grag nodded. "The troops are assembled in the tunnel, awaiting my command. If the hammer is found, the dwarves will take it to the location they call the Temple of the Stars. Once the Thanes have assembled, we can seal the exits, trapping them and the hammer inside."

"After his lordship has met his sad end," Dray-yan said, "and the hammer is safely in my hands, I will have a little talk with the Thanes. I will let them know who is going to be in charge from now on." He cast a baleful glance at Realgar.

"We draconians will be the first in the Dark Queen's service to conquer a nation of Ansalon," Grag observed. "Emperor Ariakas cannot choose but to grant us the respect we deserve. Perhaps someday a draconian will be the one to wear the Crown of Power."

Dray-yan could almost feel that crown upon his own scaly head. He reluctantly tore himself away from his dream and returned to business.

"Grag and I have spoken," said Dray-yan to the Theiwar. "We agree to your terms."

"I thought you lizards might," said Realgar with a sneer.

"We have devised a plan to deal with His Lordship," Dray-yan continued, "but first, Grag and I are concerned about these six assassins who have entered your realm. These men are in the pay of the elves. They were sent into Pax Tharkas to try to kill His Lordship. He survived the attack, but they managed to escape."

"You sound as though you're afraid of these criminals," said Realgar.

Dray-yan's claws twitched. He had something very special in mind for Realgar once he took over.

"I do not *fear* them," Dray-yan said. "I do respect them, however, as should you. They are clever, and they are skilled, and they have the blessings of their gods."

"*And* they are dead," said Realgar smugly. "You need not worry about them."

Dray-yan's tongue flicked in and out. He didn't believe Realgar.

"Dead? How?" he asked sharply.

He was interrupted by a dwarf, who came running into the Thane's sinkhole of a dwelling place. The dwarf began gabbling in his own language. Realgar listened with interest. His scraggly beard parted in a rotted-toothed grin. At almost the same moment, a baaz draconian entered. He saluted and waited for Grag to acknowledge him.

The baaz made his report, who relayed the news to Dray-yan.

"A small band of humans are approaching the Northgate. It looks like a scouting party."

"My fugitive slaves?"

"Almost certainly. One of them is that extremely tall Plainsman who fought Verminaard. He leads others like him, all dressed in animal skins—six total. An elf lord travels with them. He was also seen at Pax Tharkas."

"I take it we have received the same news," said Realgar, who was watching the draconians closely. "Human warriors have arrived at Northgate."

"Yes," Dray-yan responded. "The same criminals who escaped us in Pax Tharkas."

"Praise Her Dark Majesty," said Realgar, rubbing his dirty hands together in satisfaction. "They will not escape us here."

"I will send my forces to destroy them," Grag began.

"No, wait!" Realgar interposed. "They're not to be slain. I want at least two of them captured alive."

"A live enemy is a dangerous enemy," said Grag. "Kill them and be done with it."

"Normally, I would agree," said Realgar, "but I need this scum as proof to Hornfel and the other Council members that a human army is planning to invade us. I will bring these spies before the Council, exhibit them, and make them confess. Hornfel will have no choice but to close the Northgate, which will ensure that our secret dealings with the dragonarmy will continue. The Theiwar will grow rich and powerful. The Hylar will starve. I will soon be ruler under the mountain—hammer or no hammer."

"You know, of course, that there is no human army," Grag said. "They are merely desperate slaves. Why should these humans say otherwise?"

"When I am finished with them, they will not only claim they are leaders of an army sent here to attack us, they will believe their confessions, and so will all who hear them. In the meantime, you and your troops will go down into the forest, track down these other humans, and kill them."

"I do not take my orders from you—" Grag began, his clawed hand reaching for the hilt of his sword.

"Patience, Commander," Dray-yan counseled, adding in their own language, "This Realgar may be a weasel, but he is a cunning weasel. Do as he commands in regard to the slaves. Take them alive. We will let him think he is in control for the time being. Meanwhile, I want you to make certain he is telling the truth. Find out if the assassins have been slain, as he claims. If not, you deal with them."

"Stop hissing at each other! From now on, you'll speak Common when you're in my presence. What did you just say to him?" Realgar demanded suspiciously.

"What you told me to say, Thane," Dray-yan replied humbly. "I relayed your orders to Grag, tellling him his men are to capture the Plainsmen alive."

Realgar grunted. "Take them to the dungeons once you have them. I will be there to question them."

"Commander, you heard the Thane's orders," said Dray-yan in Common. He glanced back at Realgar. "You have no objection, I take it, to allowing Commander Grag to view the bodies of the six assassins?"

"Nothing easier," said Realgar. "I will send some of my people to escort him." He gestured to a couple of Theiwar, who stood lurking in the shadows.

"I suppose this Grag is capable of handling my orders?" Realgar added, casting the draconian commander a disparaging glance.

"He's very intelligent," Dray-yan replied dryly, "for a lizard."

16

Duncan's Tomb. Yet another Kharas.

The helm *was* cursed," Arman said, his voice trembling with anger and fear. He rounded on Flint. "You have lured us to our doom!"

Flint's gut twisted. He imagined for one terrible moment what it would be like to be imprisoned here, left to die, then he remembered touching the stone hand of the Prince, the feeling of peace that had stolen over him.

"You didn't expect to walk in and find the Hammer lying on the floor, did you?" he asked Arman. "We'll be tested, like as not, before we find it. We might well die, but we weren't sent here to die."

Arman considered this. "You are probably right," he said more calmly. "I should have thought of that. A test, of course, to see which of us is worthy."

Sunlight edged in through the slit windows. Arman reached into a leather pouch he wore on his belt and drew out a folded piece of yellowed parchment. He carefully opened the folds, then walked over to the light to study it.

"What have you got there?" Flint asked curiously.

Arman did not reply.

"It's a map," said Tasslehoff, crowding close beside the dwarf, peering over his elbow. "I love maps. What's it a map of?"

Arman shifted his position so that his back was to the kender.

"The tomb," he answered. "It was drawn up by the original architect. It has been in our family for generations."

"Then all we have to do is use the map to find the Hammer!" said Tas excitedly.

"No, we can't, you doorknob," said Flint. "The Hammer was placed in the tomb *after* Duncan was buried here. It wouldn't be on the map." He eyed Arman. "Would it?"

"No," said Arman, studying the map, then glancing around at their surroundings, then going back to the map.

"Mind if I take a look?" Flint asked.

"The map is very old and fragile," said Arman. "It should not be handled." He folded the map and slid it back into his belt.

"But at least it will show us the way out," said Tas. "There must be a front door."

"And what good will that do when we're a mile in the air, you doorknob?" Flint demanded.

"Oh," said Tas. "Yeah, right."

The magical archway through which they had passed would also have been added after Duncan's death, undoubtedly put there by the same powerful force that had ripped the tomb out of the ground and hoisted it into the clouds. The same force that might still be lurking inside the tomb, waiting for them.

Arman paced the chamber, peering into shadowy corners and glancing out the arrow slits to the ground far below. He turned to Flint. "The first thing you should do is search for the exit."

"I'll search," said Flint grimly, "for what I came for—the Hammer."

As if conjured up by the word, the musical note sounded again. The note was no longer faint as it had been below, but rich and melodious. Long after the sound ceased, the vibrations lingered on the air.

"That noise goes all the way through me. I can even feel it in my teeth," said Tas, charmed. He stared at the ceiling and pointed. "It's coming from up there."

"There are stairs over here, leading up," Arman reported from the far side of the chamber. He paused, then said stiffly, "I'm sorry I lost my nerve. It won't happen again, I assure you."

Flint nodded noncommittally. He intended to conduct his own inspection of the room. "Where does the map say we are?"

"This is the Hall of Enemies," said Arman. "These trophies honor King Duncan's battles."

Various weapons, shields, and other implements of war were on display, along with etched silver plaques relating the triumphs of King Duncan over his enemies, including his exploits in the famous war against the ogres. There were no trophies from the last war, however, the most bitter and terrible war fought against his own kind.

Flint caught the kender in the act of trying to pick up a large ogre battle-axe.

"Put that down!" Flint said, incensed. "What else have you stuck in your pouches—"

"I don't have any pouches," Tas pointed out sadly. "I had to leave them behind to put on the dwarf armor."

"Your pockets, then," Flint spluttered, "and if I find that you've stolen something—"

"I never stole in my life!" Tas protested. "Stealing is wrong."

Flint sucked in a breath. "Well, then if I find that you've 'borrowed' anything or picked up something that someone's dropped—"

"Stealing from the dead is extremely wrong," Tas said solemnly. "Cursed, even."

"Would you let me finish a sentence?" Flint roared.

"Yes, Flint," said Tas meekly. "What was it you wanted to say?"

Flint glared. "I forget. Come with me."

He turned on his heel and walked to the corner where Arman had reported finding the stairs. Tas sidled over to one of the displays and put down a small bone-handled knife that had somehow managed to make its way up his shirt sleeve. He gave the knife a pat and sighed, then went to join Flint, who was staring intently at several hammers stacked up against a wall.

"I guess it's all right if *you* steal from the dead," said Tas.

"Me?" Flint said, incensed. "I'm not—"

He paused, not sure what to say.

"What about the Hammer?" Tas asked.

"That's not stealing," said Flint. "It's . . . *finding*. There's a difference."

"So if I 'find' something I can take it?" Tas asked. He had, after all, found that bone-handled knife.

"I didn't say that!"

"Yes, you did."

"Where's Arman?" Flint realized suddenly that he and Tas were alone.

"I think he's gone up those stairs," said Tas, pointing. "When you're not shouting, I can hear him talking to someone."

"Who in blazes could he be talking to?" Flint wondered uneasily. He cocked an ear, and sure enough, he heard what sounded like two voices, one of which was definitely Arman's.

"A ghost!" Tas guessed, and he started to race up the stairs.

Flint seized hold of the kender's shirttail. "Not so fast."

"But if there is a ghost, I don't want to miss it!" Tas cried, wriggling in Flint's grasp.

"Shush! I want to hear what they're talking about."

Flint crept up the narrow stairs. Tas sneaked along behind him. The staircase was steep, and they couldn't see where the steps led. Soon, Flint's breath began to come in gasps and his leg muscles started to cramp. He pressed on and suddenly came to an abrupt halt. Two of the stone stairs jutted outward at an odd angle, leaving an opening about the size of a large human. Light glimmered from within.

"Huh," Flint grunted. "Secret passage."

"I love secret passages!" Tas started to crawl inside.

Flint grabbed hold of his ankle and dragged him out.

"Me first."

Flint crawled into the passage. At the other end, a small wooden door stood open a crack. Flint peeked through. Tas couldn't see for the dwarf's bulk, and he squirmed and wriggled to wedge his head in beside him.

"The burial chamber," said Flint softly. "The king lies here." He removed his helm.

An ornate marble sarcophagus stood in the center of the room. A carven figure of the king graced the top. At the far end two immense doors of bronze and gold were sealed shut. The great bronze doors would have been opened only on special occasions, such as the yearly anniversary of the High King's death. Statues of dwarven warriors ranged around the tomb, standing silent and eternal guard. Light gleamed off a golden anvil placed in front of the tomb and on a stand of armor made of gold and steel.

Arman was on his knees, his own helm beside him on the floor.

Standing over him, gazing down at him, was a dwarf with white hair and a long, white beard. The dwarf was stooped with age, but even stooped, he was taller than Flint and massively built.

"It's not a ghost," Tas whispered, disappointed. "It's just an old dwarf. No offense, Flint."

Flint gave the kender a kick. "Quiet!"

"I am honored to be in your presence, Great Kharas," Arman said, his voice choked with emotion.

Flint's eyes opened wide. His eyebrows shot up to his hair line.

"Kharas? Did he say Kharas?" Tas asked. "We've already got two Kharases—Arman and the dead one. Is this another? How many are there?"

Flint kicked him again and Tas subsided, rubbing bruised ribs.

"Rise up, young man," said the ancient dwarf. "You should not bow before me. I am not a king. I am merely one who guards the rest of the king."

"All these centuries you have stayed here," said Arman, awed. "Why did you not come back to your people, Great Kharas? We are in sore need of your guidance."

"I offered guidance to my people," said the ancient dwarf bitterly, "but it wasn't wanted. I am not in this tomb of my own choosing. You could say I was exiled to this place, sent here by the folly of my people."

Flint's eyes narrowed. He tugged on his beard. "Funny way of talking," he muttered.

Arman bowed his head in shame. "We have been foolish, Kharas, but all that will change now. You will come back to us. You will bring the Hammer to us. We will be united under one king."

The ancient dwarf regarded the younger. "Why have you come here, Arman Kharas?"

"To . . . to pay homage to King Duncan," Arman stammered.

Kharas smiled sadly. "You came for the Hammer, I think."

Arman flushed. "We need the Hammer!" he said defensively. "Our people are suffering. The clans are divided. The Northgate, closed for centuries, has been opened. There is talk of war in the world above, and I fear there will be war beneath the mountain. If I could bring back the Hammer to Thorbardin, my father would be High King and he would—" He paused.

"He would do what?" Kharas asked mildly.

"He would unite the clans. Welcome our Neidar cousins back to the mountain. Open the gates to humans and elves, and reestablish trade and commerce."

"Laudable goals," Kharas said, nodding his head sagely. "Why do you need the hammer to accomplish them?"

Arman looked confused. "You said yourself long ago, before you left: 'Only when a good and honorable dwarf comes to unite the nations shall the Hammer of Kharas return. It will be his badge of righteousness.'"

"Are you that dwarf?" Kharas asked.

Arman lifted his head and stood straight and tall. "I am Arman Kharas," he said proudly. "I found the way here when no one could find it for three hundred years."

Flint scowled. "*He* found the way here!"

Now it was Tas who kicked him. "Shush!"

"Why name yourself after Kharas?" the ancient dwarf asked.

"Because you are a great hero, of course!"

"He didn't mean to be a hero," said Kharas softly. "He was only a man who held true to his beliefs and did what he thought was right."

He regarded Arman intently, then said, "What is your name?"

"Arman Kharas," answered the young dwarf.

"No, that is what you call yourself. What is your name?" Kharas persisted.

Arman frowned. "I don't know what you mean. That is my name."

"The name given to you at birth," said Kharas.

Arman flushed an ugly red. "What does that matter? My name is what I say it is. I chose my name and when I did so, a blessed red light flashed—"

"Yes, yes." Kharas said impatiently. "I know all about that. What is your name?"

Arman opened his mouth. He shut it again and swallowed. His face went even redder. He mumbled something.

"What?" Kharas leaned toward him.

"Pike," said Arman in sulky tones. "My name was Pike, but Pike is not the name of a hero!"

"It might be," said Kharas.

Arman shook his head.

Flint grunted. At the sound, the ancient dwarf turned his head, casting a sharp glance in the direction of the secret passage. Flint ducked back into the shadows and hauled the kender with him.

Kharas smiled and ran his fingers through his white beard. Then he turned back to Arman.

"You did not come alone, did you?" he said.

"Two others came with me," Arman, adding carelessly, "My servants."

"Servants!" Tas gasped. "Did you hear that, Flint?"

He expected Flint to explode in anger, or rush out and bash Arman with the hammer, or burst into flame, or maybe all three at once.

Flint just sat there, tugging on his beard.

"Did you hear him, Flint?" Tas whispered loudly. "He called you his servant!"

"I heard," said Flint. He quit tugging on his beard and smoothed it with his hand.

"Servants, huh. I guess they don't need to be tested then," stated Kharas.

A gust of wind blew the wooden door shut, nearly catching the kender's topknot in it.

"How rude!" Tasslehoff exclaimed, twitching his hair back just in time.

"Open it!" said Flint, frowning.

Tasslehoff gave the door handle a jiggle, and it came off in his hand. "Oops."

"You have a lock pick, don't you?" Flint growled. "For once, it might prove useful."

Tas felt through all his pockets.

"I must have left it in one of my pouches."

"Oh, for the love of Reorx!" Flint grumbled. "The only reason you're any use to anyone is for picking the occasional lock, and now you can't even do that!"

He put his ear to the keyhole.

"Can you hear anything?" Tas asked.

"No."

"We'd better go!" Tas urged, tugging on Flint's sleeve. "The really, really old Kharas will probably lead our Kharas to the hammer! We have to beat him to it!"

"It's not a race," Flint said, but he suddenly turned around and began to clump rapidly down the stairs, moving so fast that he caught the kender flat-footed. Tas had to scramble to catch up.

"Arman's real name is Pike, and his brother is Pick. Pick and Pike!" The kender giggled. "That's funny!"

Flint had no comment. Reaching the floor of the Hall of Enemies, he began searching the room, poking at walls and stomping on the floor to see if there might be a trap door. "Blast it! How do we get out of here?"

Tas fished about in his pocket. "Would this help?" He brought forth a piece of parchment. "It's Arman's map. I *found* it," he added, with emphasis.

He held out the map to Flint.

The dwarf hesitated, then seized hold of it.

"Arman must have dropped it," Flint muttered.

17

Caramon skips breakfast.
Grag is late for lunch.

istening to Sturm's prayer, Tanis felt suddenly soothed and restful. His worries left him alone for a moment, and he drifted off to sleep. Raistlin's coughing woke him.

Raistlin had not suffered a bad coughing spell in some time. He ordered Caramon out of bed to fix his special herbal brew. This involved stirring up the fire and searching about for a kettle, and then boiling the water, all of which, thankfully, kept Caramon occupied and caused him to at least quit talking about food. The dwarves had not yet brought them anything to eat, and Caramon was growing worried.

Raistlin sipped at the tea, and his cough eased. He sat dozing in the chair, huddled as close to the fire as he could get. Sturm remained on his knees, finding solace in his prayers. Tanis envied his friend. He wanted to believe, he truly did. How comforting it would be to put Flint's fate into the hands of the gods, having faith that they would watch over him and guide him. The same faith would reassure him that Hornfel would be made to see the truth, causing him to have a change of heart and open the gates to the refugees.

Instead of faith, Tanis was walking each step of the way with Flint in his mind and seeing darkness and danger at every turn. He stirred restlessly and rolled over, and he was about to try to go back to sleep, when Caramon asked a question that jolted Tanis to alarmed wakefulness.

"Hey, has anyone seen Tas?"

Tanis was on the move as soon his feet hit the floor, searching the room. To no avail. "Damn it! He was here only moments ago!"

"I dunno," said Caramon, shaking his head. "I haven't seen him in a while, not since Flint left. But then I've been fixing Raist's tea. . . ."

"Sturm," said Tanis, breaking in on the knight's prayers, "have you seen Tasslehoff?"

Sturm rose stiffly to his feet. He cast a swift glance around the room. "No. I have not been watching over him. I saw him last before Flint left."

"Search upstairs," Tanis ordered.

"Why?" Raistlin asked in a whispered gasp. "You know where he has gone! He went after Flint."

"Search anyway," said Tanis grimly.

They looked under crates, inside cupboards, and in the upstairs rooms, but there was no sign of the kender. Sturm took the opportunity, when Tanis and Caramon were roaming about the second level, to speak to Raistlin.

"Tas could ruin our plan! What do we do?"

"Nothing we can do about it now," Raistlin said with a grimace.

"The only nuisances up there are rats," Caramon reported as he and Tanis came back down the stairs. "We could question the guards to see if they saw him."

"And we draw attention to the fact that he's gone missing," Tanis said. "We're already in enough trouble without telling Hornfel we've unleashed a kender on his unsuspecting populace. Besides, Tas might come back on his own."

"And I might walk through this solid stone wall," said Sturm, "but I doubt it."

Raistlin was about to say something but was interrupted by a dwarf opening the door.

They froze, waiting for the dire news that Tasslehoff had been found and tossed in the lake, or the dungeons, or worse.

"Breakfast," the dwarf announced.

The guard held the door while two more dwarves walked in bearing trays laden with heavy wooden bowls. Caramon sniffed the fragrant aroma and immediately took his seat at the table.

The others exchanged glances, wondering if the guards would notice they were one person short. The guards did not take a head count, however. They unloaded the bowls from the tray and handed them about, laid out two loaves of dark bread, and a couple of pitchers of ale, then departed, shutting the door behind them.

Everyone breathed a sigh.

"Those were different guards," said Tanis. "They're not the same ones who were here when Flint left. They must have changed shifts. Apparently none of them noticed Tas is missing. Let's keep it that way as long as we can."

Sturm sat at the table. Tanis did the same. Caramon was already ladling out the food.

"Smells good," he said hungrily. He picked up a bowl and took it over to his brother. "Here, Raist. It's mushrooms in brown gravy. I think there's onions in there, too."

Raistlin averted his head.

"You need to eat, Raist," said Caramon.

"Put it there," said Raistlin, indicating a table near his chair.

Caramon set the bowl down. Raistlin glanced at it and started to turn away. Then he looked at it more intently.

The meal did smell good. Tanis had not thought he was hungry, but he picked up his spoon. Sturm was praying to Paladine to bless this meal. Caramon, tearing off a hunk of bread, dipped it in the gravy and was bringing it, dripping, to his mouth when the staff of Magius lashed out, struck his hand, and knocked the bread to the floor.

"Don't eat that!' Raistlin gasped. "Any of you!"

He swung the staff again and struck Sturm's bowl, sending it to the floor, and then smashed Tanis's bowl just as he was digging his spoon into it.

Crockery broke. Gravy splattered. Mushrooms went sliding across the table and fell to the floor.

Everyone stared at Raistlin.

"It's poison! Those mushrooms! Deadly poison! Look!" He pointed.

Attracted by the food on the floor, rats had come slinking out of their holes to take their share. One started to lap up the spilled gravy. It took no more than a couple of slurps before its small body quivered, then stiffened. The rat flopped over sideways, its limbs writhing. Froth bubbled on its mouth, and after a moment's agony, it went limp. The other rats either took warning from their comrade's terrible fate, or they didn't like the smell, for they skittered back to their holes.

Caramon went white, and jumping from the table, he made another trip to the slop bucket.

Sturm stared, transfixed, at the dead rat.

Tanis dropped his spoon. His hands were shaking. "How did you know?"

"If you remember, I studied the mushrooms when we passed through the forest," said Raistlin. "Some of you thought my interest quite amusing, as I recall. Arman and I were discussing dwarf spirits, which, you know, are made of mushrooms. What I found most interesting is that the mushrooms used to make dwarf spirits are safe to ingest if allowed to ferment but poisonous if eaten either raw or cooked. I'd never come across any other plant or fungi with this characteristic, and I took special note of it. I recognized the dwarf spirit mushrooms in the stew. Whoever tried to kill us assumed we would not know the difference."

"And we wouldn't have," Tanis admitted. "We are grateful, Raistlin."

"Indeed," Sturm murmured. He was still staring at the dead rat.

"Who tried to kill us, I wonder?" Tanis said.

"Those dwarves who brought the food!" Sturm cried, jumping to his feet. He ran to the door, yanked it open, and darted out. He returned, bringing with him his sword and Caramon's.

"They're gone," he reported, "and so are the guards. At least we can now retrieve our weapons. We'll be ready if they come back."

"Our first concern should be about Flint," said Raistlin sharply. "Has it not occurred to you that if we came seeking the hammer, then others might be seeking it as well, others such as the Dark Queen and her minions?"

"The dragonlance was responsible for driving Takhisis back into the Abyss," Sturm said. "You may be sure she would try to keep them from being forged again."

"They tried to kill us. Flint might already be dead," Tanis said quietly.

"I do not think so. They would wait to kill him until *after* he's found the hammer," said Raistlin.

"Perhaps all the dwarves are in league with darkness," Sturm said grimly.

"Once the dark dwarves worshipped Takhisis, or so it is written," Raistlin said, "and if you remember, Tanis, I asked you how the Theiwar knew the refugees were in the forest. You brushed it off at the time, but I think we have to look no farther than the Theiwar thane. What is his name—"

"Realgar. I agree," said Tanis. "Hornfel may not trust us or like us, but he doesn't seem the type to stoop to murder. I don't see how we prove it, or how we catch them."

"Easy," said Caramon, coming back to the table, wiping his mouth with the back of his hand. "Whoever did this will return to make sure it worked. When they come, they'll get a surprise."

Raistlin, Tanis, and Sturm looked at Caramon, then looked at each other.

"I am impressed, my brother," said Raistlin. "Sometimes you show glimmerings of intelligence."

Caramon flushed with pleasure. "Thanks, Raist."

"So we pretend we're dead, and when the murderer enters—"

"We grab him and then we make him talk," said Caramon.

"It could work," Sturm conceded. "We take the murderer to Hornfel, and this provides proof that Flint is in danger."

"And Tas," Caramon reminded them.

"Wherever he is," Tanis sighed. He'd momentarily forgotten the missing kender.

"Hornfel will have to let us go after Flint," Sturm concluded.

Tanis wasn't sure about that, but at least this attempt on their lives would put the Thanes on the defensive, unless the Thanes were all in on this together.

"The murderer will be expecting to find our bodies. How would we look if we'd been poisoned?"

"Too bad the bowls are broken," Sturm said. "That will give it away."

"Not at all," Raistlin said coolly. "We would have knocked the bowls about in our death throes. Now, if you will allow me, I will arrange your corpses for best effect."

* * *

The more Realgar thought about it, the less he liked the idea of Grag traipsing off to the Life Tree to see the bodies of the murdered assassins. The Theiwar Thane had argued long, vehemently and quite logically that Grag—being a "lizard" as Realgar termed him, complete with wings and tail—would stand out in a crowd. The bodies weren't going anywhere. Grag could wait to view them once the hammer was safely in Theiwar hands.

Dray-yan insisted, however. He did not trust these assassins, nor did he trust the Theiwar. He wanted to make certain the assassins were dead as promised. Grag would go in disguise, cloaked and hooded. The dwarves would notice the tall bozak; that couldn't be helped. The word had spread that humans were in Thorbardin. Grag would be taken for one of them.

Realgar gave in because he had to give in. He detested the "lizards," but he needed them and their army to conquer and subdue the other clans. Grag's lizard-warriors had already proven their worth by ambushing a party of human barbarians who had entered Northgate. Not only had the draconians captured the humans, they'd taken an elf lord prisoner as well.

The captives had been given to the Theiwar for interrogation. Grag would have liked to have been present, but Dray-yan had told him there was no need. He knew all he needed to know about these humans. Realgar had only to convince one or two to tell the "truth," forcing the humans to admit they had come to Thorbardin with the intention of invading the dwarven kingdom, and that would be the end of them. Having spent a moment or two watching the dwarves' "questioning" methods, Grag had to admit the Theiwar knew what they were about when it came to torture. He had no doubt they would soon have a confession.

Realgar was going to a lot of trouble for nothing, Grag reflected. Once Thorbardin was secure, he and his troops were going to kill the slaves anyway. Still, as Dray-yan pointed out, fostering distrust between humans and dwarves could only aid their cause. Let the Hylar believe that humans had been about to invade their kingdom. They would far less likely to trust any human after that.

Satisfied that all was proceeding as planned, Grag accompanied four dark dwarves to the inn. Realgar himself did not go along. Realgar had asked for a meeting of the Council of Thanes on an emergency matter. He was planning to take two of the captives with him and exhibit them to the other Thanes.

"This revelation will throw the Thanes into turmoil," Dray-yan told Grag, "giving you time to marshal your forces and bring them into position. We will have the Thanes all neatly trapped in the same bottle."

"Including Realgar," said Grag, his claws twitching.

"Including that filthy maggot, and when the hammer of Kharas is brought forth, 'His Lordship' will be there to receive it."

"Verminaard has thought up an excellent plan," said Grag, grinning. "Too bad he's going to bungle it. Fortunately, his two brilliant subcommanders will be there to save the day."

"Here's to his brilliant subcommanders." Dray-yan raised a mug of dwarf spirits.

Grag raised his own mug. They toasted each other, then both drank deeply. The draconians had only recently discovered this potent liquor made by the dwarves, and both agreed that while dwarves might be a race of loathsome, hairy cretins, they could do two things right: forge steel and brew a fine drink.

Grag could still taste the spirits on his tongue and feel the fire burning in his belly as he left the boat that had carried him and his Theiwar companions across the lake to the Life Tree of the Hylar. Realgar and his two captives—both battered and bloody—traveled in the same boat.

The captives were wrapped in burlap bags to keep their identities concealed until Realgar's big moment before the Thanes. The two men lay unconscious in the boat's bow, though occasionally one would moan, at which sound one of the Theiwar would kick him into silence. One of the captives was a barbarian, an extremely tall man, identified as the leader of the refugees. The other was the elf lord. Grag's scales clicked at the stink of elf blood. Grag hoped Realgar didn't kill him. Grag hated all the people of Ansalon, but there was a special place in his heart for elves.

Grag noted that blood was starting to seep through the burlap bag. He wondered how Realgar planned to haul the captives through the city up to the Court without attracting too much attention.

Realgar wasn't worried about such details, apparently. Peering out from the eye slits in his mask at the Life Tree, the thane talked in smug tones about the day his clan would leave their dank caves and move to this choice location. He pointed to certain prime businesses already marked for take-over by his people. As for his dwelling place, he would live in the home in which Hornfel was currently residing. Hornfel wouldn't need it. He'd be dwelling in the Valley of the Thanes.

Grag listened to the dark dwarf boast and brag, and the draconian smiled inwardly.

Few dark dwarves made the crossing from the Theiwar realm to the Life Tree, for there was little trade carried on between the Theiwar and the Hylar these days. The dock where the Theiwar usually landed was empty. Realgar and his men hauled the captives out of the boat without notice. Once they entered the streets, however, they ran into crowds of dwarves stilling milling about, talking in heated tones about the detested Neidar seeking "their" hammer. Few paid any attention to the Theiwar or the blood-stained burlap bags. Those who did were told that the Theiwar had been "butchering hogs."

Grag and his guides took their leave of Realgar. The dwarves who were out in the streets stared balefully at Grag, and as a Tall, he came in for his share of verbal abuse. Grag paid no attention. He just kept walking, his clawed feet—wrapped in rags—shuffling over the cobblestones, and he just kept smiling.

The Theiwar led Grag to the part of the city where the Talls resided. They had not gone far before two shadowy figures detached themselves from a building and hastened over to talk to the Theiwar. They all jabbered in dwarven for long moments, the two Theiwar gesturing at the inn, smirking and chortling. They pointed out two Hylar dwarves lying in an alley, bound hand and foot, with bags over their heads.

Grag waited impatiently for someone to tell him what was going on. Finally one of the Theiwar turned to him.

"It's done. You can report back to your master that the Talls are dead."

"My orders are to see for myself," said Grag. "Where are the bodies?"

The Theiwar scowled. "In an inn at the end of the street, but it's a waste of time, and we might be discovered. The Hylar could come at any moment."

"I'll run the risk," said Grag. He started to walk toward the building, then stopped and pointed to the Hylar dwarves. "What about them? Are they dead?"

"Of course not," said the Theiwar scornfully. "We're going to take them back with us."

"Easier to kill them," Grag pointed out.

"But less profitable," said the Theiwar with a grin.

Grag rolled his eyes.

"Are you sure the Talls inside are dead," he asked grimly, "or are you planning to hold them for ransom?"

"See for yourself, lizard," the Theiwar sneered, and he pointed to a cracked window.

Grag peered inside. He recognized the humans from Pax Tharkas. There was the Solamnic knight, not looking so knightly anymore, sprawled under the table. The half-elf lay alongside him. The wizard was slumped over in a chair. Grag was glad to see the mage was among the dead. He'd been a weak and sickly fellow, as Grag remembered, but wizards were always trouble. The big, muscle-bound warrior lay by the door. The poison had probably been slower to work on him. Perhaps he'd tried to go for help.

"They look dead," he admitted, "but I need to check the bodies to make certain."

He started for the door and suddenly found all the Theiwar lined up in front of him, their squinty little eyes glaring at him.

"What's the matter now?" Grag demanded.

One of the Theiwar jabbed a filthy finger at him. "Don't go looting the bodies. Anything of value on them is *ours*."

The other Theiwar all nodded emphatically.

Grag regarded them with disgust and started to push past them. The Theiwar seemed inclined to argue, but Grag made it clear that he was not going to put up with any nonsense. He put his hand to the hilt of his sword, and the Theiwar, grumbling, moved away from the door. As Grag opened it, two of the Theiwar dashed in immediately. They crouched beside the big fellow by the door and began tugging on his leather boots. The other two hurried inside after them, heading straight for the dead wizard.

Grag entered more slowly, keeping his eyes on the knight. The damned Solamnics were hard to kill. In fact, it seemed to Grag that the Solamnic looked a little too healthy for a corpse. Grag had drawn his sword and was bending over the knight to feel for a life-beat when squeals of terror erupted from behind him; squeals cut short by a sickening sound like the squishing of over-ripe melons—two Theiwar heads being bashed together.

This was followed almost immediately by a dazzling flash, a shriek, and a curse. The knight and the half-elf both leaped to their feet. Half-blinded by the flash of light, Grag slashed at them with his sword. The half-elf overturned the table, effectively blocking the blow.

"It's a draconian!" the knight shouted, swinging his sword.

Grag ducked the blow.

"Don't kill him! Take him alive!" someone yelled.

Grag guessed he was on his own in this battle and a glance out the window proved him right. Two surviving Theiwar, their hair and beards singed, were running as fast as they could down the street.

Grag swore at them beneath his breath. He had two competent and skilled warriors in front of him, but he was more worried about the wizard behind him. Grag was just about to overpower the half-elf, when he heard chanting. He felt suddenly drowsy and staggered on his feet. Grag knew a magic spell when he heard one and he fought against it, but the magic overcame him.

The last thing he remembered, as he slumped to the floor, was rose petals drifting down around his head.

"*This* is how the dark dwarves knew about us and about the refugees," said Raistlin.

He was standing over the comatose draconian, watching as Sturm and Caramon bound the creature's clawed hands and feet. "I told you at the Council meeting, Tanis, that it was important to find out."

"I've said twice I was sorry," Tanis said impatiently. "Next time I will listen to you, I promise. The question is now—what does this mean? What are draconians doing in Thorbardin?"

"What it means is that Verminaard and his troops are in league with the dwarves," said Sturm.

Tanis shook his head. Turning away, he kicked suddenly and viciously at a table leg. "Damn it all! I urged the refugees to leave the valley where they were safe and led them right into a trap! How could I have been so stupid?"

"Some of the dwarves may be in league with the Dark Queen," said Raistlin slowly, thinking out loud, "but I do not believe Thorbardin has fallen. We would not have been brought before the Council if that were the case. I doubt if Hornfel or the other Thanes have any knowledge of this, and if you want further proof, Tanis, this draconian wears a disguise. If the draconians were in control of Thorbardin, he would not try to conceal his identity. My guess is that Verminaard is allied with the dark dwarves. That means Realgar and possibly that other Thane, Rance."

"That would make sense, Tanis," said Sturm. "Hornfel and the others probably know nothing about this."

"Which is why the Theiwar tossed those boulders at us when we came into Thorbardin," said Caramon, "and why they tried to poison us now. They're afraid we'll tell Hornfel!"

"Which is exactly what we must do," said Raistlin. "We must show him this specimen—one reason I urged you to keep the draconian alive."

"I agree we have to get word to Hornfel," Tanis said, "but how?"

"That part will be easy," Sturm said grimly. "Simply walk out that door. The dwarves who catch you will take you immediately to the Thanes."

"Provided they don't kill him first," Raistlin observed.

"I'll go," Sturm offered.

"You don't speak Dwarvish," Tanis said. "Give me enough time to find Hornfel. Wait here a short time, then bring the draconian to the Court of the Thanes."

He looked down at the bozak, who was starting to stir. "I think he's waking up. You should cast another sleep spell on him."

"I must conserve my strength," Raistlin said. "A bash over the head would take less toll on me."

Caramon flexed his big hands. "He won't cause any trouble, Tanis. Don't worry."

Tanis nodded. He climbed over the broken furniture and the bodies of the two dark dwarves who lay on the floor, then paused at the door.

"What about Flint? And Tas?"

"They are beyond our reach," said Raistlin quietly. "There is nothing we can do to help them now."

"Except pray," added Sturm.

"I'll leave that up to you," said Tanis, and he walked out of the inn to get himself arrested.

18

Tasslehoff's find. Flint's wall. More stairs.

lint and Tas squatted on the floor of the Hall of Enemies, the map spread out before them. The bright sunlight that had been shining through the arrow slits had dimmed, submerged in an eerie fog that had an odd reddish tinge to it. Flint had the strange feeling that he was wrapped up in a sunset. Wisps of fog seeped into the chamber, making it difficult to see.

"I wish I could read Dwarvish," said Tas, holding up a lantern that Flint had brought with him from the inn and shining the light down on the map. "What does that squiggle mean?"

Flint slapped the kender's hand away. "Don't touch! And quit jiggling. You're jostling the light about."

Tas put his hand in his pocket so that it would behave itself and tried hard not to jiggle.

"Why do you think Arman called you a servant, Flint? That wasn't very nice, especially after all you've done for him."

Flint grumbled something beneath his breath.

"I didn't catch that," Tas said, but before Flint could repeat himself, the musical note sounded again, ringing loudly throughout the room.

Tas waited until the reverberations had died away, then he tried again, "What do you think, Flint?"

"I think the Hammer is here." Flint put his stubby finger on the map.

"Where?" Tas asked eagerly, bending over.

"You're jiggling again!" Flint glowered at him.

"Sorry. Where?"

"The very top. What they call the Ruby Chamber. At least, that's where I'd put a hammer if I wanted to put it somewhere where no one could find it." Rising stiffly to his feet, Flint massaged his aching knees. Carefully folding the map, he tucked it into his belt. "We'll go there after we search for Arman."

"Arman?" Tas repeated in astonishment. "Why are we looking for him?"

"Because he's a young fool," said Flint gruffly, "and someone needs to look after him."

"But he's with Kharas, and Kharas is a good and honorable dwarf, at least that's what everyone keeps saying."

"I agree with the kender," said a voice from out of the shadows. "Why are you worried about the Hylar? He is your long-time enemy, after all."

Flint snatched the hammer from its harness, forgetting, in his haste, that he was supposed to pretend it was heavy.

"Step into the light," Flint called. "Where I can see you."

"Certainly. You don't need your weapon," said the dwarf, moving into the lantern light.

He had a long white beard and white hair. His face was wrinkled as a shriveled apple. His eyes were dark and penetrating, clear as the eyes of a newborn babe. His voice was strong, deep, and youthful.

"Remarkable hammer you've got there." The ancient dwarf squinted at it in the bright light. "I seem to remember one just like it."

"You'll feel this hammer on your head if you come any closer," Flint warned. "Who are you?"

"He's another Kharas, like the one in the tomb with Arman!" Tasslehoff said. "How many does this make? Three or four?"

The ancient dwarf took a step nearer.

Flint raised the hammer. "Stop right there."

"I'm not carrying any weapons," Kharas said mildly.

"Ghosts don't need weapons," said Flint.

"He looks awfully substantial for a ghost, Flint," Tas said in a whisper.

"The kender is right. What makes you think I'm not who I say I am?"

"Humpf!" Flint snorted. "What do you take me for? A gully dwarf?"

"No, I take you for a Neidar by the name of Flint Fireforge. I know a lot about you. I had a chat with a friend of yours."

"Arman isn't a friend," Flint said dourly. "No mountain dwarf is my friend, and I'm not his servant either!"

"I never thought that, and I wasn't referring to Arman."

Flint snorted again.

"Never mind that now," said the latest Kharas. A smile caused all the wrinkles in his face to crinkle. "I'm still interested to know why you are going to search for Arman. You came here to find the Hammer of Kharas."

"And I'll leave here with the Hammer of Kharas," stated Flint stoutly, "and with young Arman. Now you tell me what you've done with him."

"I haven't done anything to him." Kharas shrugged. "I told him where to find the Hammer. It may take him awhile, however. It seems he's lost his map."

"He dropped it," Tas said sadly.

"Yes, that's what I thought might have happened," Kharas said with a slight smile. "What if I told you, Flint Fireforge, that I can take you straight to the Hammer?"

"And throw us into a pit or shove us off the top of some tower? No thanks." Flint shook the hammer at the dwarf. "If you truly mean us no harm, go on about your business and leave us alone, and you leave Arman alone, too. He's a not a bad sort, just misguided."

"He needs to be taught a lesson," said Kharas. "The mountain dwarves all need to be taught a lesson, don't they? Isn't that what you've been thinking?"

"Never you mind what I'm thinking!" Flint said, scowling. "Just take yourself off and do whatever it is you do around here."

"I will, but first I'll make you a wager. I'll bet you your soul that Arman ends up with the Hammer."

"I'll take your bet," said Flint. "It's all nonsense, anyway."

"We'll see," Kharas said, his smile broadening. "Remember, I offered to show you where to find the Hammer, and you turned me down."

The ancient dwarf stepped backward into the red swirling mists and vanished.

Flint shivered all over. "Is he gone?"

Tas walked over to where the dwarf had been standing and flapped his hands about in the mists. "I don't see him. Say, if he does take your soul, Flint, can I watch?"

"You're a fine friend!" Flint lowered the hammer, but he kept it in his hand, just in case.

"I hope he doesn't," said Tas politely, and he truly meant it. Well, he mostly truly meant it. "But if he does—"

"Oh, just shut your mouth. We've wasted enough time palavering with that thing, whatever it was. We have to find Arman."

"No, we have to find the Hammer," Tas argued, "otherwise Kharas will win the bet and take your soul."

Flint shook his head and walked off, heading for the stairs again.

"Are we going back inside the secret passage?" Tas asked as they were climbing. "Say, you know, we never went all the way to the top of these stairs. Where do you suppose they lead? What do you think is up there? Was it on the map?"

Flint stopped on one of the stairs, turned around and raised his fist. "If you ask me another question, I'll . . . I'll gag you with your own hoopak!"

He began to clump up the stairs again, stifling a groan as he did so. The stairs were steep, and as Raistlin had reminded him, Flint wasn't a young dwarf anymore.

Tas hurried along after, wondering how someone could be gagged with a hoopak. He'd have to remember to ask.

They arrived at the place where the secret passage had been, only to find that it wasn't there any longer. The stairs behind which it was hidden had been shoved back into place, and try as he might, Flint could not open them again. He wondered how Arman had discovered the passage. The ancient dwarf who claimed to know Kharas probably had something to do with it. Glowering and muttering to himself, Flint climbed the stairs to the top.

Once there, he consulted the map. They'd reached the second level of the tomb. Here were galleries, antechambers, a Promenade of Nobles, and a banquet hall.

"The Thanes would have attended a grand feast in honor of the fallen king," Flint murmured. "At least, that was what Duncan intended, but his burial feast was never held. The Thanes were fighting for the crown. Kharas was the king's sole mourner." Flint glanced about the darkness and added grimly, "And whoever lifted up the tomb and set it floating among the clouds."

"If they didn't hold the feast, maybe there's some food left," said Tas. "I'm starving. Which way's the banquet hall? This way?"

Before Flint could answer, the kender was off, racing down the hall.

"Wait! Tas! You doorknob! You've got the lantern!" Flint shouted into the fog-ridden gloom, but the kender was out of sight.

Heaving a sigh, Flint stamped off in pursuit.

———————————————

"Drat," said Tas, looking over the banquet table that was empty of everything except dust. "Nothing. I suppose mice ate it, or maybe that Kharas did. Oh well. After three hundred years, the food probably wouldn't have tasted that good anyhow."

Tas wished again he'd brought his pouches. He could generally find something to snack on in there—the odd meat pie, muffin, or grapes that weren't bad once you removed the bits of fluff. Thinking of food made him hungrier, however, and so he put the thought out of his mind.

The banquet table held nothing interesting. Tas wandered about, searching for a forgotten crumb or two. He could hear Flint bellowing in the distance.

"I'm in the banquet hall!" Tas called out. "There's no food, so don't hurry!"

That prompted more bellowing, but Tas couldn't understand what Flint was saying. Something about Arman.

"I guess I'm supposed to look for him," Tas said, so he did call out his name a couple of times, though not with much enthusiasm. He peered under the table and poked about in a couple of corners.

He didn't find Arman, but he did find something, and it was a lot more interesting than an arrogant young dwarf who always said the word "kender" as though he'd bitten down on a rotten fig. In a corner of the room was a chair, and beside the chair was a table. On the table was a book, pen, and ink, and a pair of spectacles.

Tas held the lantern close to the book, which had squiggles on the cover. He guessed it was something else written in Dwarvish. Then it occurred to him that maybe the writing was magic and this might be a magic spellbook, like those Raistlin kept with him that Tas was never allowed to even get a little tiny peek at, no matter that he promised he would be extra, extra careful, and not crease the pages, or spill tarbean tea on it. As for the spectacles, they were ordinary looking, or would have been ordinary if the glass inside them had been clear like other spectacles the kender had seen and not ruby-colored.

The kender was torn. He started to pick up the book, then his hand hovered over the spectacles, then went back to the book. At last it occurred to him that he could do both—he could put on the spectacles and look at the book.

He picked up the spectacles and slid them over his ears, noting, as he did so, that they appeared to have been made just for him. Most spectacles were way too big and slid down his nose. These stayed put. Pleased, he looked out through the glass and saw that the ruby glass made the red-tinged fog even redder than it had been before. Other than that, the spectacles didn't really do anything. They didn't make his eyes go all blurry as did other spectacles. Thinking that these spectacles weren't good for much, Tas picked up the book.

He scrutinized the title. "'Being a History of Duncan, High King of Thorbardin, with Full and Complete Accounts of the Ogre Battles, the Dwarfgate Wars, and Subsequent Tragic Ramifications Involving Civil Unrest.' Whew!" Tas paused to straighten out his tongue that had gotten all tangled up over that last bit.

Flint came peering through the fog. "Tasslehoff, you rattle-brain, where have you gotten to?"

Tas snatched off the spectacles and thrust them in one of his pockets. He had found them lying about, which made them fair game, but he wasn't certain Flint would see it that way, and Tas didn't want to waste time arguing.

"I'm over here," he called.

"Doing what?" Flint demanded, seeing the light and bearing down on him.

"Nothing," Tas said, hurt. "Just taking a look at this old book.

I can read Dwarvish, Flint. I can't speak it or understand it, but I can read it. Isn't that interesting?"

Flint took away the lantern and glanced at the book. "That's not Dwarvish, you ninny. I don't know what it is. Any sign of Arman?"

"Who? Oh, him. No, but take a look at this book. It's about King Duncan. The title says so, along with a bunch of other stuff about rams and civil unrest."

He stopped talking, because suddenly he couldn't read the title. The words had gone back to being squiggles, whorls, dots, dashes and curlicues. When he'd seen them through the spectacles, they had been words. When he looked at them now, with the spectacles tucked in his pocket, they weren't. Tas had a sneaking hunch he knew what was going on.

He glanced about to see if Flint was watching. The dwarf was calling out Arman's name, but no one answered.

"I don't like this," Flint muttered.

"If he is out there searching for the Hammer, he wouldn't be likely to tell us where, would he?" Tas pointed out. "He wants to beat us to it."

Flint grunted and rubbed his nose, then muttered again and pulled out the map. Holding it in his hand, he went over to stare and poke at a wall. He looked at the map, then looked back, frowning, at the wall. "Must be a hidden door here somewhere." He started to tap the wall with his hammer. "According to the map, the Promenade of Nobles is on the other side, but I can't figure out how to get to it."

Tas took out the spectacles and held them to his eyes and looked down at the book. Sure enough, the Ramifications and Subesquents were back. Tas peered through the spectacles at Flint, to see if they made the dwarf look different.

Flint looked the same, rather to Tas's disappointment. The wall, however, had changed a good deal. In fact, it wasn't a wall at all.

"There's no wall, Flint," Tas told him. "Just keep walking and you'll be inside a dark hall with statues all lined up in a row."

"What do you mean there's no wall? Of course, there's a wall! Look at it!"

As Flint turned to glare at him, Tas whipped off the spectacles and held them behind his back. This was more fun than he'd had in a long time. The wall was there once again. A solid stone wall.

"Whoa!" breathed Tas, awed.

"Quit wasting time," Flint snapped, "and come over and help me look for the secret door. On the other side of this wall is the Promenade. We walk down it, go up some stairs and then go up some more stairs, and we're at the entrance to the Ruby Chamber with the Hammer!" He rubbed his hands. "We're close. Really close! We just have to find some way past this blasted wall!"

He went back to tapping at the stone work. Tas held up the spectacles, took one last look, then, secreting them in his pocket, he walked boldly up to the wall, closed his eyes—in case the spectacles might be wrong and he was going to smash his nose—and walked straight into the stones.

He heard Flint bellow, then he heard the bellow get stuck in the dwarf's windpipe so that it turned into a choke, and then Flint was yelling. "Tas! You rattle-brain! Where did you go?"

Tas turned around. He could see Flint quite clearly, but apparently the dwarf couldn't see him, because Flint was running up and down in front of a stone wall that wasn't there.

"I'm on the other side," Tas called. "I told you. There's no wall. It just looks like there's a wall. You can walk through it!"

Flint hesitated, dithered a little bit, then he put the hammer back in its harness and set down the lantern on the floor. Holding one hand over his eyes and thrusting the other hand in front of him, he walked forward slowly and gingerly.

Nothing happened. Flint took away his hand from his eyes. He found himself, just as Tas had said, in a long, dark hallway lined with statues of dwarves, each standing in its own niche.

"You forgot the lantern," said Tas, and he went back to fetch it.

Flint stared at the kender in wonder. "How did you know that wall wasn't real?"

"It was marked on the map," Tas said. He handed Flint the lantern. "Where does this corridor lead?"

Flint looked back at the map. "No, it isn't."

"Bah!" Tas said. "What do you know about maps? I'm the expert. Are we going down this hall or not?"

Flint looked at the map and scratched his head. He looked back at the wall that wasn't there, then stared at the kender. Tas smiled at him brightly. Flint frowned, then walked off down the corridor, flashing the light over the statues and muttering to himself, something he tended to do a lot when he was around the kender.

Tasslehoff put his hand into his pocket, patted the spectacles, and sighed with bliss. They were magic! Not even Raistlin had such a wonderful pair of spectacles as this.

Tas meant to keep these marvelous spectacles forever and ever, or at least for the next couple of weeks, which, to a kender, amounts to roughly the same thing.

———————————————

As Flint walked the Grand Promenade, flashing the lantern light here and there, he forgot Tasslehoff and the mystery of the vanishing stone wall. The Hammer was as good as his.

In each niche he passed stood a statue of a dwarven warrior clad in the armor of the time of King Duncan. Moving down the long row, Flint imagined himself surrounded by an honor guard of dwarven soldiers, clad in their ceremonial finery, assembled to pay him homage. He could hear their cheers: Flint Fireforge, the Hammer-Finder! Flint Fireforge, the Unifier! Flint Fireforge, the Bringer of the Dragonlance! Flint Fireforge, High King!

No, Flint decided. He didn't want to be High King. Being king would mean he'd have to live under the mountain, and he was too fond of fresh air, blue sky, and sunshine to do that. But the other titles sounded fine to him, especially the Bringer of the Dragonlance. He came to the end of the rows of dwarven soldiers and there was Sturm, splendid in his armor, saluting him. Next to him stood Caramon, looking very solemn, and Raistlin, meek and humble in the great dwarf's presence.

Laurana was there, too, smiling on him and giving him a kiss, and Tika was there, and Otik, promising him a life-time supply of free ale if he would honor the inn with his presence. Tasslehoff popped up, grinning and waving, but Flint banished him. No kender in this dream. He passed Hornfel, who bowed deeply, and came to Tanis, who regarded his old friend with pride. There, at the end of the row, was the flashily dressed dwarf from his dream. The dwarf winked at him.

"Not much time . . ." said Reorx.

Flint went cold all over. He came to a halt and wiped chill sweat from his brow.

"Serves me right. Daydreaming when I should be keeping an eye out for danger." He turned around to yell at the kender. "What do you think you're doing, lolly-gagging about when we're on an important quest!"

"I'm not lolly-gagging," Tas protested. "I'm looking for Arman. I don't think he's been here. We'd see his footprints in the dust. He probably didn't know that wall wasn't a wall."

"Most likely," said Flint, feeling a jab of conscience. In his dream of glory, he'd forgotten all about the young dwarf.

"Should we turn around and go back?" Tas asked.

The line of statues came to an end. A short corridor branched off from the promenade to the left. According to the map, this corridor led to one set of stairs that led to a second set of stairs. Hidden stairs. Secret stairs. Young Arman would never find them. He could manage to make his way to the Ruby Tower without climbing up these stairs, but the route was longer and more complicated. Unless, of course, that dwarf claiming to be Kharas showed him the way.

"We'll find the Hammer first," Flint decided. "We've come this far, after all, and we're close to where it might be, according to the map. Once we have the Hammer safe, then we'll search for Arman."

He hurried down the corridor, with the kender at his heels, and there were the stairs. Flint started climbing, and the aches came back to his leg muscles, and the pain returned to his knees, and there was that annoying shortness of breath in his chest again. He distracted himself by trying to decide what he was going to do with the Hammer once he found it.

He knew what Sturm and Raistlin wanted him to do. He knew what Tanis wanted him to do. What he didn't know yet was what he, Flint, wanted to do, though the ancient dwarf that called himself Kharas had been pretty near the mark.

Teach them a lesson. Yeah, that sounded good to him, really good. He'd teach them all a lesson—dwarves, Sturm, Raistlin . . . everyone.

He reached the top of this first flight of stairs and emerged into a very small, very dark, and very empty chamber. Flint held up the lantern and shone it along the wall until he found a narrow archway that had been marked on the map. He peered inside, holding the lantern high.

Tasslehoff, peering with him, gave a sigh. "More stairs. I'm getting awfully tired of stairs. Aren't you, Flint? When they build my tomb, I hope they make it all one level so that I won't have to climb up and down all the time."

"Your tomb!" Flint scoffed. "As if anyone would build a tomb for you! You'll most likely end up in the belly of a bugbear, and if you're dead you won't be climbing up and down anything."

"I might," said Tas. "I don't plan to stay dead. That's boring. I plan to come back as a lich or a wraith or a relevant, or something."

"Revenant," Flint corrected.

He was putting off the evil moment when he would have to make his aching legs climb this next staircase which, according to the map, was about three times as long as any of those they had climbed previously.

"Maybe I won't die at all," Tasslehoff said, giving the matter some thought. "Maybe everyone will think I'm dead, but I won't be dead, not really, and I'll come back and give everyone a big surprise. You'd be surprised, wouldn't you, Flint?"

Deciding that the pain of climbing stairs was not nearly so bad as the pain of listening to the kender's yammering, Flint heaved a sigh, grit his teeth, and once more began to climb.

19

Prisoners of the Theiwar.
Tanis warns the Thancs.

iverwind regained consciousness when the cold water slapped his face. He sputtered, gasped, then groaned, as the pain twisted inside him. Opening his eyes and seeing himself surrounded by enemies, he clamped his teeth down on the groan, unwilling to let them see how much he was suffering.

Bright light lanced through his aching head. He longed to shut his eyes against it, but he needed to find out what was going on and he forced himself to look.

He was in a large chamber with stone walls, lined with columns, with the feel of an assembly room about it, for there were nine large throne-like chairs arranged in a semi-circle on a dais near where he lay, bound hand and foot, on the floor.

Several dwarves stood over him, arguing loudly in their deep voices. Riverwind recognized one of the dwarves—a skinny little runt who wore a helm with a smoked glass visor, who was doing most of the talking. He'd been the one asking the questions, the same questions, over and over. Then, when he didn't get the answers he wanted, he had ordered them to make the pain come again.

Hearing another groan, Riverwind turned his gaze from the dwarves. Gilthanas lay beside him. Riverwind wondered if he looked as bad as the elf lord. If so, he must be close to death.

Gilthanas's face was streaked with blood from cuts on his forehead and his lip. One eye was swollen shut, he had a lump on his jaw and a massive bruise on one side of his face. His clothes were torn, and his skin was burned and blistered from where they'd pressed red hot irons into his flesh.

They had treated the elf worse than they'd treated the humans. Riverwind had the feeling that the filthy dwarves had tormented Gilthanas more for the fun of it than because they wanted information from him. A gully dwarf of grandiose appearance was now throwing cold water in the elf's face and slapping him solicitously on the cheek, but he still remained unconscious.

Riverwind lay back and cursed himself. He'd taken precautions. He and his men—six all told—had entered the gate armed and wary, intending to look about, trying to determine if this was, in truth, the fabled gate to Thorbardin. He and his cohorts had never seen the attack coming. The draconians had emerged from the shadows, disarmed them and disabled them swiftly and efficiently.

The next thing Riverwind knew, he woke in pitch darkness, in a dungeon cell, with a hairy and foul-breathed dwarf bending over him, asking him in Common how many men were in the army, where they were hiding, and when did they mean to invade Thorbardin?

Riverwind said over and over there was no army, they weren't planning to invade. The dwarf told him to prove it, to tell him where the people were hiding so he could go see for himself. Riverwind saw through that ploy and told the hairy little runt to go throw himself off the mountain. They then tried to loosen his tongue, beating and kicking him until he'd lost consciousness, when they woke him up, put a bag over him, and carted him off. He rode first in a wagon, then in a boat, then he'd lost consciousness again and had awakened here. He wondered how his comrades were faring. He'd heard their screams and their moans, and he knew proudly that the other four Plainsmen were not giving the dwarves the answers they wanted.

His head was starting to clear, and he decided that he wasn't going to lie here at the feet of these dwarves like a criminal.

"Paladine, give me strength," Riverwind prayed and, gritting his teeth, he struggled to sit up.

The scrawny dwarf said something to him and kicked him in the side. Riverwind stifled a groan, but refused to lie back down. Another dwarf, this one tall with gray in his beard, said something angrily to the dwarf in the helm. Riverwind took a good look at this dwarf. He had a noble bearing and a proud mien, and though he was not regarding Riverwind with a friendly eye, he appeared to be outraged by the human's beaten and bloody condition.

This dwarf barked an order and beckoned to one of the guards. The guard left the Court, returning a short time later bearing a mug of some foul-smelling liquid. He held it to Riverwind's lips. Riverwind looked up at the noble looking dwarf, who gave a reassuring nod.

"Drink it," he said in Common. "It will not hurt you." To prove it, he took a drink himself.

Riverwind sipped at the brew, spluttering and coughing as the fiery liquid burned its way down his throat. Warmth flooded his body, and he felt better. The throbbing pain eased. He shook his head when offered another drink, however.

The noble looking dwarf did not waste time on pleasantries. "I am Hornfel," he said, "Thane of the Hylar. Realgar, Thane of the Theiwar, the dwarf who took you and the others prisoner, says that you arrived here with an army of humans and elves prepared to invade us. Is that true?"

"No, lord, it is not true," said Riverwind, talking slowly through swollen lips.

"He lies!" Realgar snarled. "He admitted the truth to me himself not an hour ago!"

"He lies," said Riverwind, fixing the Theiwar with a baleful stare. "I am the leader of a group of refugees, former slaves of the evil Dragon Highlord of Pax Tharkas. We have women and children with us. We were sheltering in a valley not far from here, but then dragons and dragonmen attacked us and we were forced to flee."

He watched the Thane's expression, and when he spoke of the dragons and dragonmen, he saw Hornfel's face harden into disbelief.

"We have heard such lies before, Hornfel," Realgar said, "the exact same tale told to us by the other Talls."

Riverwind lifted his head. Other Talls. That could only mean his friends. He wondered where they were, if they were safe, what was going on. The questions were on his tongue, but he did not ask them.

He would find out more from the dwarves before saying something that might be entirely the wrong thing to say.

The dwarves went back to arguing among themselves, however, and Riverwind could not understand a word. He had the impression the dwarf known as Hornfel did not trust or like the dwarf he called Realgar. Unfortunately, Hornfel did not trust Riverwind either. One other Thane appeared to be siding with Realgar, and another with Hornfel. The rest seemed to be having trouble making up their minds.

Gilthanas stirred and groaned, but the dwarves ignored him. Riverwind could do nothing to help the elf. He could do nothing to help anyone. He sat, watched, and waited.

———————————◆————

Tanis had no trouble getting himself apprehended, though he first had to free his captors to do so. He was walking down the street near the inn when he came upon two Hylar guards bound hand and foot, with gags over their mouths. He cut their bonds and helped them stand, then told the guards he needed to speak to Hornfel on a matter of the utmost urgency. The dwarves were clearly furious, but not at Tanis. They, too, wanted to talk to their Thane, and after a moment's deliberation, they decided to take Tanis with them.

The dwarven guards hustled him into one of the lifts. Other dwarves stared at him and scowled, and several called out, wanting to know what was going on. His guards had neither the time nor the inclination to answer. They kept fast hold of him, though he assured them he wasn't going to try to escape; he wanted to see Hornfel. When the lift stopped, the guards stopped to question other guards, asking where Hornfel could be found.

"The Court of Thanes," was the answer.

———————————◆————

Tanis was in no very good humor. He'd had little sleep and nothing to eat. He was outraged at the attempt on their lives, deeply concerned about Flint and Tas and the knowledge that draconians were in Thorbardin. He entered the Court of Thanes determined to make Hornfel understand his peril. He planned to have his say first and give the Thanes time to digest his words. When his friends arrived with the draconian prisoner, he would use the monster to emphasize his point. He would demand that he and his friends be allowed to seek out Flint and Tas in the Valley of the Thanes. Tanis was convinced Flint had been, or was going to be, lured into some sort of trap.

These words were in his head and on his tongue, and he forgot them all in dismay and amazement when he walked into the Court of the Thanes to find Riverwind bound, bruised, and bleeding, and Gilthanas barely conscious.

Tanis stopped and stared at his friends. The Thanes stopped and stared at him, wondering what he was doing here. The most astonished was Realgar, who had been convinced Tanis and the rest were dead. Realgar foresaw trouble, but he didn't know how to combat it, for he had no idea what had gone wrong.

Tanis tried to speak, but the guards launched into their grievances. Hornfel grimly asked for an explanation for why the prisoner was loose. The guards explained with furious gestures at Realgar, while the other Thanes added to the confusion by loudly demanding to know what was going on.

Tanis saw that for the moment, his guards were defending him better than he could. He hastened over to Riverwind, who was sitting up, his back propped against a column. Gilthanas lay on the floor beside him, more dead than alive.

"What happened? Who did this?"

"An ambush," Riverwind answered, grimacing in pain. He drew breath haltingly. "Draconians. Waiting for us at the gate. Don't worry. The refugees are safely hidden. I left Elistan in charge . . ."

"Hush, don't talk. I'll sort this out."

Riverwind seized hold of him with a bloody hand. "That dwarf, the one in the helm, he tried to make us admit we were here to invade . . ." Riverwind sank back, breathing hard. Sweat beaded his brow and ran down his face.

Tanis put his hand to Gilthanas's neck, felt for the life beat. The elf lord needed care.

Hornfel managed to shout down the other Thanes and obtain some semblance of order. The dwarf guards started their tale by relating first how the kender had escaped and knocked them out (they glossed over this fairly quickly), then, in mounting rage, they stated that when they'd regained consciousness, they were set upon by four Theiwar. The next thing they knew, the Tall (Tanis) was cutting loose their bonds and insisting on seeing Hornfel.

Hornfel glowered at Realgar. "What is the meaning of this?"

"I will tell you, Thane," said Tanis, rising to his feet. "The Theiwar wanted our guards out of the way so they could poison us."

"That's a lie," Realgar snarled. "If someone tried to poison you, human, it was not me or my people. As for these guards, my men caught them drunk on their watch and decided to teach them a lesson."

The guards were vehement in denial. One leaped at Realgar, and his companion had to drag him back.

"We have evidence to prove our claim," said Tanis. "We have the poisoned mushrooms and the bodies of two Theiwar who came to gloat over their handiwork, and we have further evidence of an even more serious matter than the attempt on our lives, great Thanes."

"What of our evidence?" Realgar demanded, pointing at Riverwind. "This human and those with him admit that they are with an army of humans and elves planning to invade our realm."

"If he or any of those with him said this, they did so to escape the pain of their torment. Look what has been done to them!" Tanis said. "Is this how men of honor of any race treat their captives?

"I bring you this warning, Thanes of Thorbardin," Tanis continued grimly, "there *is* an army prepared to invade your realm, but it is not an army of humans. It is an army of the Dark Queen's dragonmen."

"He would have us believe this wild tale to distract us so that he and his humans can take us unaware! I, for one, will not waste my time by staying around to listen to this human's lies. I must go prepare my forces to repel the human army's invasion—"

Realgar started walking toward the door.

"Stop him, Thanes!" Tanis warned. "He has betrayed you. He is in league with these dragonmen and their evil master, Lord Verminaard. He has opened the gates of Thorbardin to them."

"Realgar," said Hornfel sternly, "you must remain to answer these charges—"

"You are not High King, Hornfel!" Realgar retorted. "You can't order me about!"

"Guards, detain him!" Hornfel commanded.

Realgar opened his palm, exhibited a ring of black jet, and slipped it on his finger. Foul-smelling smoke billowed out from the ring, driving back the soldiers, who began to gasp and cough. Realgar disappeared.

"The Theiwar is telling the truth, Hornfel," Rance stated. "These humans and their friends the elves are the real danger. Don't listen to the lies of this Tall."

"I have proof!" Tanis countered. "My friends and I have captured one of the dragonmen. They are bringing the monster here so that you can see for yourselves!"

"I will not wait," said Hornfel decisively. "I will go see for myself. You will come with me, Half-Elven."

"I will come, Thane," Tanis answered, "but first I must see to my friends. Their injuries are serious. They need healing care."

"I have already summoned physicians," Hornfel said. "Your friends will be taken to the Houses of Healing, but," he added in grim tones, "you will all remain prisoners until I have determined the truth of what is going on."

He left the Court of the Thanes, and Tanis had no choice but to accompany him. The other Thanes decided to go with them, including Rance, who was starting to think that he, too, had been betrayed by Realgar.

The Highbluph came along, but only because he was under the mistaken impression they were all going to lunch.

20

Flight. A swim. War beneath the mountain.

he draconian lay sprawled on the floor. Caramon stood over
him, sucking on his bruised knuckles.

"That thing has a hard skull," he complained. "What I
want to know is why we just don't kill it and show the dwarves the
body? It would be a lot easier."

"I take back everything I said about your intelligence, my
brother," Raistlin said. He was feeling sick and weak, the after-
effects of his spell casting, and that put him in a bad temper.

"Huh?" Caramon was puzzled.

"There wouldn't be a body to show," Sturm explained patiently.
"You remember what happens if we kill one of these things. They
either blow up, turn to dust, or—"

"Oh, yeah, right. I forgot." Caramon thumped himself good-
naturedly on the head.

"We should go now," Raistlin said. "Tanis has had time enough to
speak to the Thanes."

"The sight of this beauty should make the Thanes sit up and
take notice," Sturm said. "Bring over the table, Caramon, and help

---

381

me hoist him onto it."

They had tried to lift the draconian, but the monster's wings made carrying the creature awkward. Caramon came up with the idea of knocking the legs off the table and turning the wooden board into a make-shift litter. He now hauled it over and set it down next to the unconscious draconian.

Grunting at the effort, he shoved the draconian over on his belly, so that the wings would not be an impediment. The draconian had kept his wings close to his body in order to cover them with the robes, but when he'd been hit by the sleep spell, the wings had relaxed and now flopped out on either side. Between Caramon and Sturm, they heaved and wrestled the creature onto the wooden table top.

"This thing weighs as much as a small house!" Sturm gasped.

Caramon, who could probably have picked up a small house had he been inclined to do so, nodded in agreement and wiped sweat from his face. Not only was the draconian heavy, it was wearing armor beneath its robes, as well as a sword. Sturm removed the weapon and tossed it aside.

"We have to haul this demon-spawn clear to the top of the Life Tree?" Caramon asked, shaking his head. "Uh, Raist, I don't suppose you could—"

"No, I could not," Raistlin snapped. "I am already weakened from the spells I've cast this day. You must do the best you can."

"You take the head," said Sturm to Caramon.

The big man bent down, took hold of the table with the monster on top of it and, with a grunt, lifted it off the floor. Sturm took hold of his end, and they managed to maneuver table and draconian out the door.

"Wait!" Raistlin ordered. "We should cover it with a blanket. We'll draw enough attention to ourselves as it is, without being seen hauling a monster through the streets."

"Hurry up!" Sturm gasped.

Raistlin grabbed up two blankets and draped them over the draconian.

"I'll walk ahead of you," Raistlin offered, "to clear the way."

"You're sure that won't take too much out of you?" Sturm said bitterly.

Either Raistlin did not hear him, or he chose to ignore him. He preceeded them through the street, the light of his staff shining brightly.

Sturm and Caramon had to stop every so often to rest and shift position to ease cramps in their backs and shoulders. They made relatively good time until they reached the populated parts of Thorbardin. At the sight of the Talls, dwarves immediately surrounded them and demanded to know where they were going and why.

Raistlin managed to find a dwarf who spoke enough Common to carry on a limited conversation. Raistlin explained that one of their number had been taken ill, and they wanted to transport him to the upper levels, where he said they had been told there were Houses of Healing.

The dwarf wanted to take a look at the sick Tall, and he reached for the blanket. Raistlin laid his hand on the blanket-covered head.

"You don't want to touch him," he said softly, in his whispering voice. "We fear it might be the plague."

The dwarf fell back, glaring darkly at the companions, and crying out a warning to the other dwarves, who regarded them with even more distrust than before, if that were possible.

"What did you tell them?" Sturm demanded. "By the looks of them, they mean to kill us all!"

"Never mind," said Raistlin. "We'll sort it out later. For the moment they'll stay clear of us. Keep moving."

The dwarves gave them a clear path, but they fell in behind them, forming a grim and silent escort. The companions arrived at the lift, and this presented their next problem.

"The table won't fit in the bucket," Caramon pointed out.

"Dump the draconian into the bottom," said Sturm.

"They are watching us," Raistlin warned. He gestured to the crowd of dwarves growing larger by the moment. "Be careful to keep the monster covered."

He climbed into the lift. Sturm and Caramon tilted the table and the draconian slid off, landing in a heap at the bottom of the bucket. Raistlin hurriedly arranged the blanket over him. As many dwarves as could fit crowded into a second lift and rode up alongside them, keeping an eye on them.

Sturm sank back against the side of the bucket, massaging his shoulders. Caramon flexed his hands and then arched his back, trying to ease a kink in his muscles. Raistlin kept watch on the dwarves in the lift. The dwarves kept their eyes fixed on him.

None of them noticed the faint quivering of the blanket covering the draconian until it was too late.

━━━━━━━━━━━━━━━━━━

Grag had come to his senses to find himself being hauled off to some unknown destination by his enemies. He had continued to feign unconsciousness, biding his time, and cursing the Theiwar, who had managed to bungle everything. The draconian would have to reveal himself for what he was, and that was a pity, but it couldn't be helped. Grag had to return to his command and let Dray-yan know what had happened, so they could alter their plans accordingly.

Being dumped into the bottom of the bucket gave Grag his chance. Flinging off the blanket, he leapt to his feet. His first care was to fell the wizard. An elbow to the gut rendered him harmless. The wizard gasped in agony and crumpled. The two warriors were reaching for their swords. Grag whirled about, catching both of them with his lashing tail, knocking the knight backward and nearly flipping the other out of the lift.

Grag would have liked to have settled the score and finished off these three humans, especially the knight, but he didn't have time. He jumped onto the edge of the bucket and perched there for a moment, getting his bearings. He looked down the lift shaft to see the base of the Life Tree far, far below. His idea had been to try to coast down on his wings, but the shaft was narrow, and he feared he might strike his wings on the stone sides and damage them.

The dwarves in the second lift were raising a ruckus, pointing and shouting and bellowing in horror at the sight of the monster. Those dwarves waiting for the lift on the next level, hearing the commotion echoing up the shaft, saw the draconian poised on the edge of the bucket, wings spread, tail twitching. One quick-thinking dwarf seized the control lever, shoved it in place, halting the lift.

Grag jumped out of the bucket when it was still swinging. He landed on his feet on the ground and came face-to-face with Hornfel and Tanis.

Hornfel took one look at the monster, drew his sword and ran to the attack. Tanis looked into the lift, saw Caramon helping Raistlin to his feet, and Sturm trying to extricate himself. Seeing they were all right, Tanis went with Hornfel. The Daewar Thane, Gneiss, was slower off the mark, but soon caught up with the Hylar and the wild-eyed Klar. Shouting a piercing battle cry and swinging an enormous axe, he ran to join them. The soldiers were startled at the sight of the monster, but inspired by their Thanes' courageous example, they rallied and raced after them.

Grag had no intention of fighting. He was outnumbered, and besides, this was neither the time nor the place. He cast a quick look around and saw what appeared to be a garden with a balcony overlooking the lake. Grag took to his heels. Using his wings to skim over the ground and any obstacles in his way, he easily outdistanced the pursuing dwarves.

Arriving at the balcony, he leapt on it and teetered there a moment, while he figured out where he was in relation to where he wanted to be. He glanced back at his pursuers, spread his wings, and jumped off.

Grag was at the top level of the Life Tree when he leaped, and his training in jumping from the back of a dragon proved invaluable. He could not fly, but as he had learned when jumping off the dragon, he could use his wings to slow his descent. He located the Theiwar wharf from the air, and though it was far off to his left, he could maneuver a little in the air in order to land in the water as near the Theiwar realm as possible.

Glancing up, Grag saw the dwarves peering over the edge of the balcony. More dwarves—hundreds of dwarves—were down below, staring up at him.

So much for their plans for secrecy.

Grag shrugged and gave his wings a twitch. As a commander, he was accustomed to sudden and unexpected shifts in battle. He couldn't waste time bemoaning mistakes made in the past. He had to think about the future, decide what to do and how to do it, and he had determined his next course of action by the time he was half-way down. He struck the water with a large splash.

Draconians don't like water, but they can swim if they have to. Grag set out for the Theiwar side of the lake, propelling his scaly body through the cold lake with powerful strokes of his strong legs and using his arms to dog-paddle.

Grag reached the wharf and pulled himself, dripping, out of the water. He tore off his robes, leaving them in a sodden heap on the dock.

Then, loping and flying, he headed for the secret tunnels where his army waited for him.

———————————————

"Is that one of the monsters of which you spoke?" Hornfel leaned over the balcony, watching the draconian drift through the air as gently as a falling feather.

"These draconians are powerful beings," said Tanis, "capable of using magic as well as steel. Their armies have conquered large sections of Ansalon. They have driven the Qualinesti from their lands and seized Pax Tharkas and our land of Abanasinia."

"Where did these fiends come from?" Hornfel asked, horrified. "I have never seen or heard of the like of them before!"

"They are new to Ansalon," Tanis replied, shaking his head. "We do not know what spawned this evil. All we know is that their numbers are great. They are intelligent and fierce warriors, as dangerous dead as they are alive."

"And you believe they have invaded Thorbardin? Perhaps there is only this one . . ."

"They are like mice," said Sturm. "If you see one, there are twenty more hiding in the walls."

"You're bleeding," said Tanis.

"Am I?" Sturm lifted his hand to his face, bringing it back smeared with blood. "The creature's tail hit me." He shook his head ruefully. "I am sorry he got away, Tanis. He fooled us completely."

"How are Raistlin and Caramon?" Tanis asked, looking worriedly about.

"Raistlin had the worst of it. He took an elbow to the gut. He'll have a belly ache for awhile, but he'll be all right. The draconian nearly knocked Caramon out of the lift. He's more shaken than hurt, I think."

Tanis turned to see the twins coming toward him. Raistlin was slightly stooped and his breathing was ragged. His expression was one of grim determination.

"Are you all right?" Tanis asked in concern.

"Never mind me," Raistlin returned impatiently. "What are we going to do about Flint and the hammer?"

Tanis shook his head. He'd seen Raistlin grow faint and nearly pass out over a stubbed toe, yet after suffering a blow that would have sent stronger men to their beds, he could brush it off as though nothing had happened.

Caramon came trialing up after his twin. He looked at Tanis and winced.

"Sorry we lost him," he said, chagrined.

"No harm done, and maybe some good. We accomplished what we set out to do. The dwarves have seen the truth for themselves. However, we now have new problems."

As Tanis was telling his friends about Riverwind and Gilthanas, Hornfel was deep in discussion with the Thanes of the Daewar and Klar. The Highbluph was nowhere to be found. The draconian had, unfortunately, leapt straight at him when making his escape, leading the terrified Highbluph to think his last moments had come. He had turned and fled, running to the darkest, deepest pit he could find, and there he would remain until the supply of rats ran low and he was obliged to come out of hiding.

The absence of the Aghar Thane concerned no one. It is doubtful if they noticed. They did take note—grimly—of the absence of Rance, the Thane of the Daergar. No one had witnessed his departure. There was little doubt in Hornfel's mind that his worst fears were realized. His hopes for unification of the clans beneath the mountain were dashed. A Theiwar and Daergar alliance would have been bad enough, but now there was evidence the renegade dwarves had secretly opened the gates of Thorbardin to forces of darkness. The very tragedy he had worked so hard to avoid—civil war—appeared inevitable.

The Daewar Thane, who had been the most reluctant to think ill of his cousins, was now the most militant, ready to summon his army and battle them on the spot. The wild-eyed Klar would follow Hornfel's lead and do whatever he was commanded to do. Klar military forces were not entirely reliable, however. They were vicious fighters, but undisciplined and chaotic.

The Theiwar were not warriors, but the dark Daergar were. Their numbers were plentiful, and they were fierce, loyal, and consumed with hatred for their cousins, especially the Hylar. If they were joined by an army of monstrous beings, Hornfel foresaw ruin and disaster.

After discussing the situation with the Thanes and making what plans they could, Hornfel walked over to speak to Tanis, to offer his apologies for his earlier treatment.

"I would be glad to provide safe haven for the refugees in your care, Half-Elven," Hornfel said, adding grimly, "but I fear there will be no safe haven for anyone beneath the mountain—humans or dwarves."

"Perhaps all is not as dire as you think, Thane," Tanis said. "What if the Daergar have not allied with the Theiwar? I saw Rance's face when he first set eyes on the draconian, and he did not look smug. He looked as shocked and horrified as the rest of you."

"When I saw him, he wore a look of fury," said Raistlin. "He passed us on the way to the lift, and his expression was dark with rage. His brows were lowered and his fists were clenched, and he was muttering to himself. My guess is that he had no knowledge that the Theiwar had brought in these terrible new allies and that he is not happy about it."

Hornfel looked grateful. "You give me hope, friends, and food for thought. Much now depends on the recovery of the Hammer of Kharas. If the hammer is returned to us, along with proof that Reorx has also returned, the Daergar would, I think, refuse to side with the Theiwar. The Daergar are not evil and twisted, as the Theiwar have become. Their clan was hurt badly by the mine closings and many have sunk to crime, but deep inside they are loyal to Thorbardin. They could be convinced to listen to reason and they would be as glad as any to welcome Reorx back to his shrines. The reemergence of the true hammer would be a most fortuitous event now!"

"Not fortuitous," said Sturm. "Divine intervention. The gods brought us here for this reason."

Did they? Tanis found himself wondering. Or did we come here through stumblings and missteps, wrong turns and right choices, accidents and failures, and here and there a triumph? I wish I knew.

"We have to reach Flint and Arman," he said, "for the very reasons you stated, Thane."

"Impossible, I fear," Hornfel returned gravely. "My people reported to me that the bronze doors to the Valley of the Thanes have closed and no matter what we do, they will not reopen."

2I

A hero's death. Flint makes up his mind.

lint sat on the steps in the dark, rubbing his thighs and his poor old creaking knees. His legs had given out, refusing to climb one more stair. He'd climbed the last few half-blinded by tears from the pain that burned through his muscles like liquid fire. He was hurting and in a bad mood, and he took it as a personal affront that Tasslehoff was so cheerful. The kender came clattering down the stairs.

"The staircase ends right up there—What are you doing sitting here?" the kender asked, amazed. "Hurry up! We're almost at the top."

At about that time, the gong struck, and it did sound quite loud, much louder than before. The musical tone resonated through the stairwell and seemed to jar right through Flint's head.

"I'm not budging," he grumbled. "Arman can have the hammer. I'll not take one more step."

"It's only about twenty stairs and then you're there," Tasslehoff urged. He tried to slide his arms underneath Flint's shoulders with the intent of dragging him. "If you scoot along on your bottom—"

"I'll do no such thing!" Flint cried, outraged. He batted the kender away. "Let go of me!"

"Well, then, if you won't go up, let's go back down," Tas said, exasperated. "The map shows other ways to reach the top—"

"I'm not going down either. I'm not moving."

Secretly, Flint was afraid he couldn't move. He didn't have the strength, and that dull ache was back in his chest.

Tas eyed him thoughtfully then plunked himself down on the steps.

"I guess staying here forever won't be so bad," said Tas. "I'll have a chance to tell you all my very best stories. Did you hear about the time I found a woolly mammoth? I was walking along the road one day, and I heard a ferocious bellowing coming out of the woods. I went to see what the bellowing was, and it turned out to be—"

"I'm going!" said Flint. Gritting his teeth, he put his hand on the kender's shoulder and, groaning, hauled himself upright. His head spun, and he tottered on his feet and had to steady himself with a hand on the kender.

"Put your arm around my shoulder," Tas suggested. "No, like this. There you go. You can lean on me. We'll go up together. One stair at a time."

This was highly undignified. Flint would have refused, but he feared he could not make it without assistance, and he was driven not so much by the hammer but by the terrifying prospect of hearing the woolly mammoth story for the umpteenth time. Assisted by the kender, Flint began to stagger up the stairs.

"I don't mind you leaning on me, Flint," said Tas after a moment, "but could you not lean quite so heavily? I'm practically walking on my knees!"

"I thought you said there were only twenty stairs!" Flint growled, but he eased up on the kender. "I've counted thirty and I still don't see the end."

"What's a few stairs more or less?" Tas asked lightly, then, feeling Flint's arm tighten around his neck in a choking manner, Tas added hurriedly, "I see light! Don't you see light, Flint? We're near the top."

Flint raised his head, and he had to admit that the stairwell was much lighter than it had been before. They could almost dispense with the lantern. Flint was forced to practically crawl up the last few stairs, but he managed it.

An arched wooden door banded with iron stood at the top of the stairs. Sunlight gleaming through the slats lit their way. Tas pushed on the door, but it wouldn't budge. He jiggled the handle, then shook his head.

"It's locked," he reported. "Drat! That will teach me never to leave my pouches behind again!"

The kender slumped down. "All these stairs for nothing!"

Flint couldn't believe it. His aching legs didn't want to believe it. He gave the door an irritated shove and it swung open.

"Locked!" Flint said, glaring in disgust at the kender.

"I tell you it was!" Tas insisted. "I may not know much about fighting, politics, the return of the gods, or all that other stuff, but I do know locks, and that lock was *locked.*"

"No, it wasn't," said Flint. "You don't know how to work a door handle, that's all."

"I do so, too," Tas said indignantly. "I'm an expert on door handles, door knobs, and door locks. That door was bolted shut, I tell you."

"No, it wasn't!" Flint shouted angrily.

Because if the door had been locked, that meant that someone—or some thing—had opened it when he pushed on it, and he didn't want to think about that.

Flint walked out into the sunshine. Tasslehoff followed, giving the offending door an irritated kick in passing.

They had reached the battlements at the top of the tomb. Across from them was a crenellated stone wall. A tower lined with rows of windows rose to Flint's left. A short, squat tower was to his right. Beyond the towers and the stone wall was azure blue sky.

"I don't want to hear anymore about it— Great Reorx's beard!" He gasped.

"Oh, Flint!" Tasslehoff let out a soft breath.

The sunlight gleamed off a cone-shaped roof made of faceted panels of ruby-colored transparent glass. The pain in Flint's legs and the burning in his chest were subsumed in wonder and in awe.

He pressed his nose to the glass, and so did the kender, both of them trying to see inside.

"Is that it?" asked Tas softly.

"That's it," said Flint, and his voice was choked.

A bronze hammer attached to what appeared to be a thin rope hung suspended from the apex of the cone. The hammer swung slowly from one side of the chamber to the other. Around the ceiling were twenty-four enormous gongs made of bronze. Each of the gongs was inscribed with a rune. Each rune represented the hours of a day from Waking Hour to First Eating Hour; First Working Hour to Second Eating Hour; and around to the Sleep Hours. The Hammer swung back and forth, shifting position with each swing, timed so that it struck a gong at the start of the hour, then continued on in a never ending circle.

Flint had never seen anything so wonderful.

"That's truly remarkable," said Tasslehoff, sighing. He drew his head back and rubbed his nose, which had been pressed flat against the glass. "Did dwarves set the Hammer to swinging like that?"

"No," said Flint, adding hoarsely. "It's magic. Powerful magic." Though the sun was uncomfortably hot on the back of his neck, he shivered at the thought.

"Magic!" Tas was thrilled. "That makes it even better. I didn't know dwarves could do magic like that."

"They can't!" Flint said crossly. He waved his hand at the swinging Hammer. "No self-respecting dwarf would even dream up something like that, much less do it. The same magic that yanked this tomb out of the ground and set it floating in the sky has turned the Hammer of Kharas into a Palanthian cuckoo clock and—" he sighed glumly and peered up again at the Hammer— "whoever wants the Hammer has to find out a way to get inside there, then stop it from swinging, and then haul it down from the ceiling. From where I stand, it can't be done. All this way for nothing."

The moment he said it, he was suddenly, secretly, vastly relieved.

The decision whether or not to switch hammers had been taken out of his hands. He could go back to Sturm, Raistlin and Tanis and tell them the Hammer was out of reach. He'd tried. He'd done his best. It wasn't meant to be. Sturm would have to get along without his dragonlances. Tanis would have to find some other way to persuade the dwarves to let the refugees inside the mountain. He, Flint Fireforge, was never cut out to be a hero.

At least, he thought with a certain amount of grim satisfaction, Arman Kharas won't be able to get to the Hammer either.

———

Flint was about to start back down the stairs, when he looked about and realized he was alone. He felt a twinge of panic. He'd forgotten the first rules of traveling with a kender. Rule Number One: never allow the kender to grow bored. Rule Number Two: never let a bored kender out of your sight.

Flint groaned again. This was all he needed. A kender loose in a magic-infested tomb! He let out a roar: "Tasslehoff Burrfoot— Oh, there you are!"

The kender popped out from around the corner of the small, squat tower.

"Don't go running off like that!" Flint scolded. "We're going back down to find Arman."

"You're standing in the wrong place, Flint," Tas announced.

"What?" Flint stared at him.

"You said that from where you stood, you couldn't reach the hammer, and you're right. From where you are standing, you can't reach the hammer. You're standing in the wrong place. But if you walk around to the other side of this tower, there's a way. Here, look inside again."

Tas pressed his nose to the glass and, reluctantly, yet feeling a twinge of excitement, Flint did the same.

"See that ledge over there, the one sticking out of the wall above the gongs."

Flint squinted. He thought he could make out what Tas was talking about. A long stone ledge thrust out into the chamber.

"If it is a ledge, it's not much of one," he muttered.

Tas pretended he hadn't heard. Flint was such a pessimist! "I figured if there was a ledge, there had to be some way to reach the ledge, and I found it. Come with me!"

Tas dashed around the squat tower. Flint followed more slowly, still searching for a way off this tomb. He looked out over the crenellations, but all he could see down below were curls and whorls of red-tinged mist.

"Not there, Flint. Over here!" Tas called.

The kender stood in front of a double door made of wood banded with iron.

"They're locked," Tas said, and he fixed the doors with a stern eye.

Flint walked up, pushed on one of the doors, and it swung silently open.

"How do you keep doing that!" Tasslehoff wailed.

Sunlight poured eagerly inside, as though it had been waiting all these centuries to illuminate the darkness.

Flint took a few steps and came to a sudden halt. Tasslehoff, coming behind, stumbled right into him.

"What is it?" the kender asked, trying to see around him in the narrow hall.

"A body," said Flint, shaken. He'd nearly trod on it.

"Whose?" said Tas in a smothered whisper.

Flint had trouble speaking for a moment. "I think it's Kharas."

The body had been sealed in a windowless vestibule shut off by two sets of double-doors and was well-preserved. The body was intact, the skin like parchment or old leather, drawn tight over the bones. It was that of a dwarven male, unusually tall, with long flowing hair, but only a very short scruff of a beard. Flint remembered hearing that Kharas had shaved his beard in grief over the Dwarfgate Wars and had never allowed it to grow back. The corpse was clad in ornate, ceremonial armor, as befitted the warrior who had borne the king to his final rest. The harness that had held the hammer for which he was famous was empty. He had no weapons in his hands. There was no sign of a wound on his body, yet he appeared to have died in agony, for his hand clasped his throat, the mummified mouth gaped wide.

"Here's the killer," said Tas, squatting down by the body. He pointed to the remains of a scorpion. "He was stung to death."

"That's no way for a hero to die," Flint stated angrily. "Kharas should have died fighting ogres, giants, dragons, or something."

Not felled by a bug.

Not felled by a weak heart . . .

"But if this is Kharas and he's dead," said Tas, "who's that other Kharas? The one who told Arman he'd show him how to find the Hammer?"

"That's what I'm wondering," said Flint grimly.

At the end of the vestibule was another set of double doors. Beyond the two doors was the Ruby Chamber and inside the chamber was the Hammer of Kharas. Flint knew those doors were locked and he also knew the locked doors would open for him, as the other locked doors had opened. Having seen the ledge, he had figured out a way to obtain the Hammer.

He looked down at the corpse of Kharas, the great hero, who had died an ignoble and meaningless death.

"May his soul be with Reorx," Flint said softly. "Though I'm guessing the god took him to his rest a long, long time ago."

Flint gazed down at the corpse and made a sudden resolve.

By Reorx, I won't go out like this, he vowed to himself.

"Hey," he said aloud. "Where do you think you're going?"

Tasslehoff was standing impatiently in front of doors at the end of the vestibule, waiting for Flint to come open them. "I'm going to help you get the Hammer."

"No, you're not," said Flint gruffly. "You're going to find Arman."

"I am?" Tas was amazed, pleased but amazed. "Finding Arman is awfully important, Flint. No one ever lets me do anything awfully important."

"I'm going to this time. I don't have much choice. You're going to find Arman and warn him that the thing he thinks is Kharas isn't Kharas, and you're going to tell Arman you know where the Hammer is. Then you're going to bring him back here."

"But if I do that, he'll find the Hammer," Tas argued. "I thought you wanted to be the one to find the Hammer."

"I have found it," said Flint imperturbably. "No more arguments. There isn't time. Off you go."

Tas thought it over. "Warning Arman *is* awfully important, but I guess I'll pass. I really don't like him all that much. I'd rather stay here with you."

"You're going," said Flint firmly, "one way or another."

Tas shook his head and took hold of the door handle and held on tight. After a brief tussle, Flint managed to pry the kender's fingers loose. He got a good grip on Tas's shirt collar and dragged the wriggling, protesting kender across the floor and tossed him bodily out the door.

"And," Flint added, "I'll need this."

He deftly twitched the hoopak out of the kender's hand, then slammed the door in his face.

"Flint!" Tas's voice sounded muffled and far away through the bronze doors. "Open up! Let me in!"

Flint heard him rattling the door handle, kicking the door and beating on it with his fists. Hefting the hoopak, Flint turned and walked off. Tas would get bored with the door soon enough, and for lack of anything better to do, he'd go in search of Arman.

Flint did feel a twinge of guilt at sending the kender off to encounter that ghost, ghoul, or whatever it was that was claiming it was Kharas. He quickly banished the guilt by reminding himself that the kender had a remarkable talent for survival.

"He just gets other people killed. If anything," Flint muttered, "I should be worried for the ghost."

The truth was that Flint could not risk having the kender witness what he was about to do. Tasslehoff Burrfoot had never ever kept a secret. He would solemnly swear on his topknot that he would never ever tell, and five minutes later he would be blabbing it to everyone and his dog, and this secret had to be kept. Lives depended on the keeping of it. Countless thousands of lives . . .

Flint struck the double doors with his hand, and they opened with a resounding boom, and he walked inside the Ruby Chamber.

22

FliNT's secRet. The haMMeR.
Tas makes aN amaziNG discoveRy.

 nside the Ruby Chamber, sunlight gleamed red through the
ruby-colored glass ceiling, filling the room with a warm glow.
Flint walked out onto the ledge and marveled that he was
here. He was humble, overwhelmed, triumphant.

He watched the Hammer swing back and forth in a slow arc, as it
had done for three hundred years. Had Kharas suspended it from the
ceiling? Flint craned his neck to see. The rope on which the Hammer
was suspended hung from a simple iron hook. Flint had the impression that perhaps Kharas had suspended the Hammer, but that other
hands had added the magic. Other hands had fashioned the gongs
that struck the hour and had crafted the beautiful ruby ceiling. The
same hands had dragged the tomb out of the Valley of the Thanes and
set it floating in the sky, hands that were somewhere around here still,
perhaps waiting to close around Flint's throat.

He watched the Hammer count the minutes as they passed, as
the Hammer had counted all the minutes of Flint's life as they had
passed, from birth to this moment, as it counted the beating of his
weak old heart.

Each dwarf dreams that he or she will be the one to find the fabled Hammer of Kharas. They talk of it over their mugs of ale. They tell the story to their children, who make hammers out of wood and play at being the dwarven hero. Flint had dreamed of it, but he'd been pragmatic enough to know that his was nothing more than a dream. How could he, metal-smith, toy-maker and wanderer, alienated from his own kind, ever be the hero of his race?

But he had. Somehow. By some miracle, the gods had brought him here. They had brought him for a reason, and he was certain he knew what that reason was.

The Hammer swinging above him made a gentle whooshing sound as it sailed through the air. He could feel the breath of its passing on his face, and he fancied it was the breath of Reorx. Moving stiffly, grimacing at the pain, Flint knelt down awkwardly on the ledge. His old knees creaked in protest. He hoped he could get up again.

"Reorx," he said, gazing into the ruby glow, "you're not one of the Gods of Light, like Paladine and Mishakal. You're a god who sees both the light and the darkness in a man's soul. You know why I'm here, I guess. You know what I mean to do. Paladine would frown at it, if he were here. Mishakal would throw up her pretty hands in horror.

"I am being dishonest, I suppose," Flint added, stirring uncomfortably, "and what I propose to do is not honorable, though Sturm did go along with it and he's the most honorable person I know.

"You see, Reorx," Flint explained, "I'm only borrowing the Hammer. I'm not stealing it. I'll make sure the dwarves get it back. I just want to use it to forge the dragonlances, and once that's done and we win the battle against the Dark Queen, I'll return the Hammer, switch the true one for the false. The dwarves will never know the difference. Because they think *they* have the real Hammer, they'll choose a High King, open the gates to the Thorbardin to the world, bring in the refugees and all will be well. There's no harm to anyone and much good.

"That's my plan," said Flint, struggling to stand again. He managed, but only by propping himself up with the kender's hoopak. "I guess if you don't like it, you'll knock me off this ledge or deliver some such punishment."

Flint waited, but nothing happened. The double doors shut behind him, but so slowly and so softly that he never noticed.

Taking silence for a sign that he could proceed with the god's sanction if not his blessing, Flint walked out to the very end of the ledge. He stared down into the shaft below. All he could see was red light. He wondered how far the drop was then, shrugging, put the thought out of his mind. He gazed up at the Hammer and calculated the distance from the Hammer to the ledge. He eyed the hoopak, then eyed the Hammer again, and thought his plan just might work.

Flint stretched out flat on his belly on the ledge. Grasping the hoopak, he held out his arm as far as it would go and made a swipe at the rope with the forked end of the hoopak as the Hammer whistled past.

He missed, but he was close. He had to scoot out over the ledge just another couple of inches. He clutched the end of the stone ledge with his hand and waited for the Hammer to pass him again.

Flint swung his arm with all his might, and his momentum almost carried him off the ledge. For a heart stopping moment, he feared he was going to fall, but then the hoopak snagged the rope, and like an angler with a fish on the line, Flint gave the hoopak a sharp jerk.

The leather sling dangling from the end of the hoopak tangled itself around the rope, and Flint, his heart beating fast and wild, slowly and carefully drew in the hoopak and the rope attached to the Hammer.

Dropping the hoopak, Flint grabbed the Hammer and hauled it up onto the ledge. At that point he had to pause, for he couldn't quite catch his breath. He was light-headed and dizzy, and strange swirling lights were dancing in front of his eyes. The sensation passed quickly, however, and he was able to sit up and take the blessed Hammer in his lap and gaze at it in reverence and awe.

"Thank you, Reorx," said Flint softly. "I'll do good with it. I'll use the hammer to bring honor to your name. I swear it by your beard and mine."

The Hammer was a wonder and a marvel. He could not stop looking at it. The false hammer was like the true but did not feel like it. He put his hand on the Hammer of Kharas, and he felt it quiver with life. He felt himself connected to an intelligence that was good, wise and benevolent, grieving over the weaknesses of mankind, yet understanding of them and forgiving. Some dwarves swore Kharas had carried the Hammer for so long that it was imbued with his spirit, and Flint could almost believe it.

He realized, then, that any dwarf who had ever touched the real Hammer of Kharas could never mistake the false for the true. Fortunately, no dwarf now living had ever touched the real Hammer. Not even Hornfel would know the difference. The counterfeit looked the same, and it weighed about the same, since Raistlin had magicked it. Both hammers were light-weight, easy to carry. The runes were same on both. The color was nearly the same. The true Hammer had a golden sheen that the other did not. He'd just have to keep the real one concealed in his harness.

As for other differences, the false hammer would probably not strike as hard or hit its mark as surely as this Hammer would do. Flint longed to test it, for he had heard that the Hammer of Kharas fused with the dwarf who wielded it, reacting to mind, more than touch; however, Flint would have to wait until he and his friends had put the dwarven kingdom far behind them before he could try it out.

Remembering that Arman might show up at any moment. Flint took the false hammer from his harness—thinking, as he did so, how cheap and shoddy it looked in comparison to the true. He slid the Hammer of Kharas into the harness on his back, tied the false hammer onto the end of the rope then, pulling back the rope as far as it would go, he let loose of the hammer and set it swinging again.

The false hammer swung back and forth as its momentum carried it. But then, slowly, it came to a stop and hung motionless from the ceiling. Flint experienced a moment of panic. Now that it had quit swinging, the hammer might well be out of reach!

He lay down and extended the hoopak. He couldn't touch it, and for a moment he despaired. Then he remembered that Arman's arms were far longer than his, and Flint breathed easier. This was actually good, for it provided him with an excuse for why he'd failed.

Flint walked over to the double doors and opened one and peeped out into the vestibule. No sign of Arman. Just the body of Kharas. The empty eyes seemed to stare at him accusingly. Flint didn't like that, so he shut the door and went to sit down on the ledge. The Hammer of Kharas pressed against his spine, sending a glow of warmth through his body that eased his aches and pains.

Flint waited.

———◆———

After Flint had so very rudely banished him from the Ruby Chamber, Tasslehoff wasted several moments trying every trick he knew to open the doors, with no result. He then spent a few moments lamenting the loss of his hoopak, the crankiness of dwarves, and the general unfairness of life. Then, seeing as how the doors were not going to open, Tas decided he'd do as Flint had told him and go off to find Arman.

The kender did not have far to look. He had only to turn around, in fact, and there was Arman emerging from a tower to the kender's right.

"Arman!" Tas greeted him with joy.

"Kender," said Arman.

Tas sighed. Liking Arman was hard work.

"Where is Flint?" Arman demanded.

"He's in there," said Tas, pointing at the doors. "We've made the most wonderful discovery! The Hammer of Kharas is inside."

"And Flint is in there?" Arman asked, alarmed.

"Yes, but—"

"Get out of my way!" Arman gave the kender a shove that sent him sprawling on the flagstones. "He must not get the Hammer! It is mine!"

Tas stood up grumpily, rubbing a bruised elbow.

"There's a body in there, too," he said. "The body of *Kharas*!" He laid emphasis on that. "Kharas is dead. Quite dead. Been dead a long time, I should imagine."

Arman either wasn't paying attention, or he didn't catch the connection, or maybe it didn't bother him that he'd been hobnobbing with a Kharas who was lying in a mummified state in the vestibule. Arman walked up to the double doors and put his hand on the handle.

"They're locked," Tas started to tell him.

Arman flung the doors open wide and walked in.

"How do they keep doing that?" Tas demanded, frustrated.

He made a spring at the door, just as Arman Kharas shut it in his face.

Tasslehoff gave a dismal wail and pulled on the handles and pushed on the doors. They wouldn't budge. He slumped down disconsolately on the door stoop and sulked. Dwarves opening doors left and right, and he, a kender, shut out. Tas vowed from then on that he would carry his lock picks in his smalls if he had to.

After a moment, he realized that even if he couldn't be present, he could at least see what was happening inside the chamber. He ran over to the roof and pressed his nose against the ruby glass. There was Arman and there was Flint, standing off to one side, and there was the hammer hanging from the rope that wasn't swinging anymore. Arman had something in his hand.

"My hoopak!" Tas cried indignantly. He beat on the glass. "Hey! You put that down!"

"I don't think he can hear you," said Kharas.

Kender are not subject to fear, so it couldn't have been fear that made Tasslehoff leap several feet into the air. It must have been because he felt like leaping. He gave a few more light-hearted leaps after that, just to prove it.

Tas turned to confront the white-haired, white-bearded, stooped-shouldered dwarf. The kender raised a scolding finger. "I'm sorry if I hurt your feelings when I say this, but I don't believe you are Kharas. He's dead inside that vestibule. I saw his corpse. He was stung to death by a scorpion, and it's been my experience that a person can't be alive here and dead there at the same time."

"Perhaps I'm the ghost of Kharas," suggested the dwarf.

"I thought you might be, at first," Tas poked his finger into the dwarf's arm, "but ghosts are insubstantial, and you're substantial."

He was quite proud of those long words. They ranked right up there with Ramification and Speculation.

That gave him an idea. His glasses! The ruby glasses had let him read writing he couldn't read and see through a wall that wasn't there. Perhaps they would reveal the truth about this mysterious dwarf.

"Hey! Look behind you! What's that?" Tas cried, and pointed past the dwarf's left shoulder.

The dwarf turned to look.

Tas whipped out his spectacles and put them on his nose and stared through the ruby glass.

He was so amazed by what he saw that he forgot to take them off again. He stood staring, his body going limp, his mind stumbling about in a foggy daze.

"You're . . ." he began weakly. "You're a . . ." He swallowed hard, and the word came out. "Dragon."

The dragon was an enormous dragon, the biggest Tasslehoff had ever seen, bigger even than the horrible red dragon of Pax Tharkas. This dragon was also the most beautiful. His scales glittered gold in the sunlight. He held his head proudly, his body was powerful, yet his movements were made with studied grace. He didn't appear to be a ferocious dragon, the kind who considered kender a toothsome midday snack. Although Tas had a feeling this dragon could look very fierce when he wanted to. Right now the dragon only looked troubled and disturbed.

"Ah," said the dragon, his gaze fixed on the ruby spectacles perched on the kender's nose, "I wondered where I'd put those."

"I found them," said Tas immediately. "I think you must have dropped them. Are you going to kill me?"

Tas wasn't really afraid. He just needed to be informed. While he didn't want to be killed by a dragon, if he was going to, he didn't want to miss it.

"I should kill you, you know," the golden dragon said sternly. "You've seen what you're not meant to see. There'll be hell to pay over this, I suppose."

The dragon's expression hardened. "Still, I don't much care. Queen Takhisis and her foul minions have returned to the world, haven't they?"

"Does this mean that you're *not* a foul minion?" Tas asked.

"You could say that," said the dragon, with the hint of smile in his wise, shining eyes.

"Then I *will* say that." Tas was relieved. "Yes, the Dark Queen is back, and she's causing a great deal of trouble. She's driven the poor elves out of their beautiful homeland and killed a lot of them, and she and her dragons killed Goldmoon's family and all her people, even the little children. That was really sad." The kender's eyes filled with tears. "And there are these creatures called draconians who look like dragons except they don't, because they walk on two legs like people, but they have wings, tails, and scales like dragons and they're really nasty. There are red dragons who set people on fire, and black dragons who boil the flesh off your bones, and I don't know how many other kinds."

"But no dragons like myself," said the dragon. "No gold dragons or silver . . ."

Tasslehoff had a squirmy feeling then. He had seen gold and silver dragons somewhere. He couldn't quite place it. It had something to do with a tapestry and Fizban . . . The memory almost came back, but then it was gone. Disappeared in a puff ball.

"Sorry, but I've never seen anyone like you before." Tas brightened. "I saw a woolly mammoth once, though. Would you like to hear about it?"

"Perhaps some other time," said the dragon politely. He looked even more troubled and very grim.

"I'm Tasslehoff Burrfoot, by the way," said Tas.

"I am called Evenstar," said the dragon.

"What are you doing here?" Tas asked curiously.

"I am the guardian of the Hammer of Kharas. I have kept it safe until the gods returned and a dwarven hero of honor and righteousness came to claim it. Now my duty is done, my punishment is ended. They cannot keep me here."

"You talk like this was a prison," said Tas.

"It was," Evenstar replied gravely.

"But,"Tasslehoff spread his arms, looked up at the wide blue sky— "you could fly anywhere!"

"I was bound to my promise, a promise I've kept for three hundred years. Now I am free to go."

"You could fight alongside us," Tas suggested eagerly. "Why, I'll bet you could tie one of those red dragons in knots and make him swallow his tail!"

Evenstar smiled.

"I wish I could help you, little friend. I would like nothing better. I cannot, however. We dragons took a vow, and although I opposed it and advised against it, I will not break the vow. Though I cannot fight at your side, I will do what I can to aid you. These draconian creatures you describe trouble me greatly."

"What are you going to do? Make them swallow their tails?"

"That would spoil my surprise. Farewell, Tasslehoff Burrfoot," said Evenstar. "I would ask you to keep my secret, for the world must not yet know that my kind exists, but I understand that secrets can be a great burden on one with such a light and merry heart. Therefore it is a burden I will not inflict."

Tas didn't understand. He barely heard. He was wrestling with a choke in his throat that wouldn't go away. The dragon was so wonderful and beautiful, and he looked so unhappy, that Tasslehoff took off the ruby spectacles and held them out in his small hand.

"I guess these belong to you."

The dragon reached down an enormous claw, a claw that could

have engulfed the kender, and gently snagged the spectacles with a tip.

"Oh, before I forget," Tas said, sadly watching the spectacles disappear in the dragon's grasp, "how do we get off this tomb? Not that I'm not enjoying my stay here," he added quickly, thinking the dragon might be offended, "but I left Tanis and Caramon and the others on their own, and they tend to get into trouble when I'm not there to watch over them."

"Ah, yes," said Evenstar gravely. "I understand."

The dragon drew a large rune on the flagstones. He breathed on the rune and it began to glow with a shimmering golden light.

"When you are ready to depart, step onto this rune, and it will take you to the Temple of the Stars where the dwarven Thanes are gathered to await the Hammer's return."

"Thank you, Evenstar," said Tas. "Will I see you again?"

"Who knows? The gods hold the fates of all in their hands."

Evenstar's body began to shimmer with the same golden light. The light grew dim, then faint, then vanished altogether in a radiant haze. Tas had to blink several times and snort a great deal to clear some snuffles from his eyes and nose. He was still not seeing all that well, when he felt a tap on his shoulder.

A white-bearded, stoop-shouldered dwarf stood in front of him. The dwarf held a pair of ruby-colored spectacles in his hand.

"Here," said the dwarf, "you dropped these. And mind that you don't lose them! Spectacles like this don't grow on trees, you know."

Tas started to say he would treasure them forever, but he didn't, because the dwarf wasn't there to say it to. The dwarf wasn't anywhere.

"Oh, well," Tas said, cheering up, "I have the spectacles back! I'll be very careful of them. Very careful."

He tucked the spectacles into his pocket, made sure they were safe and secure, then went back to the red glass roof.

Flint and Arman were gone, and so was the Hammer. Tas was wondering what could have happened to them and was seriously considering trying to break the glass, so he could crawl inside and find out, when the double doors flew open.

Arman walked into the sunlight. "I have the Hammer of Kharas!" he proclaimed in triumph. He was so pleased with himself, he even smiled at Tas. "Look, kender! I have the sacred Hammer."

"I'm glad for you," said Tas politely, and he was, in a way; Arman did look very proud and happy. If he was happy for Arman, he was sad for Flint, who came trailing out the door after Arman. Flint looked subdued, but not as crushed and disappointed as Tas had feared.

"I'm sorry, Flint," said Tas, resting a consoling hand on the dwarf's shoulder, a hand the dwarf promptly removed. "I think you should have been the one to take the Hammer. Oh, by the way, can I have my hoopak back?"

Flint handed it over. "The gods made their choice," he said.

Tas didn't quite see how the gods had anything to do with finding the Hammer, but he didn't like to argue with Flint in his unhappy state. Tas changed the subject.

"I met a golden woolly mammoth, Flint! He showed me the way out," he said.

Flint glared at him. "No more woolly mammoths. Not now. Not ever."

"What?" Tasslehoff was confused. "I didn't say woolly mammoth. There's no such thing as a golden woolly mammoth. I met a golden . . . woolly mammoth."

Tasslehoff clapped his hands over his mouth.

"Why did I say that? I didn't see a woolly mammoth. I saw a golden . . . woolly mammoth."

Tas slapped himself on the head, hoping to jolt his brain. "It was big, it was gold, it had wings and a tail, and it was a . . . woolly mammoth."

No matter how hard he tried, he couldn't manage to say the word . . . woolly mammoth.

Tas heaved a deep sigh. He'd been looking forward to telling Flint, Tanis and all the rest how he, Tasslehoff Burrfoot, had spoken to a golden . . . woolly mammoth, and now he couldn't. His brain knew what he wanted to say. It was his tongue that kept confusing things.

Flint had walked off in disgust. Arman Kharas was marching about the battlements, holding the hammer and shouting to the world that he, Arman Kharas, had discovered it. Tas trailed after Flint.

"I did find the way out," he said. "I met a . . . er . . . someone who showed me. All we have to do is step on that golden rune over there, and it will take us to someplace or other. I forget."

He pointed to the brightly glowing rune, glistening on the flagstones.

"Oh, yes! The Temple of the Stars. Your father's there," Tas said to Arman, "waiting the return of the Hammer."

Flint looked astonished and skeptical. Arman was tempted, but suspicious.

"Where did this rune come from?" he demanded.

"I told you. I met someone. The guardian of the tomb. He was a . . ." Tas tried his very best to say it. The word "dragon" was in his throat, but he knew perfectly well what it would come out as "woolly mammoth," and so he swallowed it. "I met Kharas. He showed me the rune."

Arman's face darkened, and so did Flint's.

"Kharas is dead," said Arman. "I paid homage to his spirit. I will return when I may and see to it that he is entombed with honor. I do not know who or what that apparition was—"

"It was his restless, roving spirit," said Tas, now enjoying himself, "doomed to wander the tomb of his king in unhappy torment, weeping, wailing, and wringing his hands, unable to depart until a true hero of the dwarves returns to free him. That hero is you," Tas said to Arman. "The spirit of Kharas is now free. He left me with a blessing and floated up into the air like a soap bubble. Poof, he was gone."

Flint knew the kender was lying through his teeth. He didn't dare say a word, however, because Arman had listened to the outlandish tale with reverent respect.

"We will honor the last wishes of the spirit of Kharas." Removing his helm, Arman walked over and stood with bowed head on the golden rune.

"Where did this rune really come from?" Flint asked in a harsh whisper, adding indignantly, "No dwarf ever went 'poof'!"

"I'd tell you the truth, Flint," said Tas, sighing, "but I can't. My tongue won't let me."

Flint glared at him. "And you expect me to stand on a strange rune and let it magic me to Reorx knows where?"

"The Temple of the Stars, where they're awaiting the return of the Hammer."

"Make haste!" called Arman impatiently. "This is my moment of triumph."

"I have a feeling I'm going to regret this," Flint muttered into his beard, but he stomped off and went to stand beside Arman on the golden rune.

Tasslehoff joined them. He was the keeper of a marvelous secret, one of the biggest secrets of the past couple of centuries, a secret that would astound and amaze everyone . . . and he couldn't tell a soul. Life was very unfair.

The rune began to glow. Tas's hand went to his pocket and closed over the ruby spectacles and felt something tickle his fingers. He fished it out. The rune began to shine bright gold, and the red mist closed in around them, and he couldn't see the tomb anymore. All he could see was Flint, Arman, and a white chicken feather. Then Tas understood.

Hope. That was the secret, and it was one he could share. Even if he couldn't say a word to anyone about there being golden . . . woolly mammoths.

When word spread through the dwarven realms that the doors leading to the Valley of the Thanes had closed and would not open, the dwarves of Thorbardin came at last to believe that some momentous event was at hand. The Eighth Road was reopened, and dwarves traveled by wagon and on foot to take up their vigil outside the Guardian Hall.

The day was drawing to close when suddenly the great doors swung open. A solitary dwarf appeared, an elderly dwarf with long white hair and a long white beard. He was not Arman Kharas, nor was he the Neidar dwarf, and the assembled dwarves regarded him warily.

The elderly dwarf stood before them. He raised his hands, calling for silence, and silence fell.

"The Hammer of Kharas has been found," the dwarf announced. "It is being carried to the Temple of the Stars to dedicate it to Reorx, who has returned and now walks among you."

The dwarves stared at him in suspicion and amazement. Some shook their heads. The elderly dwarf raised his voice, his tone stern.

"The Hammer hung suspended from a thin piece of rope. It swung back and forth, counting out the minutes of your lives. The rope has been cut, the Hammer freed. It is you, the dwarven clans of Thorbardin, who hang suspended from that same fragile lifeline, swinging between darkness and light. Reorx grant that you choose well."

The strange dwarf turned and walked back inside the great bronze doors. Some of the bolder dwarves followed him into the Valley of the Thanes, hoping to be able to speak to him, ask questions, demand answers. But upon entering the doors, the dwarves were momentarily dazzled by the sunlight shining into the Valley, and they lost sight of the dwarf in the glare. When they could see again, the strange dwarf was nowhere to be found.

It was then they saw the miracle

The Tomb of Duncan no longer floated among the clouds. The tomb stood on the site where it had been built three hundred years before. The sunshine gleamed on white towers and glowed on a turret crafted of ruby glass. The lake was gone, as though it had never been.

The dwarves knew then the identity of the strange dwarf who had appeared to them, and they took off their helms and sank to their knees and praised Reorx, asking his forgiveness and his blessing.

The statue of Grallen stood guard before the tomb, where, inside, they would find the final resting place of King Duncan and the remains of the hero, Kharas. A stone helm was on the statue's stone head, and an expression of infinite peace was on the stone face.

23

The Temple of the Stars.
The Hammer returns. The dead walk.

anis and his companions were with Riverwind and Gilthanas in the dwarven House of Healing when Hornfel brought them word that the Hammer had been found.

Riverwind and Gilthanas were now both conscious and feeling somewhat better. Raistlin had made a study of the healing arts in his youth, and not entirely trusting the dwarven physicians, he examined their injuries and found that none were serious. He advised them both to remain in bed and to refrain from drinking any of the potions the dwarven healers wanted to feed them.

"Drink only this water," Raistlin cautioned them. "Caramon fetched it from the well himself, and I can attest to its purity."

Hornfel was impatient to leave for the Temple of the Stars, but he was gracious enough, and perhaps feeling guilty enough, to take time to ask after the health of the two captives and to offer his apologies for the rough way in which they had been treated. He posted members of his own personal guard beside their beds with orders to watch over the human and the elf with as much care as they would guard him. Only then did Tanis feel comfortable leaving his friends.

"Do you think that Flint has really found the Hammer of Kharas?" Gilthanas asked.

"I don't know what to think," Tanis returned. "I don't know what to hope—that he has found the Hammer, or he that he hasn't. It seems to me that finding the Hammer will cause more problems than it solves."

"You walk in darkness, Half-Elven," said Riverwind quietly. "Look to the light."

"I tried it," Tanis said quietly. "It hurt my eyes."

He left his friends, not without some misgivings, but he couldn't be in two places at once, and he and the others needed to be at the Temple of the Stars to witness, and perhaps defend, Flint's return. If he had found the Hammer of Kharas, there were many who would try to take it from him.

———————◆————————

The Temple of the Stars was the most holy site in all of Thorbardin, which, for the dwarves, meant all the world. For the dwarves believed that in this temple was a shaft that led to the city where dwelt Reorx.

The shaft was a natural phenomenon discovered during the construction of Thorbardin. None could plumb its depths or determine how far below the earth it went. Rocks tossed into it never hit bottom. Thinking perhaps that they just couldn't hear them, the dwarves had thrown an anvil into the pit, knowing that when it hit, they would hear a resounding crash.

The dwarves listened. They listened for hours. They listened for days. Weeks went by, followed by months, and they still heard no sound. It was then the dwarven priests decreed that the shaft was a holy site, for it obviously connected this world to the realm of Reorx. It was also said that if you had nerve enough to look straight down into the pit, you would see the lights of Reorx's magnificent city sparkling like stars far below. The dwarves built a grand temple around the pit and named it Temple of the Stars.

A platform extended out over the pit and here the dwarves placed an altar dedicated to Reorx. They built a waist-high wall around the pit, though no dwarf would have ever dreamed of committing the sacrilege of either climbing or jumping into it. Dwarf priests conducted their most sacred rituals here, including marriage and naming ceremonies. Here the High Kings were crowned.

The dwarves held the temple in reverence and awe, going there to offer humble prayers to Reorx, to ask for his blessing and praise him. But as time passed and the might of Thorbardin grew, the dwarves thought better of themselves. Who were they, powerful and mighty, to beg to a god? They came to demand, rather than ask, often writing down their demands on stones and tossing these into the pit. Some dwarven priests found this practice reprehensible and preached against it. The dwarves refused to listen, and thus Reorx was pelted with demands that he give his people everything from wealth to eternal youth to an unfailing supply of dwarf spirits.

Apparently Reorx grew weary of this, for when the Cataclysm struck, the ceiling of the temple caved in, blocking all the entrances. The dwarves attempted to remove the rubble, but every time they shifted a boulder or a beam, another crashed down, and eventually they gave up.

It was Duncan, High King, who reopened the temple. He hoped to find Reorx by doing so, and he devised a plan to use the great Ukhar worms to chew through the rubble. His detractors said the worms would not stop there but would chew through the temple walls as well, and the worms did in some places before the worm wranglers could stop them. These holes were easily repaired, however, and dwarves could once more enter the temple.

King Duncan did not find Reorx there, as he had hoped. Legend has it that the king flattened himself on his belly and peered into the pit, hoping to see the famed stars. He saw nothing but darkness. Still, he held that the temple was a sacred place and the memory of the god was here, even if the god himself was gone. He banned the tossing of stones into the pit. Once again, important ceremonies and functions were held in the Temple of the Stars and thus it was deemed to be the most suitable place for the Thanes to witness the recovery of the Hammer of Kharas. Hornfel prayed it might happen soon, for already the mountain kingdom was in turmoil.

Word of the monstrous winged lizard-man had spread rapidly throughout all the realms, creating a sensation. A laconic race, dwarves are not given to rumor-mongering. They do not embellish stories or exaggerate the facts, leaving that to humans. A dwarf caught dressing up a tale is not to be trusted. One lone draconian leaping off the lift in a human community would have turned into six hundred fire-breathing dragons invading the kingdom. The dwarves who had seen the draconian jump off the Life Tree and fly over the lake told the astonishing tale to their neighbors and relatives, and they told it accurately.

None of the dwarves knew what to make of this creature, except that it was undoubtedly evil, and each dwarf had his or her own idea on what it was and how it came to be in Thorbardin. All agreed on one thing—no monster like this had been seen in Thorbardin as long as the gate was sealed. This was what came of opening their doors to the world beyond. Tanis and the other "Talls" were viewed with even more suspicion than before.

Hundreds of dwarves were already clogging the Ninth Road in an effort to reach the Temple. There had already been several fistfights, and Hornfel feared that worse would happen. Riots would break out and dwarves would be hurt if they were allowed to crowd into the temple and its environs. Hornfel decided to close the Temple to the public. Only the Thanes and their guards would be present to witness the Hammer's return.

Having seen the draconian for himself, Hornfel came to believe that Tanis had been telling the truth—the Theiwar had betrayed Thorbardin to the forces of the Dark Queen. Hornfel feared that Realgar, knowing his perfidy had been discovered, would choose this time to attack. The Theiwar army, being little more than an armed mob, did not overly concern Hornfel, whose troops were highly trained and well disciplined. But the half-elf had warned Hornfel that an army of these dragon-men might well be prepared to invade. If that happened, they would likely attack the Temple first, in an effort to seize the Hammer. Hornfel wanted armed troops surrounding the temple, not an unruly crowd.

Hornfel was also worried about the Daergar. If Rance sided with Realgar, and they were backed up by the forces of darkness, Hornfel despaired that even the Hammer of Kharas could save his people.

The Thane of the Hylar was a dwarf of courage and nobility, whose worth was proven in these dark hours. Hornfel readily admitted that he had been taken in by Realgar's lies. He had misjudged Tanis and the others.

"I have lived too long sealed up inside the mountain," Hornfel said sadly. "I need to see the sunshine once again, breathe fresh air."

"What you need," Sturm advised, "is to look for Reorx. You won't find him at the bottom of a pit."

Hornfel thought this over. Like most dwarves, he had sworn many an oath by Reorx. The Thane had never before prayed to Reorx, however, and he wasn't certain what to say. He had been told of the words of the strange dwarf who had appeared in the entrance to the Valley, how the fate of Thorbardin hung by a slender rope. In the end, Hornfel's prayer was simple and heartfelt, "Reorx, grant me the wisdom and the strength to do what is right."

He held his troops in readiness, as did the Thane of the Daewar, Gneiss, whose thinking had agreed with Hornfel on all points except Reorx's return. If the god had come back, he would have made himself known to the Daewar first, since they had been the ones to build and tend his shrines. As of yet, Gneiss had seen no sign of him.

Tufa, the Thane of the Klar, had seen the draconian and been eager to kill it. He envisioned these monsters creeping into Thorbardin along dark and secret paths, and he sent his people, who knew their way around the darkness and the labyrinthine tunnels, to investigate.

The Thanes assembled in the Temple of the Stars, each bringing with him heavily armed guards. Hornfel had also invited the Talls to join them in the Temple. A large square building, the Temple had four entrances, one at each of the four compass points. Wide halls ran straight from the four doors to intersect in the inner chamber. This was the altar room and it was circular in shape, for it had been built around the pit—a round pool of starlit darkness beneath a domed ceiling. A hole in the ceiling was placed directly above the pit, matching it in shape and size and symbolizing the idea that the realm of the god had no beginning and no end.

The altar of Reorx, which had been considered ancient in King Duncan's time, had never been removed. Made of red granite carved in the shape of an anvil, the altar stood at the end of the platform that extended out into the pit. The dwarven Thanes eyed the altar uncomfortably, wondering if they should make some offering to acknowledge the god's return. None knew what they were supposed to do or say, so rather than risk offending the god, who was known to be touchy, they stood before it, doffed their helms, and then looked uncomfortable.

The rest of the large altar room was empty. There were no thrones, chairs, or benches. Those was entered the altar room were in the presence of the god and were meant to stand in respect. Hornfel, Gneiss, Tufa and Klar were the four Thanes in attendance. They came together, talking in low and worried voices. Tanis and his friends stood apart, saying little. The dwarves had placed torches in sconces around the walls, but the flames did little to light the vast room. Darkness seemed to flow out of the pit and drown them, for though the air was still and calm, the torches constantly flickered and went out. Even the light cast by the staff of Magius seemed dimmer than usual, shedding its light only on Raistlin, illuminating nothing else.

"Two of the Thanes are missing," said Sturm, "those of the Theiwar and the Daergar."

"The fact that Realgar is absent is no surprise," said Tanis, "but it is beginning to look as though the Daergar have joined forces with their dark cousins."

The Aghar Thane was also missing, but no one noticed.

The tension mounted as everyone waited for the Hammer. Nerves stretched taut. Conversation dwindled. No one had any idea what was going to happen, but most believed it was going to be bad. The strain proved too much for the leader of the Klar, who suddenly threw back his head and let out a hideous shriek—a feral, heart-stopping howl that echoed throughout the chamber and caused the dwarven guards to draw their weapons. Sturm, Caramon, and Tanis clapped their hands to their swords. The Klar merely snarled and waved his hand, indicating that he'd meant nothing by it, he was simply easing the tension.

"I hope he doesn't do that again," said Caramon, thrusting his sword back into its sheathe.

"I wonder what is taking so long," said Sturm. "Perhaps they were waylaid—"

"We don't even know for certain that the news about the Hammer is true," Raistlin observed. "For all we know, this may be a trap. We might have been sent here to keep us away from the Hammer."

"I don't like this any better than the rest of you," said Tanis. "I'm open to suggestions."

"I say that Tanis and I should go to Valley of the Thanes and look for Flint," said Sturm.

"No, you and I should go, Sturm," said Raistlin.

Sturm hesitated a moment, then said, "Yes, Raistlin and I should go."

Tanis was so amazed at this sudden strange alliance that he nearly forgot what he was about to say. He had started to suggest that perhaps they should all go to the Valley when suddenly there was Tasslehoff, right in front of him.

Tanis had never been so glad to see anyone. Risking the loss of his personal possessions, he gave Tas a hug. The others greeted the kender warmly, then immediately bombarded him with questions.

"How did you get here? Where's Flint? Does he have the Hammer of Kharas?"

"A magical rune made by a golden woolly mammoth," Tas answered them all in jumble. "Flint's here and no, he doesn't have the Hammer. Arman has it."

Tas pointed to Flint standing on the platform before the altar of Reorx. Arman Kharas stood beside him, holding the bronze hammer in triumph over his head.

"I, Arman Kharas, have found the Hammer of Kharas!" he thundered. "I return it to my people!"

Tanis sighed. He was glad the Hammer had been recovered, but he was concerned for his old friend. "I hope Flint's not taking this too hard."

"I was worried about that, too," said Tas. "But Flint seems really chipper. You'd almost think he found the Hammer."

Sturm and Raistlin exchanged glances.

"The gods be praised—" Sturm began, but his prayer was cut short.

Hot flame erupted from the pit and exploded in their midst. The dazzling light blinded them, the concussive blast jarred the senses and knocked many to the floor.

Half-blind and dazed, Tanis staggered to his feet, fumbling for his sword and trying to see what had happened. He had a vague impression of something monstrous crawling out of the pit. When his dazzled vision cleared, Tanis saw it was a man, fearsome in blue armor and horned helm, pulling himself with ease over the edge of the platform.

Lord Verminaard. Very much alive.

24

Seeing is believing. True metal and false.

"Verminaard was dead!" Sturm shouted hoarsely. "I stabbed him through the heart!"

"Something's not right!" Raistlin gasped.

"Yeah, the bastard can't be killed," Caramon said.

"Not that!" Raistlin whispered, felled by a fit of coughing. He tried desperately to speak, his lips were flecked with blood. "The light . . . blinded . . . a magic spell . . ." He doubled over, struggling to breathe. The coughing spasms tore at his frail body, and he could say no more.

"Where's Flint?" Tanis asked worriedly. "Can you see him?"

"The altar is in the way," said Sturm, craning his neck. "The last I saw, he was standing beside Arman."

The helmed head turned in their direction. Verminaard was aware of them; perhaps he had even heard them. He did not appear overly concerned. His attention was fixed on the Hammer of Kharas, and the dwarf who held it.

Arman Kharas had not been felled by the magical blast. He stood stalwart and firm, the hammer clasped tightly in his hands, facing

---

419

the terrible foe who towered over him, a foe who commanded the elements, who wielded fire and blinding light. A foe who had risen from the holy site that was the dwelling place of Reorx, mocking the power of the god.

"Who dares defile our sacred Temple?" Arman cried. He was pale beneath his long black beard, but resolute and determined, and he faced his enemy without fear.

"Verminaard, Highlord of the Red Dragonarmies. In the name of Ariakas, Emperor of Ansalon, and of Takhisis, Queen of Darkness, I have conquered Qualinesti, Abanasinia and the Plains of Dust. I now add Thorbardin to the list. Bring me the Hammer and bow down before me and proclaim me High King or perish where you stand."

Sturm said softly, "We should rush him. He can't fight all of us."

The Dragon Highlord shifted his hand and pointed at the knight. A ray of light shot out from the Highlord's hand, streaked through the air and struck Sturm on his metal breastplate. Lightning sizzled around the knight. He collapsed to the floor and lay writhing in agony.

All the time, Verminaard had not taken his gaze from Arman, who was staring at the stricken knight in horror, his hands clasping the hammer in a convulsive grip.

"Witness my power," Verminaard said to the young dwarf. "Bring me the Hammer, or you will be next!"

Tanis saw Caramon's hand close over the hilt of his sword.

"Don't be a fool, Caramon!" Tanis said softly. "Go see to Sturm."

Caramon glanced at his twin. Raistlin sagged against his staff. He was weak from coughing, his hand pressed over his mouth. He shook his head, and Caramon reluctantly released his hold on his weapon. He knelt beside the stricken knight.

Flint had been knocked off his feet by the power of the blast. He staggered back to the platform, coming up behind Arman. Flint could feel something sticky on his face, probably blood. He ignored it. The other Thanes were more or less on their feet, as were their guards. Between them all, they outnumbered the Dragon Highlord, but after seeing the damage inflicted on the knight, no one dared attack Verminaard.

"Give him the Hammer," Hornfel said to his son. "It is not worth your life."

"The Hammer is mine!" Arman cried defiantly. "I am Kharas!"

He shook free of the terror that had seemed to paralyze the others. Swinging the hammer, Arman Kharas sprang at the Dragon Highlord.

As the dwarf bore down on him, the Dragon Highlord fell back a step in order to bring himself into better position to repel the dwarf's attack. His foot went too close to the edge. He slipped and nearly fell, managing to save himself only by dropping his mace and grabbing hold of the granite altar.

At about this time, Tasslehoff Burrfoot reached into his pocket in search of his spectacles.

Kender, unlike humans, never doubt. Verminaard was dead. Tanis and the others had killed him, and yet here he was alive, and this made no sense, as far as Tas was concerned. Raistlin had said that something was wrong, and if anyone should know it would be him. Raistlin might not be the nicest person Tas had ever met, but the mage was the smartest.

"I think I'll just take a quick look," said Tas to himself.

He reached down into his pocket and pulled out something that might once have been a kumquat. This not being of much use, he tossed it away and after retrieving a prune pit and thimble, he located the ruby-colored spectacles and put them on his nose.

Arman Kharas struck. The blow from the hammer broke Verminaard's grip on the altar. Another blow knocked him backward. The Dragon Highlord tried desperately to save himself, but he overbalanced, and bellowing in terror and in fury, the Dragon Highlord fell into the pit.

No one moved or spoke. Arman Kharas stared into the pit in dazed disbelief. Then the realization of his triumph burst upon him. He lifted the hammer and, crying out praise to Reorx, swung the hammer joyfully through the air. The Thanes and the soldiers began to cheer wildly.

Caramon was propping up Sturm, who was dazed and in pain but alive. Caramon whooped and hollered. Sturm smiled weakly.

Raistlin stared at the pit, his eyes hard and glittering. "Something is wrong with this . . ."

"Raistlin's right, Tanis!" Tasslehoff clutched at his friend. "That's not Verminaard!"

"Not now, Tas!" Tanis said, trying to shake loose the kender. "I have to see to Sturm . . ."

"It wasn't Verminaard, I tell you!" Tas cried. "It was a draconian who looked like Verminaard!"

"Tas—"

"An illusion!" Raistlin breathed. "Now it makes sense. Verminaard was a cleric, a follower of Queen Takhisis. The spell that blinded us and the spell that felled Sturm were both spells that only a wizard could cast."

The dwarven Thanes were cheering Arman Kharas, who stood on the platform cradling the hammer in his arms and basking in his glory.

"A draconian?" said Tanis, glancing back at the altar. "Why would a draconian pretend to be Verminaard?"

"I don't know," said Raistlin softly, "but this victory was too easy."

"Look!" Caramon cried.

Clawed hands were reaching up out of the pit and grabbing hold of the edge of the platform. A draconian emerged from the pit, effortlessly pulling himself up onto the platform. Unlike other draconians, this one had no wings. His scales were a dull greenish gold. He was tall and thin with a short, stubby tail. He wore black robes decorated in whorls and runes. The draconian lifted his head, looked up at the ceiling, and raised arms as though signaling. Then he crept toward the unsuspecting young dwarf.

Arman had his back turned. He did not see his danger. The Thanes saw it and cried out in alarm. Flint did more than that. He took hold of his Hammer and ran toward the pit.

"Flint! Stop!" Tanis shouted, and he started to run to his friend's aid, when he heard Sturm cry out a warning.

"Tanis! Above you!"

Tanis looked up to see armed draconians dropping down on top of them, leaping through the hole in the ceiling. At the same time, additional draconian troops entered from the south door. A group of Theiwar, armed to the teeth, ran in through the door to the east. Sturm, pale and shivering, was on his feet, sword in hand. Caramon positioned himself next to Sturm, in case the knight faltered. Raistlin's lips were moving. Magic crackled on his fingertips. Tasslehoff, calling out jeers and insults and jumping up and down, waved his hoopak and yelled for the draconians to come and get him.

Confusion swirled about the temple as the draconians, swords slashing, hit the floor fighting. Hornfel lifted a ram's horn to his lips, and at his call, Hylar soldiers swept into the Temple from the north. The Daewar thronged in from the west, and friend and foe met in the center in a thunderous crash. Battle swirled around the pit. Steel hit steel, draconians shrieked their battle cries, angry dwarves bellowed theirs, and the dying and the wounded screamed.

Tanis looked desperately for Flint, trying to spot him in the chaos, but he could not find him. Then Tanis was forced to forget about his friend and fight for his life.

Arman Kharas was exalted. He held the hammer high, and he shook it defiantly in the beards of those who had sneered at him over the years, those who had called him Mad Kharas, those who had doubted him. He was vindicated. He had found the Hammer, and with it, he had slain the fearsome Dragon Highlord. Arman was a hero, as he had always dreamed. He gave a fierce cry of joy. In his heady elation, he did not see the monster crawling up out of the pit.

The Thanes saw the danger. Arman's father saw it and ran to help his son, but at that moment dragonmen fell out of the skies, a draconian army stormed the Temple from the south, and a rampaging mob of Theiwar burst in from the east.

Thanks to Tanis and his friends, the Theiwar and the draconians did not take the Thanes by surprise, as they had planned. The Hylar, the Daewar, and the Klar were prepared. Horn calls sounded, and their armies swarmed into the Temple to attack their foes. The battle was fierce, desperate, and furious. The Temple was soon jammed with combatants, heaving, pushing, shoving, and hacking. The floor fast became slippery with blood.

Hornfel, his battle-axe red with gore, was overwhelmed by the sheer numbers of the enemy and lost sight of his son in the confusion.

Flint had been blown off the platform when Verminaard appeared. Flint had been appalled at the sight, but there was not much he could do. The old dwarf was well nigh finished. His legs were stiff and sore, his back hurt, and his shoulders ached. He was in pain from his injuries, and he was consumed with guilt.

Arman had been duped. He thought he held in his hands a blessed weapon. He did not know the hammer he wielded was nothing more than a hunk of metal magicked up by Raistlin.

When Arman had charged at Verminaard, Flint had tried to stop him, but Arman had ignored him. Flint had turned his head, unable to watch the young dwarf's certain death. Then he'd heard Verminaard give a shout of fury and Arman yell in triumph.

Flint looked up in time to see the Dragon Highlord tumble into the pit.

"Humpf," Flint had said to himself, unknowingly echoing Raistlin, "something's not right."

Then the draconian appeared, crawling out of the pit.

Flint had stared, astounded. So far as he knew, draconians were leagues away, nowhere near Thorbardin. He had no idea how this draconian came to be here or what the monster was doing in the pit. Astonishment swiftly gave way to outrage. Draconians had no right to be in the dwarven homeland. Outrage changed to consternation, as Flint saw the greenish-gold monster pull himself with slithering grace up onto the platform behind the unsuspecting young dwarf.

The draconian wanted the hammer. Flint could see the creature's eyes fixed on it. He shouted a warning and reached for his weapon, completely forgetting in his fear for the young dwarf that he was the one who carried the blessed Hammer.

Dray-yan was nearing his moment of triumph. His charade had fooled everyone, his own draconians included. They had all seen the vaunted Lord Verminaard fall to an ignominious doom. Cloaked in the illusion of the Dragon Highlord, Dray-yan had pretended to fall off the platform. As he fell, he had caught hold of the ledge with his hands, and had hung there, waiting for Grag and his forces to storm the Temple. With the confusion of the battle covering his movements, the aurak discarded the illusion of the Dragon Highlord and pulled himself up onto the platform.

The fool young dwarf stood there all alone, his back to Dray-yan, the hammer in his hand, shouting to the world about how he'd killed the Dragon Highlord.

Dray-yan was tempted to use his powerful magicks to slay Arman, but the aurak had to be cautious. If he killed in haste, the hammer might slip out of the dwarf's hands and fall into the pit and be forever lost. While Queen Takhisis would enjoy this outcome, it would not suit Dray-yan. He envisioned himself entering the Temple at Neraka and presenting the hammer to Lord Ariakas.

Dray-yan was hampered by the fact that he did not carry a sword. Auraks generally disdained the use of weapons, preferring to rely on their magic in battle. He did, however, have a knife strapped to his leg beneath his robes.

The dwarf wore heavy armor, but that didn't faze Dray-yan. The aurak had no need to penetrate armor or hit a vital organ. A scratch on the arm would do. The knife was smeared with poison, a lethal trick he'd learned from his kapak cousins.

Blade in hand, Dray-yan crept up on Arman.

———————————

Flint took hold of the Hammer of Kharas, yanked it from the harness, and raced toward the pit, bellowing all the while at Arman to look behind him. As Flint ran, he realized suddenly that his aches and pains had vanished. Fatigue lifted from him. His arms were strong, his legs powerful. His heart beat steady and true. He was filled with life and energy. Flint was a young dwarf once more, powerful, invincible.

Arman Kharas finally heard Flint's warning shouts. The young dwarf had been about to join in the battle, but now he turned around to see, to his shock, a monstrous foe closing on him from behind.

Flint was only steps from the platform when a baaz draconian landed squarely in front of him. The baaz attacked, swinging a curved-bladed sword. Flint didn't have time for such nonsense. He had to reach Arman before the youngster got himself into serious trouble. Flint swung the Hammer with the might of his fury, and struck the baaz in the head.

The draconian disintegrated; its body changing from flesh to stone and from stone to dust so rapidly that Flint was covered in the foul mess. Flint jumped onto the platform where Arman and the draconian were locked in mortal combat, grappling for the hammer.

Steel flashed in the draconian's hand. Dray-yan tried to stab Arman with a knife with one hand and get a grip on the hammer with the other. Arman was bleeding from a few cuts on his arm, but the dwarf's heavy armor protected his body and he was not concerned about the feeble blows of his foe.

Arman was about to raise the hammer and bring it down on his enemy, when a shudder shook the young dwarf. His face went deathly pale. His eyes widened. A sheen of chill sweat covered his forehead. Pain like a thousand steel blades slicing into his vitals drove him to his knees.

Dray-yan seized hold of the hammer, intending to wrench it from the dwarf's grip. Weakened as he was, his body splintered by pain, Arman closed his hands tightly over the hammer, refusing to give it up. He fought against the monster, but his strength was failing. The poison burned through his veins. He could no longer feel his hands or his feet. His hands went limp and slid off the hammer, and Dray-yan snatched it.

His prize in hand, Dray-yan started to leap over the writhing body. He planned to flee the temple, but he found his way blocked.

Flint stood over Arman, facing the draconian. Flint gestured at the hammer in Dray-yan's hands.

"You've got the wrong one," Flint told the aurak with grim satisfaction.

Dray-yan's startled gaze went from the hammer in his hand to the Hammer the dwarf was holding. He realized immediately he'd been duped. The Hammer the dwarf held blazed with a wrathful, holy light. Dray-yan could not even bear to look at it. If he'd been thinking, he should have known at once the hammer he held was a fake. No magical life flowed through it. No magic guarded it.

Cursing dwarves for shabby little tricksters, Dray-yan flung the false hammer to the floor. He lifted his hands, his fingers flaring with magic, and lunged at Flint.

"Reorx, help me," Flint prayed and, swinging the true Hammer, he hit the draconian in the chest.

Bones cracked and snapped. Dray-yan shrieked and collapsed onto the platform. He almost rolled off, but he managed to save himself with a twist of his short, stubby tail. Flint was about to finish the aurak, when he remembered that draconians have the power to inflict harm even after they are dead. He had no idea what this strange greenish gold draconian would do, for he'd never seen one like it before, so instead he kicked the draconian, intending to push it off the platform.

Desperate, Dray-yan grabbed hold of Flint's boot and tried to yank the dwarf off his feet, hoping to grab the Hammer on the dwarf's way down, then fling him into the pit.

Flint twisted, turned and kicked frantically at the draconian. He could have slain the fiend with a single Hammer blow, but he didn't dare, for he had no idea if the creature's corpse would blow up, turn into deadly acid, or what would happen.

Then Flint realized that he might not have a choice. The draconian had managed to drag Flint near the edge of the pit. If Flint fell, the Hammer would fall with him, and that must not happen. To save the Hammer, he was going to have to kill this monster, though he himself would likely die in the process.

Flint aimed a blow at the draconian's ugly head, but before he could strike, the Hammer twisted in his hand and hit the draconian's right arm at the wrist. Bone cracked. Blood spurted. Dray-yan's hand on Flint's boot went limp.

Flint shoved the draconian, shrieking and cursing, off the platform.

His strength flagging, Flint went down on his hands and knees and stared into the darkness watching until the monster was lost to sight. Even then, Flint could still hear him screaming. Dray-yan's cries continued for a long time and never truly ended. They simply dwindled away.

"I failed . . ." said Arman, his eyes fluttering.

He lay on his back on the platform. His face was livid and contorted in pain. He shuddered and gasped for breath.

Flint, his heart wrung, crawled over to kneel beside the dwarf.

"I failed . . ." Arman murmured again. "The Hammer . . . lost."

"No, it isn't," said Flint. "You were victorious. Your foe is dead. You defeated him and saved the Hammer of Kharas. Here, I will show you."

The two hammers, one true and one false, lay side-by-side on the platform.

Flint picked up one of the hammers and thrust it into the dwarf's hands. Gently, he closed Arman's limp fingers over it. The Hammer shone with a soft and radiant light that spread over Arman.

His tortured body relaxed. His pain-twisted grimace eased. His eyes grew clear. He clasped the Hammer to his breast.

"I am a hero," he breathed, his lips barely moving. "Arman . . . Kharas."

He closed his eyes, drew in a breath, and let it out in a sigh. He did not take another.

Flint's eyes filled with tears. He was suddenly very old, weak, and tired, and he loathed himself. He stroked the young dwarf's hands that even in death still clasped the Hammer. He recalled something the ancient, white-haired dwarf had said in the tomb.

"You're not 'Arman'—a lesser Kharas," Flint told the departing soul. "You are Pike, son of Hornfel, the hero who saved the Hammer of Kharas, and that is how you will be remembered."

Flint picked up the false hammer. He held it for a moment, long enough to beg the god's forgiveness and say goodbye to his dreams. Then he glanced around to see if anyone was watching. Dwarves and draconians were stabbing and slashing, bleeding and dying. No one was watching Flint except for one. Tasslehoff was staring, wide-eyed, straight at him.

"Ah, well," Flint grunted. "No one will believe him anyway."

He flung the hammer into the pit.

The radiant light from the Hammmer of Kharas spread throughout the Temple, emboldening the dwarves and demoralizing their foes. But just when Hornfel began to think the day would be won, an army of heavily armed dwarves hundreds strong marched inside. He recognized the emblems of the Daergar on their flags, and he nearly despaired, for the Theiwar were cheering on their dark dwarf allies.

The Hammer's light did not dim, however, and Hornfel watched in astonishment as the Daegar turned on the Theiwar, cutting off the welcoming arms and trampling Theiwar bodies beneath their feet.

Hornfel had become separated from his son in the confusion of battle, but his heart swelled with pride, for he knew that somewhere Arman and the Hammer of Kharas were fighting gloriously.

25

The End of a Dream.

ven as he fought the dwarves, Grag kept an eye on Dray-yan. Generally, Grag loved nothing more than a good fight, but he was taking no pleasure in today's battle. He had enjoyed watching Dray-yan's play-acting, grinning widely at the sight of Lord Verminaard falling into a pit, listening to the hisses and chortles of his soldiers who were not in on the secret, and who thought they had truly witnessed the detested human's pitiful end. Grag had watched Dray-yan crawl out of the pit, then he'd been forced to turn his full attention to the dwarves. It was at this point when his pleasure started to diminish.

The battle was not turning out as Grag had planned. He'd expected the dwarves to be caught completely off guard by the attack. Instead, he was the one who was shocked and surprised. True, he'd been unmasked, forced to reveal the fact that a "lizard" was inside their stinking mountain, but one lizard did not an army make, and the dwarves should not have figured out that they were going to be coming under attack. Somehow, they had foreseen it. Probably tipped off by those blasted humans.

Grag found himself and his troops badly outnumbered. He had anticipated slicing up a few dwarven guards, but he was now facing four strong dwarven armies: Hylar, Daewar, Klar, and the Daergar. Grag had planned for a swift take-over, not having to fight every damn dwarf beneath the mountain.

His dubious allies, the Theiwar, proved to be even more inept fighters than Grag had expected, and he hadn't expected much. First, because of Theiwar carelessness, the Klar had discovered the secret passages and sealed up many of them with their accursed stone-chewing worms, trapping some of Grag's best men inside. During the battle, the Theiwar did more looting than fighting, leaving the fighting to swarm over the bodies of the fallen, yanking off gold rings and silver chains. The moment the Theiwar were loaded up with booty, they deserted the field, fled the temple, and ran off to skulk in their rat holes.

As Grag fought dwarves, he waited impatiently for Dray-yan to seize the blasted hammer and force the dwarves to surrender. At one point, Dray-yan had the hammer, or so Grag thought. He took his eyes away for a moment to stab his opponent in the throat. When he looked back, Dray-yan was on the platform, struggling with a single dwarf wielding a hammer that blazed with a fierce red light. Seeing the aurak was in trouble, Grag tried to make his way to him, but he found himself surrounded on all sides, fighting for his life. The next thing he knew, the dwarf with the accursed hammer had shoved Dray-yan into the pit!

As Grag listened to the aurak's terrified howls, the thought came to him that he was now the commander of the fortress of Pax Tharkas. Dragon Highlord Verminaard was, finally, dead. Dray-yan was also dead. Grag was the survivor, and he saw immediately how he could lay the blame for this unfortunate debacle in Thorbardin on both his superiors.

Unlike Dray-yan, Grag had no aspirations to be a Dragon Highlord. He wanted nothing to do with politics. His one ambition was to be a good commander and win battles for the glory of his Dark Queen. He knew when he was beaten. There was no shame in giving up the field, no sense in wasting the lives of good men in a futile cause. Grag let out a piercing call that rose above the din of battle. His draconians heard it and knew what it meant, and they slowly began an orderly retreat.

Marshalling his forces, keeping them in good order, Grag led his draconians back the way they had entered, through the south door.

A few courageous dwarves, led by two human warriors, chased after them but didn't catch them. Draconians could cover ground far more rapidly than either dwarves or humans. Grag took his forces to one of the few secret tunnels the Klar had not discovered. He left them there, while he made a small detour to take care of some unfinished business having to do with Realgar. This done, he led those troops who had survived the battle into the deep tunnels that led to Pax Tharkas. Once all were inside, Grag ordered the tunnels sealed up behind them. After praying to Takhisis and mending their hurts, the draconians began the long trek back to Pax Tharkas.

Someday Grag would return to Thorbardin.

Someday, when his queen was triumphant.

The battle in the temple ended almost as quickly as it had begun. Seeing the draconians retreating, the Theiwar, who'd had little stomach for the fighting anyway, either fled or surrendered. Realgar, as it turned out, was not among them. He had been leading from the rear, and when it looked as though he was losing, the Thane had disappeared.

When the Temple was secure, the fighting ended and the prisoners had been hauled away, Hornfel sent soldiers with orders to search every crack, crevice, and cranny in Thorbardin, until they found Realgar. Hornfel wanted the Thane alive, intending to bring him before the Council to answer for his crimes. All the while, as he was issuing commands, Hornfel asked everyone he encountered about his son. No one had seen Arman or knew what had become of him. All anyone knew was that the hammer's light had shone undimmed throughout the fight, bolstering hearts and lending strength to dwarven hands.

Hornfel was thinking with pleasure of a celebratory victory dinner with his son, when he turned to find the Neidar, Flint Fireforge, standing silently and respectfully at his side. One look at the aged dwarf's sorrowful expression, and Hornfel's heart constricted with pain.

He covered his eyes with his hands for a moment, then, lifting his head, he said quietly, "Take me to my son."

Flint led the Thane to the altar of Reorx. Arman lay on the platform, his hands clasped over the hammer, his eyes closed.

The companions were grouped nearby. Tanis had a jagged cut on his arm. Sturm had a cut over one eye and was still suffering from the effects of the magical blast. Caramon had a broken hand from having punched a draconian in the jaw. Raistlin was apparently unhurt, though no one could really tell, for he refused to answer questions and kept his cowl pulled low over his face. Tasslehoff had a torn shirt and a bloody nose. The blood mixed with the kender's tears as he looked down at the body of the dwarf.

"What happened?" Hornfel asked, grieving. "I could not see in all the turmoil."

"Your son lived as a hero and he died as a hero," said Flint simply. "A draconian who had been hiding in the pit attacked your son and tried to take the sacred hammer from him. The draconian stabbed him with a poisoned knife. Even though he knew he was dying, your son continued to fight, and he killed the draconian and flung the body into the pit."

Tasslehoff gaped at Flint in wonder at the lie. Tas opened his mouth to tell the truth about what had really hapened, but Flint fixed the kender with a look so very stern and piercing that Tas's mouth shut all by itself.

——————————◆◆◆◆——————————

The body of Arman Kharas lay in state in the Life Tree for three days. On the fourth day, Hornfel and the Thanes of the dwarven kingdom of Thorbardin, and Flint Fireforge, their Neidar cousin, carried Arman Kharas to his final rest. His body was placed next to that of the sarcophagus that held the body of his hero, Kharas, and both were placed in the tomb of King Duncan inside the Valley of the Thanes. The plaque on the tomb of the young dwarf was chiseled out of stone by Flint Fireforge. It read:

Hero of the Battle of the Temple, he recovered the Hammer of Kharas and
slew the evil Dragon Highlord Verminaard.
All honor to his name
Pike, son of Hornfel

Another body was disposed of at about the same time, though with much less ceremony. Realgar had been found murdered, his throat slit from ear to ear. Clawed footprints, discovered near the body, were the only clue to the identity of his killer.

Hornfel agreed to honor the wager made by Realgar, though Hornfel added that he would have welcomed the refugees into the safety of Thorbardin even if no wager been made. Tanis and the others were free to leave Thorbardin, to take the glad news to the refugees, and guide them to the Southgate, which would be open to receive them.

"Open to them and to the world," Hornfel promised.

———————◆———————

The night after the battle, Flint was unusually grim and dour. He kept apart form the others, refused to answer any questions, stating that he was worn out and telling everybody to leave him alone. He would not eat any dinner but went straight to his bed.

Raistlin was also in a bad temper. He shoved the plate from him, claiming that food turned his stomach. Sturm tried to eat but eventually dropped his spoon and sat with his head in his hands, his face hidden. Only Caramon was in a good mood. After assuring himself there were no mushrooms in the stew, he not only ate his meal, but he finished off his brother's and Sturm's.

Tasslehoff was also subdued. Though he was reunited with his pouches, he didn't even bother to sort through them. He sat on a chair, kicking at the legs, and fiddling with something in his pocket.

Tanis tapped the kender on the shoulder. "I'd like to have a talk with you."

Tas sighed. "I thought you might."

"Come outside, so we don't disturb Flint," said Tanis.

Feet dragging, Tas followed the half-elf out of the inn. As Tanis shut the door behind them, he saw Sturm and Raistlin rise from the table and walk over to Flint's bed.

Tanis turned to the kender.

"Tell me what happened in the Tomb of Duncan. What *really* happened," Tanis emphasized.

Tas shuffled uncomfortably. "If I tell you, Flint will be mad."

"I won't say a word to him," Tanis promised. "He'll never know."

"Well, all right." Tas gave another sigh, but this was one of relief. "It will be a burden off my mind. You can't think how hard it is to keep secrets! I found this golden woolly mammoth—"

"Not the mammoth!" said Tanis.

"But that's a very important part," Tas argued.

"The Hammer," Tanis insisted. "Flint was the one who found the Hammer of Kharas, wasn't he?"

"We both found the Hammer," Tas tried to explain, "and the body of the real Kharas and a scorpion, then Flint took my hoopak and told me to go away. That was when I met the golden woolly mammoth named Evenstar, but I won't say another word about him. I promised, you see . . ."

Sturm and Raistlin stood by the side of Flint's bed. The dwarf lay with his face to the wall, his back to them.

"Flint," said Sturm, "are you asleep?"

"Yes," Flint growled. "Go away!"

"You had the true Hammer of Kharas, didn't you?" said Raistlin. "You had it in your possession when you entered the Temple of the Stars.

Flint lay still a moment, then he reared up in bed. He faced them, his face red. "I did," he said through clenched teeth, "to my everlasting shame!"

Raistlin's mouth twisted. "And you left it in the hands of a corpse! You sentimental old fool!"

"Stop it, Raistlin" ordered Sturm angrily. "Leave Flint alone. You and I were wrong. What Flint did was honorable and noble."

"How many thousands will pay for that noble gesture with their lives?" Raistlin thrust his hands into the sleeves of his robes. He cast the knight a grim glance. "Nobility and honor do not slay dragons, Sturm Brightblade."

Raistlin stalked off. Encountering his brother, he snapped at him. "Caramon, make me my tea! I feel nauseated."

Caramon looked from Sturm to Flint—hunched up on the bed—to his twin, who was as furious as he had ever seen him.

"Uh, sure, Raist," said Caramon unhappily, and he hurried to do as he was told.

Sturm rested his hand on Flint's shoulder. "You did right," he said. "I am proud of you and deeply ashamed of myself."

Sturm cast Raistlin a dark glance, then went to confess his sins and ask forgiveness in prayer.

Tasslehoff and Tanis came back inside to find the room silent, except for Sturm's whispered words to Paladine. Tas felt so much better, now that he'd unburdened himself, that he dumped out the contents of his pouches and sorted through all his treasure, finally falling asleep in the midst of the mess.

Flint was exhausted, but he could find no solace in sleep, for sleep would not come. He lay in his bed in the darkness, sometimes drifting off, only to jerk fearfully to wakefulness, thinking that the aurak again had hold of his boot and was dragging him into the pit. At last Flint could stand it no longer. He rose from his bed, slipped out the door, and sat down upon the door stoop.

He gazed into the night. Lights sparked, but they were not the sharp, cold crystalline glitter of the stars, whose beauty never failed to pierce his heart. They were the lights of Thorbardin—larvae trapped inside lanterns until they grew old enough to chew through solid rock.

Flint heard the door open and he jumped to his feet, fearing it might be Sturm or Raistlin come to plague him. Seeing it was Tanis, Flint sat back down.

The half-elf sat beside him in silence that was comfortable between the two of them.

Flint said at last, "I had the Hammer, Tanis, the true Hammer." He paused a moment, then added gruffly, "I switched them. I let Arman think he'd found the real one, when, in truth, he found the false.

"I guessed as much," said Tanis quietly after a moment. "But in the end, you did what was right."

"I don't know. If Arman had been holding the true Hammer, maybe he wouldn't be dead."

"The Hammer couldn't have saved him from the aurak's poison. And if you had *not* been in possession of the Hammer when you fought the draconian, the Hammer of Kharas would now be in the hands of the Dark Queen," said Tanis.

Flint thought this over. Perhaps his friend was right. That didn't make what he'd done any better, but maybe, in time, he could forgive himself.

"Reorx told me the dwarf who found the Hammer would be a hero, Tanis. His name would live forever." Flint snorted. "I guess that only goes to show the gods don't know everything."

"I wouldn't be so sure of that," said Tanis.

Afterword

New readers to this series will note many unanswered questions and unresolved mysteries at the end this book, questions such as: how, why, and by whom Raistlin was led to Skullcap, and why haven't the good dragons entered the war against the Dark Queen? Since this volume is one of the "lost" stories that occurs in the middle of the series, we have deliberately left these questions and other issues unresolved for the time being. Those interested in finding out the answers, and following the further adventures of Raistlin, Caramon, Tanis, Sturm, Flint, Tasslehoff, and all the rest, are encouraged to continue their sojourn in the world of Krynn.

Suffice it to say, Hornfel was given the real Hammer of Kharas, and in return, he and the other Thanes permitted the refugees and the heroes to find safe haven in Thorbardin. The war rages on, however, and no place is truly safe for anyone. For those interested in learning what happens next, this story continues in *Dragons of Winter Night*, Volume Two of the Dragonlance *Chronicles*.

The Lost Chronicles series will continue with more stories that were never told in *Volume 2, Dragons of the Highlord Skies*, forthcoming in 2007.

Dragons of the Highlord Skies will relate the adventures of the two women who play major roles in the life of Tanis Half-Elven: the mysterious Kitiara uth Matar and Tanis's childhood sweetheart, Laurana. As the Blue Lady, Kitiara, pursues the war across Ansalon, she forms an unholy alliance with the dread death knight, Lord Soth. Meanwhile Laurana, Sturm, Flint, and Tasslehoff, divided from the rest of the companions during the battle of Tarsis, venture south into the dangerous realm of Icereach in search of one of the fabled dragon orbs.